ESTRANGED

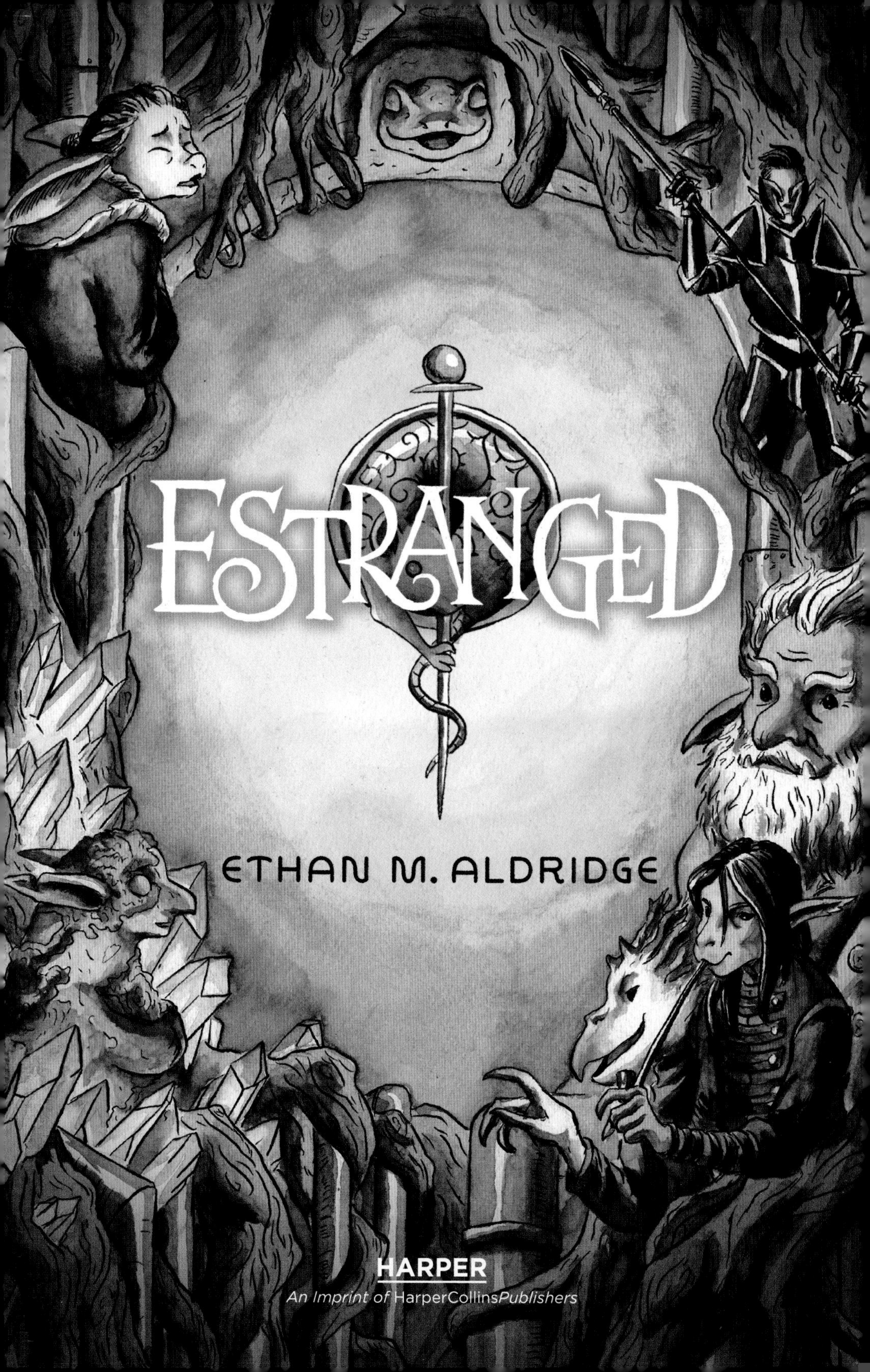

ESTRANGED

ETHAN M. ALDRIDGE

HARPER
An Imprint of HarperCollins*Publishers*

Estranged
Copyright © 2018 by Ethan M. Aldridge
All rights reserved. Manufactured in China.
No part of this book may be used or reproduced in any manner whatsoever
without written permission except in the case of brief quotations embodied in
critical articles and reviews. For information address HarperCollins
Children's Books, a division of HarperCollins Publishers,
195 Broadway, New York, NY 10007.
www.harpercollinschildrens.com

Library of Congress Control Number: 2017949551
ISBN 978-0-06-265386-4 (paperback) – ISBN 978-0-06-265387-1 (hardcover)

The artist used watercolors, ink, and Photoshop to create the illustrations
for this book.
Typography by Jim Tierney
18 19 20 21 22 SCP 10 9 8 7 6 5 4 3 2 1
❖
First Edition

To my mother and father

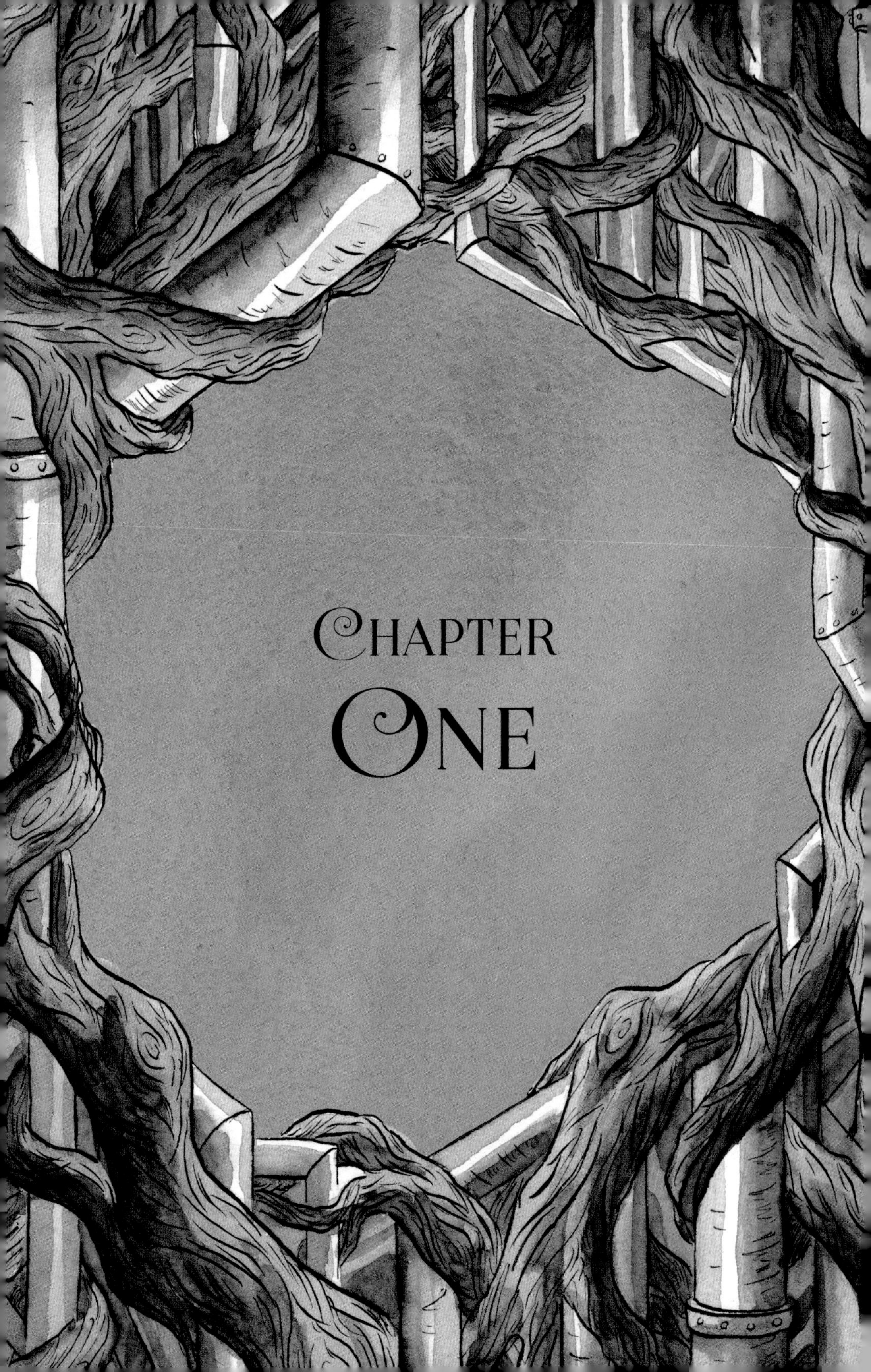

CHAPTER ONE

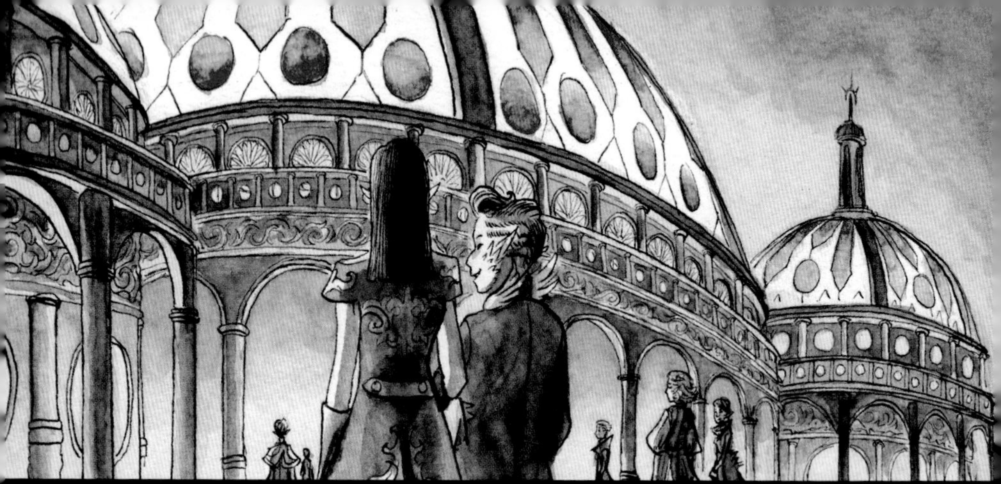

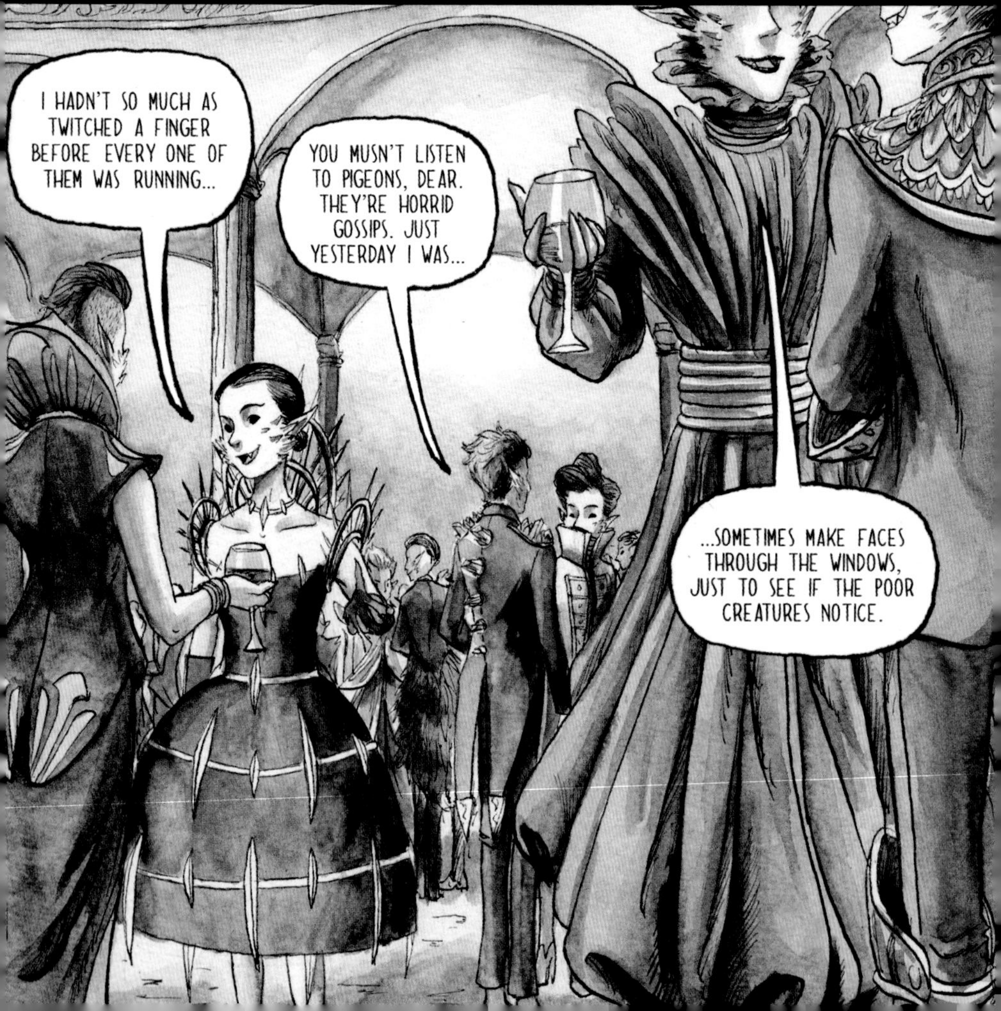
I HADN'T SO MUCH AS TWITCHED A FINGER BEFORE EVERY ONE OF THEM WAS RUNNING...
YOU MUSN'T LISTEN TO PIGEONS, DEAR. THEY'RE HORRID GOSSIPS. JUST YESTERDAY I WAS...
...SOMETIMES MAKE FACES THROUGH THE WINDOWS, JUST TO SEE IF THE POOR CREATURES NOTICE.

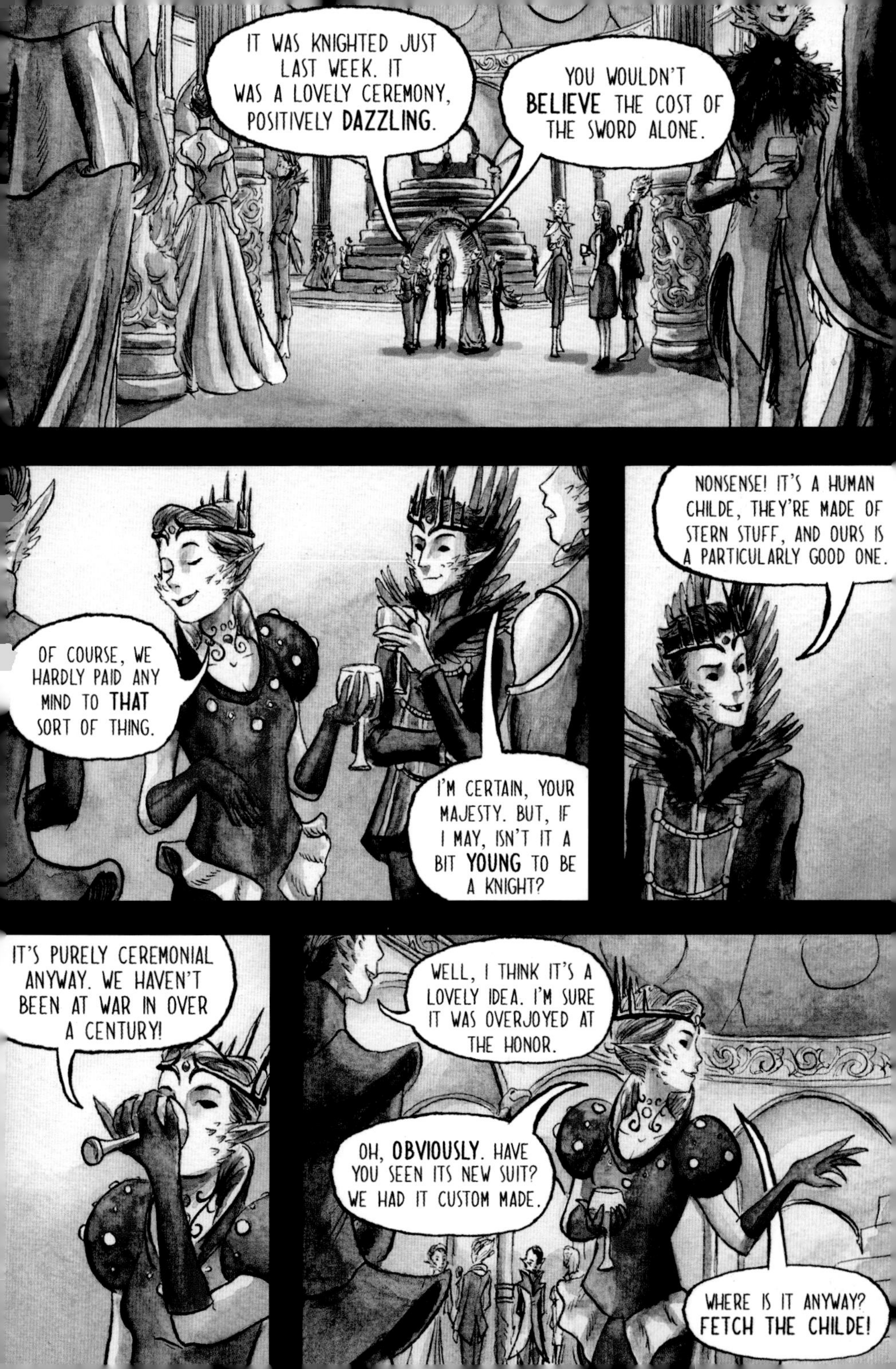
IT WAS KNIGHTED JUST LAST WEEK. IT WAS A LOVELY CEREMONY, POSITIVELY **DAZZLING**.
YOU WOULDN'T **BELIEVE** THE COST OF THE SWORD ALONE.
OF COURSE, WE HARDLY PAID ANY MIND TO **THAT** SORT OF THING.
I'M CERTAIN, YOUR MAJESTY. BUT, IF I MAY, ISN'T IT A BIT **YOUNG** TO BE A KNIGHT?
NONSENSE! IT'S A HUMAN CHILDE, THEY'RE MADE OF STERN STUFF, AND OURS IS A PARTICULARLY GOOD ONE.
IT'S PURELY CEREMONIAL ANYWAY. WE HAVEN'T BEEN AT WAR IN OVER A CENTURY!
WELL, I THINK IT'S A LOVELY IDEA. I'M SURE IT WAS OVERJOYED AT THE HONOR.
OH, **OBVIOUSLY**. HAVE YOU SEEN ITS NEW SUIT? WE HAD IT CUSTOM MADE.
WHERE IS IT ANYWAY? **FETCH THE CHILDE!**

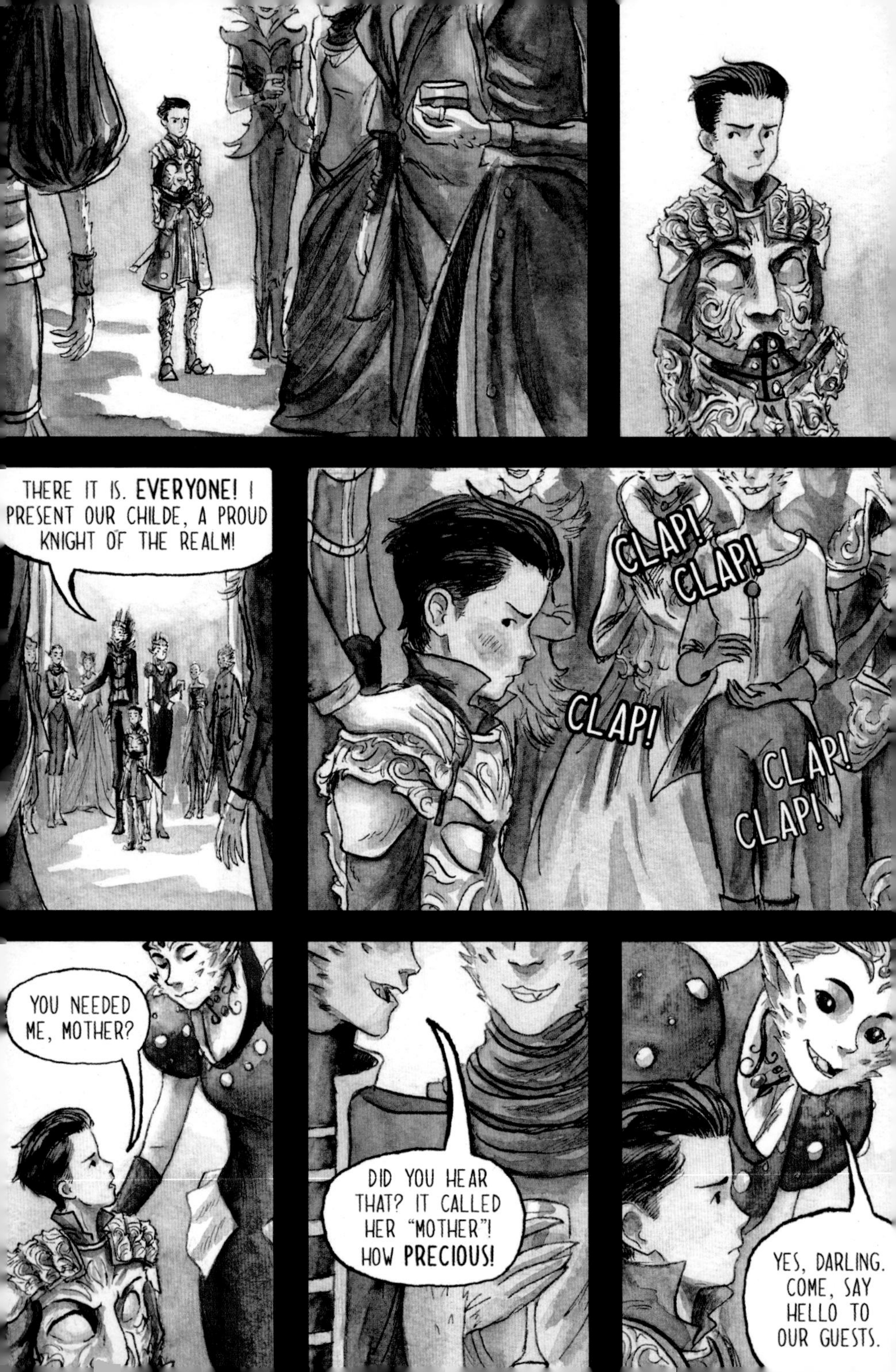
THERE IT IS. EVERYONE! I PRESENT OUR CHILDE, A PROUD KNIGHT OF THE REALM!
CLAP! CLAP!
CLAP!
CLAP! CLAP!
YOU NEEDED ME, MOTHER?
DID YOU HEAR THAT? IT CALLED HER "MOTHER"! HOW PRECIOUS!
YES, DARLING. COME, SAY HELLO TO OUR GUESTS.

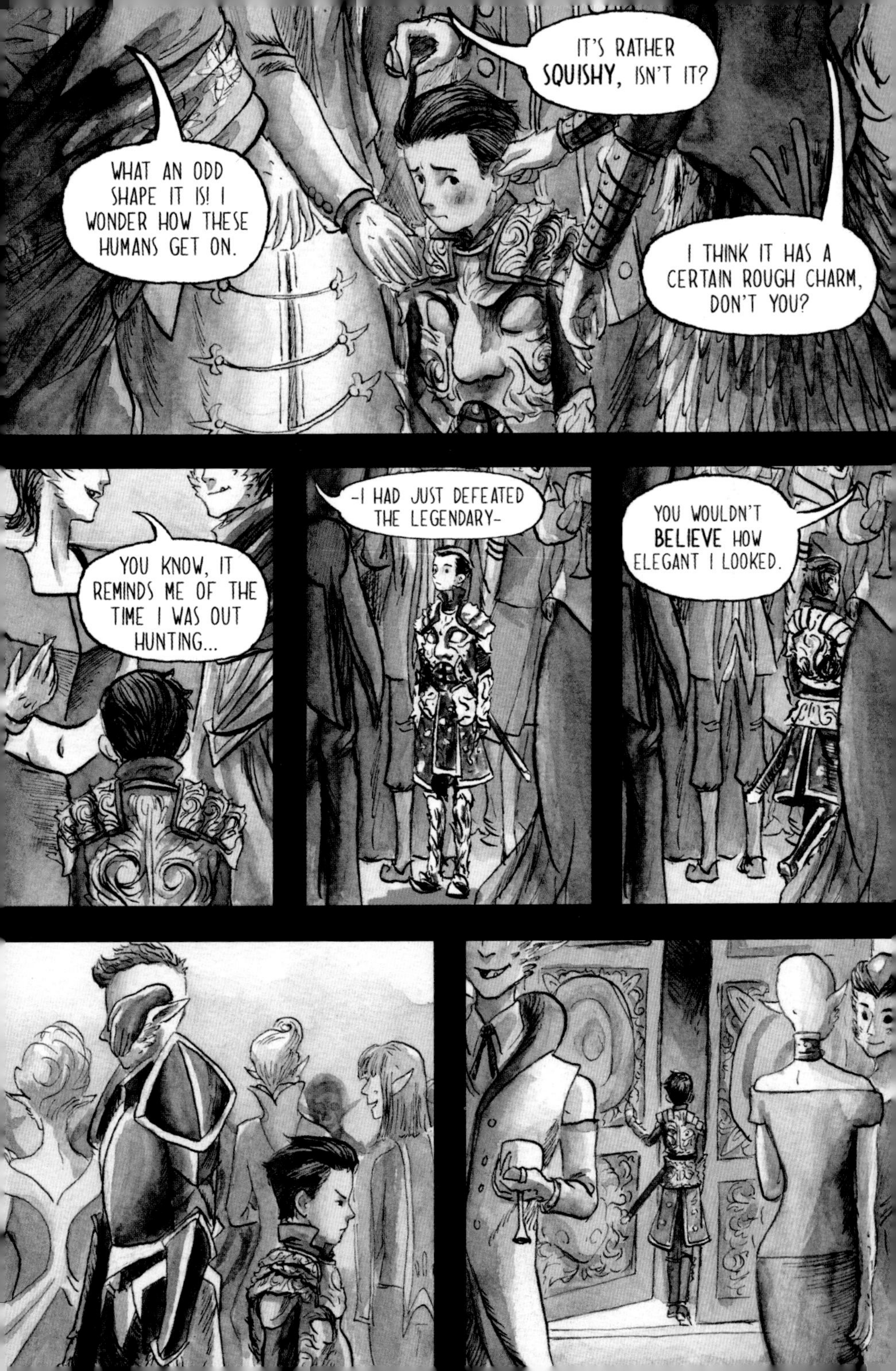
WHAT AN ODD SHAPE IT IS! I WONDER HOW THESE HUMANS GET ON.
IT'S RATHER SQUISHY, ISN'T IT?
I THINK IT HAS A CERTAIN ROUGH CHARM, DON'T YOU?
YOU KNOW, IT REMINDS ME OF THE TIME I WAS OUT HUNTING...
-I HAD JUST DEFEATED THE LEGENDARY-
YOU WOULDN'T BELIEVE HOW ELEGANT I LOOKED.

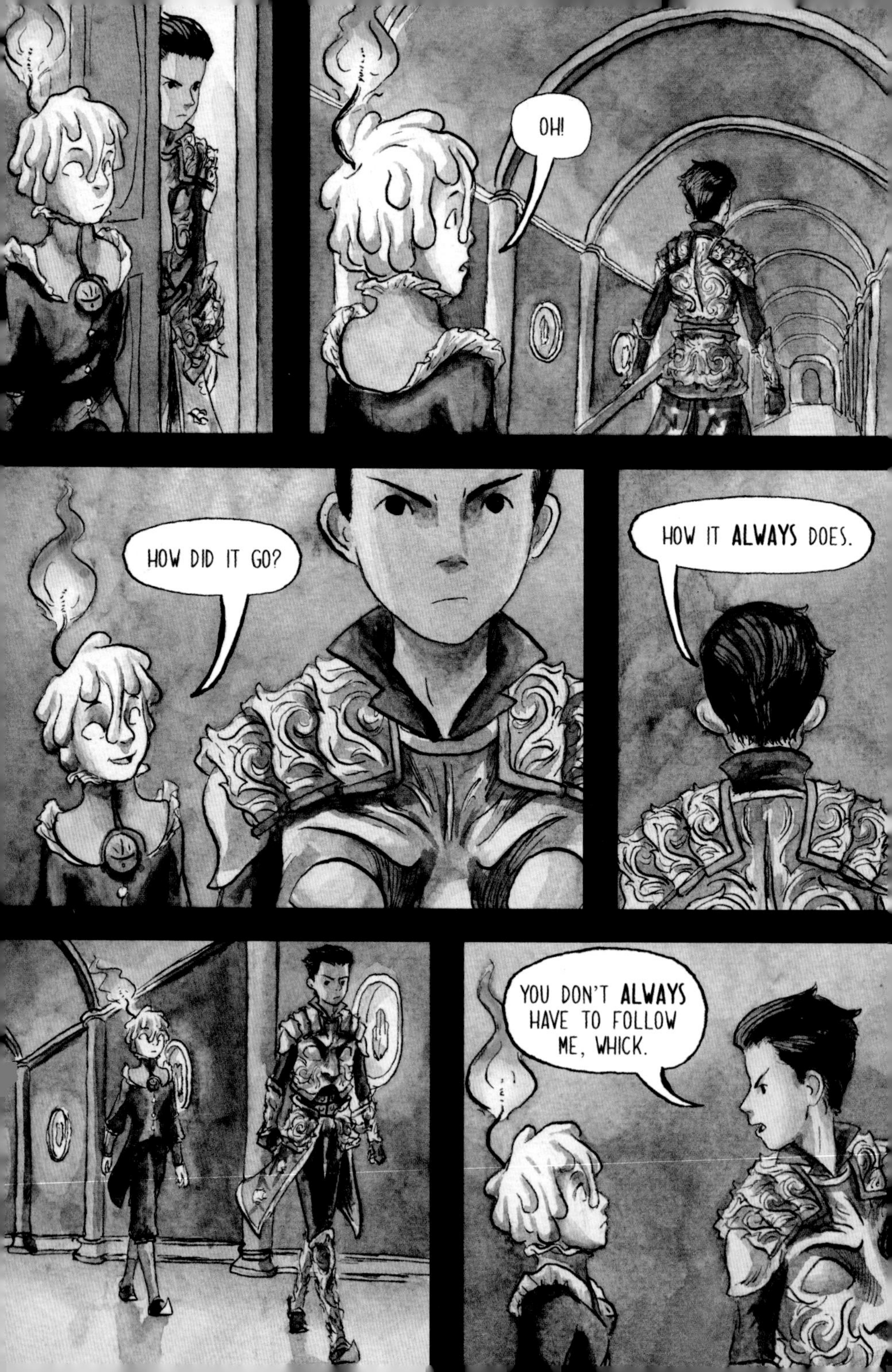
OH!
HOW DID IT GO?
HOW IT ALWAYS DOES.
YOU DON'T ALWAYS HAVE TO FOLLOW ME, WHICK.

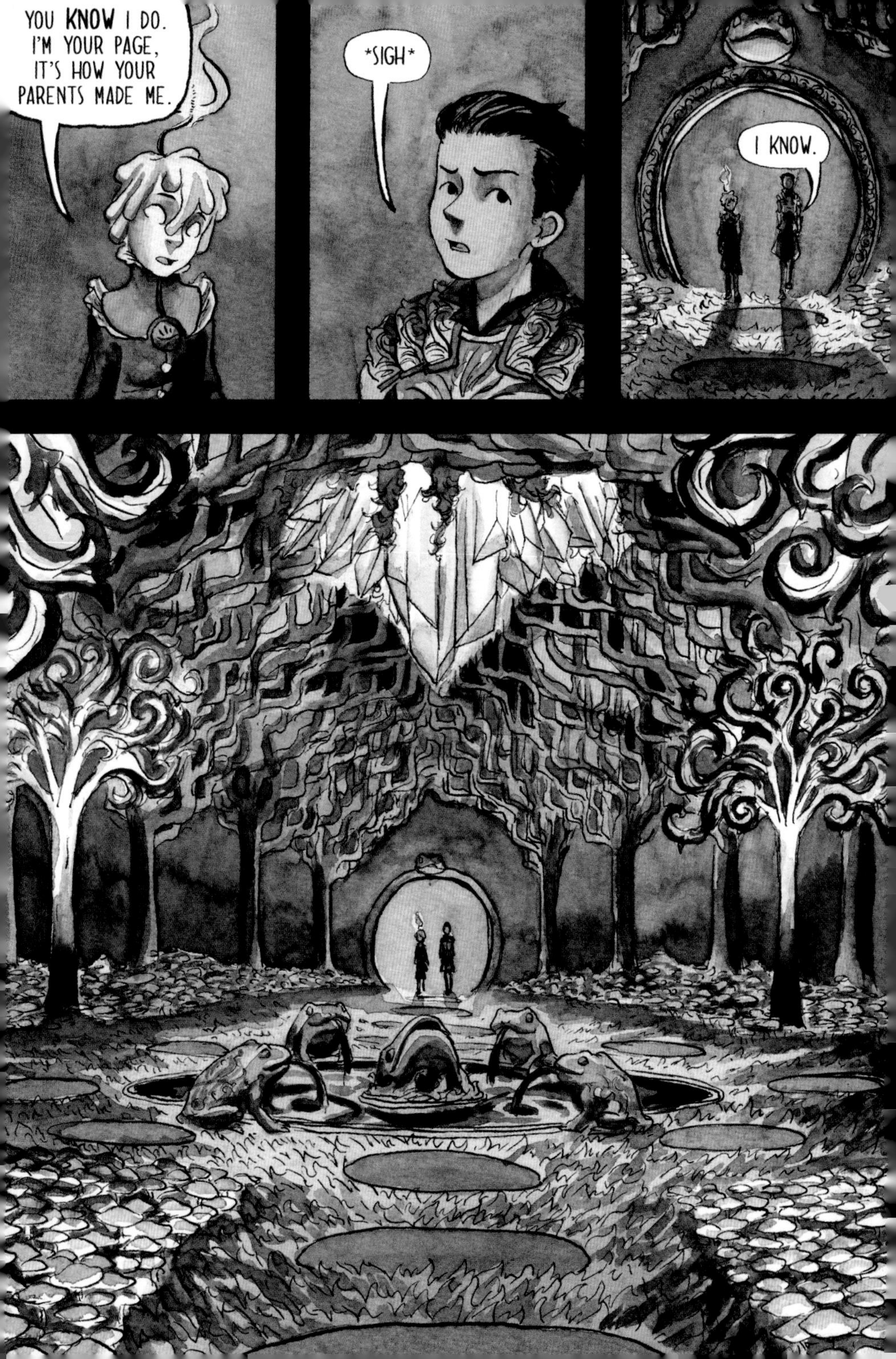
YOU KNOW I DO. I'M YOUR PAGE, IT'S HOW YOUR PARENTS MADE ME.
SIGH
I KNOW.

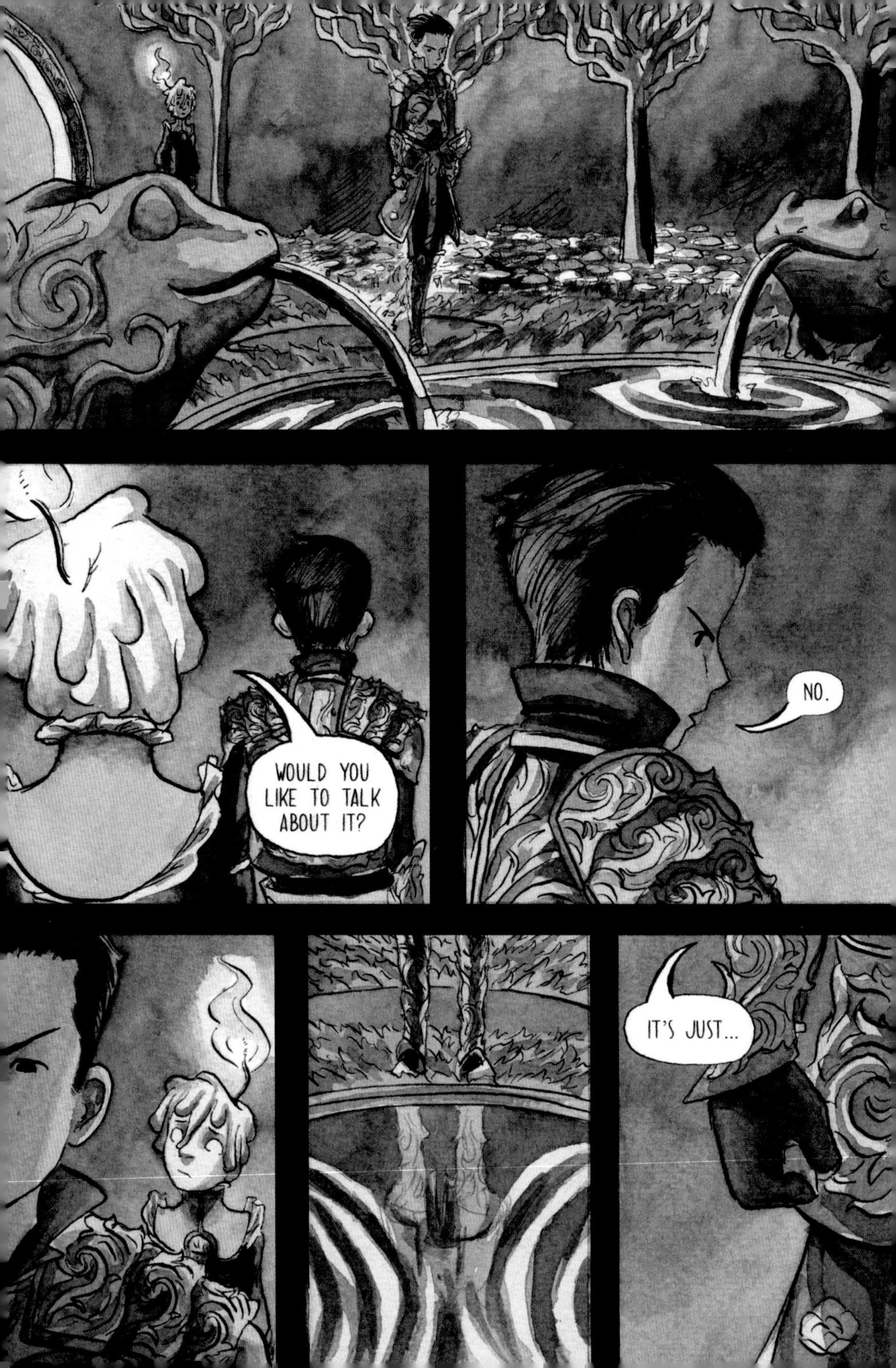
WOULD YOU LIKE TO TALK ABOUT IT?
NO.
IT'S JUST...

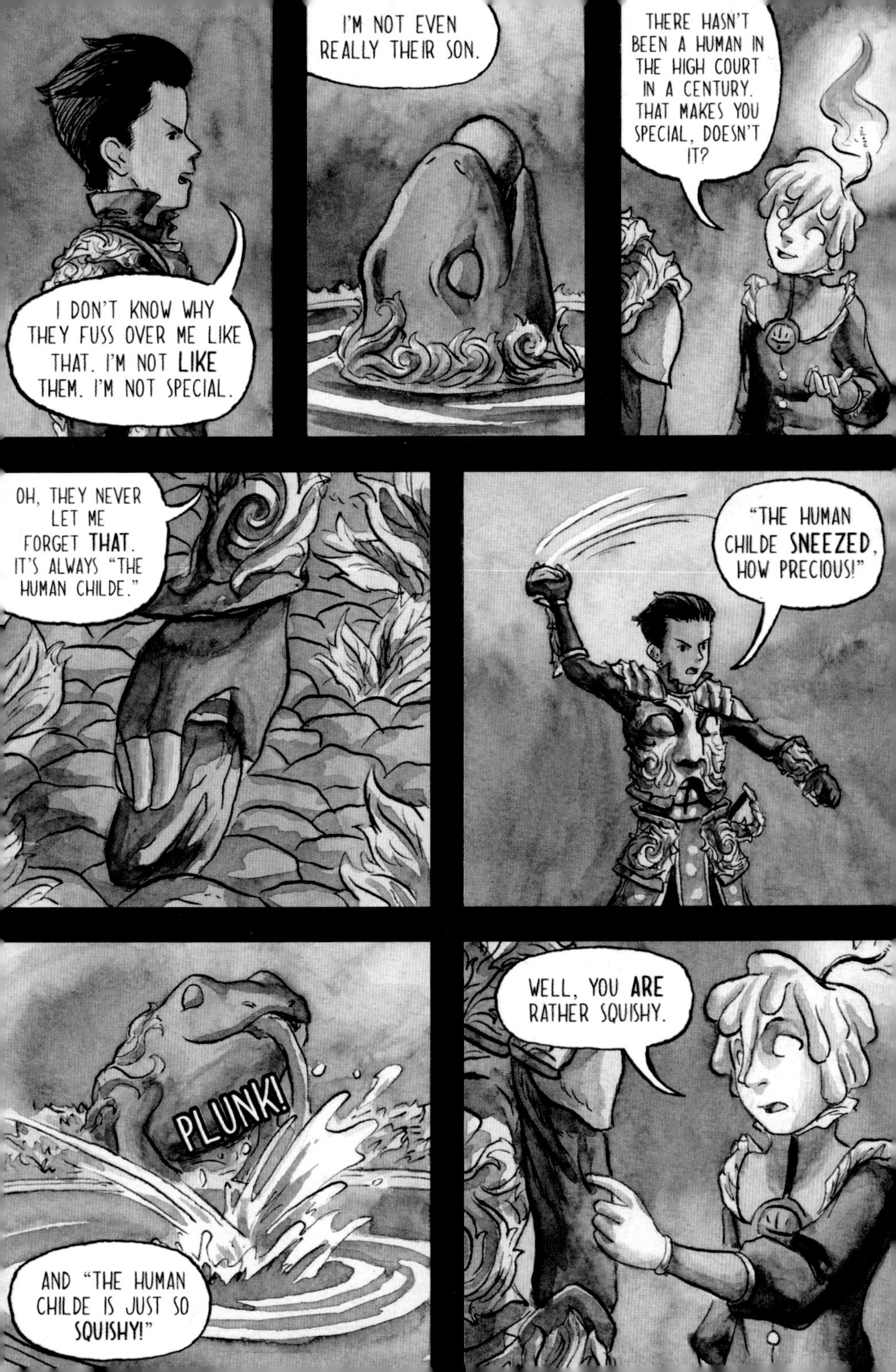
I DON'T KNOW WHY THEY FUSS OVER ME LIKE THAT. I'M NOT **LIKE** THEM. I'M NOT SPECIAL.
I'M NOT EVEN REALLY THEIR SON.
THERE HASN'T BEEN A HUMAN IN THE HIGH COURT IN A CENTURY. THAT MAKES YOU SPECIAL, DOESN'T IT?
OH, THEY NEVER LET ME FORGET **THAT**. IT'S ALWAYS "THE HUMAN CHILDE."
"THE HUMAN CHILDE **SNEEZED**, HOW PRECIOUS!"
PLUNK!
AND "THE HUMAN CHILDE IS JUST SO **SQUISHY**!"
WELL, YOU **ARE** RATHER SQUISHY.

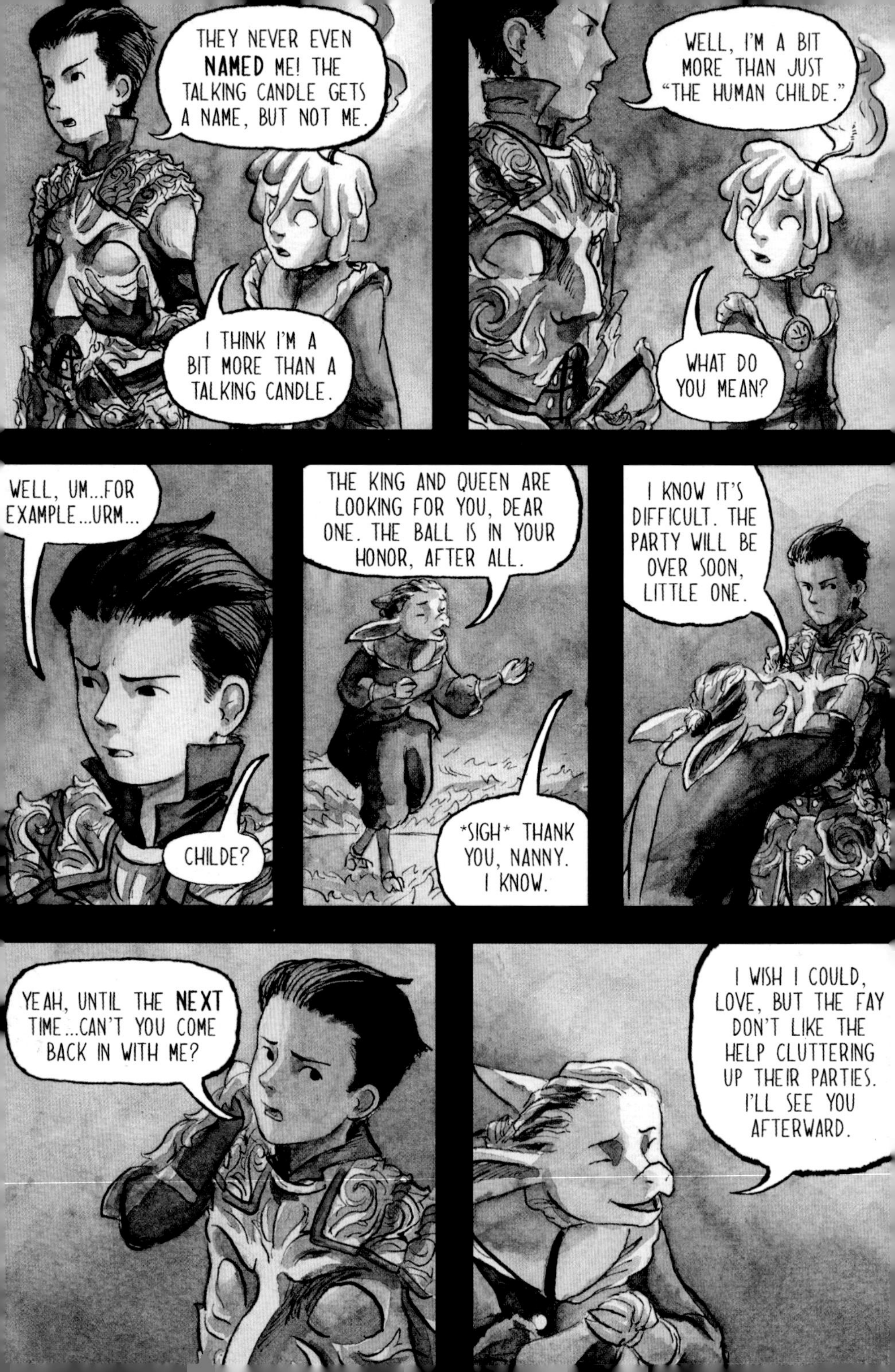
THEY NEVER EVEN **NAMED** ME! THE TALKING CANDLE GETS A NAME, BUT NOT ME.
I THINK I'M A BIT MORE THAN A TALKING CANDLE.
WELL, I'M A BIT MORE THAN JUST "THE HUMAN CHILDE."
WHAT DO YOU MEAN?
WELL, UM...FOR EXAMPLE...URM...
CHILDE?
THE KING AND QUEEN ARE LOOKING FOR YOU, DEAR ONE. THE BALL IS IN YOUR HONOR, AFTER ALL.
SIGH THANK YOU, NANNY. I KNOW.
I KNOW IT'S DIFFICULT. THE PARTY WILL BE OVER SOON, LITTLE ONE.
YEAH, UNTIL THE **NEXT** TIME...CAN'T YOU COME BACK IN WITH ME?
I WISH I COULD, LOVE, BUT THE FAY DON'T LIKE THE HELP CLUTTERING UP THEIR PARTIES. I'LL SEE YOU AFTERWARD.

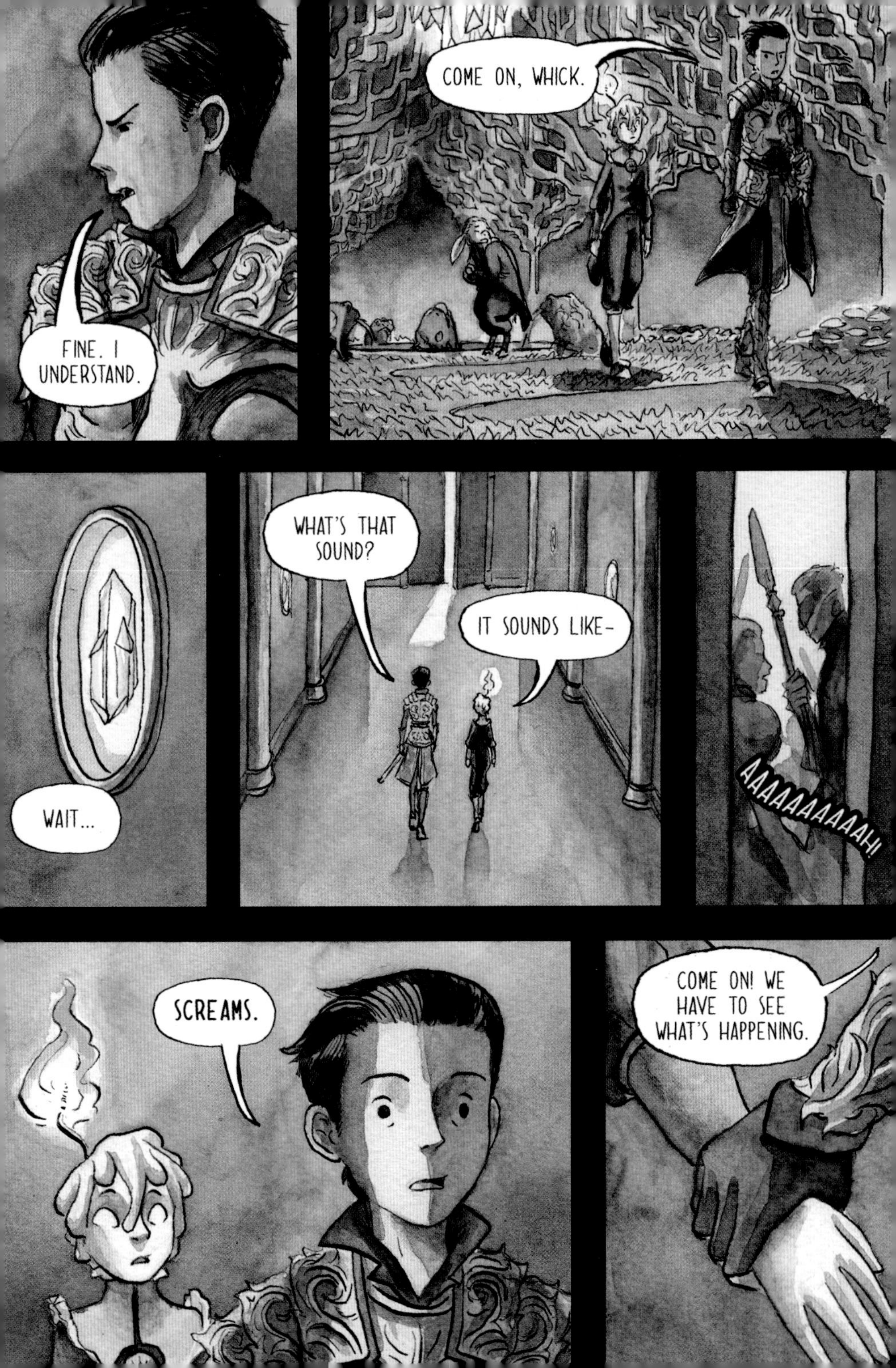
FINE. I UNDERSTAND.
COME ON, WHICK.
WAIT...
WHAT'S THAT SOUND?
IT SOUNDS LIKE-
AAAAAAAAAAH!
SCREAMS.
COME ON! WE HAVE TO SEE WHAT'S HAPPENING.

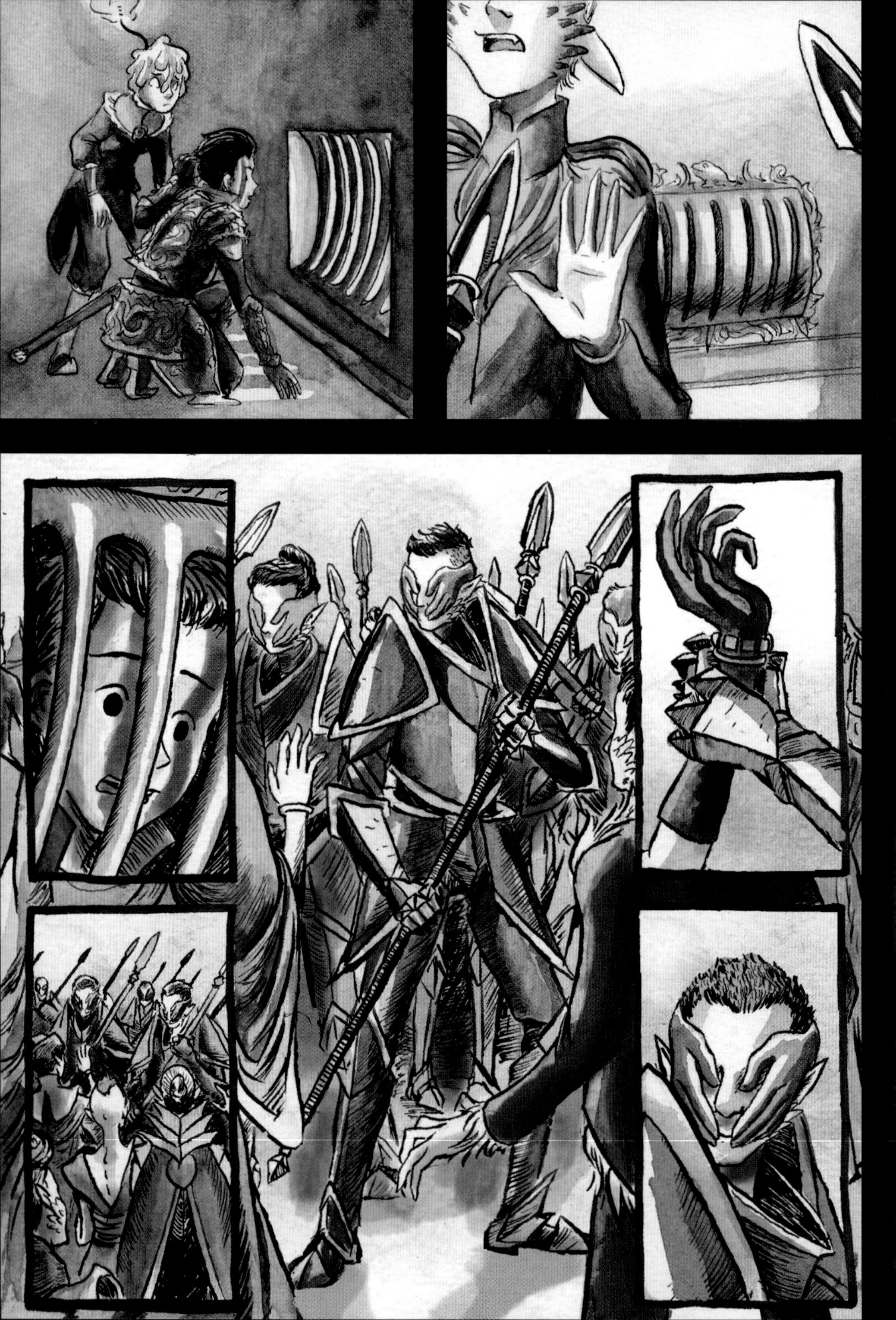

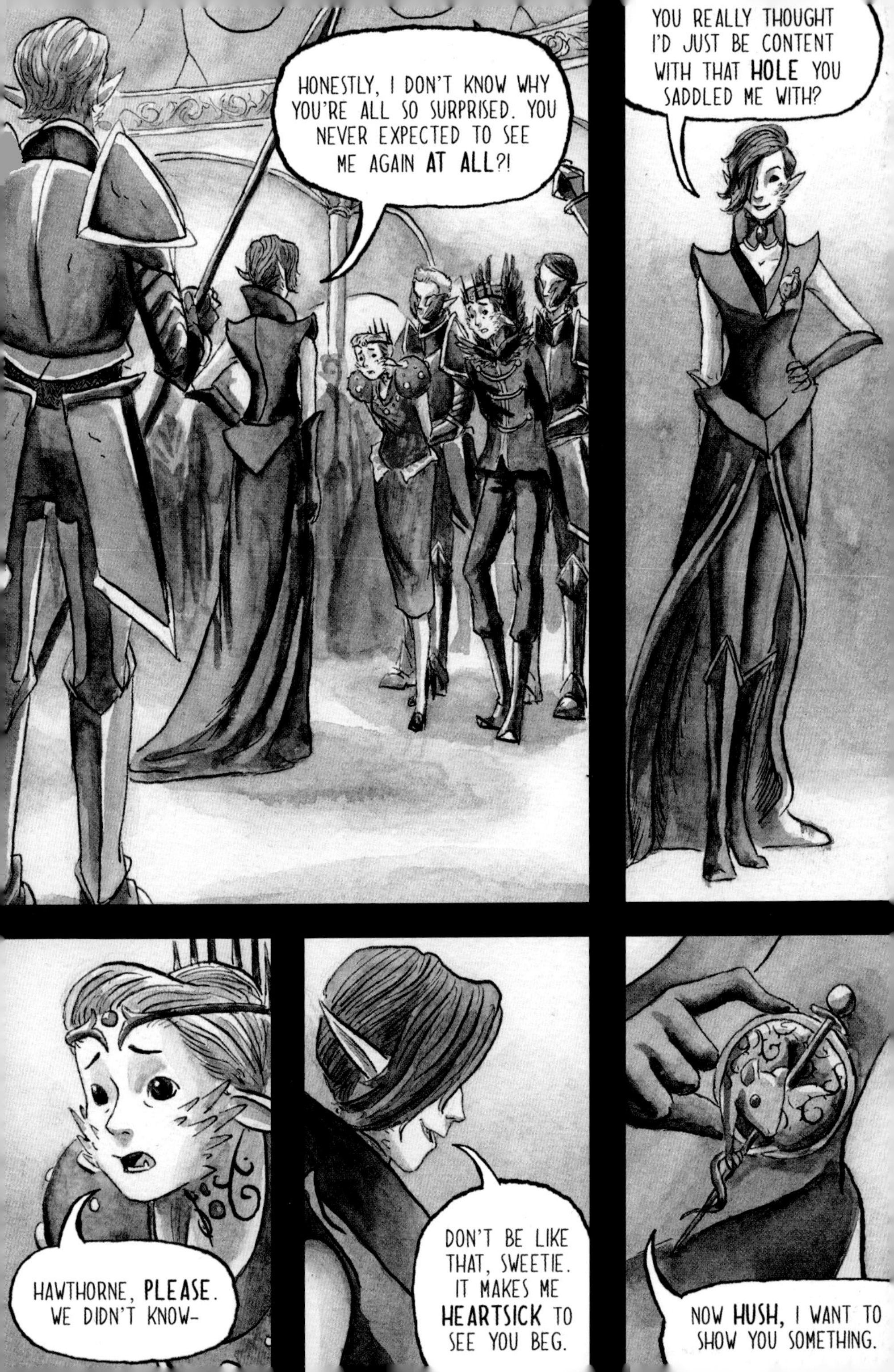
HONESTLY, I DON'T KNOW WHY YOU'RE ALL SO SURPRISED. YOU NEVER EXPECTED TO SEE ME AGAIN **AT ALL**?!
YOU REALLY THOUGHT I'D JUST BE CONTENT WITH THAT **HOLE** YOU SADDLED ME WITH?
HAWTHORNE, **PLEASE**. WE DIDN'T KNOW-
DON'T BE LIKE THAT, SWEETIE. IT MAKES ME **HEARTSICK** TO SEE YOU BEG.
NOW **HUSH**, I WANT TO SHOW YOU SOMETHING.

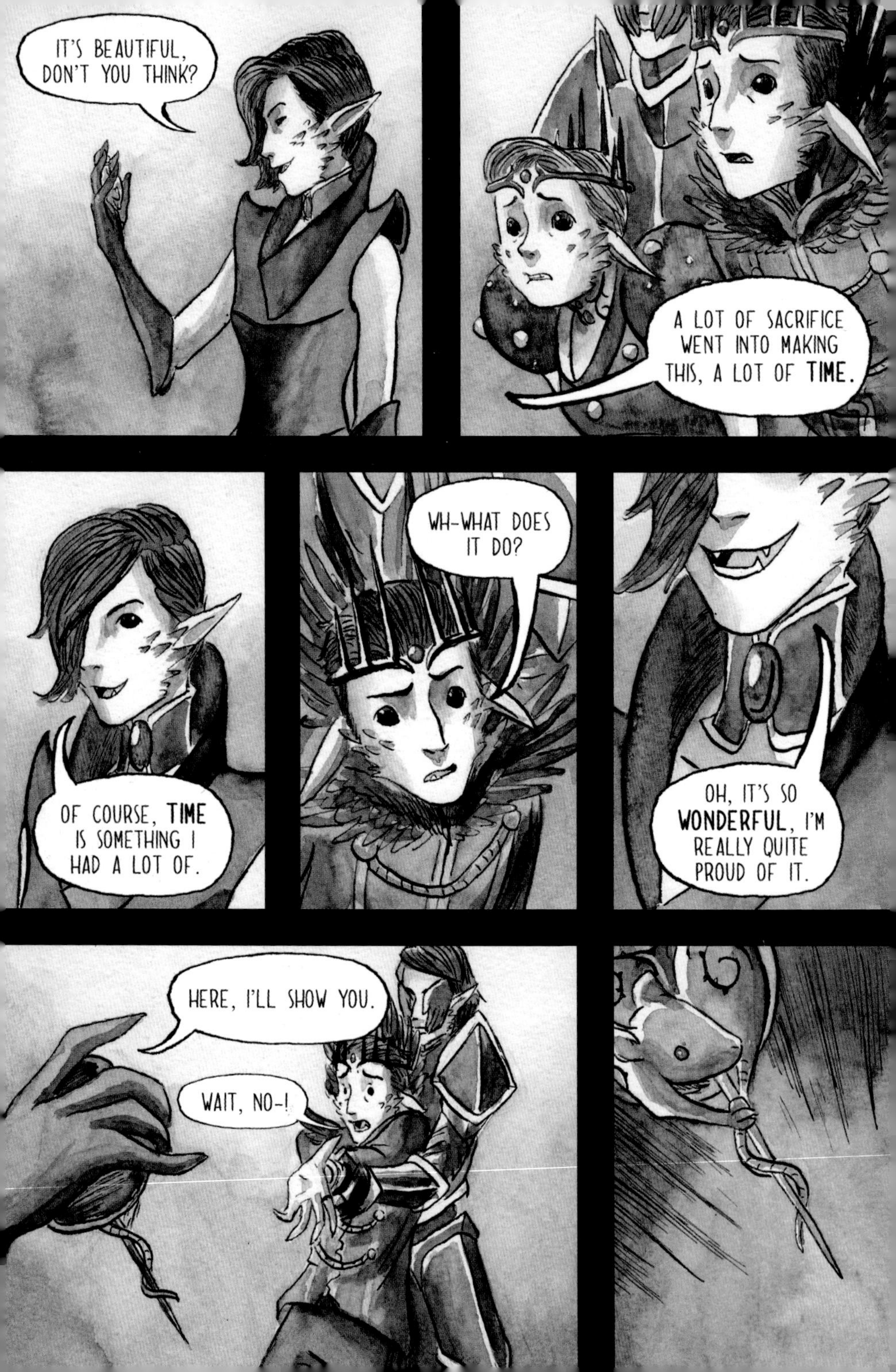
IT'S BEAUTIFUL, DON'T YOU THINK?
A LOT OF SACRIFICE WENT INTO MAKING THIS, A LOT OF **TIME**.
OF COURSE, **TIME** IS SOMETHING I HAD A LOT OF.
WH-WHAT DOES IT DO?
OH, IT'S SO **WONDERFUL**, I'M REALLY QUITE PROUD OF IT.
HERE, I'LL SHOW YOU.
WAIT, NO-!

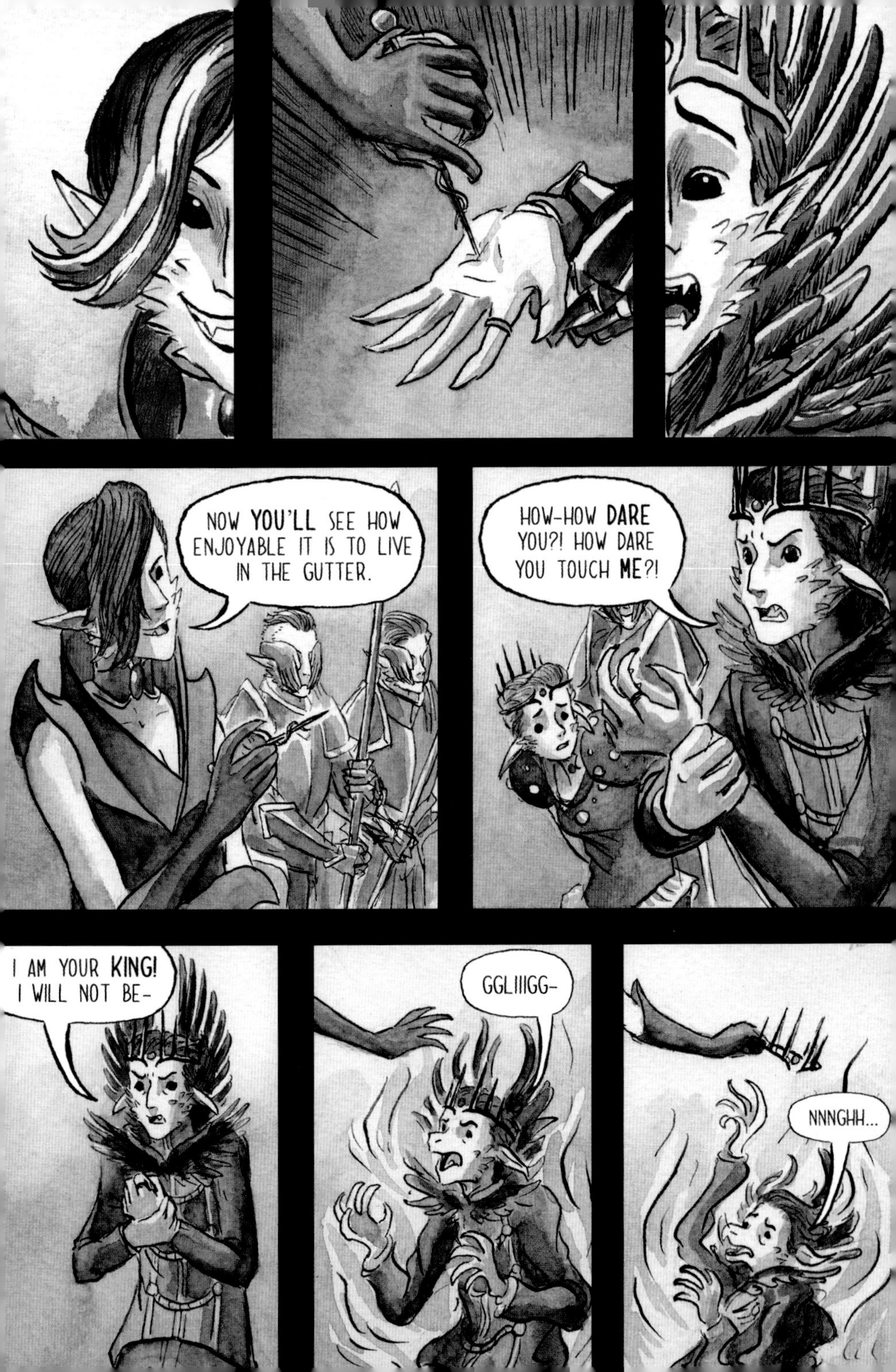
NOW YOU'LL SEE HOW ENJOYABLE IT IS TO LIVE IN THE GUTTER.
HOW-HOW DARE YOU?! HOW DARE YOU TOUCH ME?!
I AM YOUR KING! I WILL NOT BE-
GGLIIIGG-
NNNGHH...

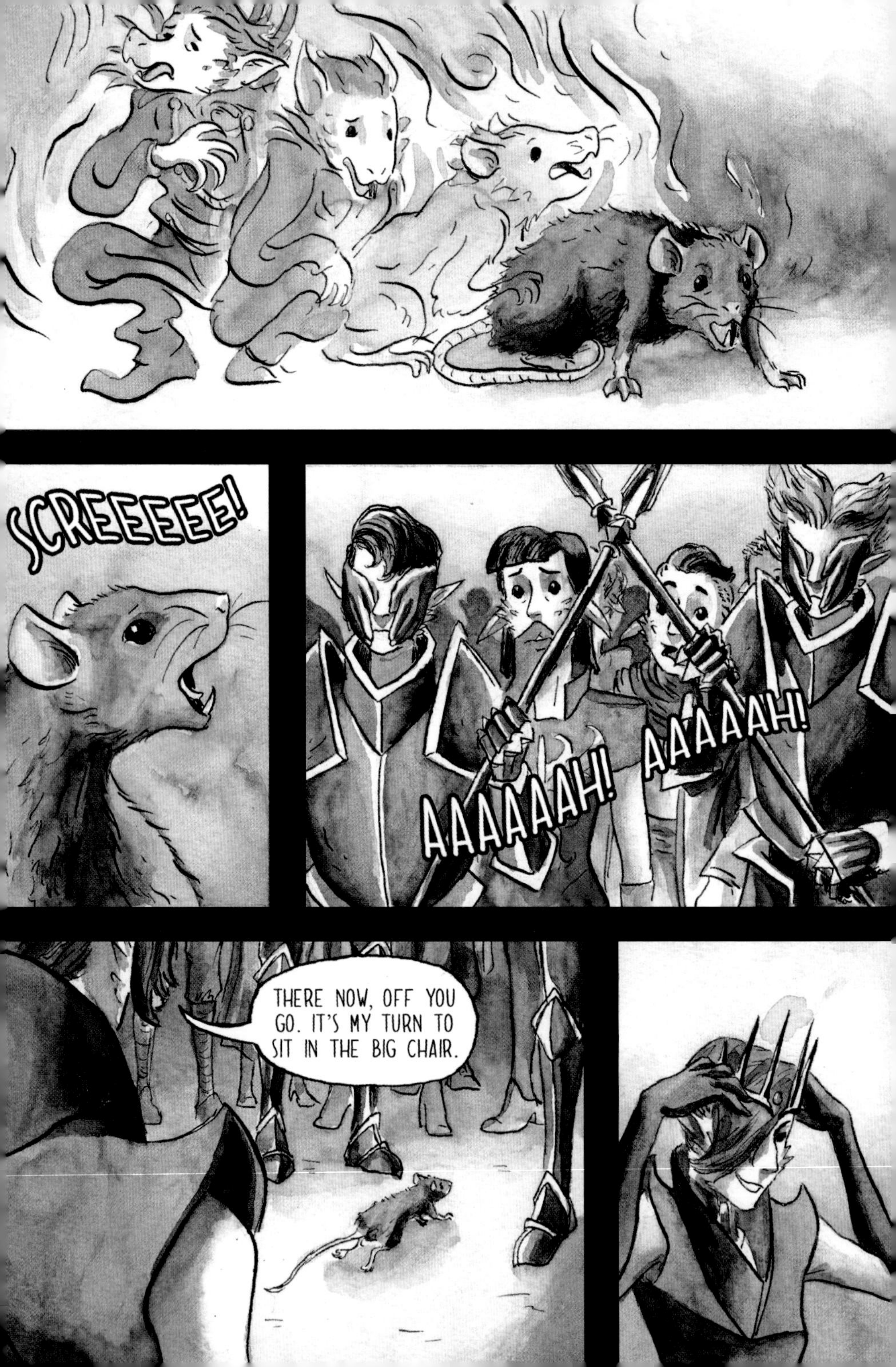
SCREEEEEE!
AAAAAAH!
AAAAAH!
THERE NOW, OFF YOU GO. IT'S MY TURN TO SIT IN THE BIG CHAIR.

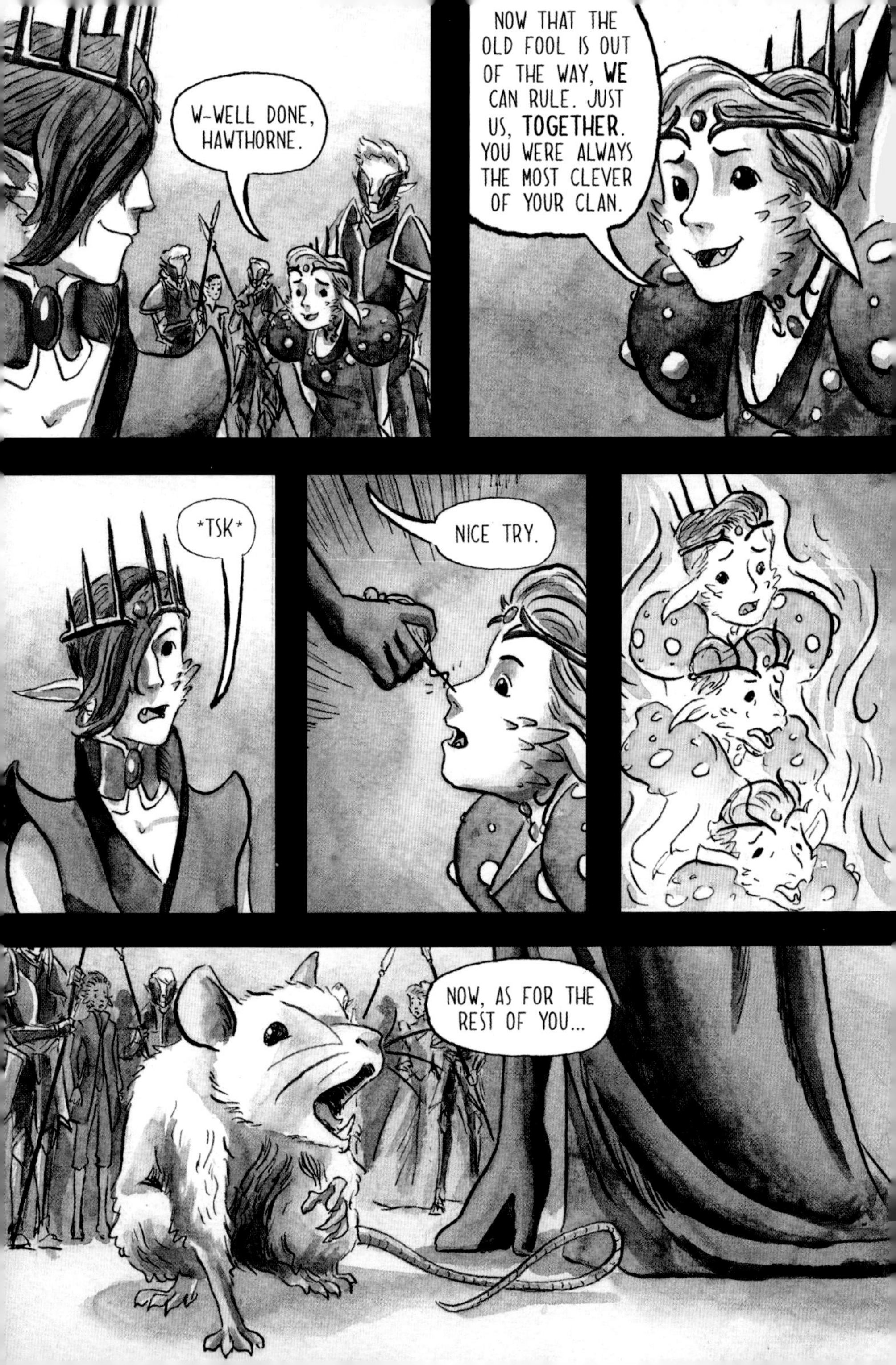
W-WELL DONE, HAWTHORNE.
NOW THAT THE OLD FOOL IS OUT OF THE WAY, **WE** CAN RULE. JUST US, **TOGETHER**. YOU WERE ALWAYS THE MOST CLEVER OF YOUR CLAN.
TSK
NICE TRY.
NOW, AS FOR THE REST OF YOU...

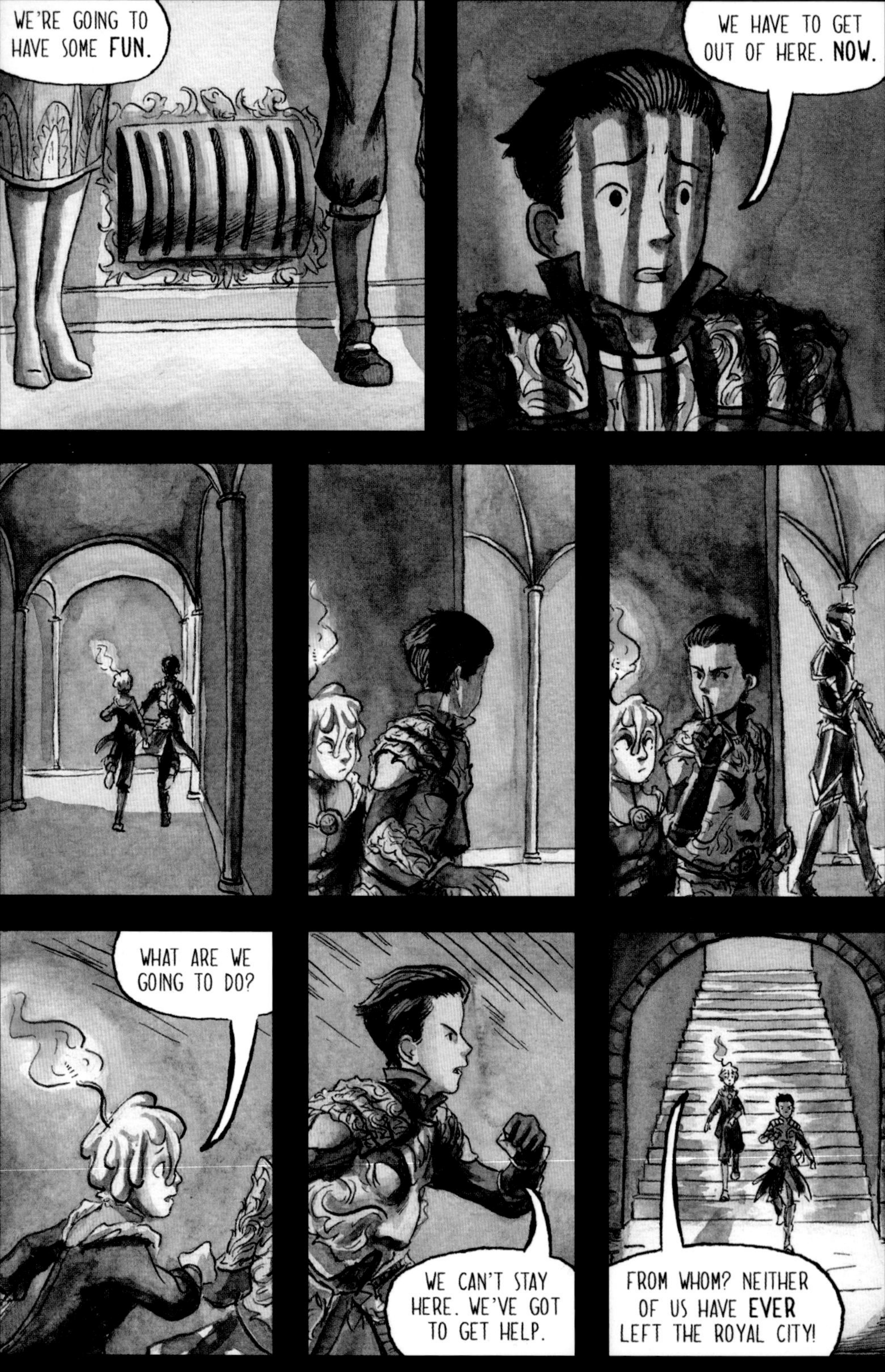
WE'RE GOING TO HAVE SOME **FUN**.
WE HAVE TO GET OUT OF HERE. **NOW**.
WHAT ARE WE GOING TO DO?
WE CAN'T STAY HERE. WE'VE GOT TO GET HELP.
FROM WHOM? NEITHER OF US HAVE **EVER** LEFT THE ROYAL CITY!

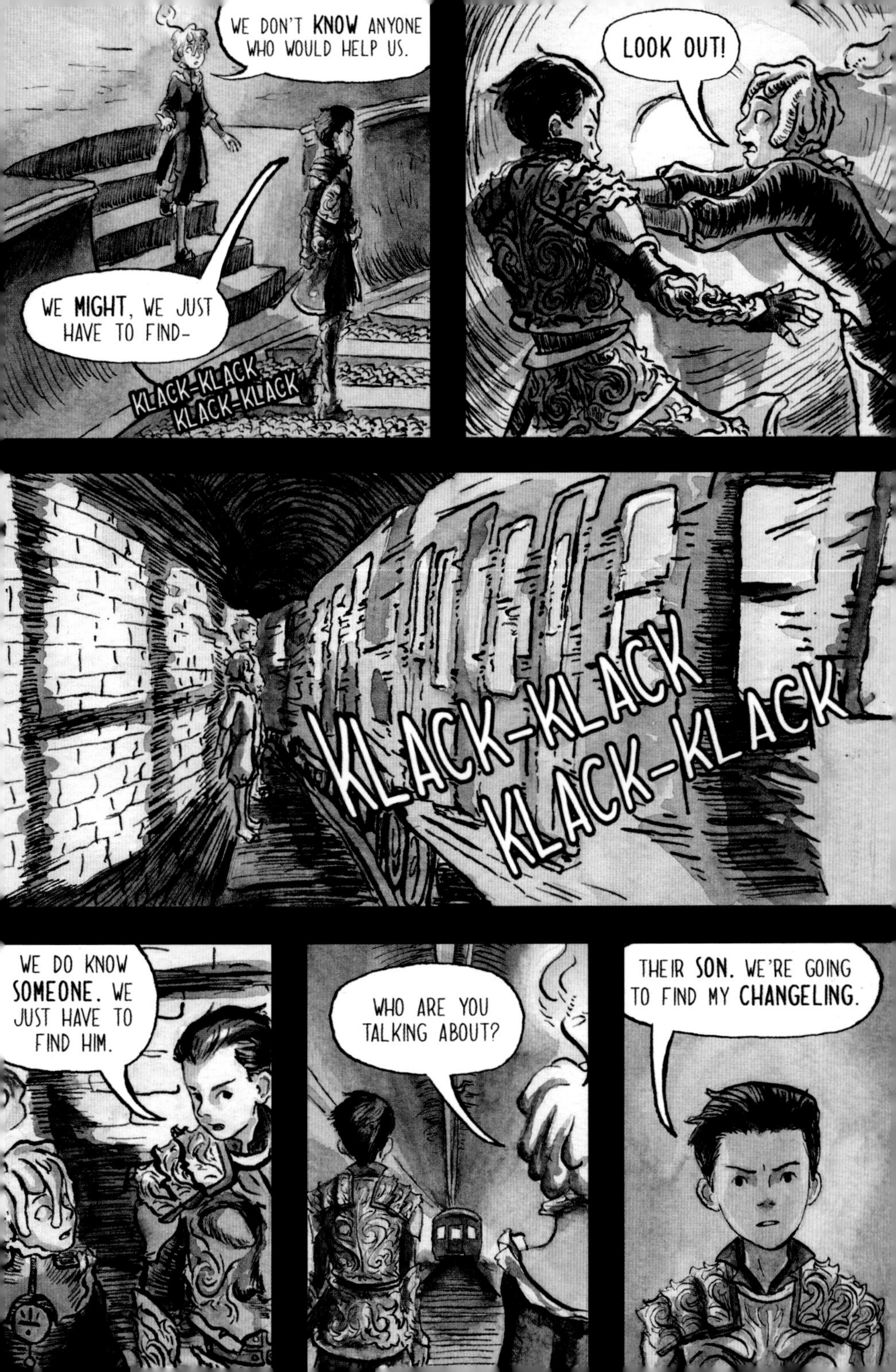
WE DON'T KNOW ANYONE WHO WOULD HELP US.
WE MIGHT, WE JUST HAVE TO FIND-
KLACK-KLACK KLACK-KLACK
LOOK OUT!
KLACK-KLACK KLACK-KLACK
WE DO KNOW SOMEONE. WE JUST HAVE TO FIND HIM.
WHO ARE YOU TALKING ABOUT?
THEIR SON. WE'RE GOING TO FIND MY CHANGELING.

Chapter Two

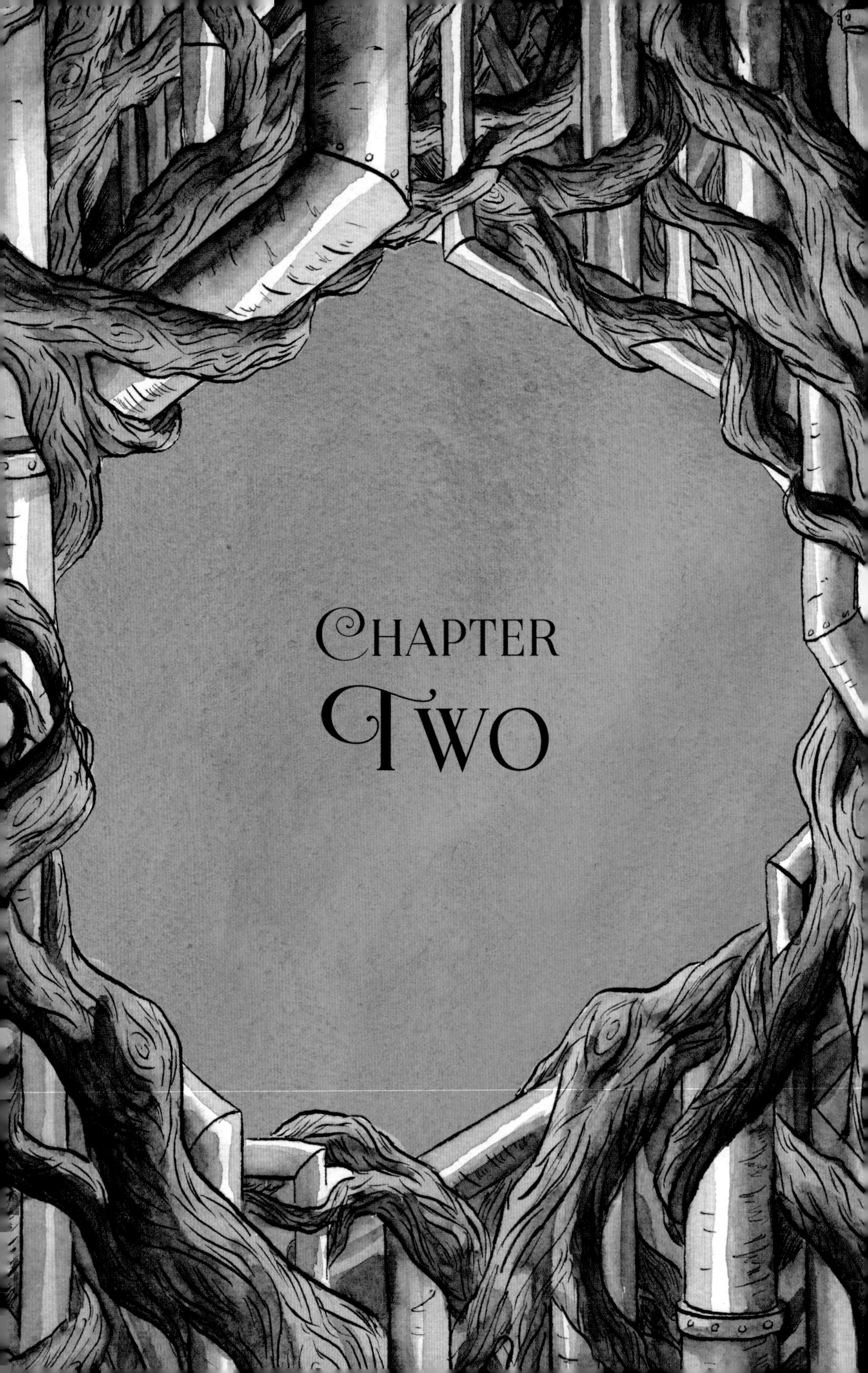

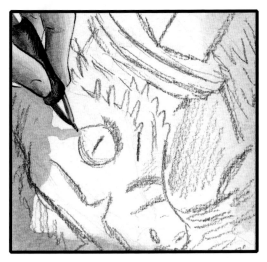

HEY, EDMUND.

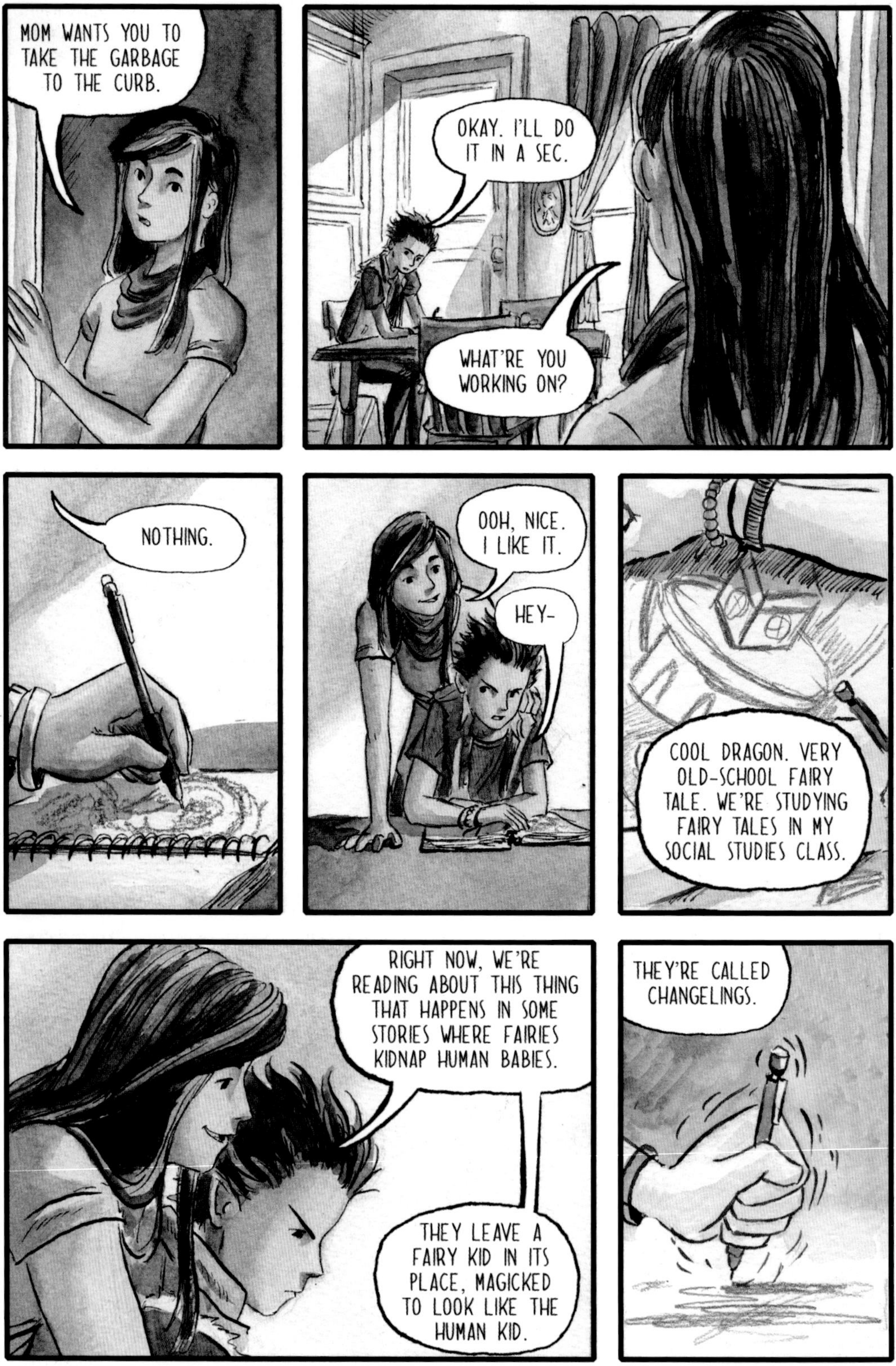
MOM WANTS YOU TO TAKE THE GARBAGE TO THE CURB.
OKAY. I'LL DO IT IN A SEC.
WHAT'RE YOU WORKING ON?
NOTHING.
OOH, NICE. I LIKE IT.
HEY-
COOL DRAGON. VERY OLD-SCHOOL FAIRY TALE. WE'RE STUDYING FAIRY TALES IN MY SOCIAL STUDIES CLASS.
RIGHT NOW, WE'RE READING ABOUT THIS THING THAT HAPPENS IN SOME STORIES WHERE FAIRIES KIDNAP HUMAN BABIES.
THEY LEAVE A FAIRY KID IN ITS PLACE, MAGICKED TO LOOK LIKE THE HUMAN KID.
THEY'RE CALLED CHANGELINGS.

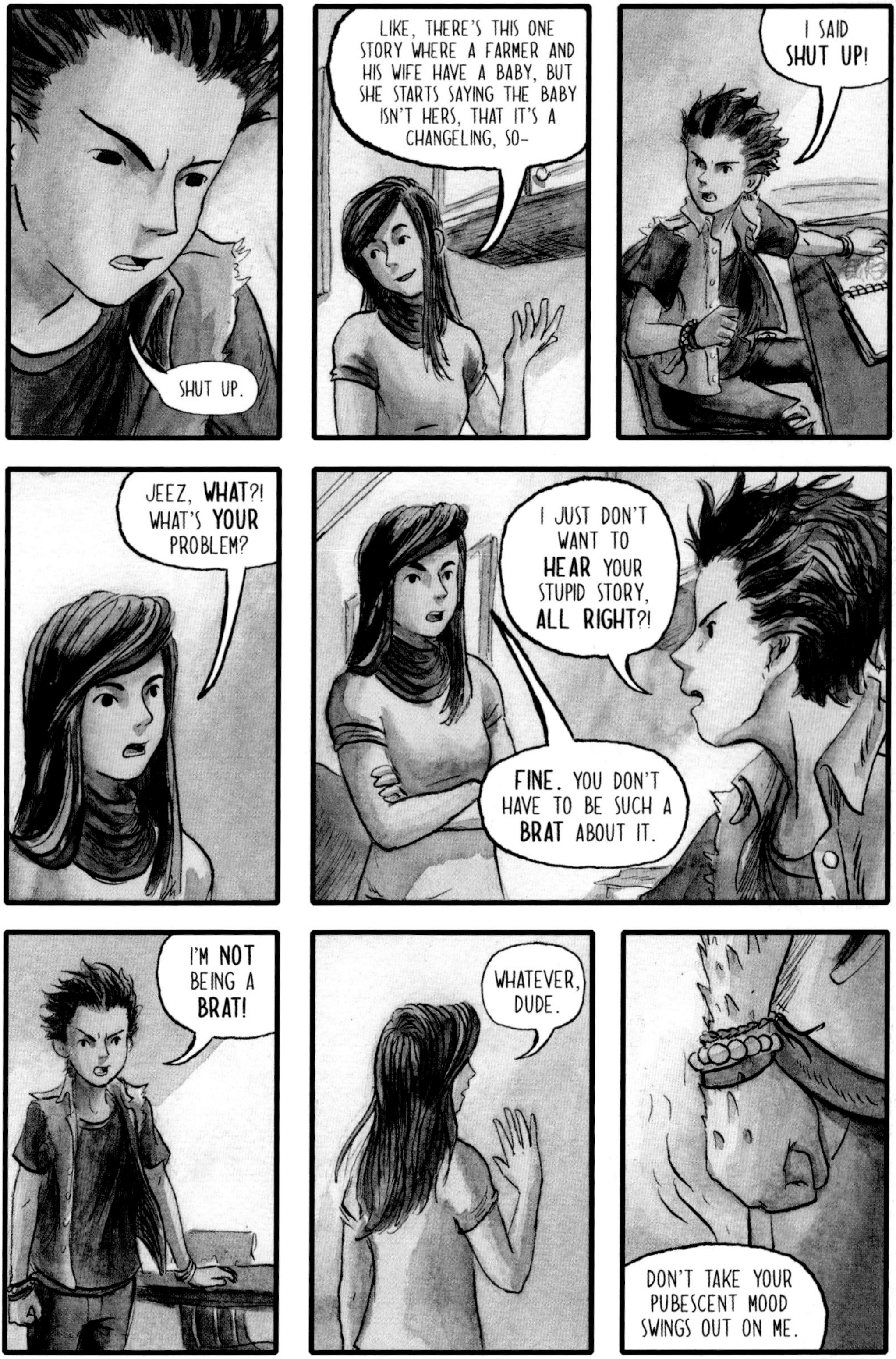
SHUT UP.
LIKE, THERE'S THIS ONE STORY WHERE A FARMER AND HIS WIFE HAVE A BABY, BUT SHE STARTS SAYING THE BABY ISN'T HERS, THAT IT'S A CHANGELING, SO–
I SAID SHUT UP!
JEEZ, WHAT?! WHAT'S YOUR PROBLEM?
I JUST DON'T WANT TO HEAR YOUR STUPID STORY, ALL RIGHT?!
FINE. YOU DON'T HAVE TO BE SUCH A BRAT ABOUT IT.
I'M NOT BEING A BRAT!
WHATEVER, DUDE.
DON'T TAKE YOUR PUBESCENT MOOD SWINGS OUT ON ME.

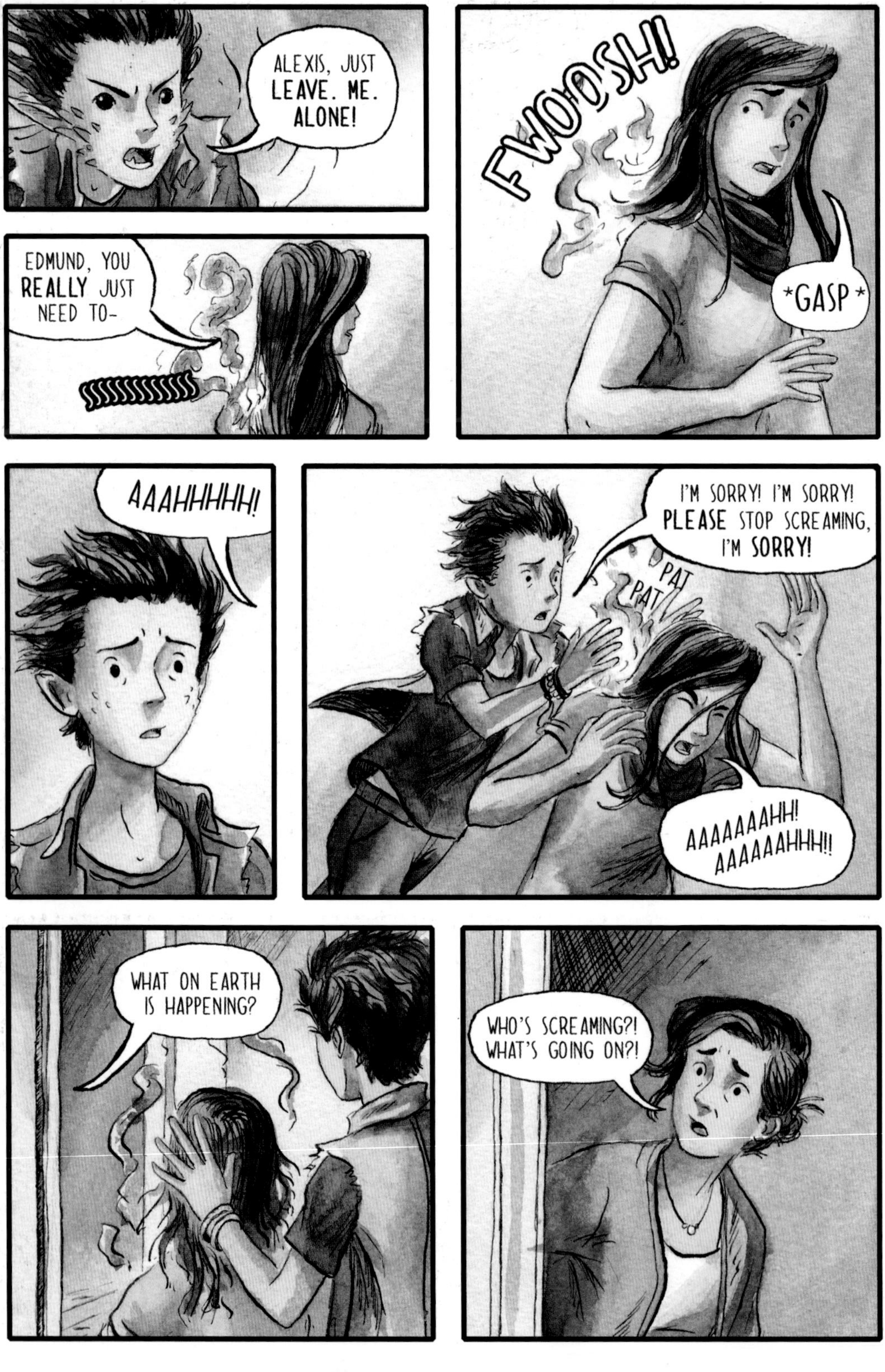
ALEXIS, JUST LEAVE. ME. ALONE!
EDMUND, YOU REALLY JUST NEED TO-
SSSSSSSSSSS
FWOOSH!
GASP
AAAHHHHH!
I'M SORRY! I'M SORRY! PLEASE STOP SCREAMING, I'M SORRY!
PAT PAT
AAAAAAAHH! AAAAAAHHH!!
WHAT ON EARTH IS HAPPENING?
WHO'S SCREAMING?! WHAT'S GOING ON?!

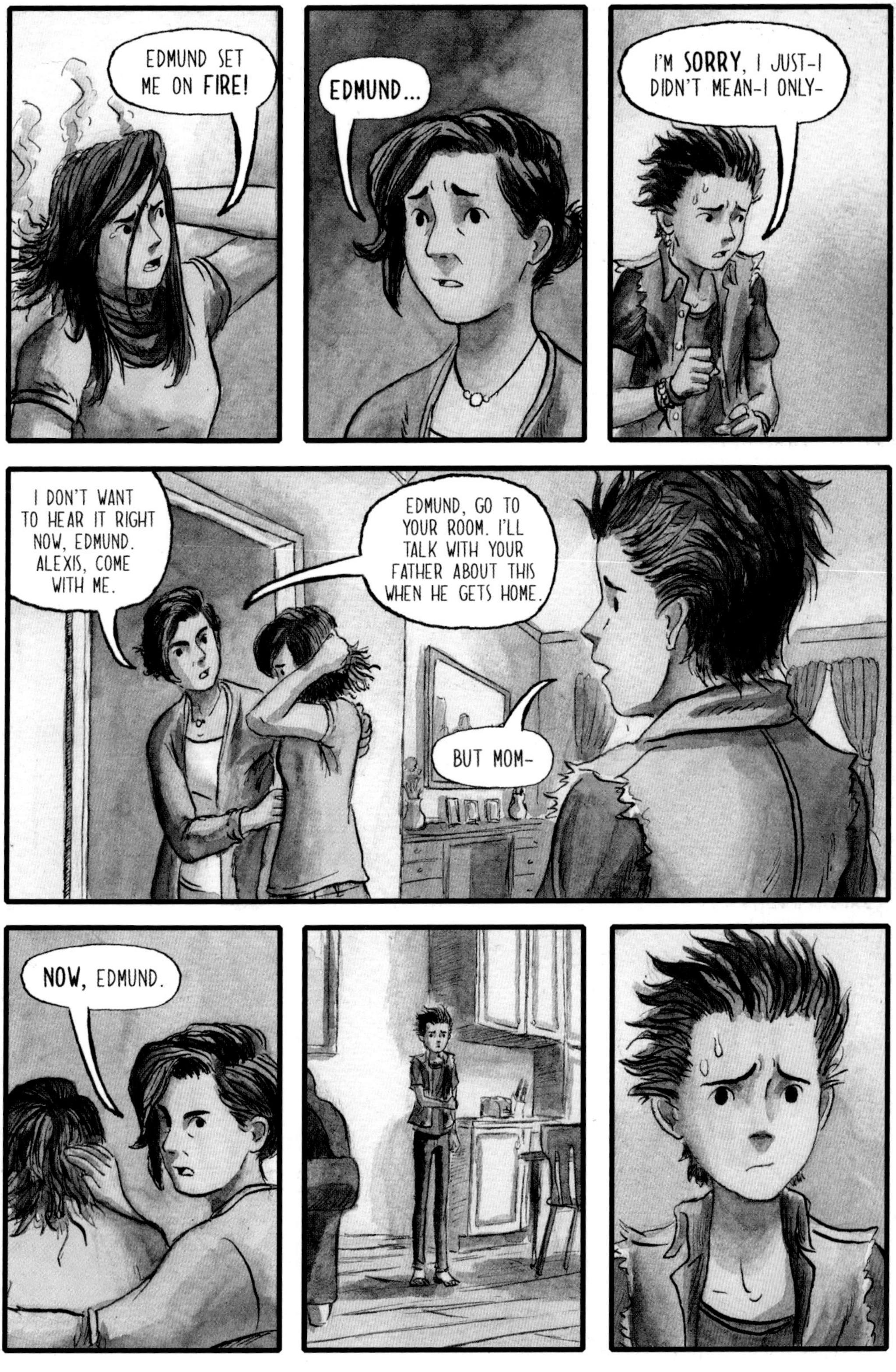
EDMUND SET ME ON FIRE!
EDMUND...
I'M SORRY, I JUST-I DIDN'T MEAN-I ONLY-
I DON'T WANT TO HEAR IT RIGHT NOW, EDMUND. ALEXIS, COME WITH ME.
EDMUND, GO TO YOUR ROOM. I'LL TALK WITH YOUR FATHER ABOUT THIS WHEN HE GETS HOME.
BUT MOM-
NOW, EDMUND.

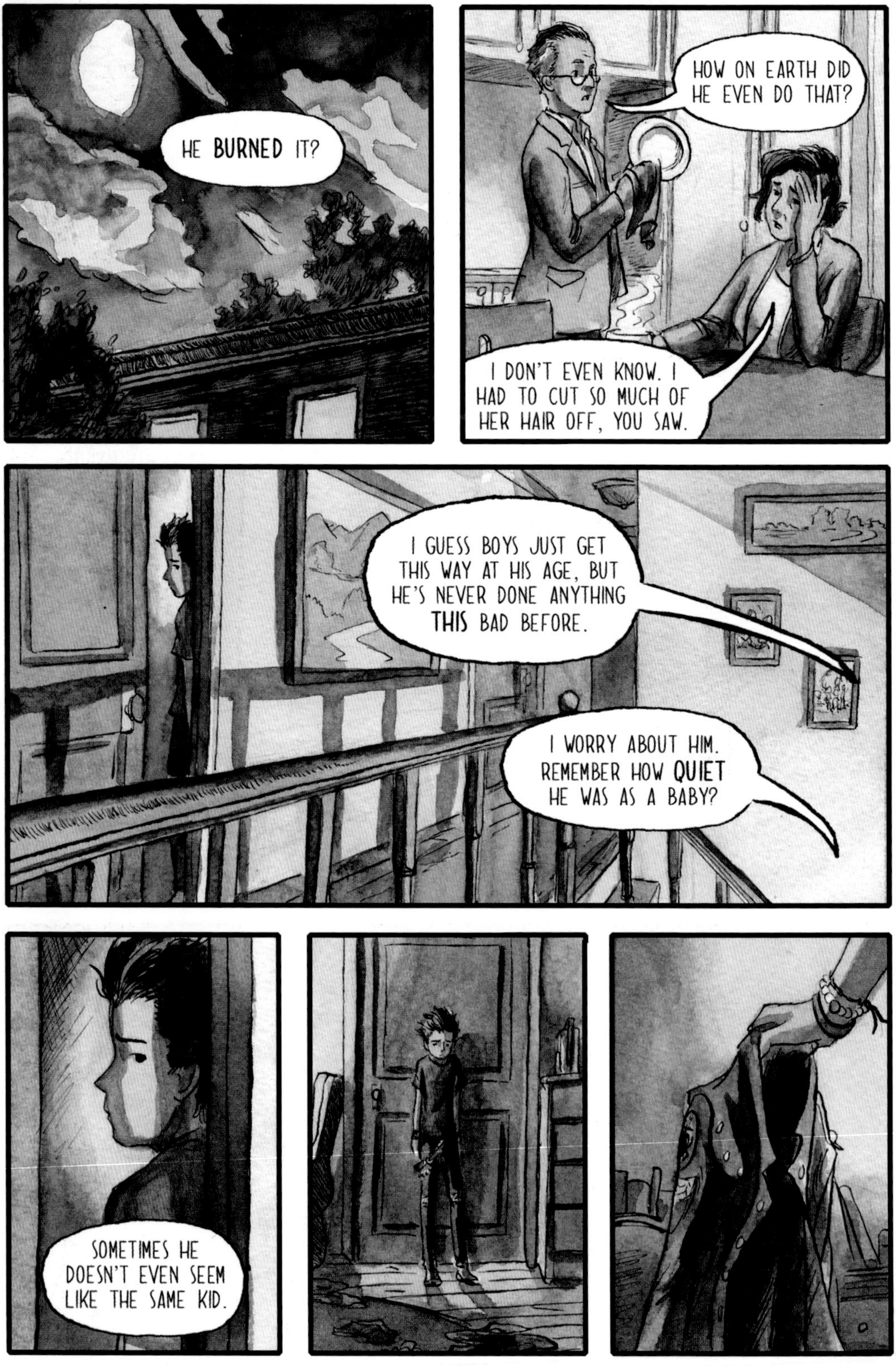
HE **BURNED** IT?
HOW ON EARTH DID HE EVEN DO THAT?
I DON'T EVEN KNOW. I HAD TO CUT SO MUCH OF HER HAIR OFF, YOU SAW.
I GUESS BOYS JUST GET THIS WAY AT HIS AGE, BUT HE'S NEVER DONE ANYTHING **THIS** BAD BEFORE.
I WORRY ABOUT HIM. REMEMBER HOW **QUIET** HE WAS AS A BABY?
SOMETIMES HE DOESN'T EVEN SEEM LIKE THE SAME KID.

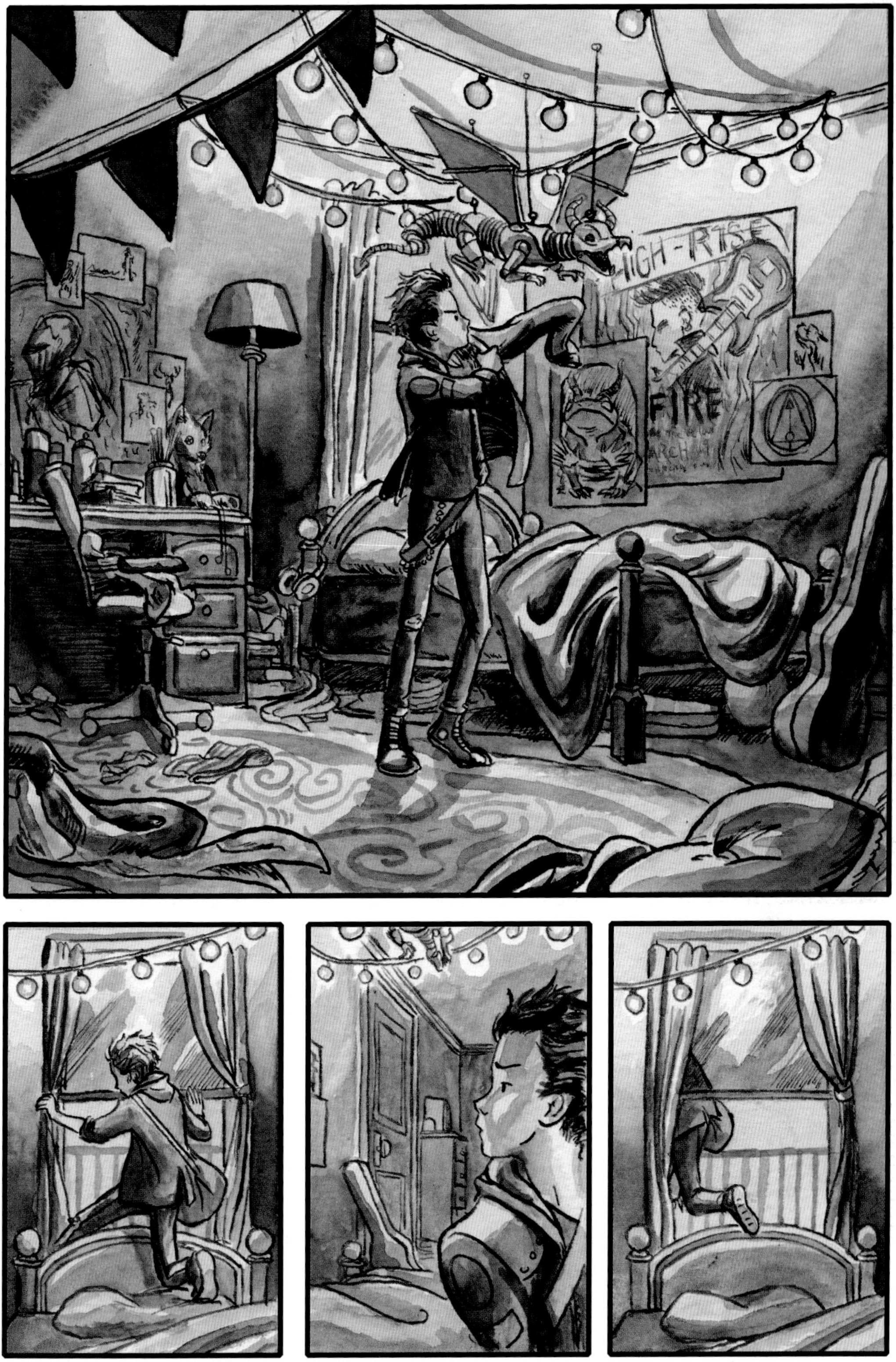
FIRE

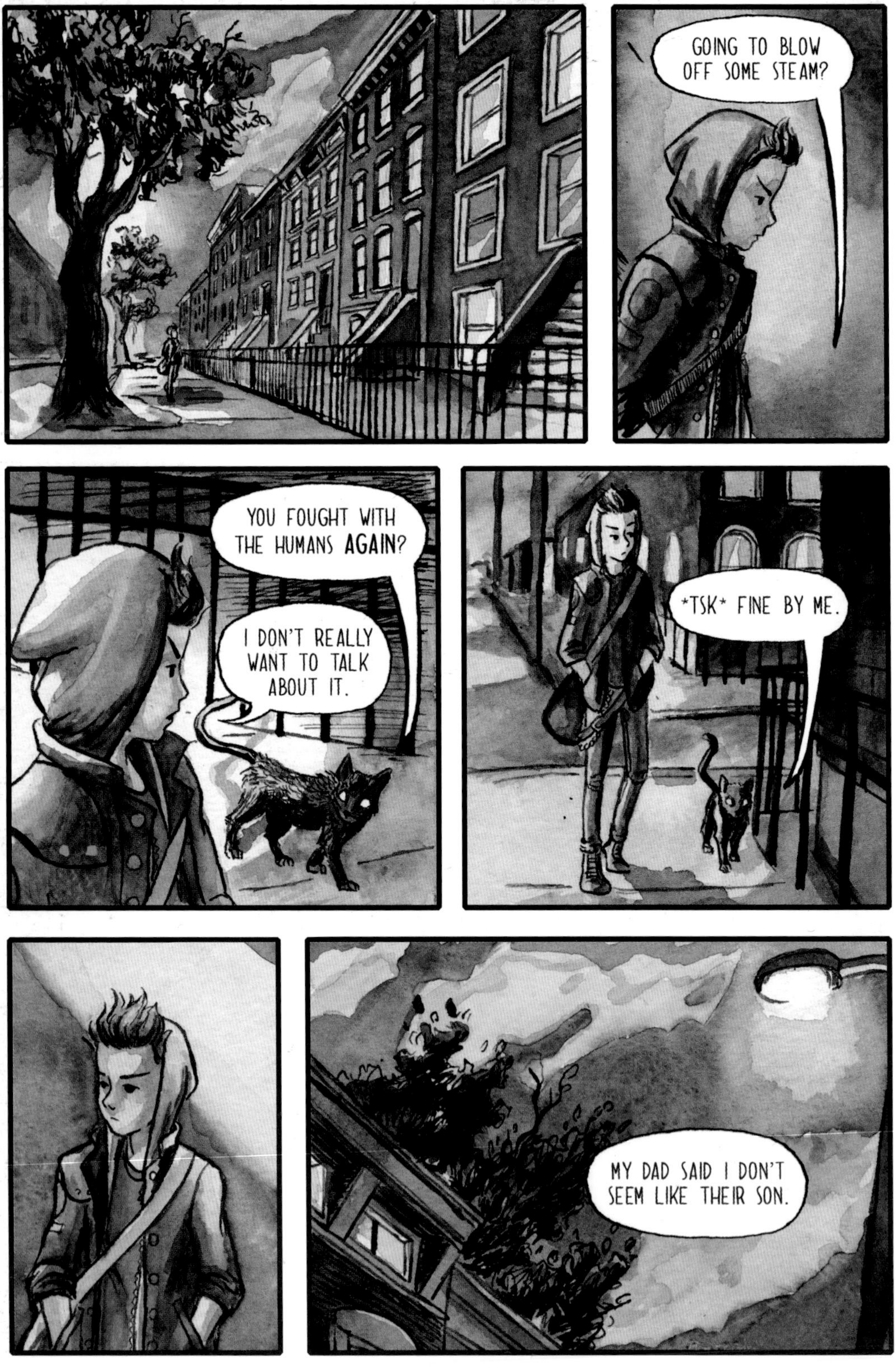
GOING TO BLOW OFF SOME STEAM?
YOU FOUGHT WITH THE HUMANS AGAIN?
I DON'T REALLY WANT TO TALK ABOUT IT.
TSK FINE BY ME.
MY DAD SAID I DON'T SEEM LIKE THEIR SON.

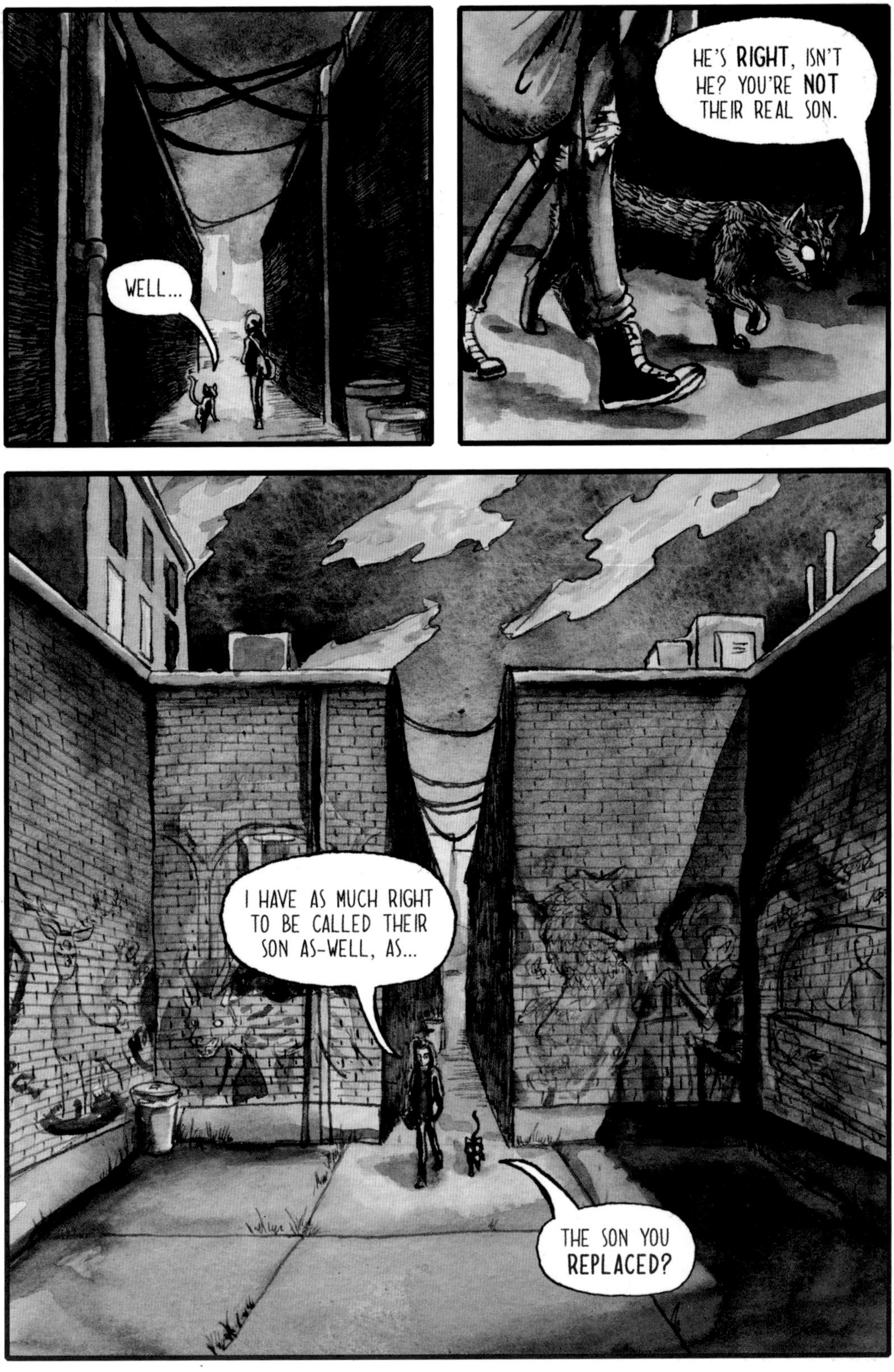
WELL...
HE'S **RIGHT**, ISN'T HE? YOU'RE **NOT** THEIR REAL SON.
I HAVE AS MUCH RIGHT TO BE CALLED THEIR SON AS-WELL, AS...
THE SON YOU **REPLACED**?

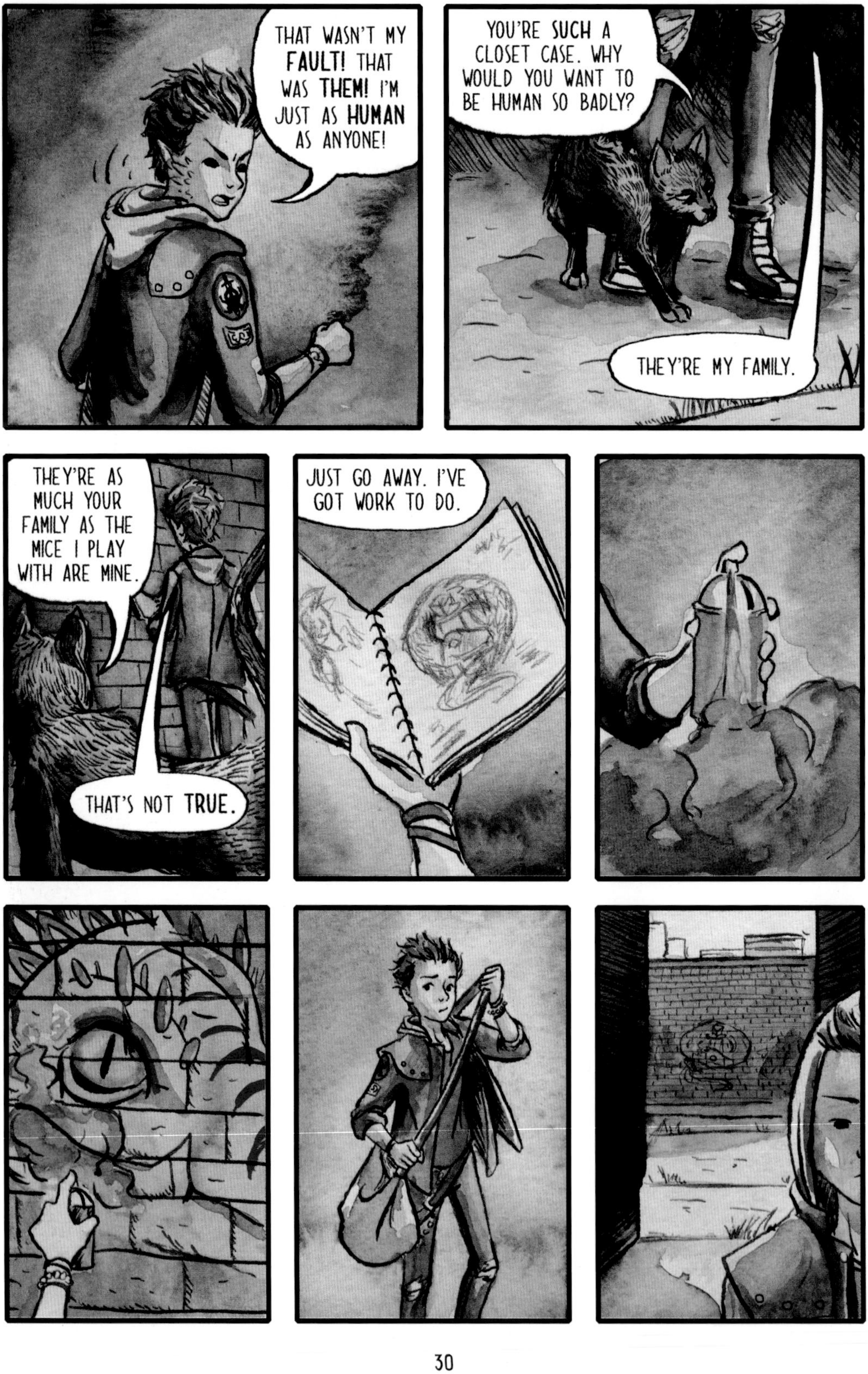
THAT WASN'T MY FAULT! THAT WAS THEM! I'M JUST AS HUMAN AS ANYONE!
YOU'RE SUCH A CLOSET CASE. WHY WOULD YOU WANT TO BE HUMAN SO BADLY?
THEY'RE MY FAMILY.
THEY'RE AS MUCH YOUR FAMILY AS THE MICE I PLAY WITH ARE MINE.
THAT'S NOT TRUE.
JUST GO AWAY. I'VE GOT WORK TO DO.

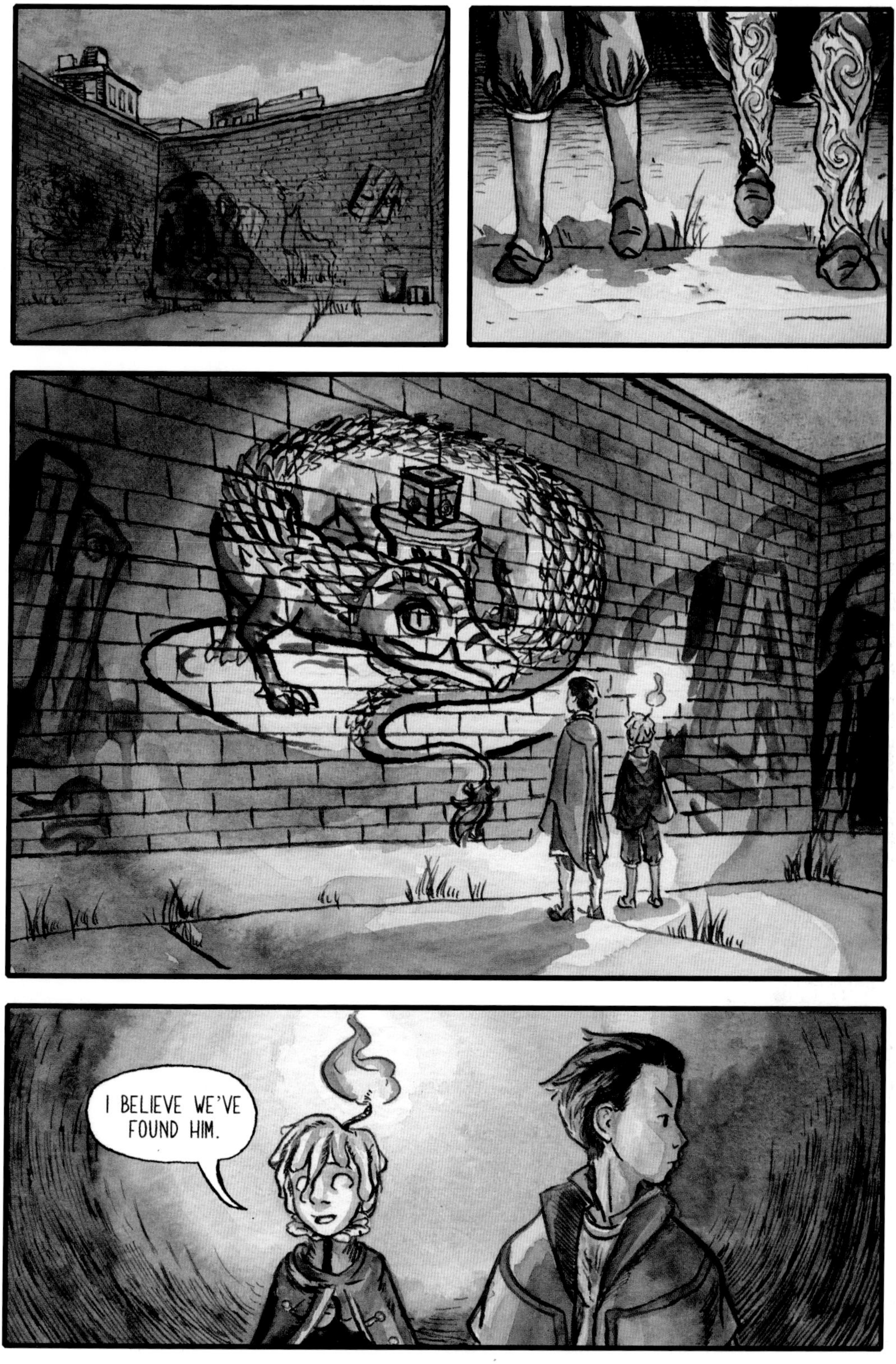
I BELIEVE WE'VE FOUND HIM.

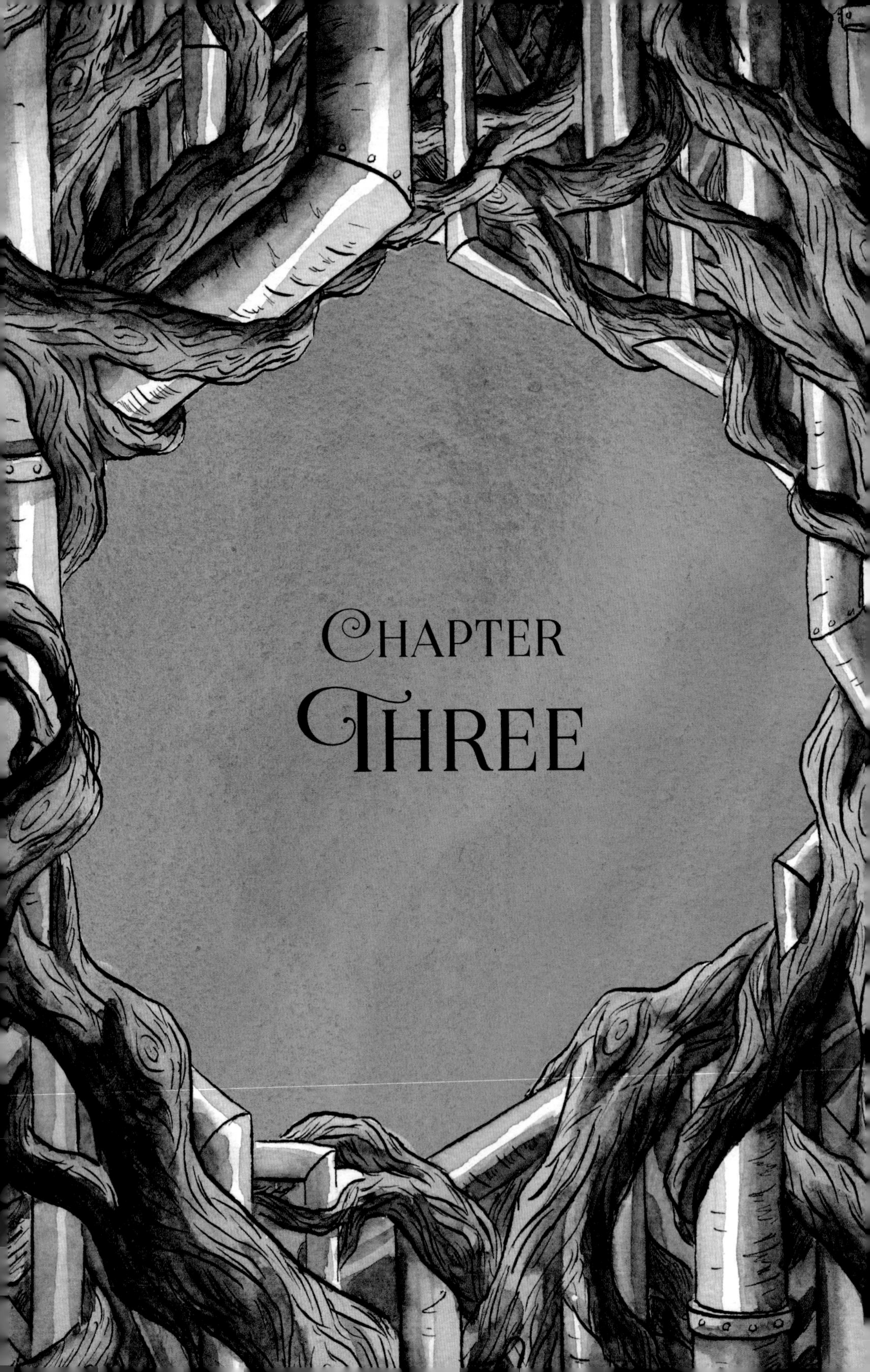

Chapter Three

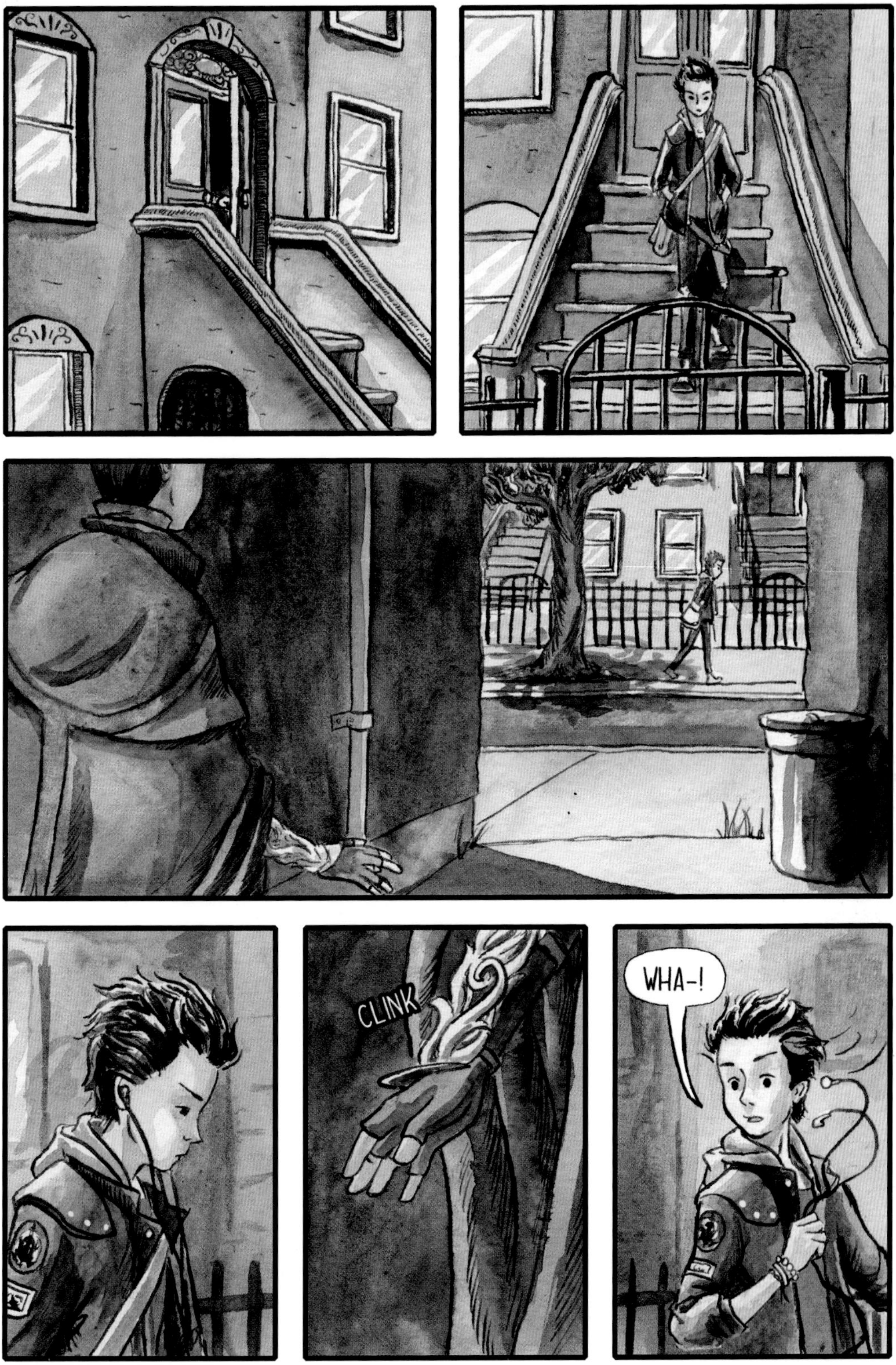
CLINK
WHA-!

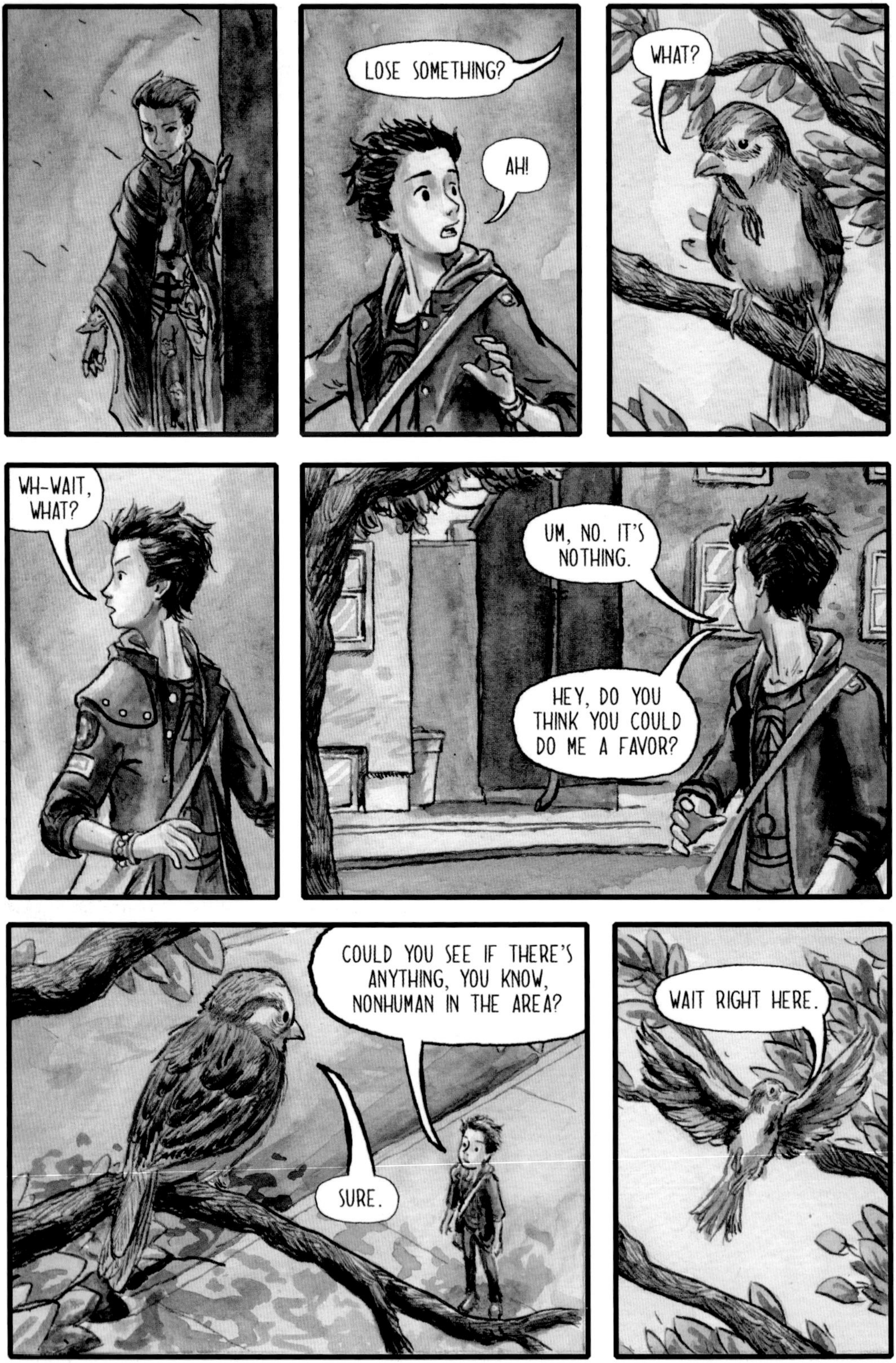
LOSE SOMETHING?
AH!
WHAT?
WH-WAIT, WHAT?
UM, NO. IT'S NOTHING.
HEY, DO YOU THINK YOU COULD DO ME A FAVOR?
COULD YOU SEE IF THERE'S ANYTHING, YOU KNOW, NONHUMAN IN THE AREA?
SURE.
WAIT RIGHT HERE.

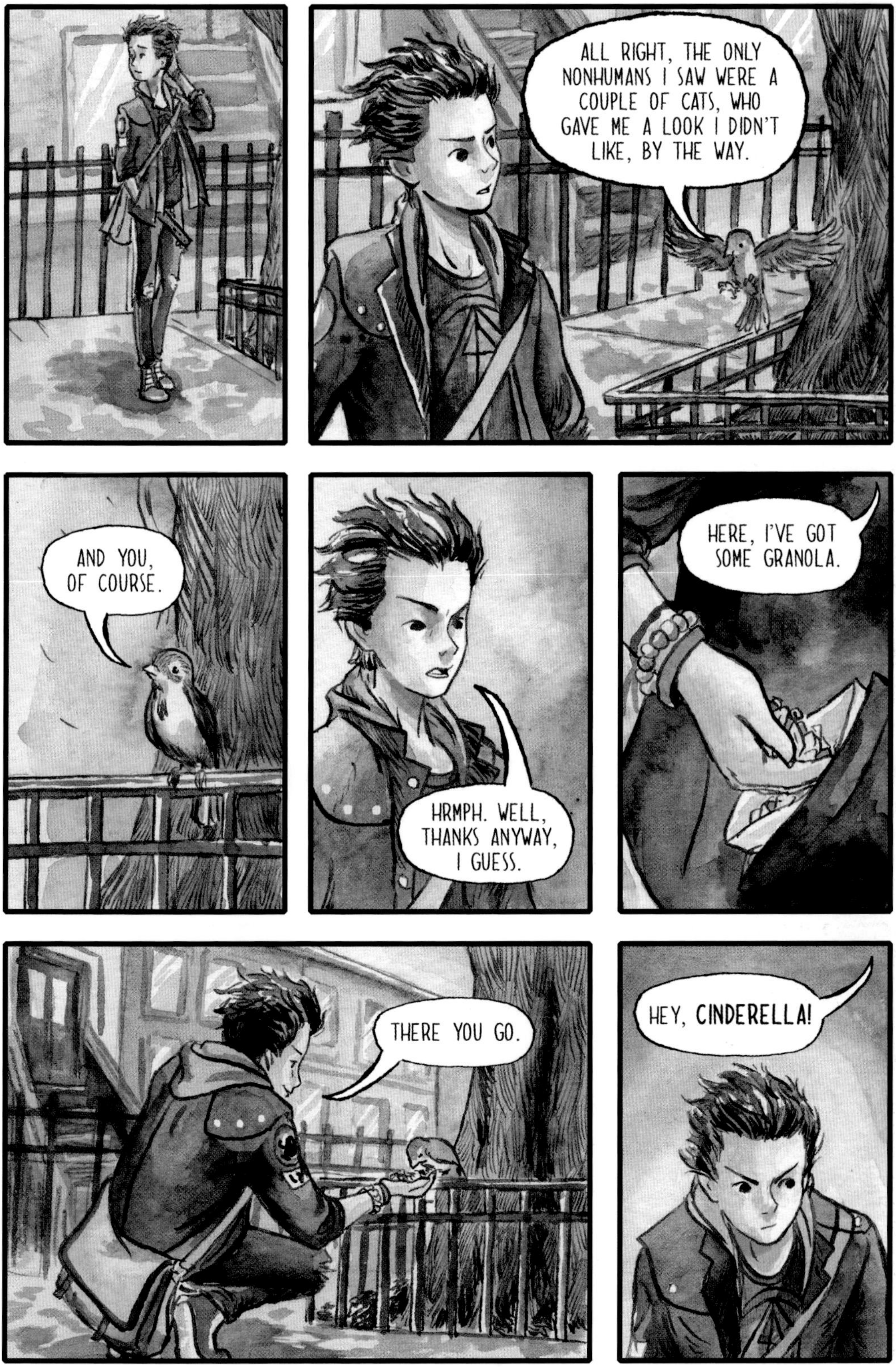
ALL RIGHT, THE ONLY NONHUMANS I SAW WERE A COUPLE OF CATS, WHO GAVE ME A LOOK I DIDN'T LIKE, BY THE WAY.
AND YOU, OF COURSE.
HRMPH. WELL, THANKS ANYWAY, I GUESS.
HERE, I'VE GOT SOME GRANOLA.
THERE YOU GO.
HEY, CINDERELLA!

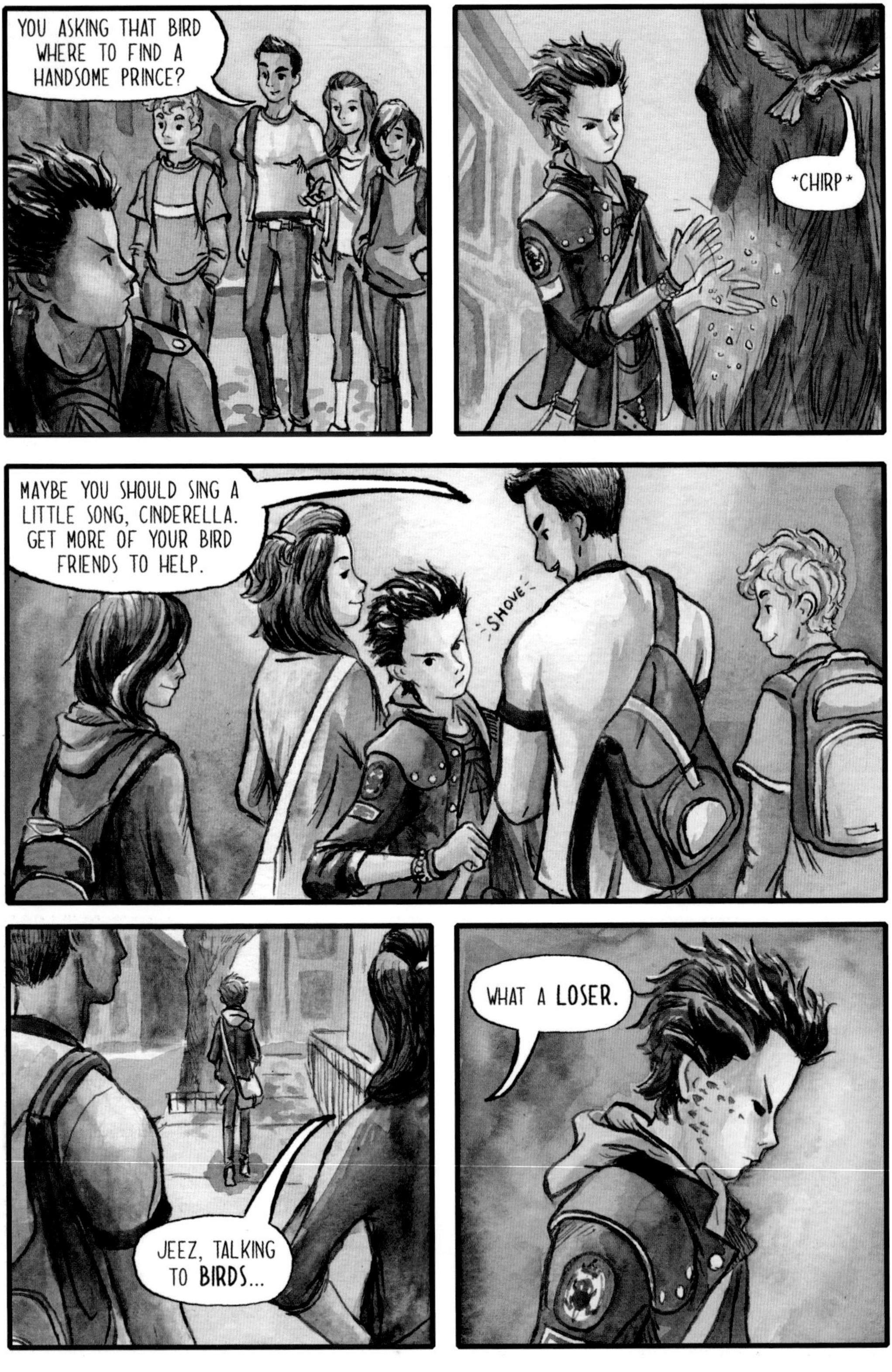
YOU ASKING THAT BIRD WHERE TO FIND A HANDSOME PRINCE?
CHIRP
MAYBE YOU SHOULD SING A LITTLE SONG, CINDERELLA. GET MORE OF YOUR BIRD FRIENDS TO HELP.
SHOVE
JEEZ, TALKING TO BIRDS...
WHAT A LOSER.

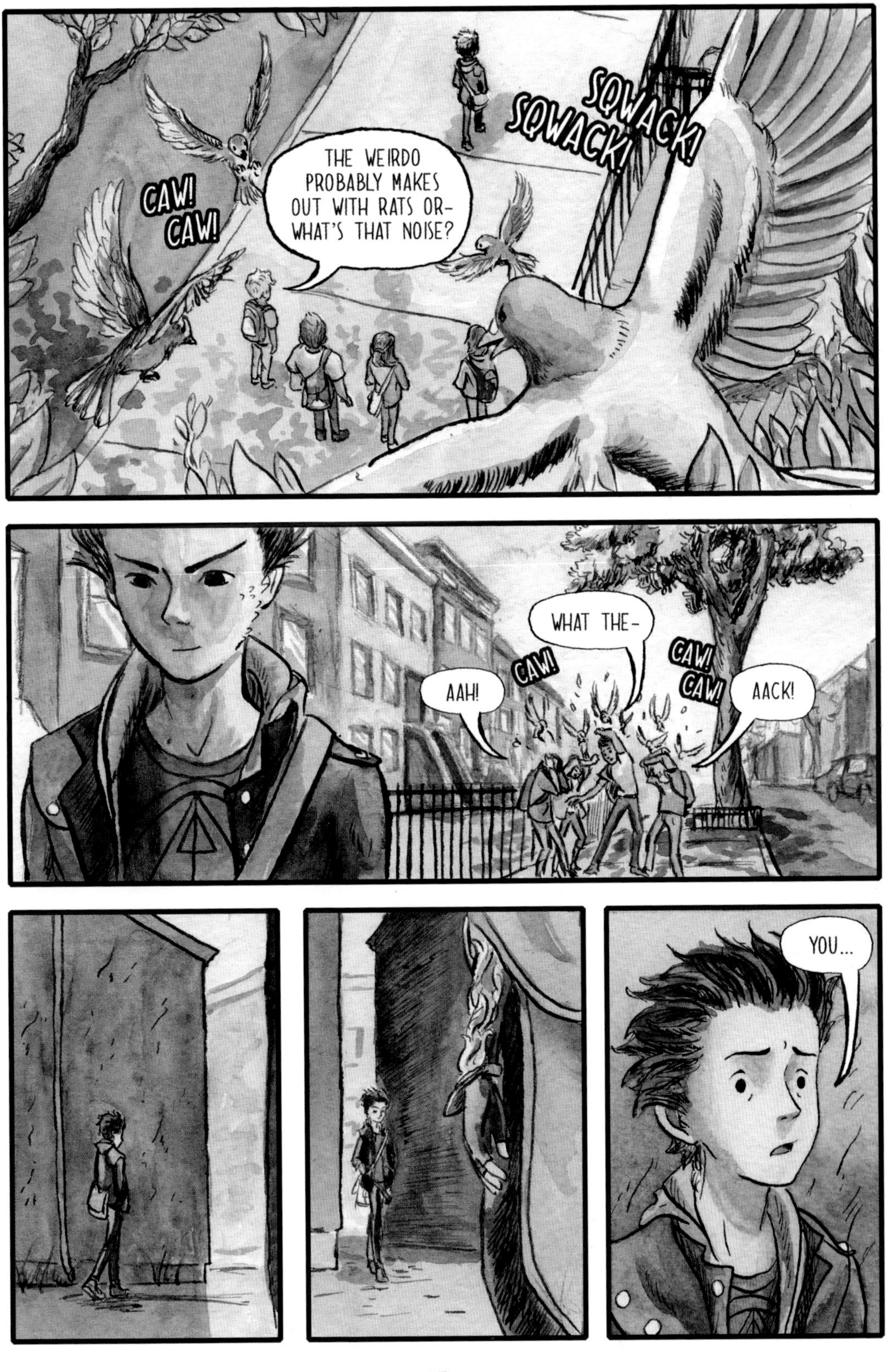
SQWACK!
SQWACK!
CAW!
CAW!
THE WEIRDO PROBABLY MAKES OUT WITH RATS OR- WHAT'S THAT NOISE?
WHAT THE-
CAW!
AAH!
CAW!
CAW!
AACK!
YOU...

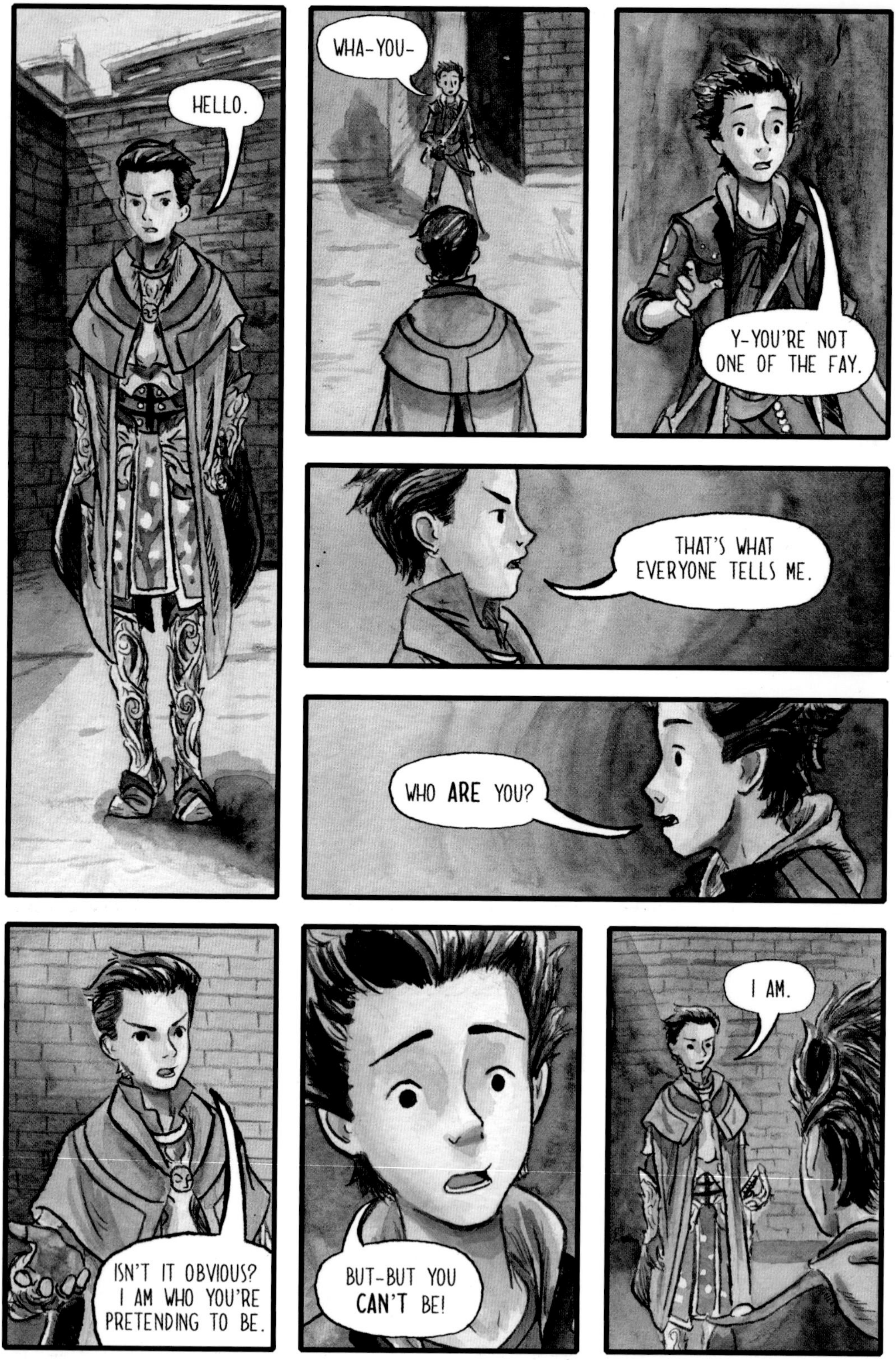
HELLO.
WHA-YOU-
Y-YOU'RE NOT ONE OF THE FAY.
THAT'S WHAT EVERYONE TELLS ME.
WHO ARE YOU?
ISN'T IT OBVIOUS? I AM WHO YOU'RE PRETENDING TO BE.
BUT-BUT YOU CAN'T BE!
I AM.

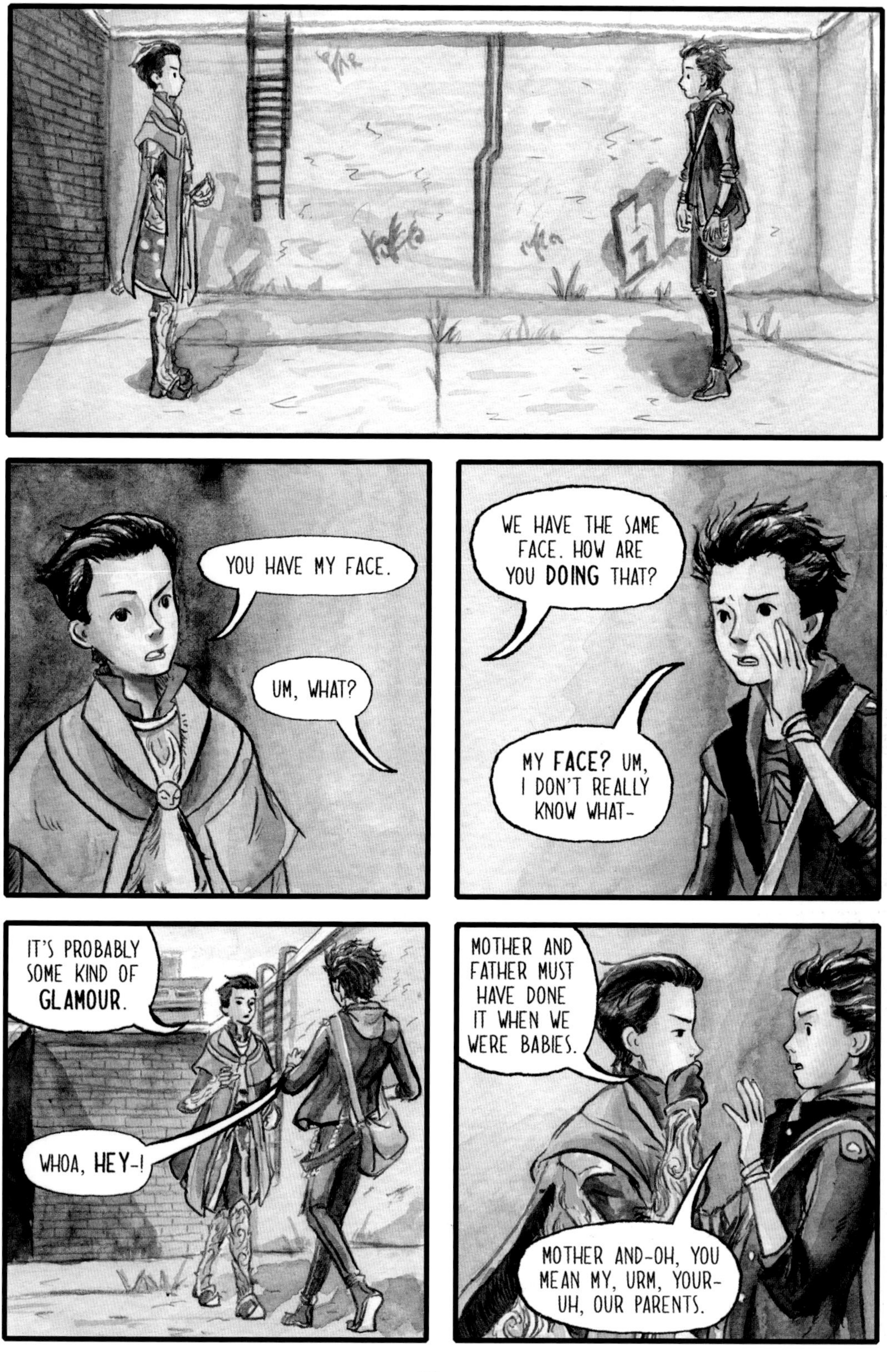
YOU HAVE MY FACE.
UM, WHAT?
WE HAVE THE SAME FACE. HOW ARE YOU DOING THAT?
MY FACE? UM, I DON'T REALLY KNOW WHAT-
IT'S PROBABLY SOME KIND OF GLAMOUR.
WHOA, HEY-!
MOTHER AND FATHER MUST HAVE DONE IT WHEN WE WERE BABIES.
MOTHER AND-OH, YOU MEAN MY, URM, YOUR-UH, OUR PARENTS.

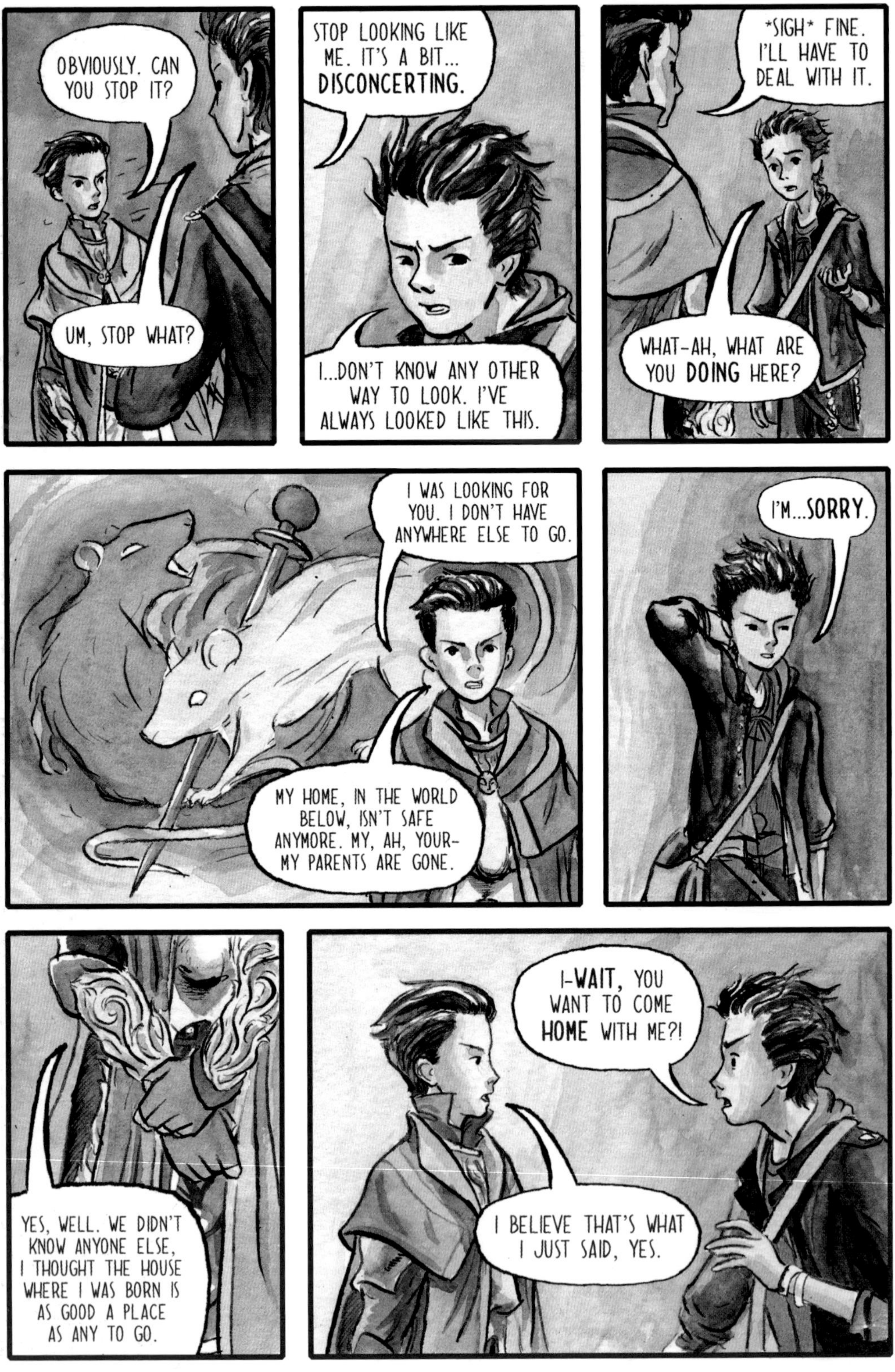
OBVIOUSLY. CAN YOU STOP IT?
UM, STOP WHAT?
STOP LOOKING LIKE ME. IT'S A BIT... DISCONCERTING.
I...DON'T KNOW ANY OTHER WAY TO LOOK. I'VE ALWAYS LOOKED LIKE THIS.
SIGH FINE. I'LL HAVE TO DEAL WITH IT.
WHAT-AH, WHAT ARE YOU DOING HERE?
I WAS LOOKING FOR YOU. I DON'T HAVE ANYWHERE ELSE TO GO.
MY HOME, IN THE WORLD BELOW, ISN'T SAFE ANYMORE. MY, AH, YOUR-MY PARENTS ARE GONE.
I'M...SORRY.
YES, WELL. WE DIDN'T KNOW ANYONE ELSE, I THOUGHT THE HOUSE WHERE I WAS BORN IS AS GOOD A PLACE AS ANY TO GO.
I-WAIT, YOU WANT TO COME HOME WITH ME?!
I BELIEVE THAT'S WHAT I JUST SAID, YES.

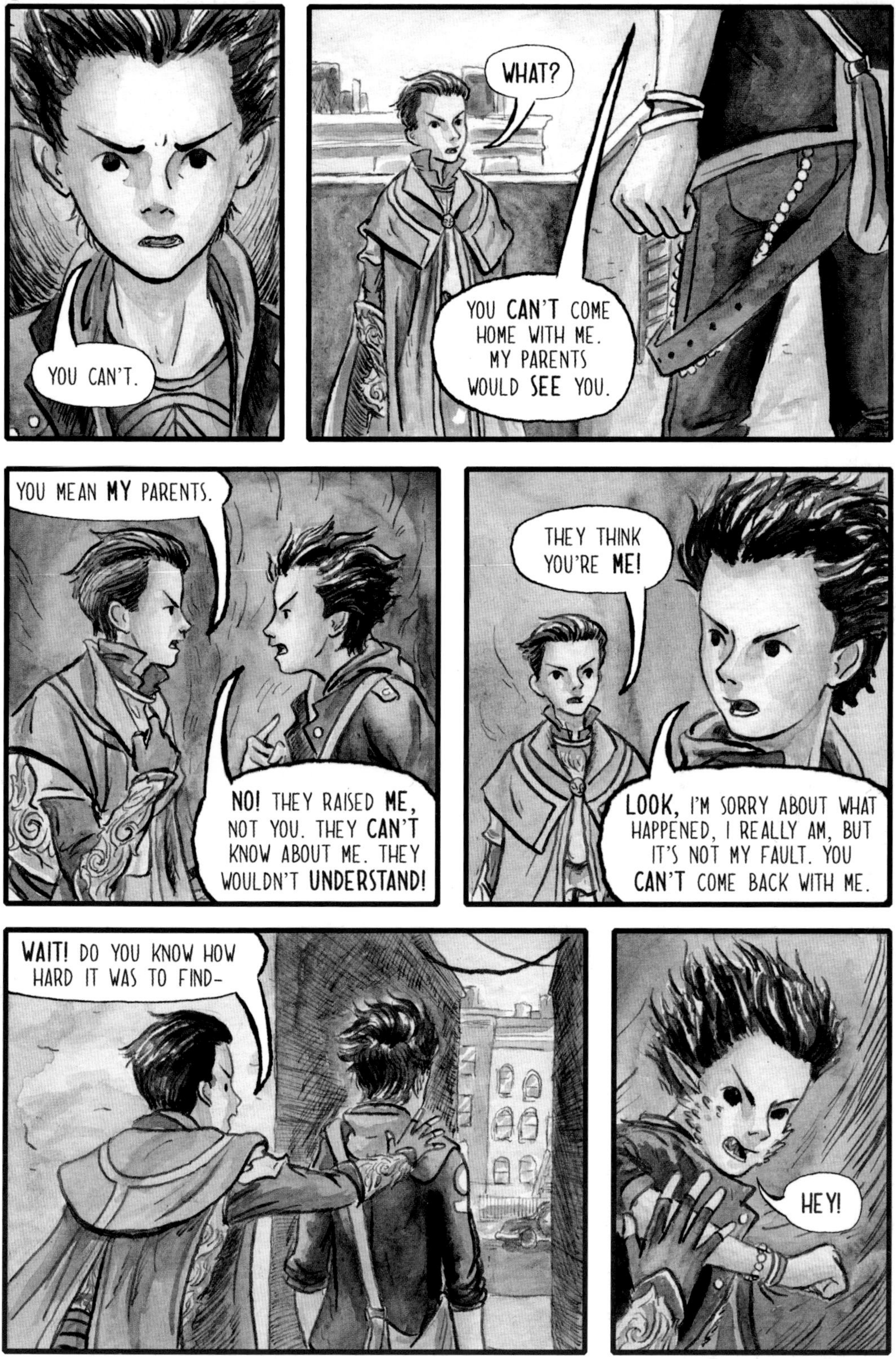
YOU CAN'T.
WHAT?
YOU CAN'T COME HOME WITH ME. MY PARENTS WOULD SEE YOU.
YOU MEAN MY PARENTS.
NO! THEY RAISED ME, NOT YOU. THEY CAN'T KNOW ABOUT ME. THEY WOULDN'T UNDERSTAND!
THEY THINK YOU'RE ME!
LOOK, I'M SORRY ABOUT WHAT HAPPENED, I REALLY AM, BUT IT'S NOT MY FAULT. YOU CAN'T COME BACK WITH ME.
WAIT! DO YOU KNOW HOW HARD IT WAS TO FIND-
HEY!

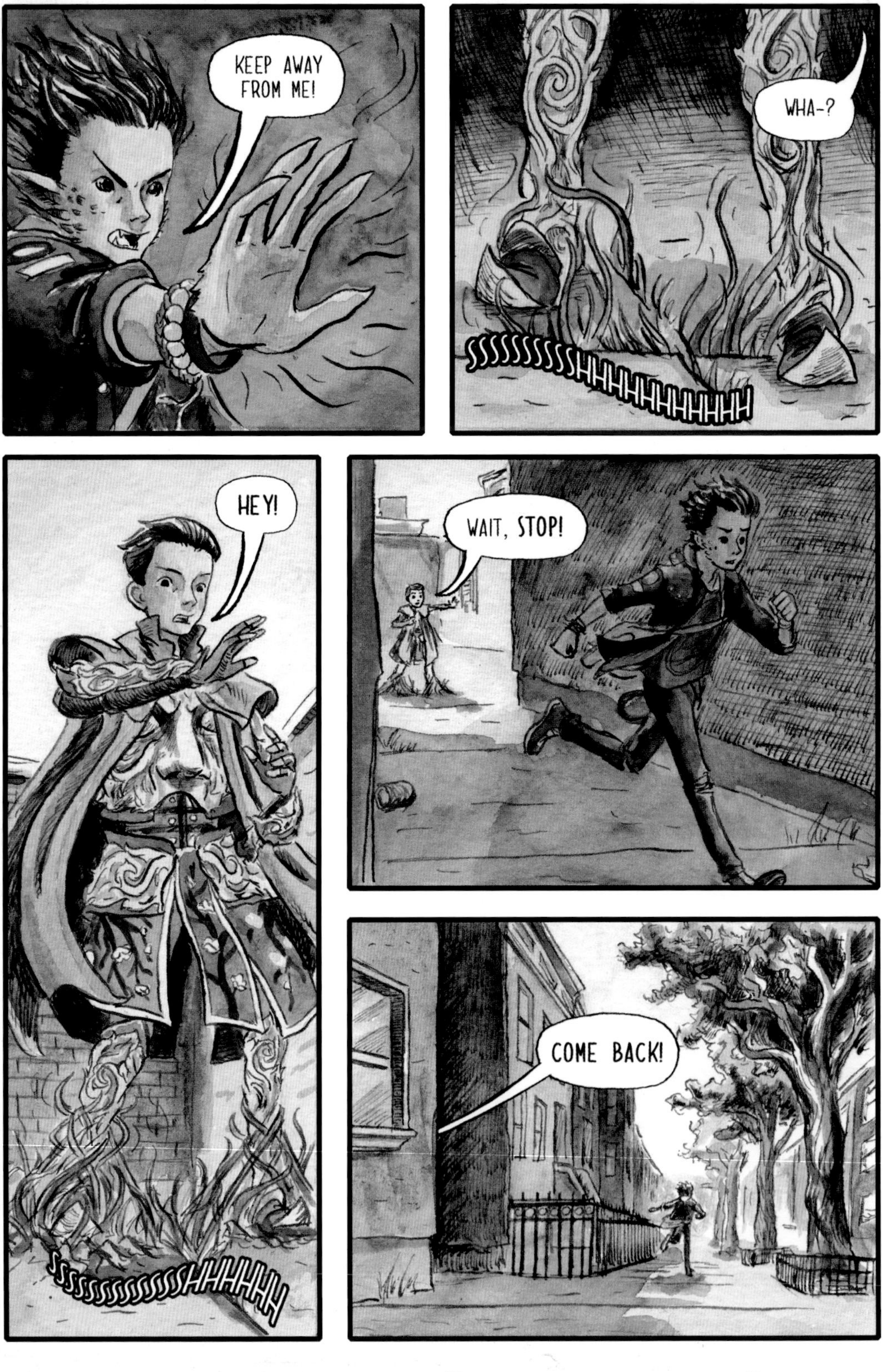
KEEP AWAY FROM ME!
WHA-?
SSSSSSSSSSHHHHHHHHHHHH
HEY!
SSSSSSSSSSSSSHHHHHHH
WAIT, STOP!
COME BACK!

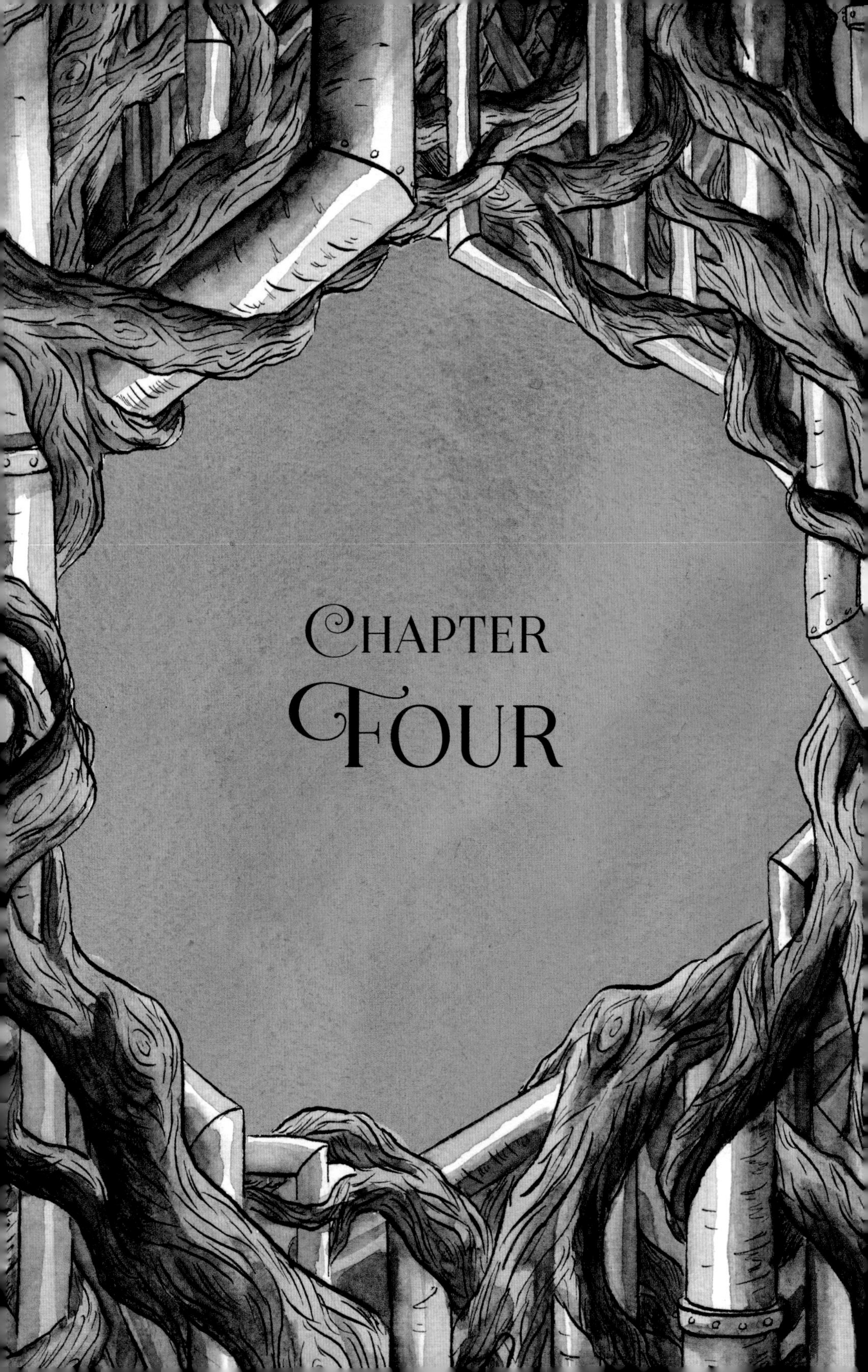

Chapter Four

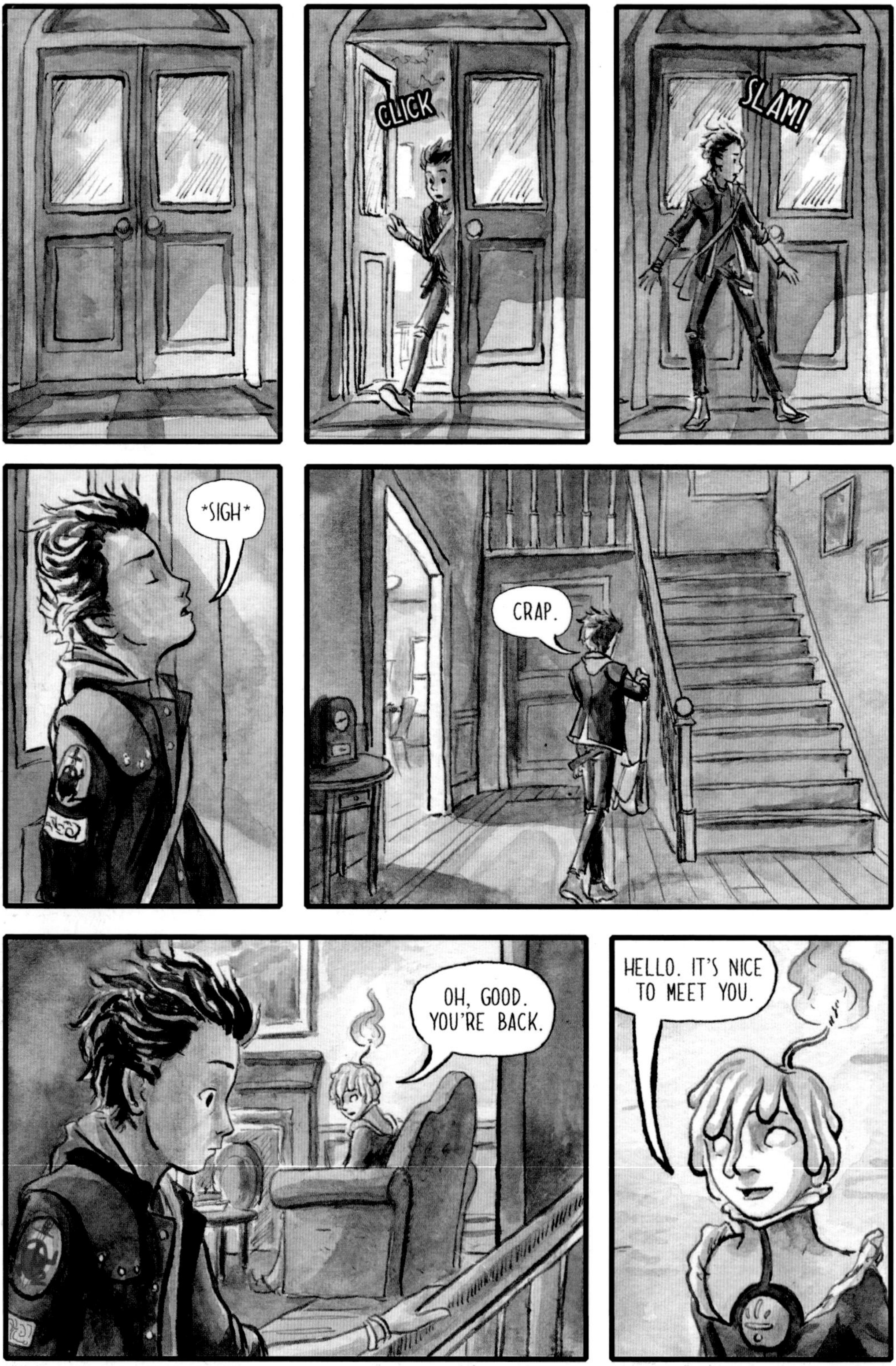
CLICK
SLAM!
SIGH
CRAP.
OH, GOOD. YOU'RE BACK.
HELLO. IT'S NICE TO MEET YOU.

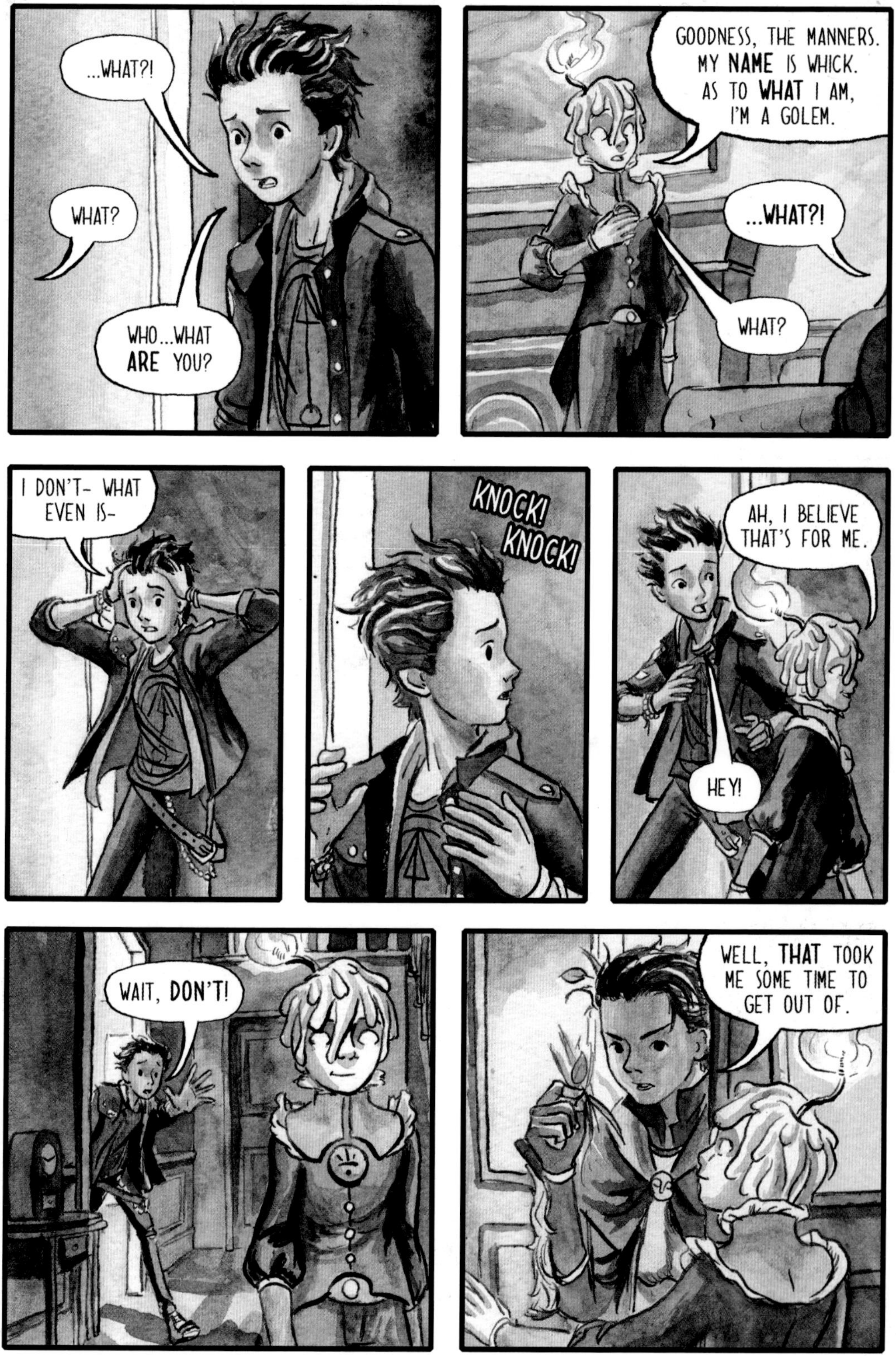
...WHAT?!
WHAT?
WHO...WHAT ARE YOU?
GOODNESS, THE MANNERS. MY NAME IS WHICK. AS TO WHAT I AM, I'M A GOLEM.
...WHAT?!
WHAT?
I DON'T- WHAT EVEN IS-
KNOCK! KNOCK!
AH, I BELIEVE THAT'S FOR ME.
HEY!
WAIT, DON'T!
WELL, THAT TOOK ME SOME TIME TO GET OUT OF.

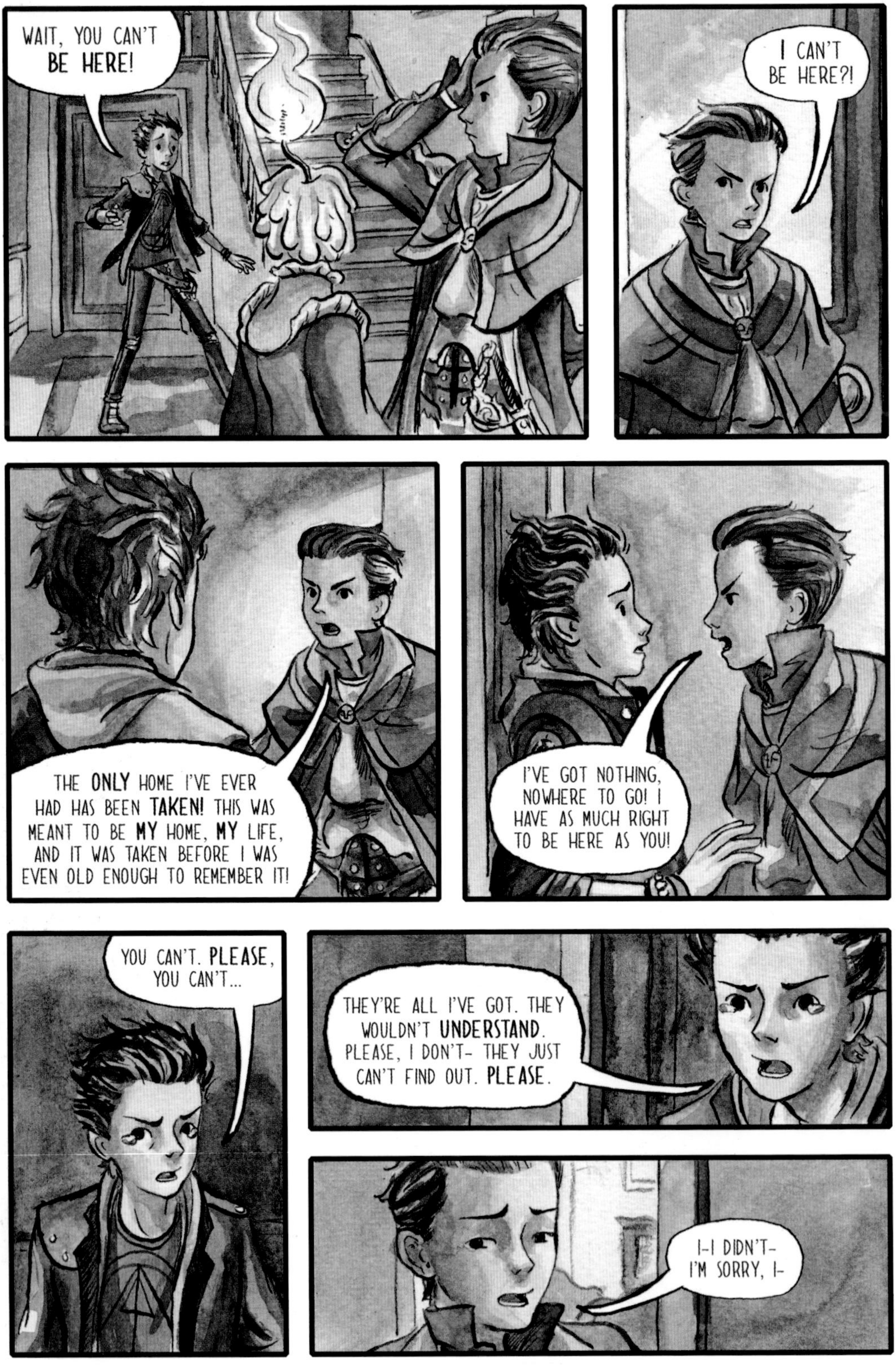
WAIT, YOU CAN'T BE HERE!
I CAN'T BE HERE?!
THE ONLY HOME I'VE EVER HAD HAS BEEN TAKEN! THIS WAS MEANT TO BE MY HOME, MY LIFE, AND IT WAS TAKEN BEFORE I WAS EVEN OLD ENOUGH TO REMEMBER IT!
I'VE GOT NOTHING, NOWHERE TO GO! I HAVE AS MUCH RIGHT TO BE HERE AS YOU!
YOU CAN'T. PLEASE, YOU CAN'T...
THEY'RE ALL I'VE GOT. THEY WOULDN'T UNDERSTAND. PLEASE, I DON'T- THEY JUST CAN'T FIND OUT. PLEASE.
I-I DIDN'T- I'M SORRY, I-

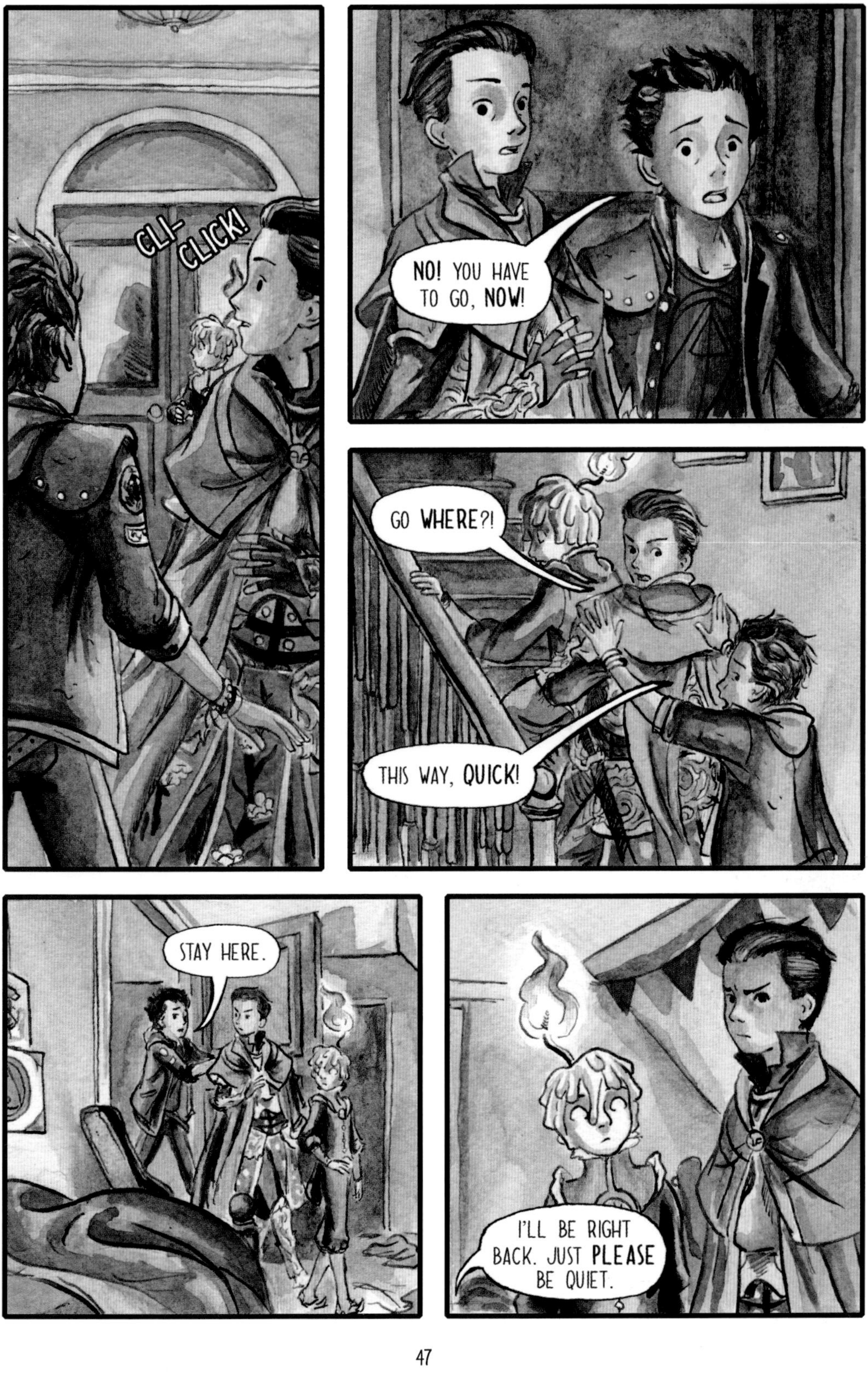
CLI-CLICK!
NO! YOU HAVE TO GO, NOW!
GO WHERE?!
THIS WAY, QUICK!
STAY HERE.
I'LL BE RIGHT BACK. JUST PLEASE BE QUIET.

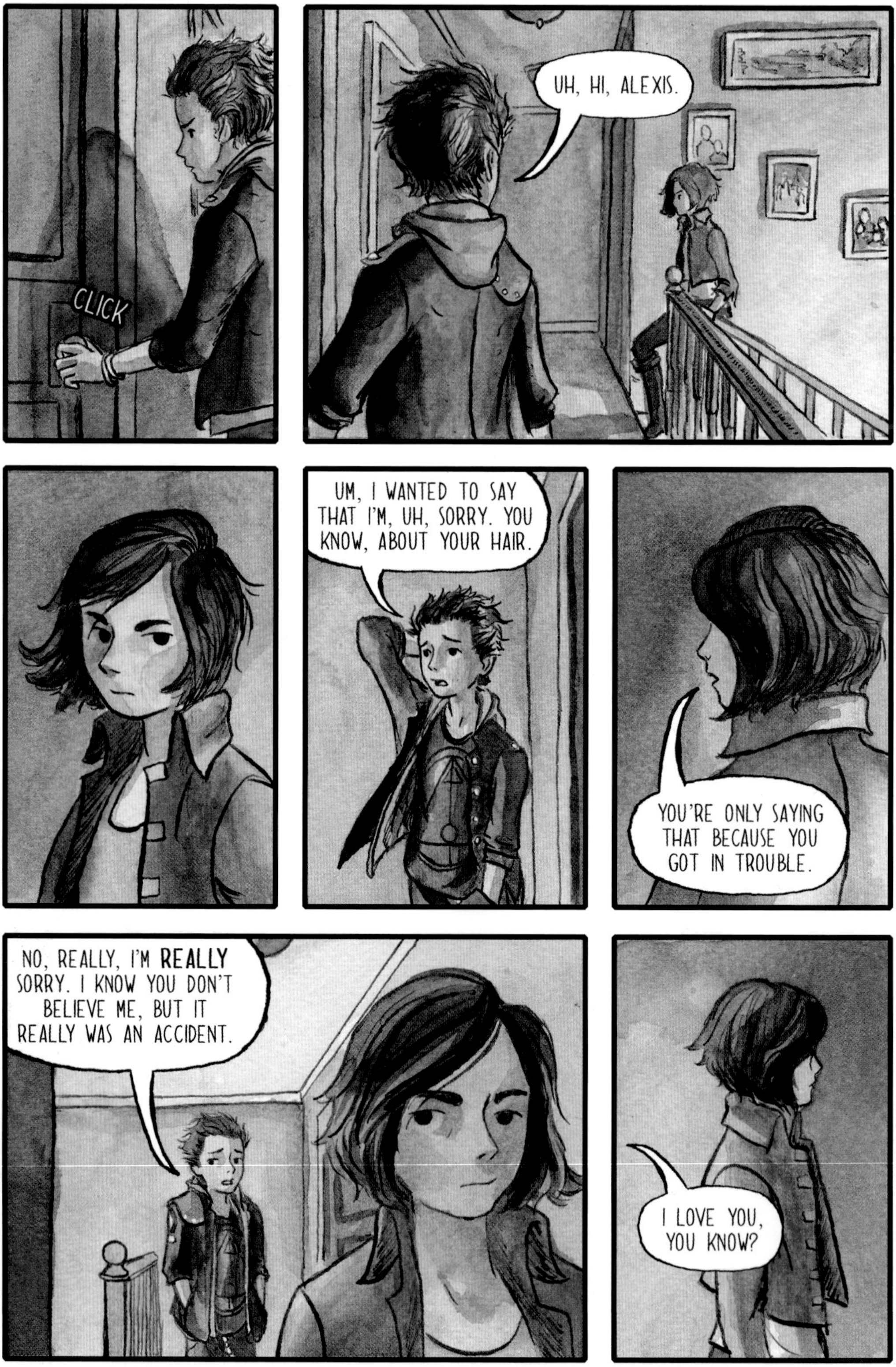
CLICK
UH, HI, ALEXIS.
UM, I WANTED TO SAY THAT I'M, UH, SORRY. YOU KNOW, ABOUT YOUR HAIR.
YOU'RE ONLY SAYING THAT BECAUSE YOU GOT IN TROUBLE.
NO, REALLY, I'M **REALLY** SORRY. I KNOW YOU DON'T BELIEVE ME, BUT IT REALLY WAS AN ACCIDENT.
I LOVE YOU, YOU KNOW?

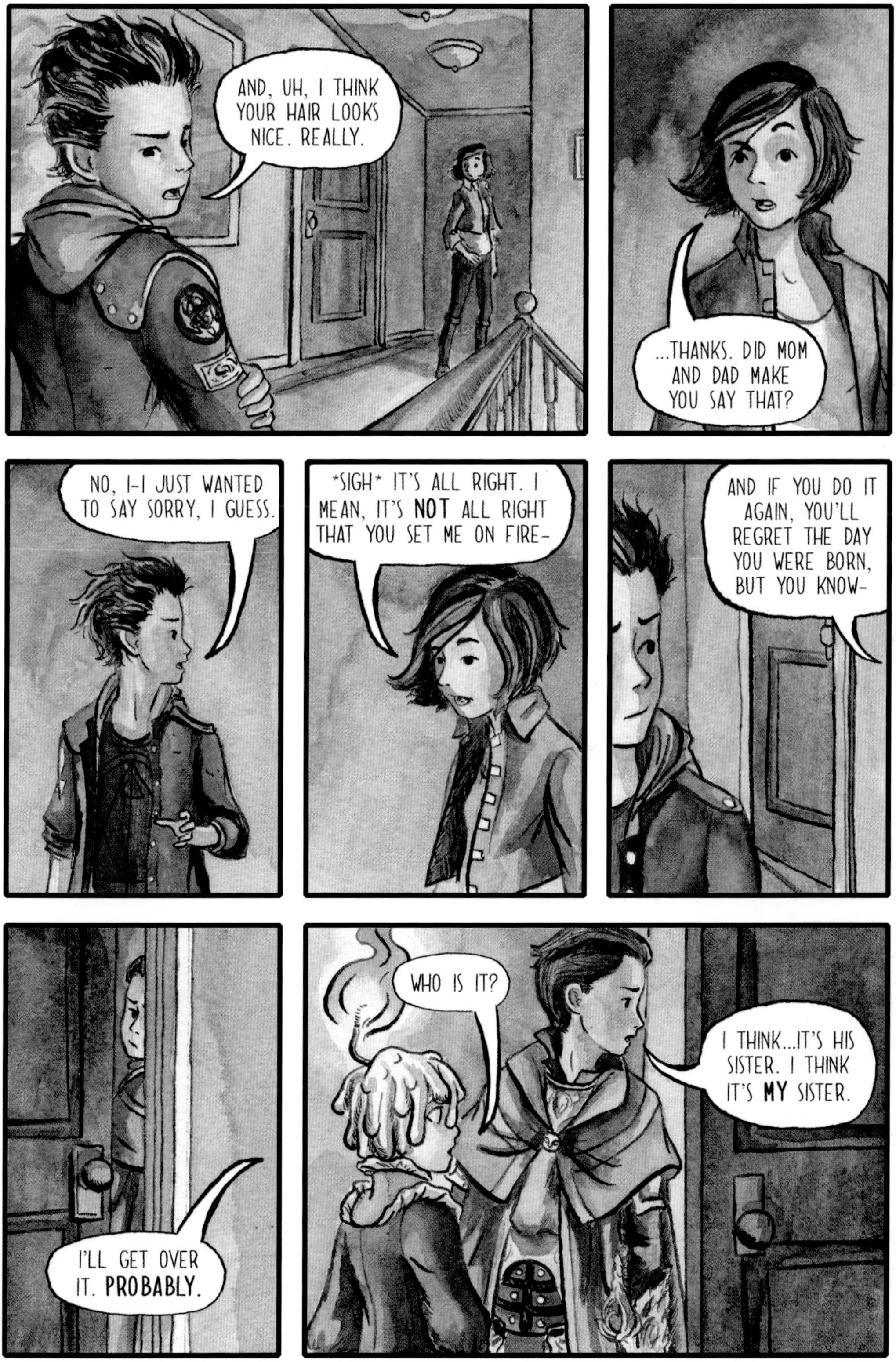
AND, UH, I THINK YOUR HAIR LOOKS NICE. REALLY.
...THANKS. DID MOM AND DAD MAKE YOU SAY THAT?
NO, I-I JUST WANTED TO SAY SORRY, I GUESS.
SIGH IT'S ALL RIGHT. I MEAN, IT'S NOT ALL RIGHT THAT YOU SET ME ON FIRE-
AND IF YOU DO IT AGAIN, YOU'LL REGRET THE DAY YOU WERE BORN, BUT YOU KNOW-
I'LL GET OVER IT. PROBABLY.
WHO IS IT?
I THINK...IT'S HIS SISTER. I THINK IT'S MY SISTER.

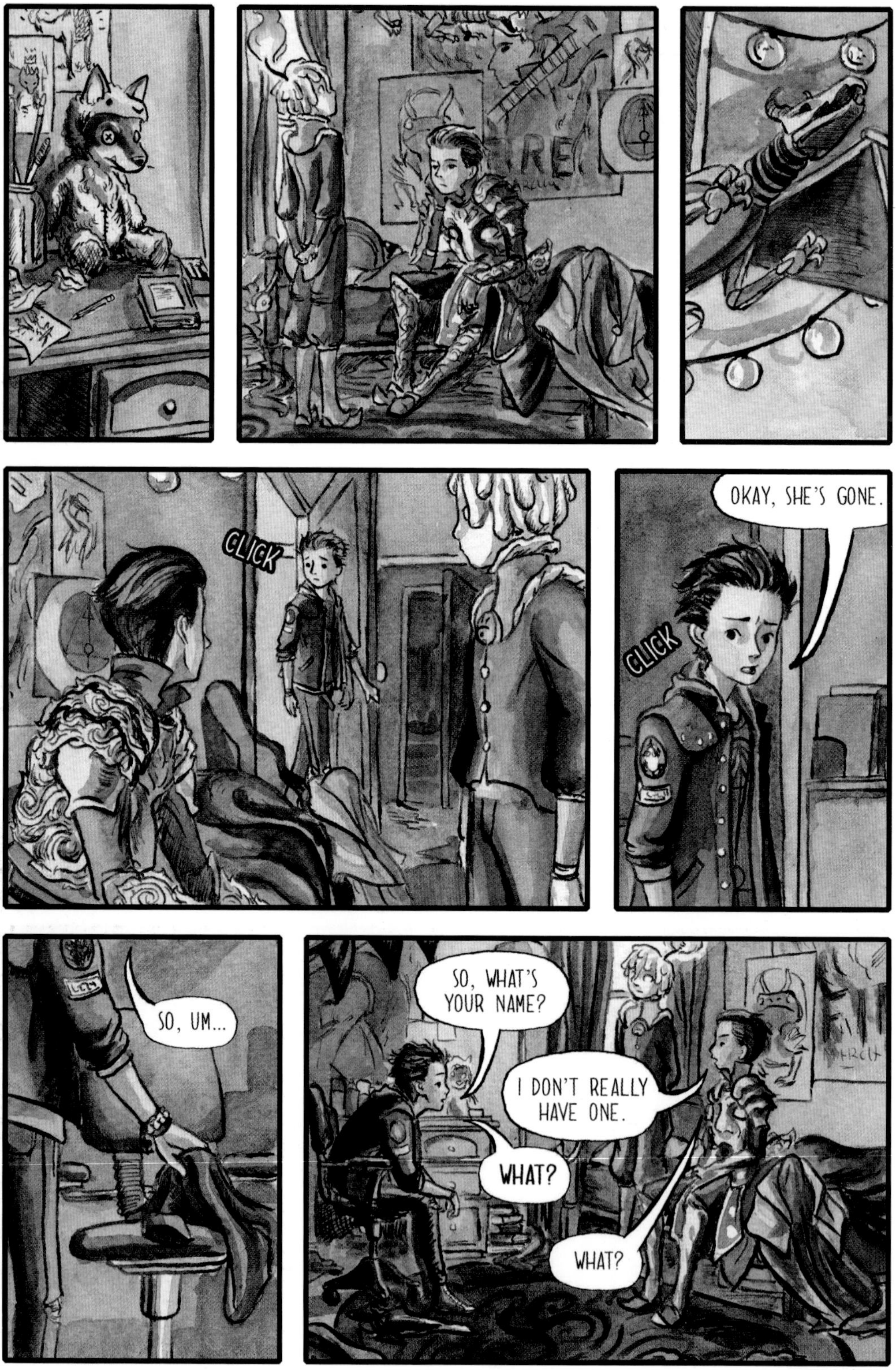
CLICK
OKAY, SHE'S GONE.
CLICK
SO, UM...
SO, WHAT'S YOUR NAME?
I DON'T REALLY HAVE ONE.
WHAT?
WHAT?

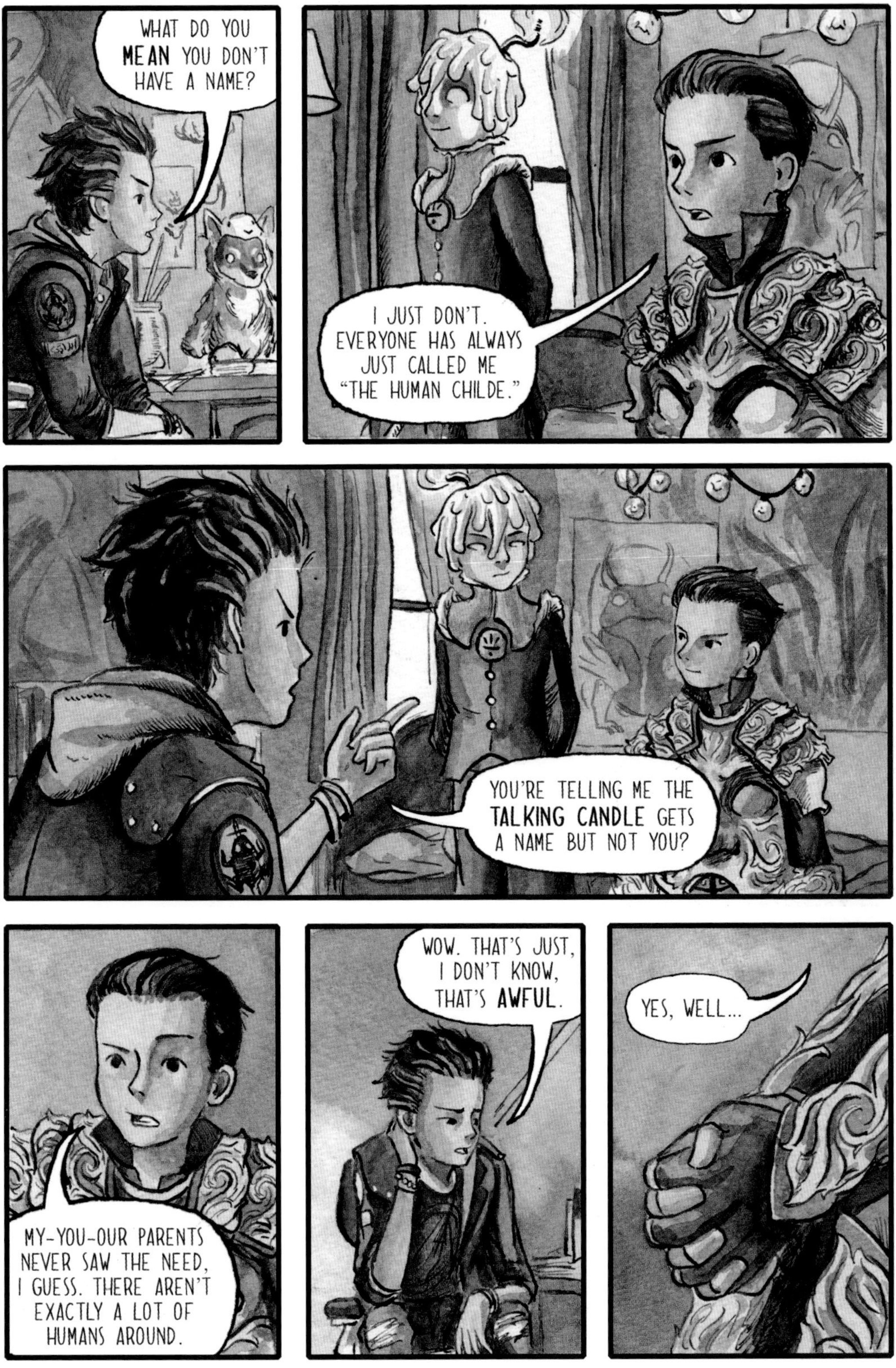
WHAT DO YOU MEAN YOU DON'T HAVE A NAME?
I JUST DON'T. EVERYONE HAS ALWAYS JUST CALLED ME "THE HUMAN CHILDE."
YOU'RE TELLING ME THE TALKING CANDLE GETS A NAME BUT NOT YOU?
MY–YOU–OUR PARENTS NEVER SAW THE NEED, I GUESS. THERE AREN'T EXACTLY A LOT OF HUMANS AROUND.
WOW. THAT'S JUST, I DON'T KNOW, THAT'S AWFUL.
YES, WELL...

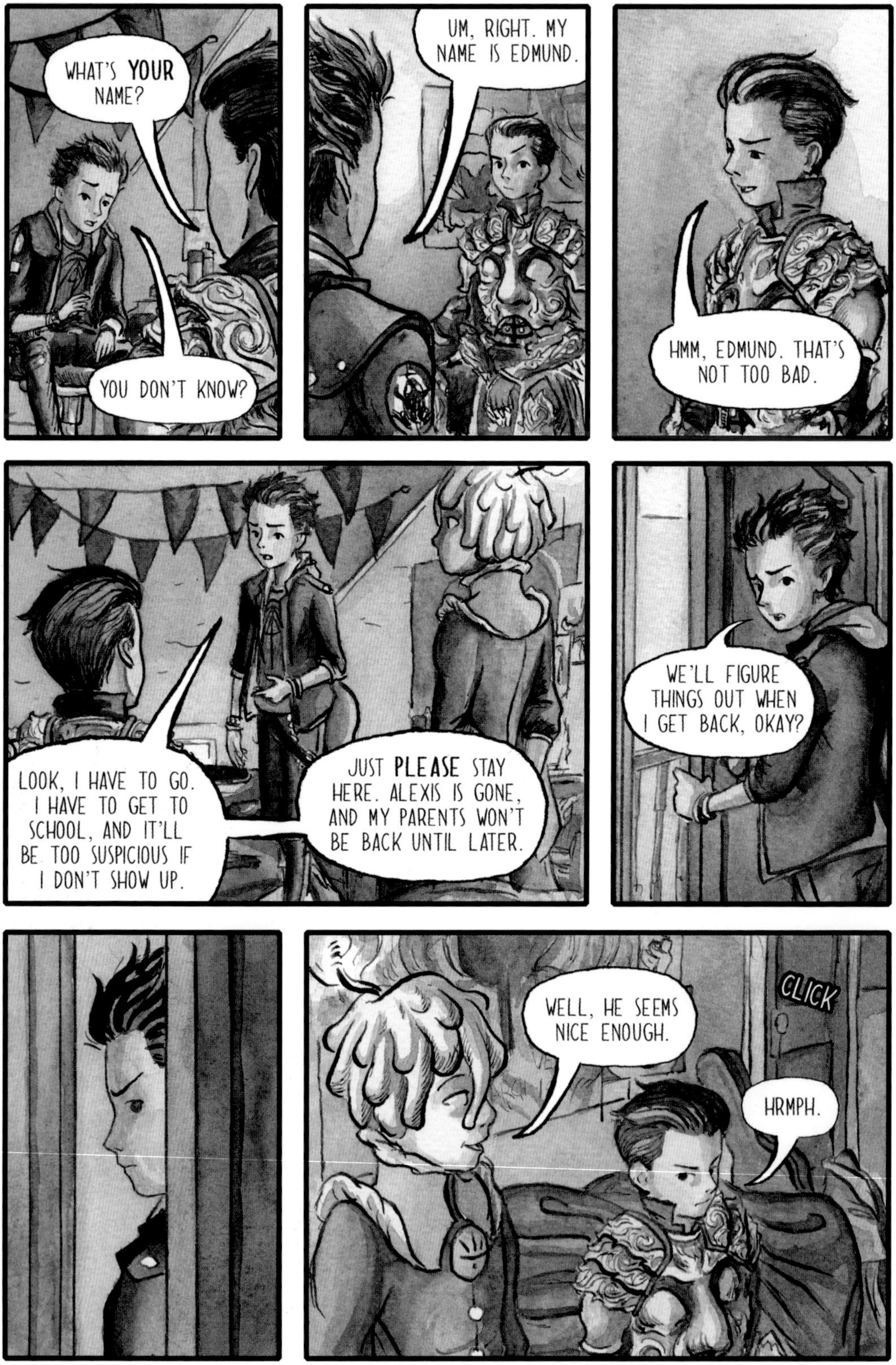
WHAT'S **YOUR** NAME?
YOU DON'T KNOW?
UM, RIGHT. MY NAME IS EDMUND.
HMM, EDMUND. THAT'S NOT TOO BAD.
LOOK, I HAVE TO GO. I HAVE TO GET TO SCHOOL, AND IT'LL BE TOO SUSPICIOUS IF I DON'T SHOW UP.
JUST **PLEASE** STAY HERE. ALEXIS IS GONE, AND MY PARENTS WON'T BE BACK UNTIL LATER.
WE'LL FIGURE THINGS OUT WHEN I GET BACK, OKAY?
CLICK
WELL, HE SEEMS NICE ENOUGH.
HRMPH.

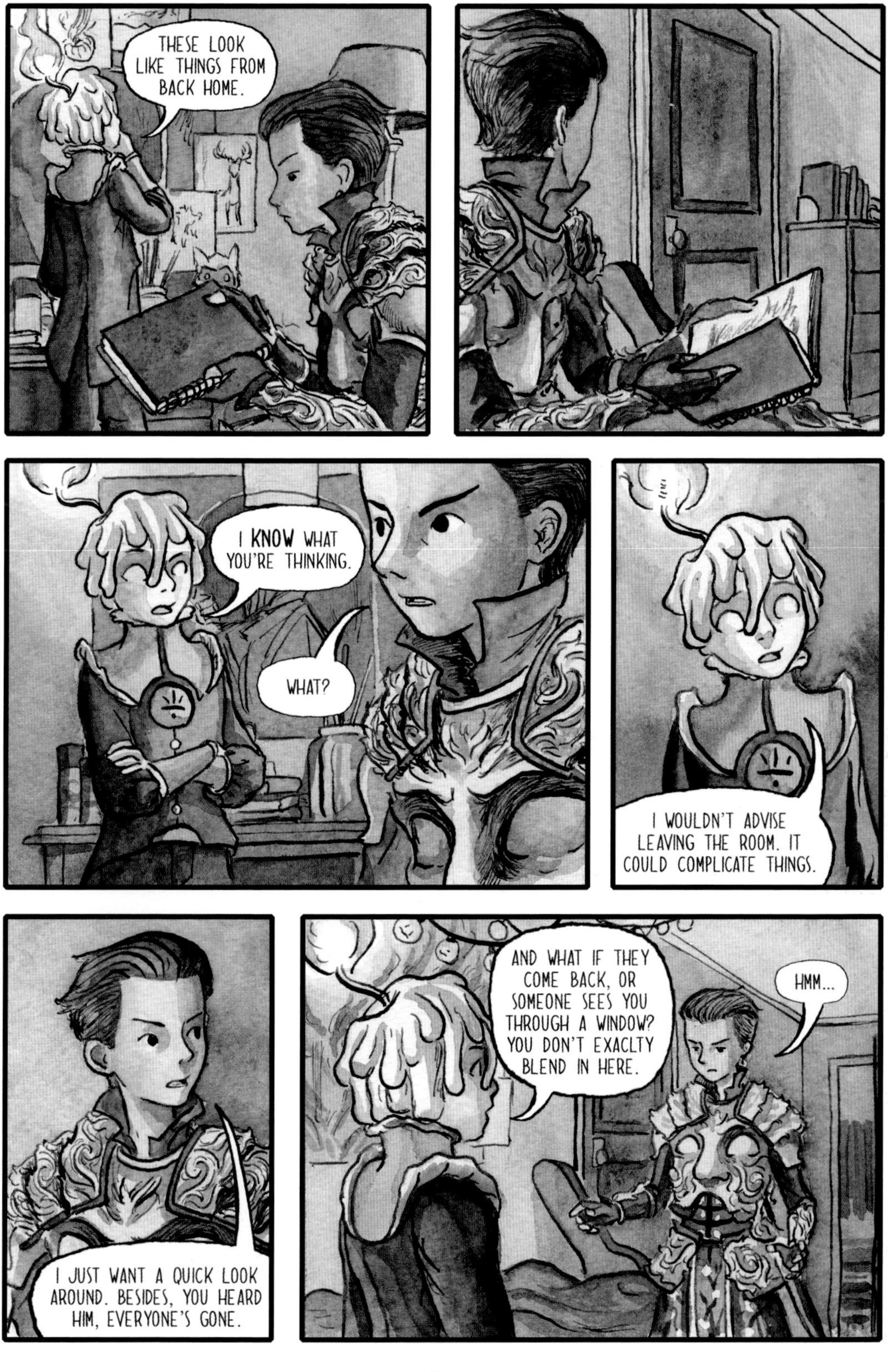
THESE LOOK LIKE THINGS FROM BACK HOME.
I KNOW WHAT YOU'RE THINKING.
WHAT?
I WOULDN'T ADVISE LEAVING THE ROOM. IT COULD COMPLICATE THINGS.
I JUST WANT A QUICK LOOK AROUND. BESIDES, YOU HEARD HIM, EVERYONE'S GONE.
AND WHAT IF THEY COME BACK, OR SOMEONE SEES YOU THROUGH A WINDOW? YOU DON'T EXACLTY BLEND IN HERE.
HMM...

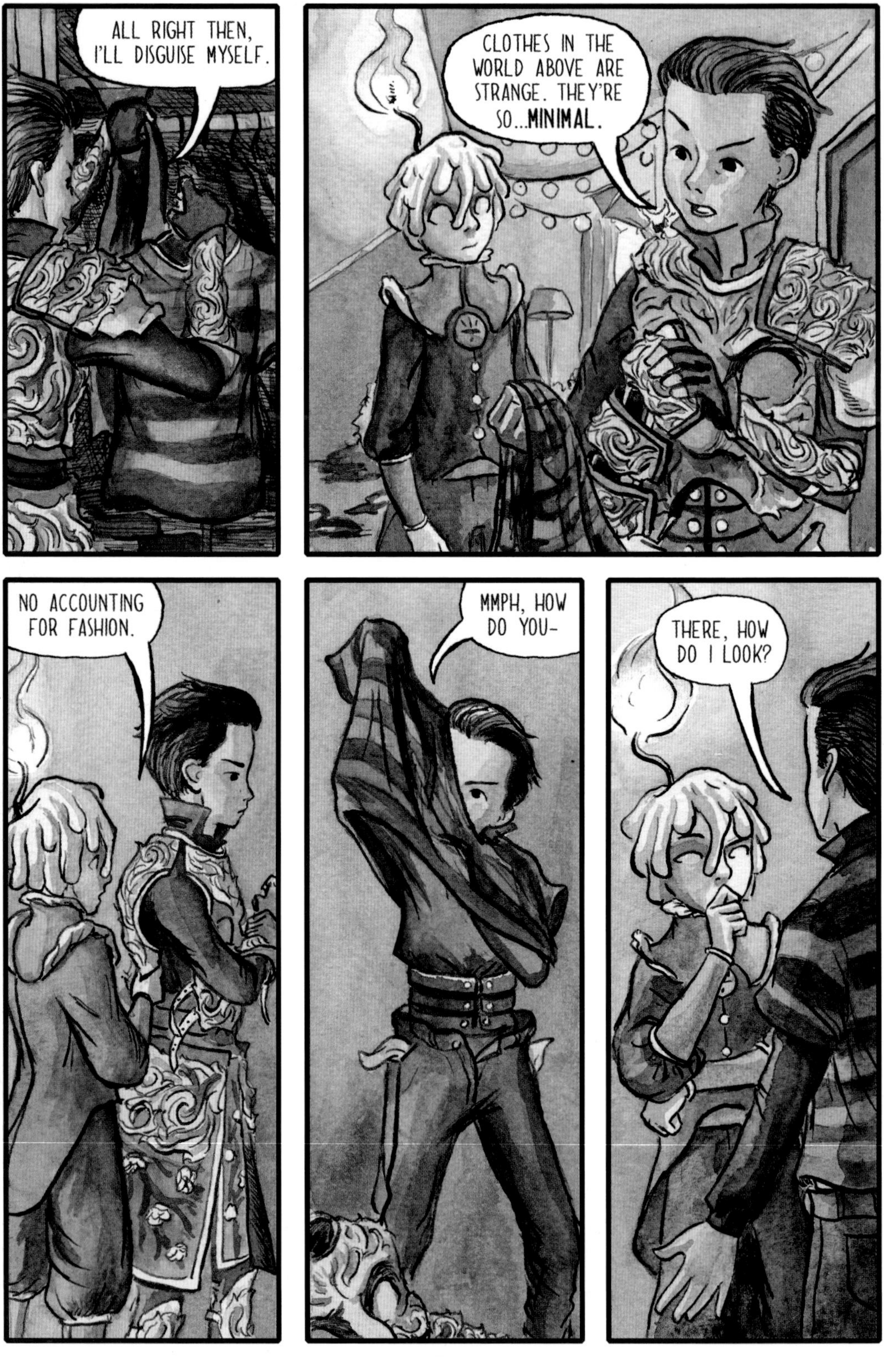
ALL RIGHT THEN, I'LL DISGUISE MYSELF.
CLOTHES IN THE WORLD ABOVE ARE STRANGE. THEY'RE SO...**MINIMAL**.
NO ACCOUNTING FOR FASHION.
MMPH, HOW DO YOU-
THERE, HOW DO I LOOK?

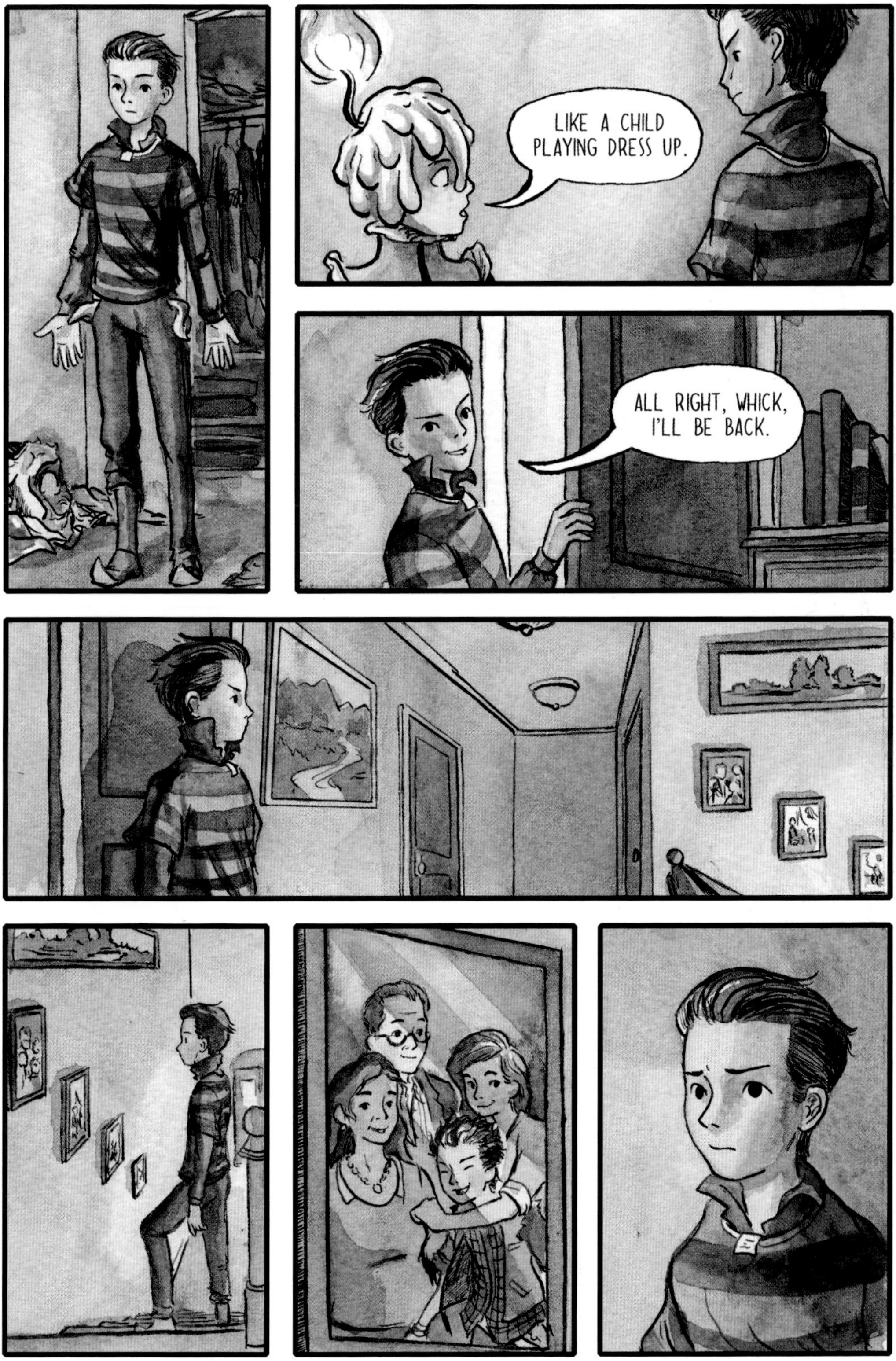
LIKE A CHILD PLAYING DRESS UP.
ALL RIGHT, WHICK, I'LL BE BACK.

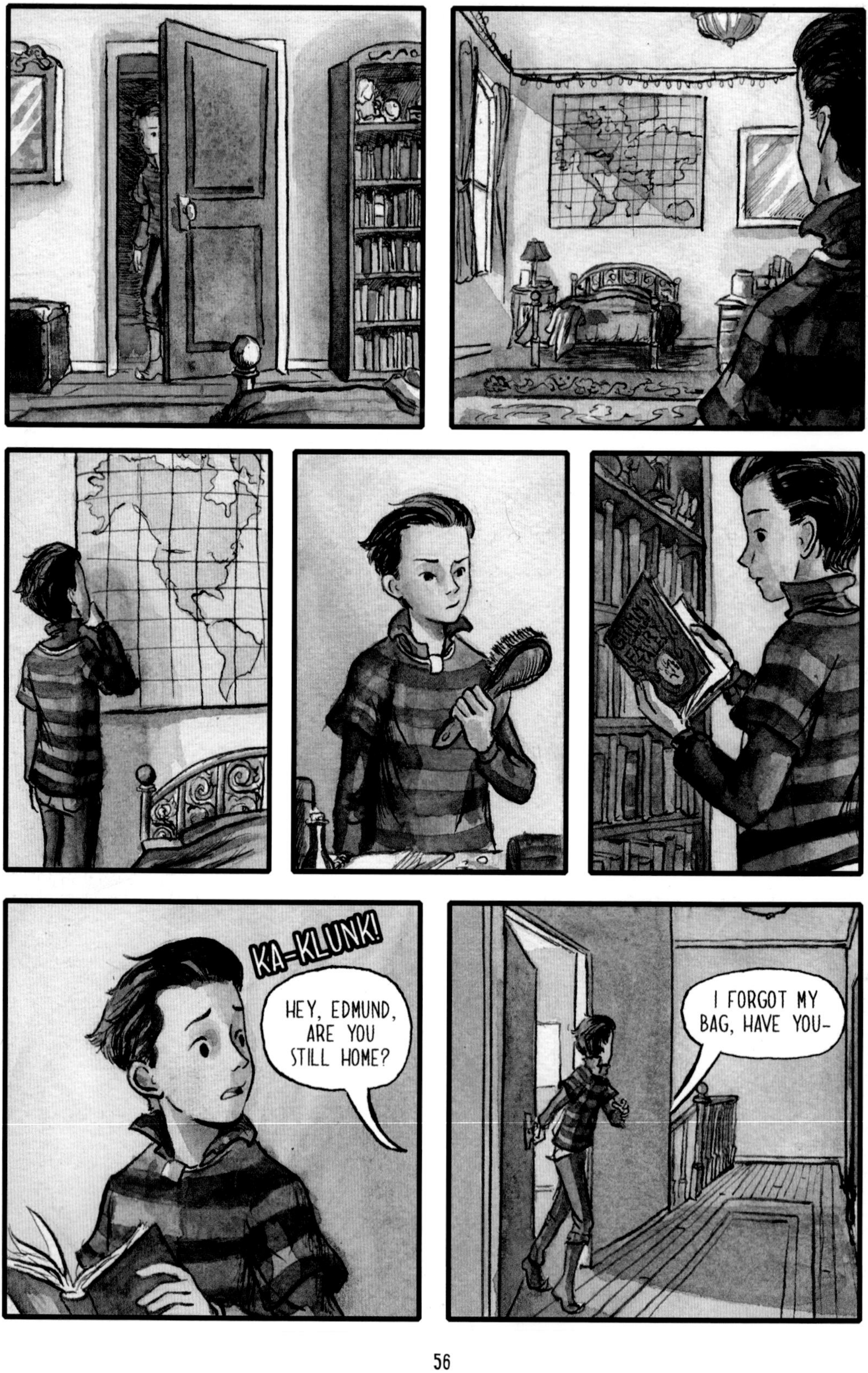
KA-KLUNK!
HEY, EDMUND, ARE YOU STILL HOME?
I FORGOT MY BAG, HAVE YOU-

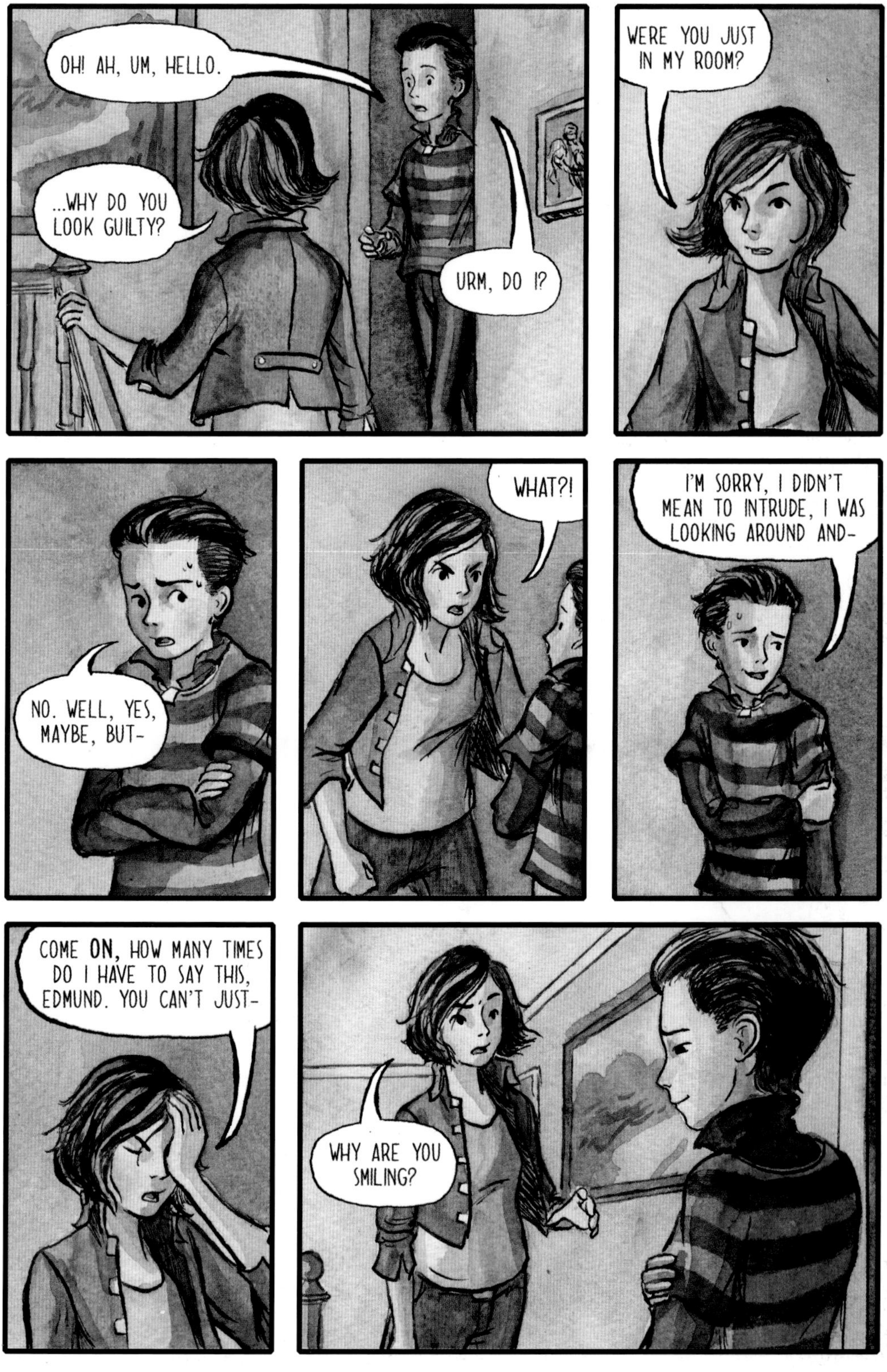
OH! AH, UM, HELLO.
...WHY DO YOU LOOK GUILTY?
URM, DO I?
WERE YOU JUST IN MY ROOM?
NO. WELL, YES, MAYBE, BUT-
WHAT?!
I'M SORRY, I DIDN'T MEAN TO INTRUDE, I WAS LOOKING AROUND AND-
COME **ON,** HOW MANY TIMES DO I HAVE TO SAY THIS, EDMUND. YOU CAN'T JUST-
WHY ARE YOU SMILING?

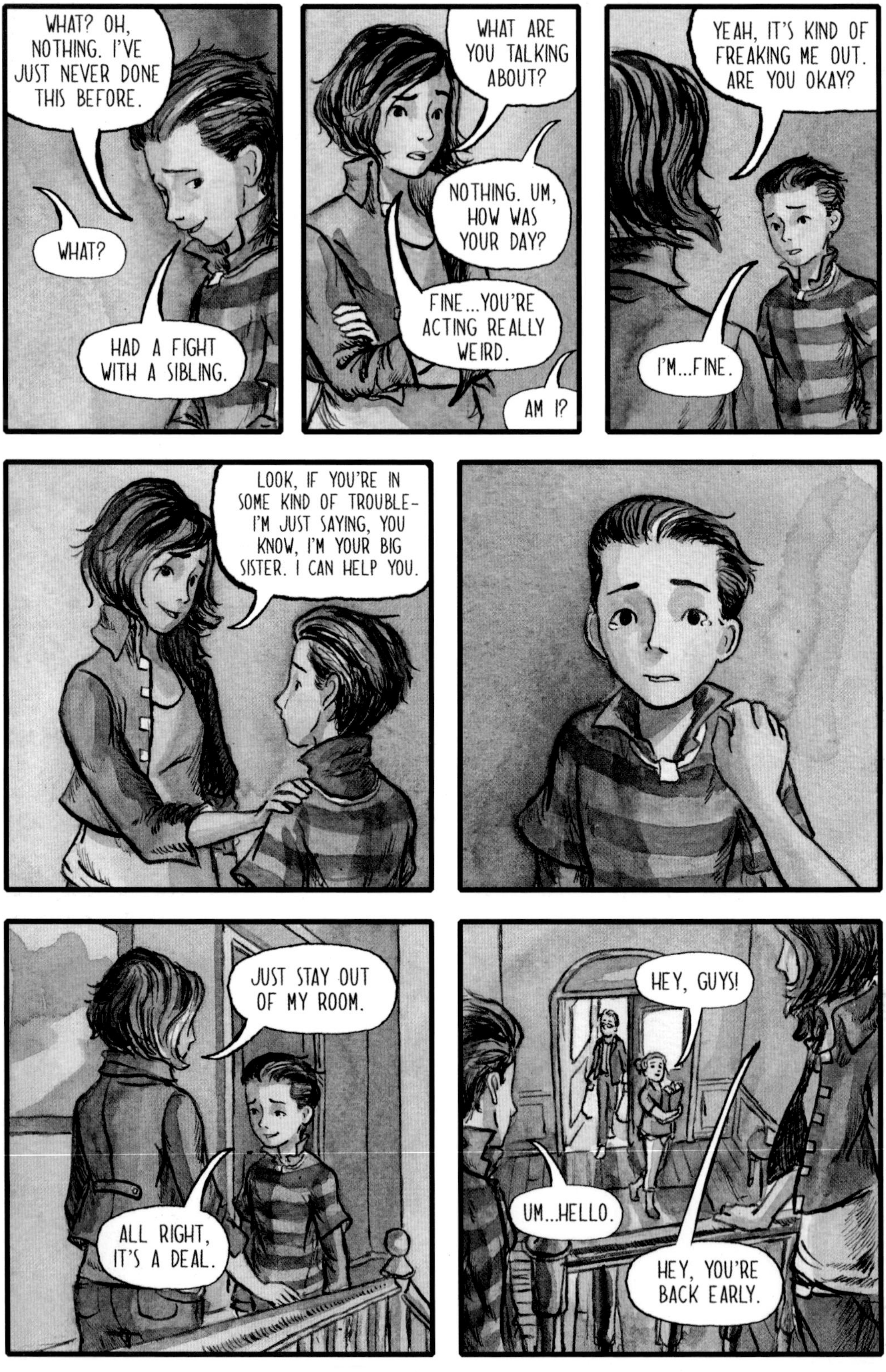
WHAT? OH, NOTHING. I'VE JUST NEVER DONE THIS BEFORE.
WHAT?
HAD A FIGHT WITH A SIBLING.
WHAT ARE YOU TALKING ABOUT?
NOTHING. UM, HOW WAS YOUR DAY?
FINE...YOU'RE ACTING REALLY WEIRD.
AM I?
YEAH, IT'S KIND OF FREAKING ME OUT. ARE YOU OKAY?
I'M...FINE.
LOOK, IF YOU'RE IN SOME KIND OF TROUBLE- I'M JUST SAYING, YOU KNOW, I'M YOUR BIG SISTER. I CAN HELP YOU.
JUST STAY OUT OF MY ROOM.
ALL RIGHT, IT'S A DEAL.
HEY, GUYS!
UM...HELLO.
HEY, YOU'RE BACK EARLY.

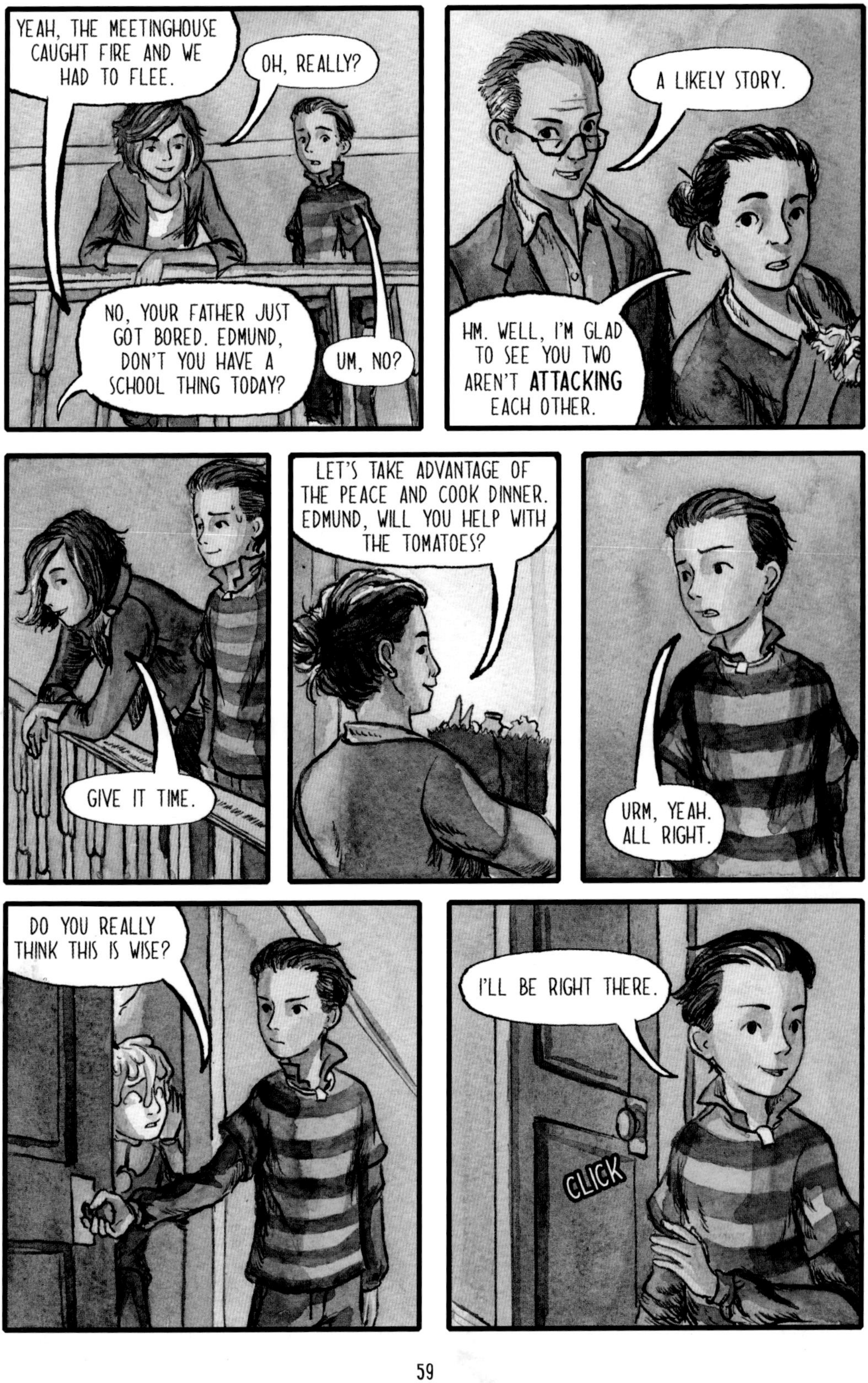
YEAH, THE MEETINGHOUSE CAUGHT FIRE AND WE HAD TO FLEE.
OH, REALLY?
NO, YOUR FATHER JUST GOT BORED. EDMUND, DON'T YOU HAVE A SCHOOL THING TODAY?
UM, NO?
A LIKELY STORY.
HM. WELL, I'M GLAD TO SEE YOU TWO AREN'T **ATTACKING** EACH OTHER.
GIVE IT TIME.
LET'S TAKE ADVANTAGE OF THE PEACE AND COOK DINNER. EDMUND, WILL YOU HELP WITH THE TOMATOES?
URM, YEAH. ALL RIGHT.
DO YOU REALLY THINK THIS IS WISE?
I'LL BE RIGHT THERE.
CLICK

Chapter Five

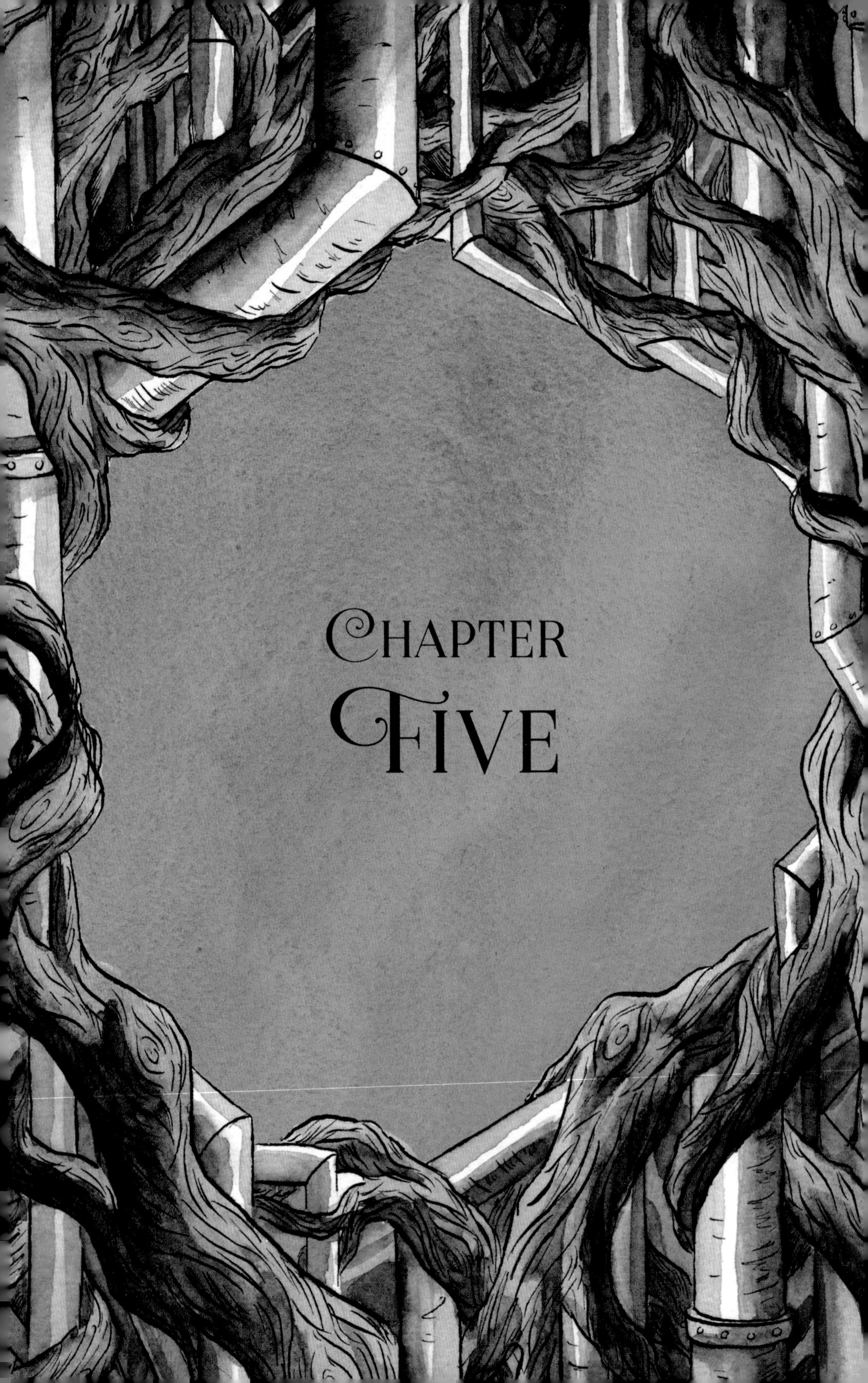

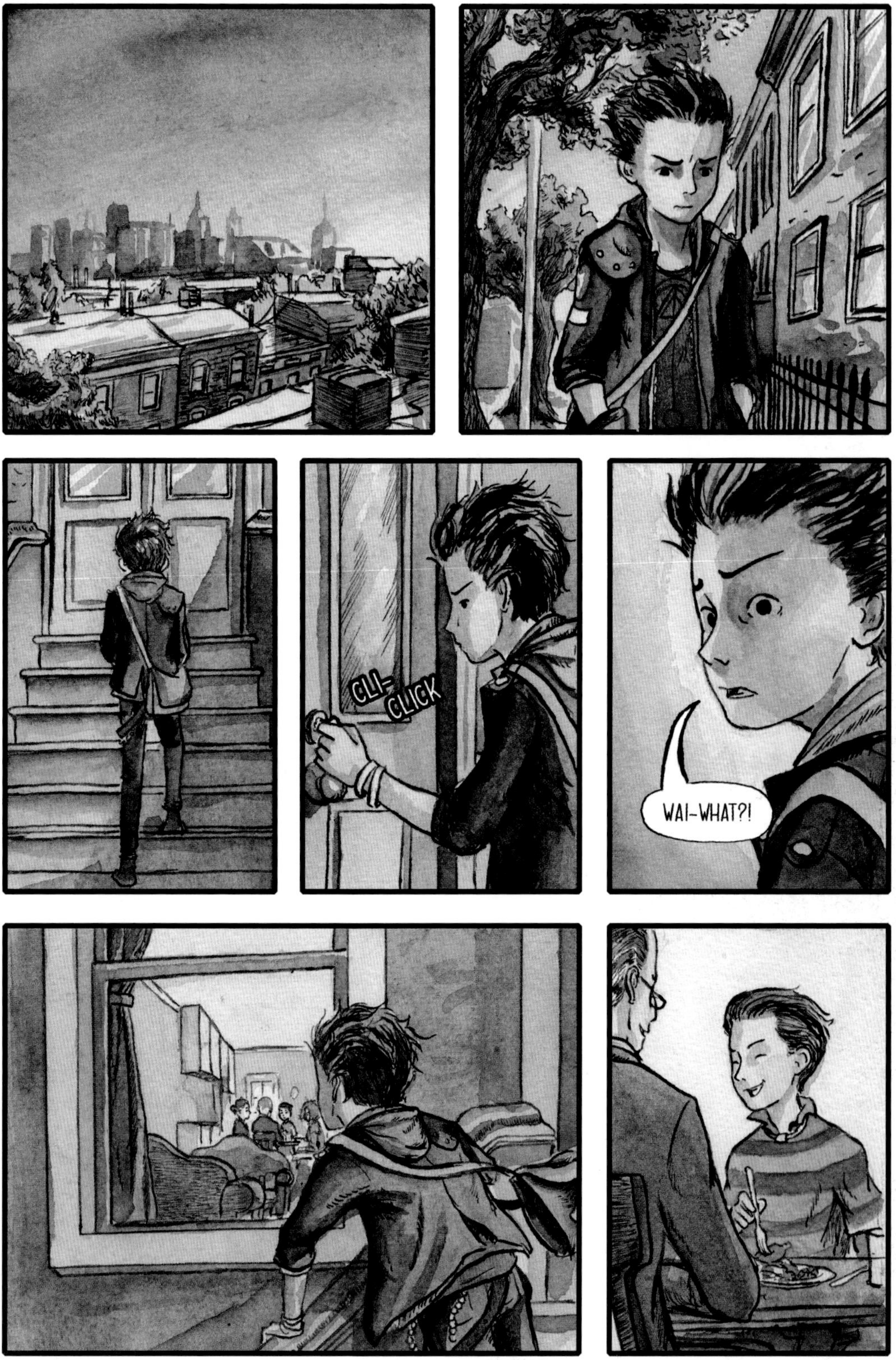
CLI-
CLICK
WAI-WHAT?!

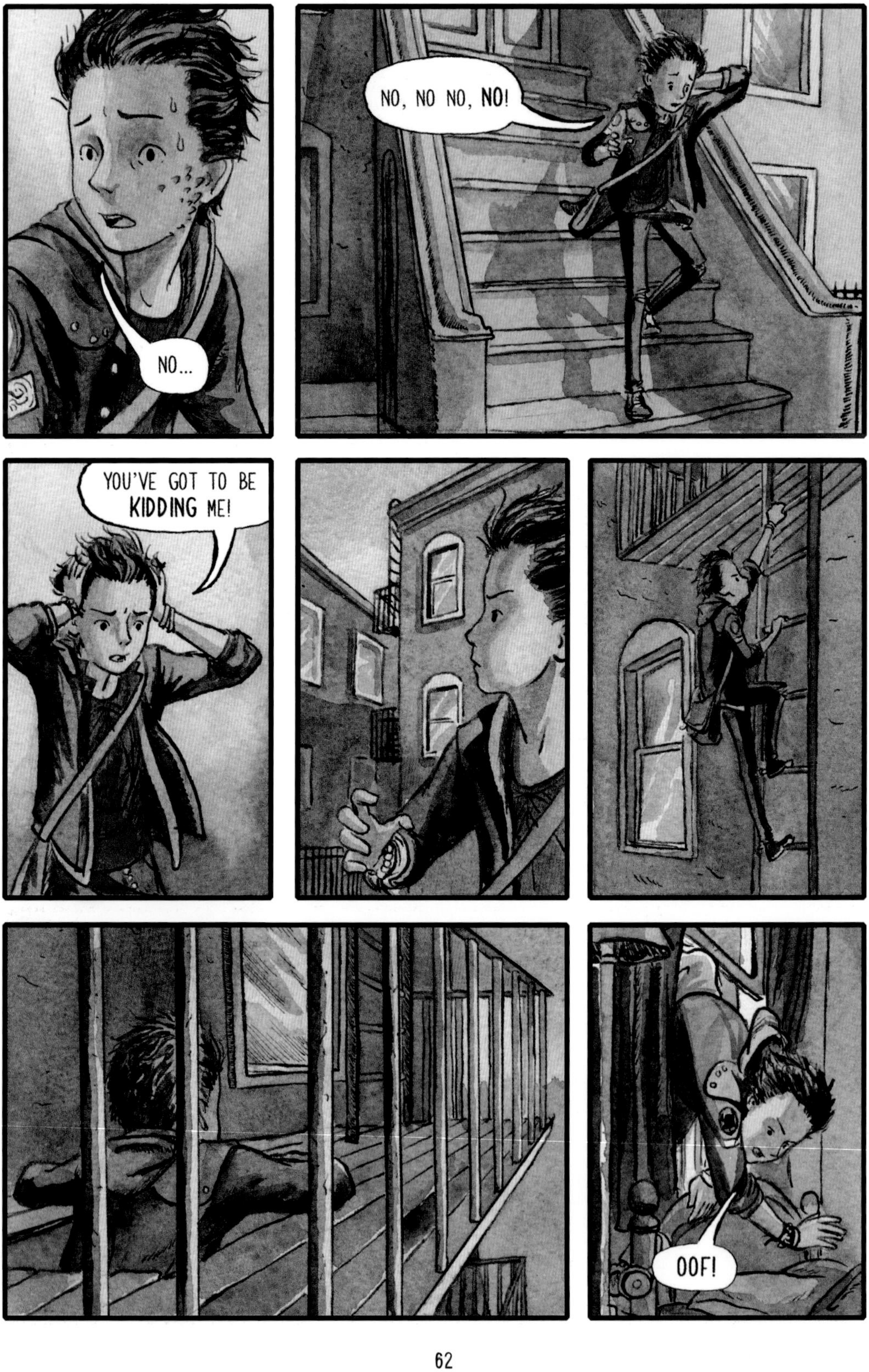
NO...
NO, NO NO, NO!
YOU'VE GOT TO BE KIDDING ME!
OOF!

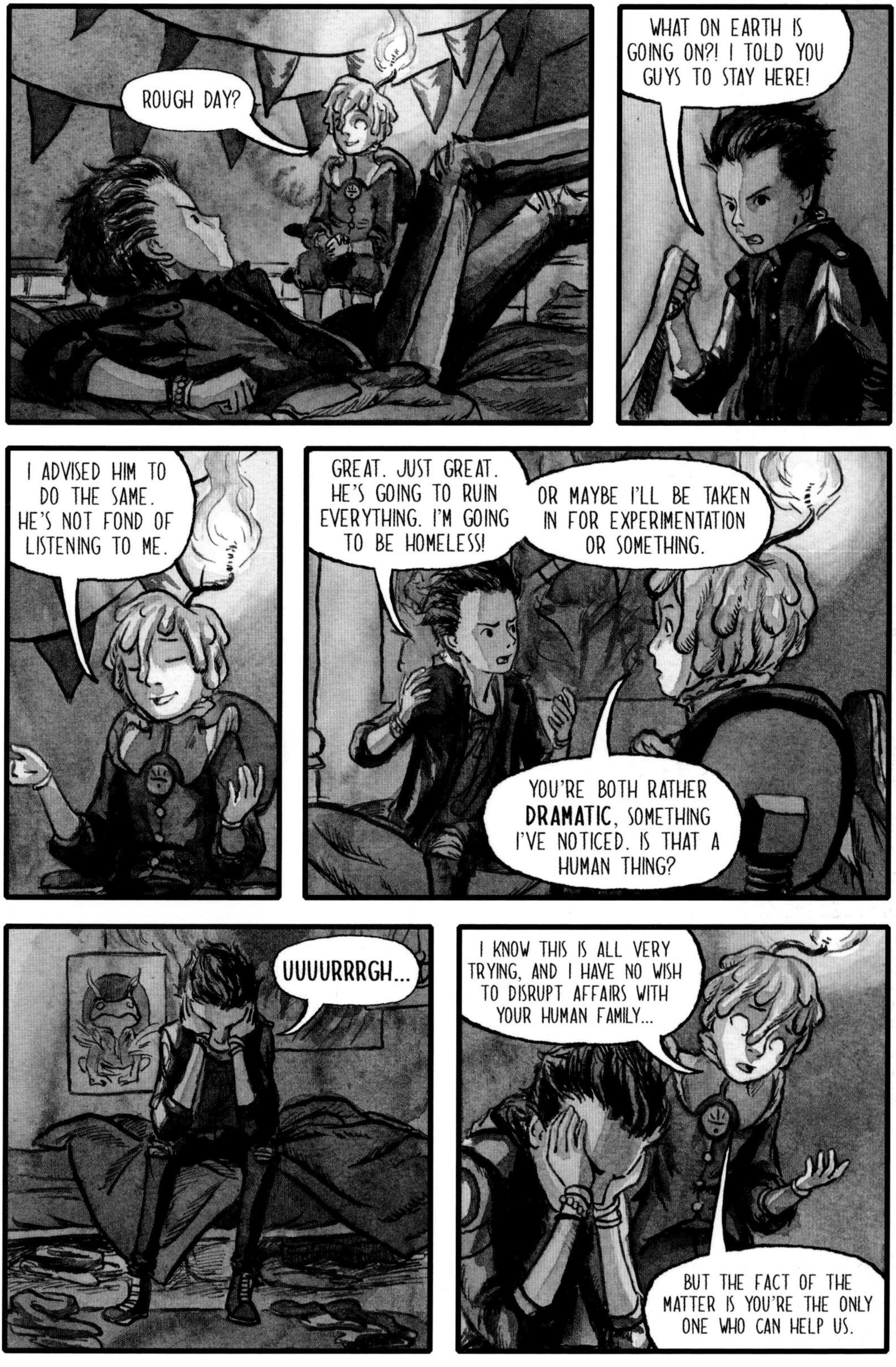
ROUGH DAY?
WHAT ON EARTH IS GOING ON?! I TOLD YOU GUYS TO STAY HERE!
I ADVISED HIM TO DO THE SAME. HE'S NOT FOND OF LISTENING TO ME.
GREAT. JUST GREAT. HE'S GOING TO RUIN EVERYTHING. I'M GOING TO BE HOMELESS!
OR MAYBE I'LL BE TAKEN IN FOR EXPERIMENTATION OR SOMETHING.
YOU'RE BOTH RATHER **DRAMATIC**, SOMETHING I'VE NOTICED. IS THAT A HUMAN THING?
UUUURRRGH...
I KNOW THIS IS ALL VERY TRYING, AND I HAVE NO WISH TO DISRUPT AFFAIRS WITH YOUR HUMAN FAMILY...
BUT THE FACT OF THE MATTER IS YOU'RE THE ONLY ONE WHO CAN HELP US.

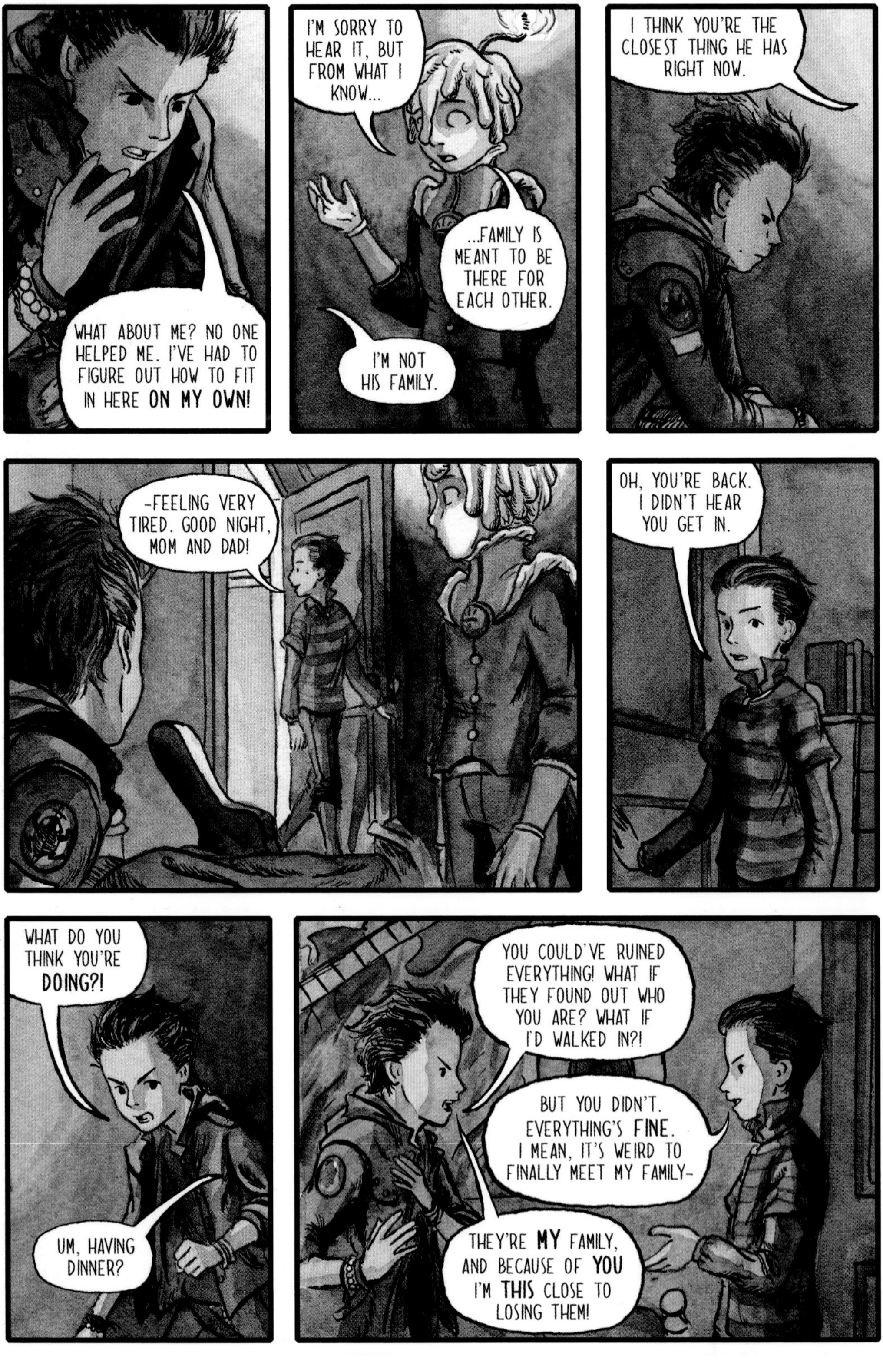
WHAT ABOUT ME? NO ONE HELPED ME. I'VE HAD TO FIGURE OUT HOW TO FIT IN HERE **ON MY OWN!**
I'M SORRY TO HEAR IT, BUT FROM WHAT I KNOW...
...FAMILY IS MEANT TO BE THERE FOR EACH OTHER.
I'M NOT HIS FAMILY.
I THINK YOU'RE THE CLOSEST THING HE HAS RIGHT NOW.
-FEELING VERY TIRED. GOOD NIGHT, MOM AND DAD!
OH, YOU'RE BACK. I DIDN'T HEAR YOU GET IN.
WHAT DO YOU THINK YOU'RE **DOING?!**
UM, HAVING DINNER?
YOU COULD'VE RUINED EVERYTHING! WHAT IF THEY FOUND OUT WHO YOU ARE? WHAT IF I'D WALKED IN?!
BUT YOU DIDN'T. EVERYTHING'S **FINE**. I MEAN, IT'S WEIRD TO FINALLY MEET MY FAMILY-
THEY'RE **MY** FAMILY, AND BECAUSE OF **YOU** I'M **THIS** CLOSE TO LOSING THEM!

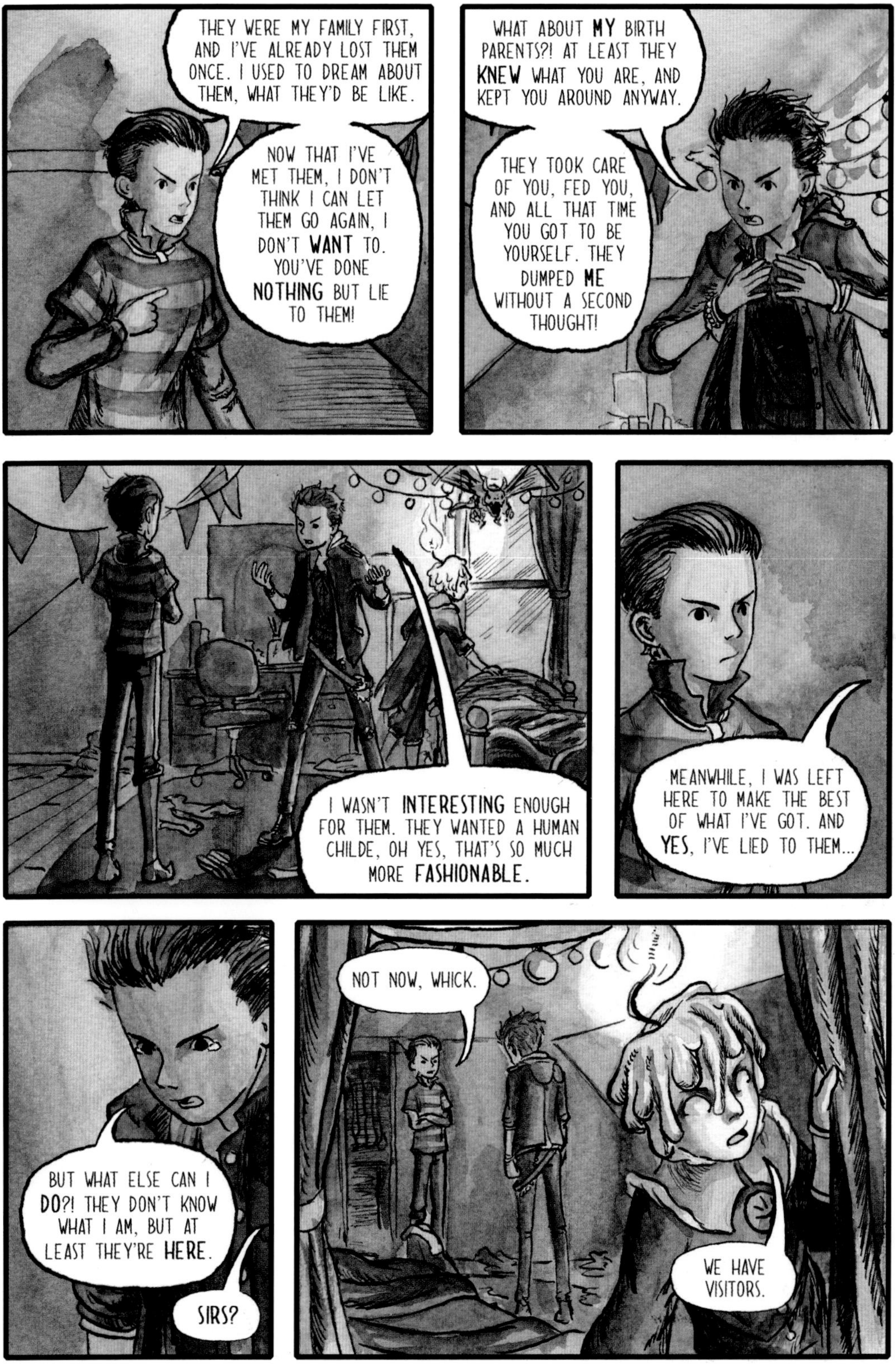
THEY WERE MY FAMILY FIRST, AND I'VE ALREADY LOST THEM ONCE. I USED TO DREAM ABOUT THEM, WHAT THEY'D BE LIKE.
NOW THAT I'VE MET THEM, I DON'T THINK I CAN LET THEM GO AGAIN, I DON'T WANT TO. YOU'VE DONE NOTHING BUT LIE TO THEM!
WHAT ABOUT MY BIRTH PARENTS?! AT LEAST THEY KNEW WHAT YOU ARE, AND KEPT YOU AROUND ANYWAY.
THEY TOOK CARE OF YOU, FED YOU, AND ALL THAT TIME YOU GOT TO BE YOURSELF. THEY DUMPED ME WITHOUT A SECOND THOUGHT!
I WASN'T INTERESTING ENOUGH FOR THEM. THEY WANTED A HUMAN CHILDE, OH YES, THAT'S SO MUCH MORE FASHIONABLE.
MEANWHILE, I WAS LEFT HERE TO MAKE THE BEST OF WHAT I'VE GOT. AND YES, I'VE LIED TO THEM...
BUT WHAT ELSE CAN I DO?! THEY DON'T KNOW WHAT I AM, BUT AT LEAST THEY'RE HERE.
SIRS?
NOT NOW, WHICK.
WE HAVE VISITORS.

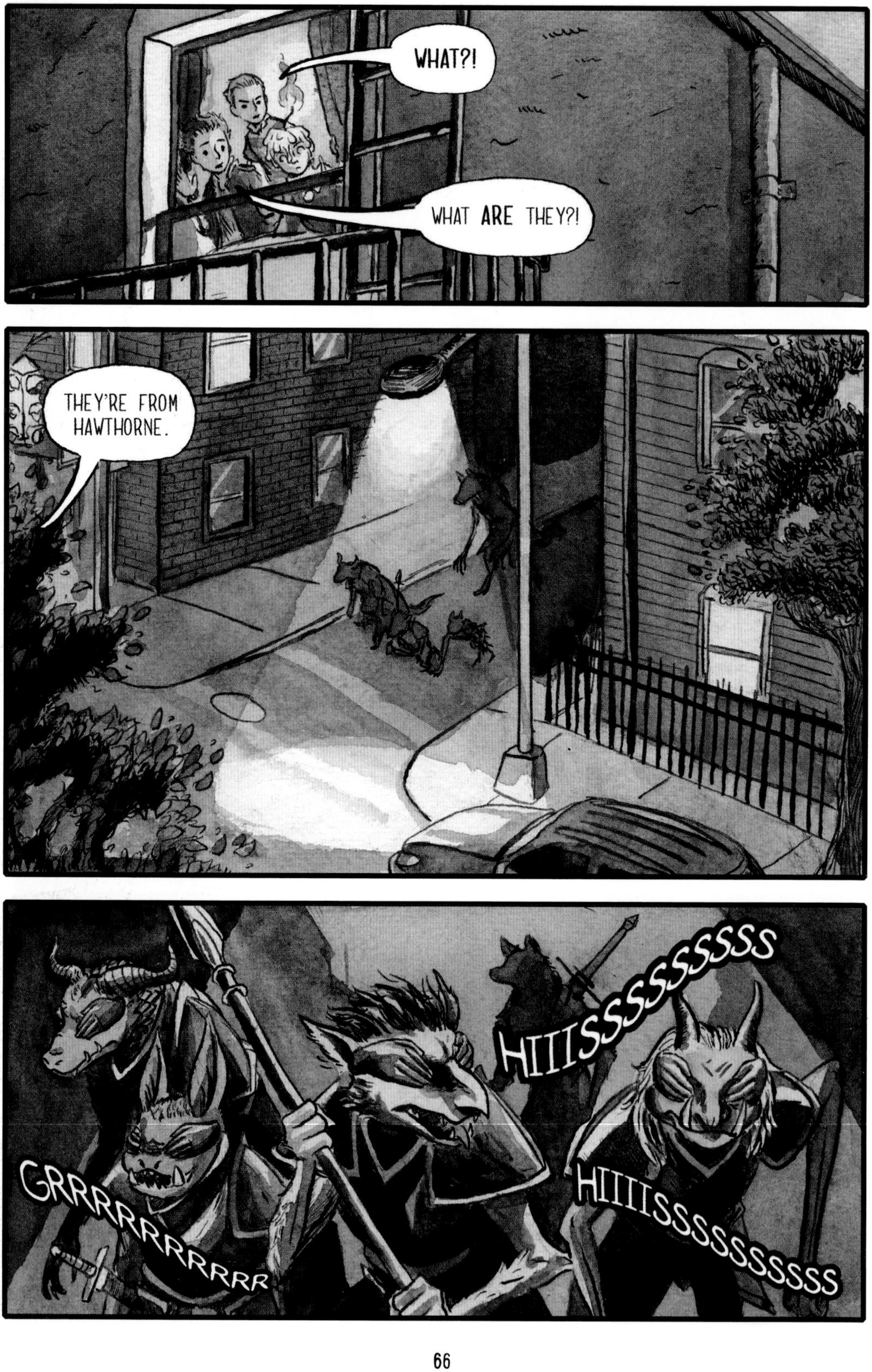
WHAT?!
WHAT ARE THEY?!
THEY'RE FROM HAWTHORNE.
HIIISSSSSSSSSS
GRRRRRRRRRRR
HIIIISSSSSSSSSSSS

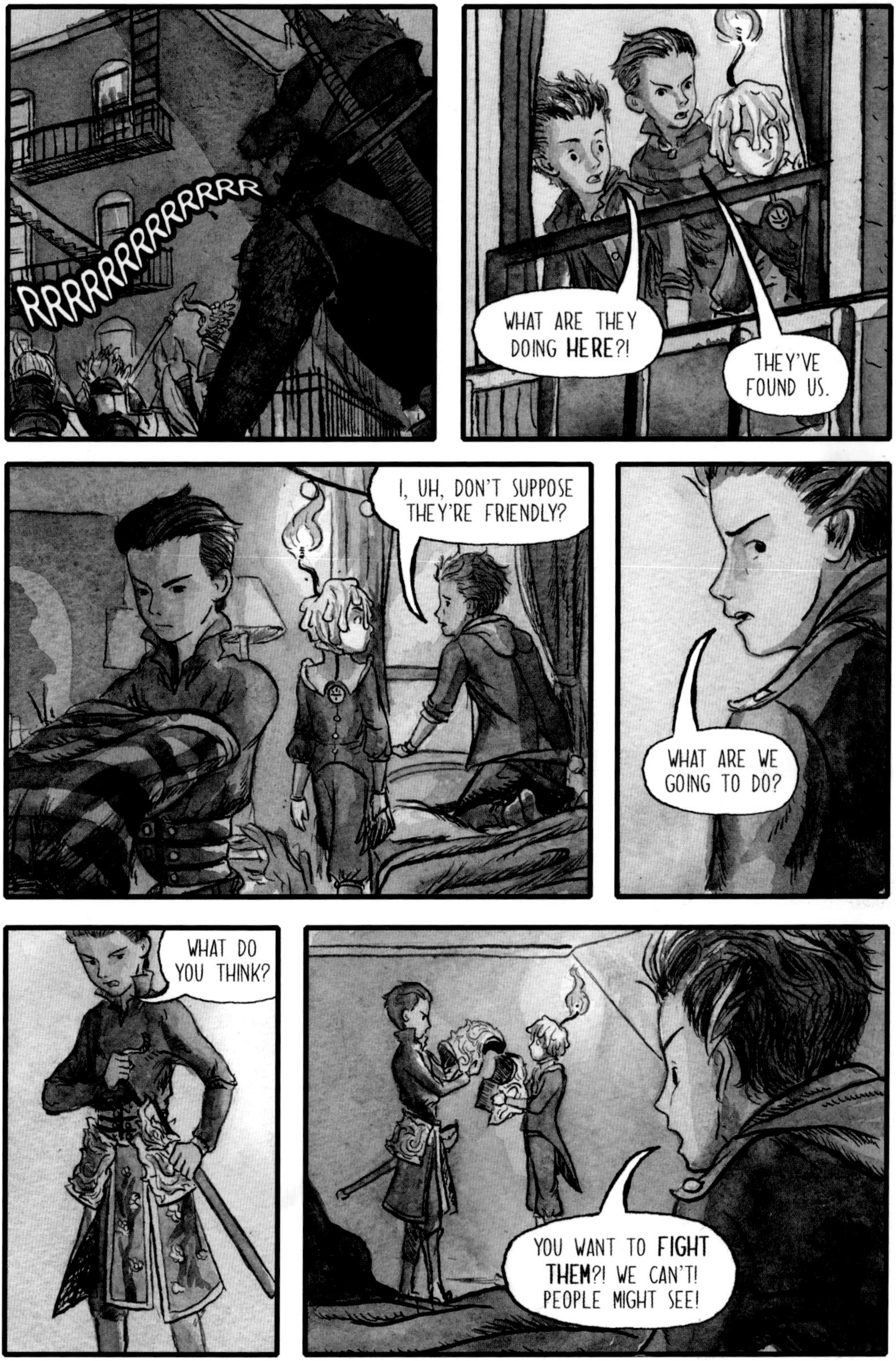
RRRRRRRRRRRRRRRRR
WHAT ARE THEY DOING **HERE**?!
THEY'VE FOUND US.
I, UH, DON'T SUPPOSE THEY'RE FRIENDLY?
WHAT ARE WE GOING TO DO?
WHAT DO YOU THINK?
YOU WANT TO **FIGHT THEM**?! WE CAN'T! PEOPLE MIGHT SEE!

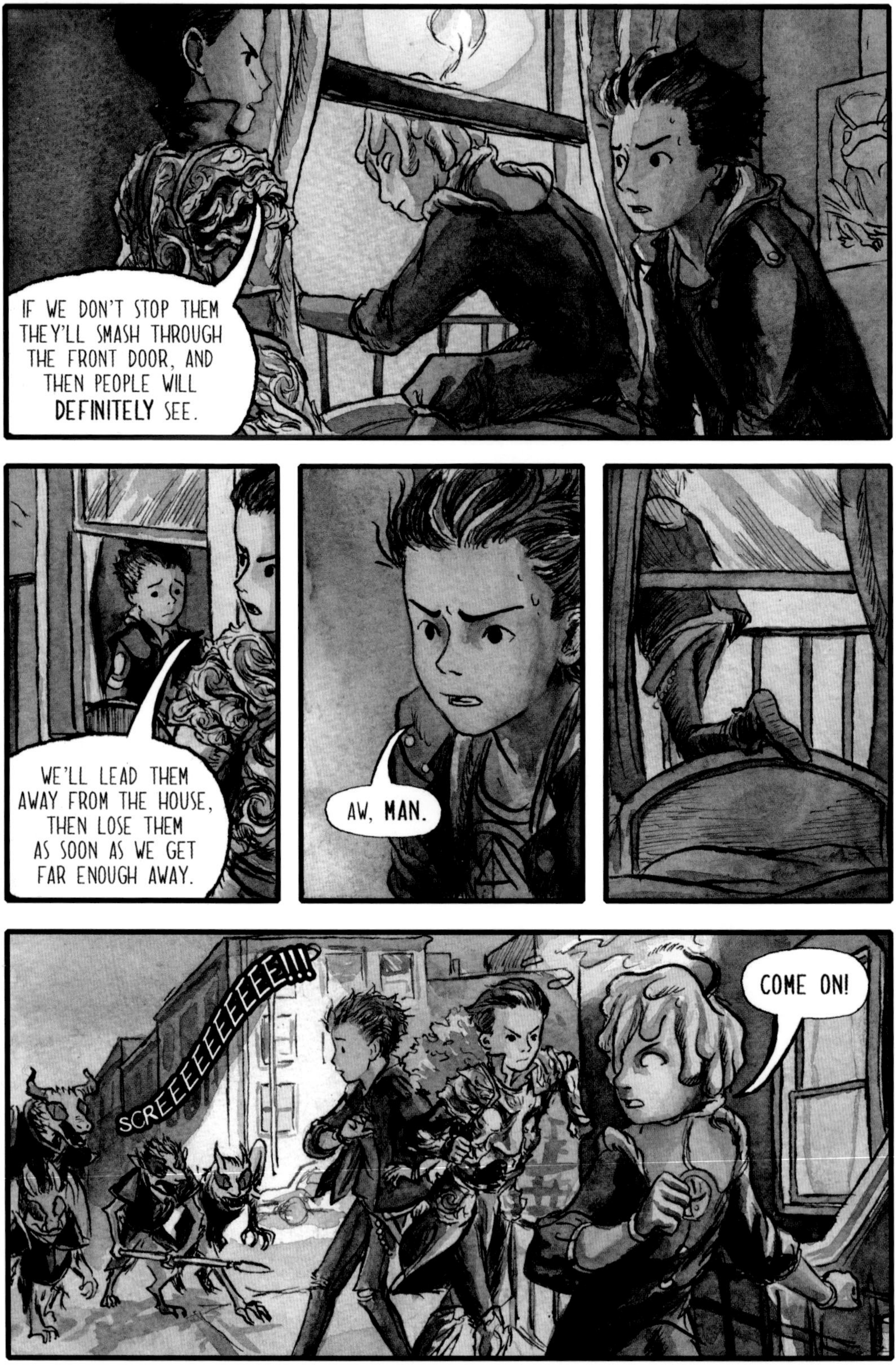
IF WE DON'T STOP THEM THEY'LL SMASH THROUGH THE FRONT DOOR, AND THEN PEOPLE WILL **DEFINITELY** SEE.
WE'LL LEAD THEM AWAY FROM THE HOUSE, THEN LOSE THEM AS SOON AS WE GET FAR ENOUGH AWAY.
AW, **MAN.**
SCREEEEEEEEEEEL!!!
COME ON!

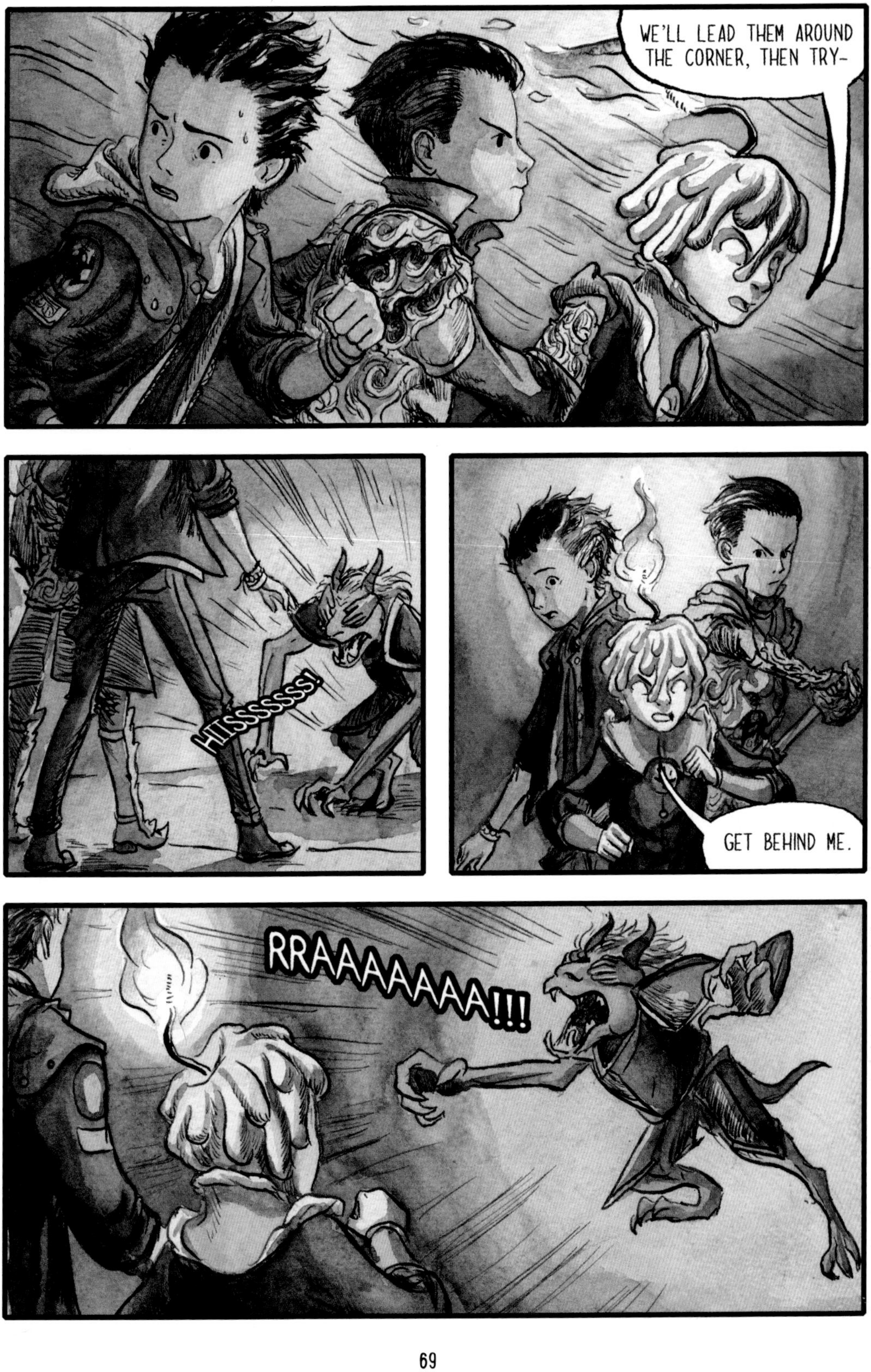
WE'LL LEAD THEM AROUND THE CORNER, THEN TRY-
HISSSSSSS!
GET BEHIND ME.
RRAAAAAAAA!!!

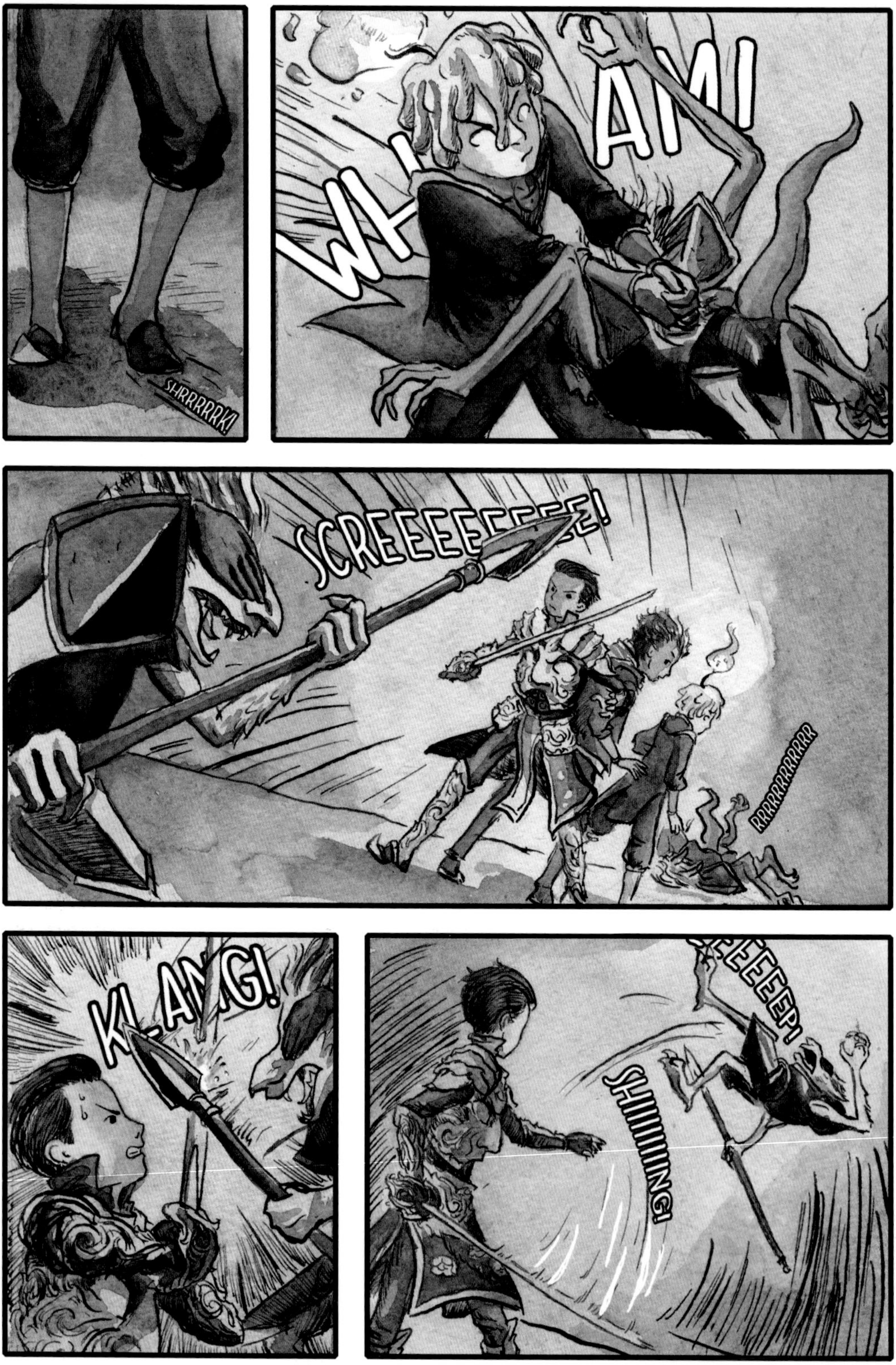
SHRRRRRK!
WH AM!
SCREEEEEEEEE!
RRRRRRRRRRRR
KLANG!
EEEEP!
SHIIIIIIING!

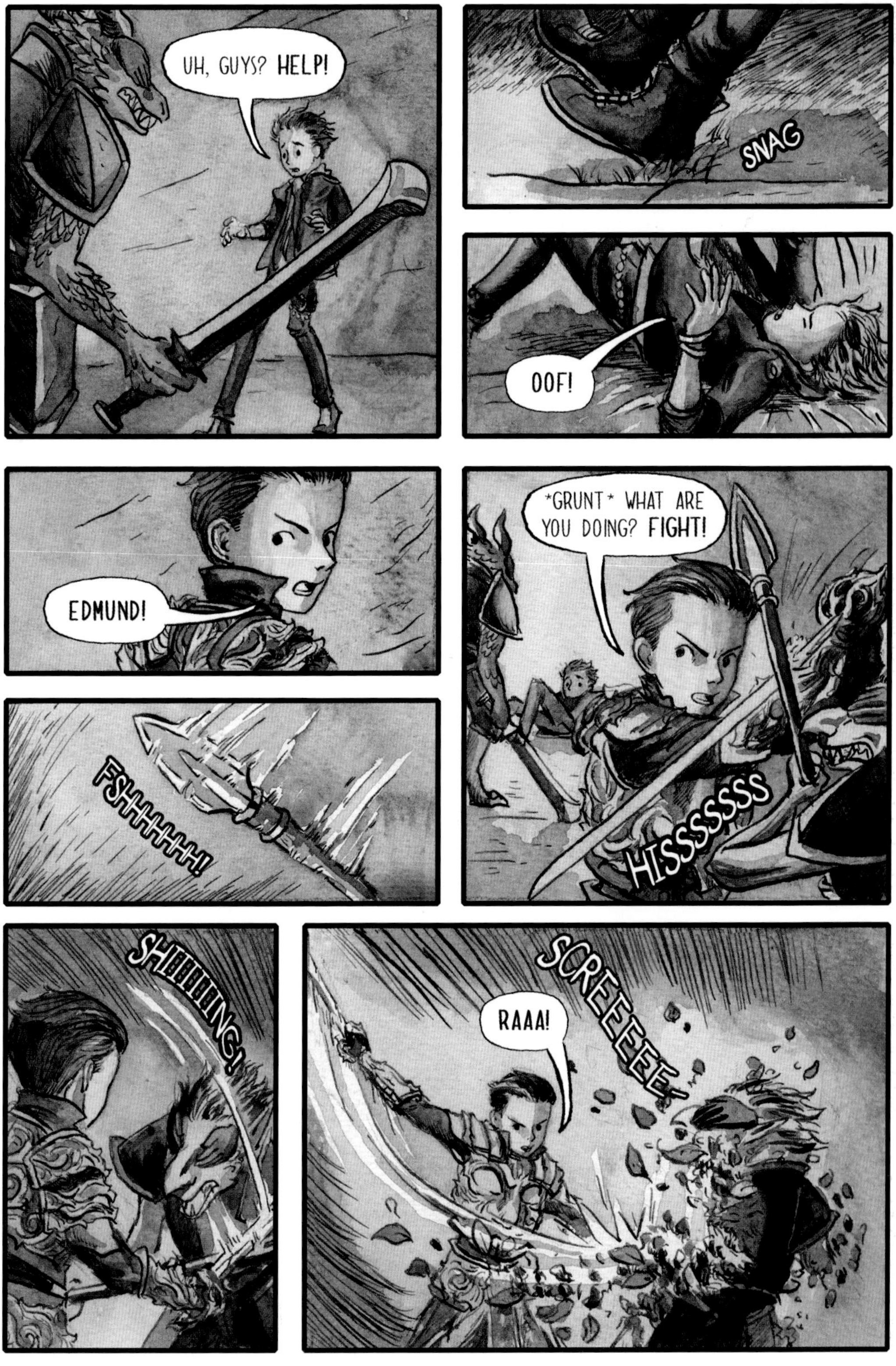
UH, GUYS? HELP!
SNAG
OOF!
EDMUND!
GRUNT WHAT ARE YOU DOING? FIGHT!
FSHHHHHH!
HISSSSSSS
SHIIIIIING!
SCREEEEEE
RAAA!

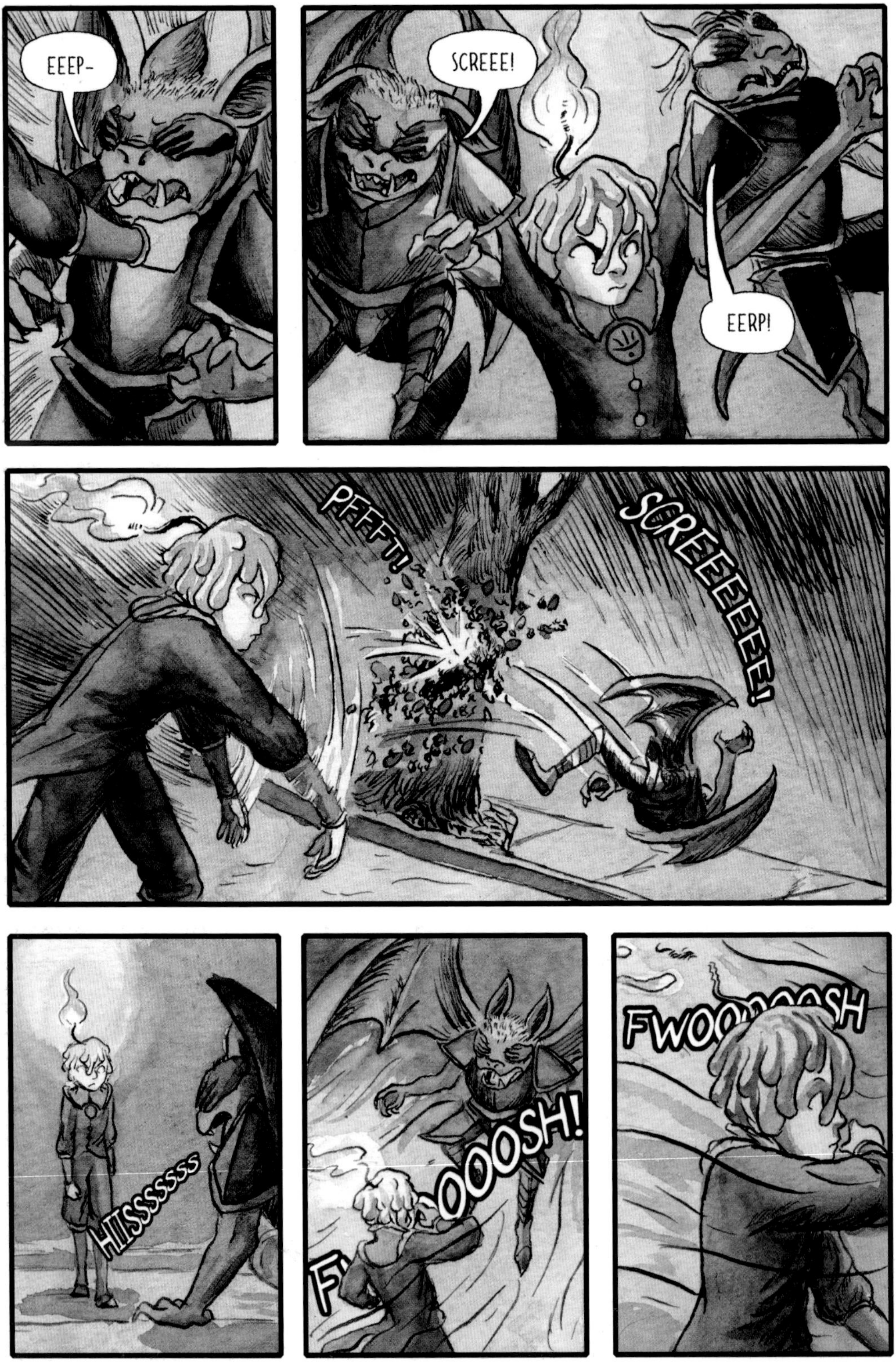
EEEP-
SCREEE!
EERP!
PFFFT!
SCREEEEEEEE!
HISSSSSSS
F
OOOSH!
FWOOOOOSH

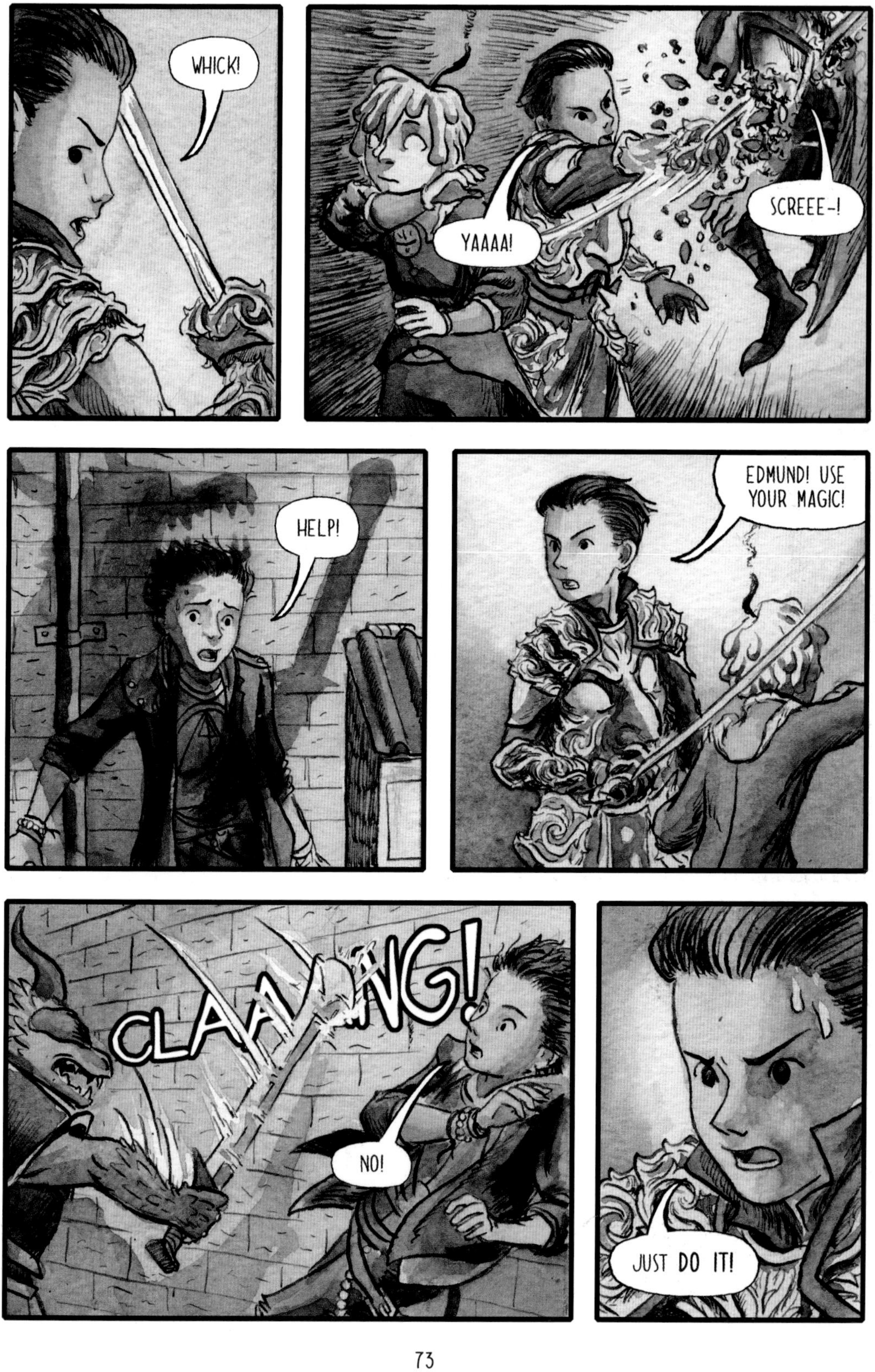
WHICK!
YAAAA!
SCREEE-!
HELP!
EDMUND! USE YOUR MAGIC!
CLAAANG!
NO!
JUST DO IT!

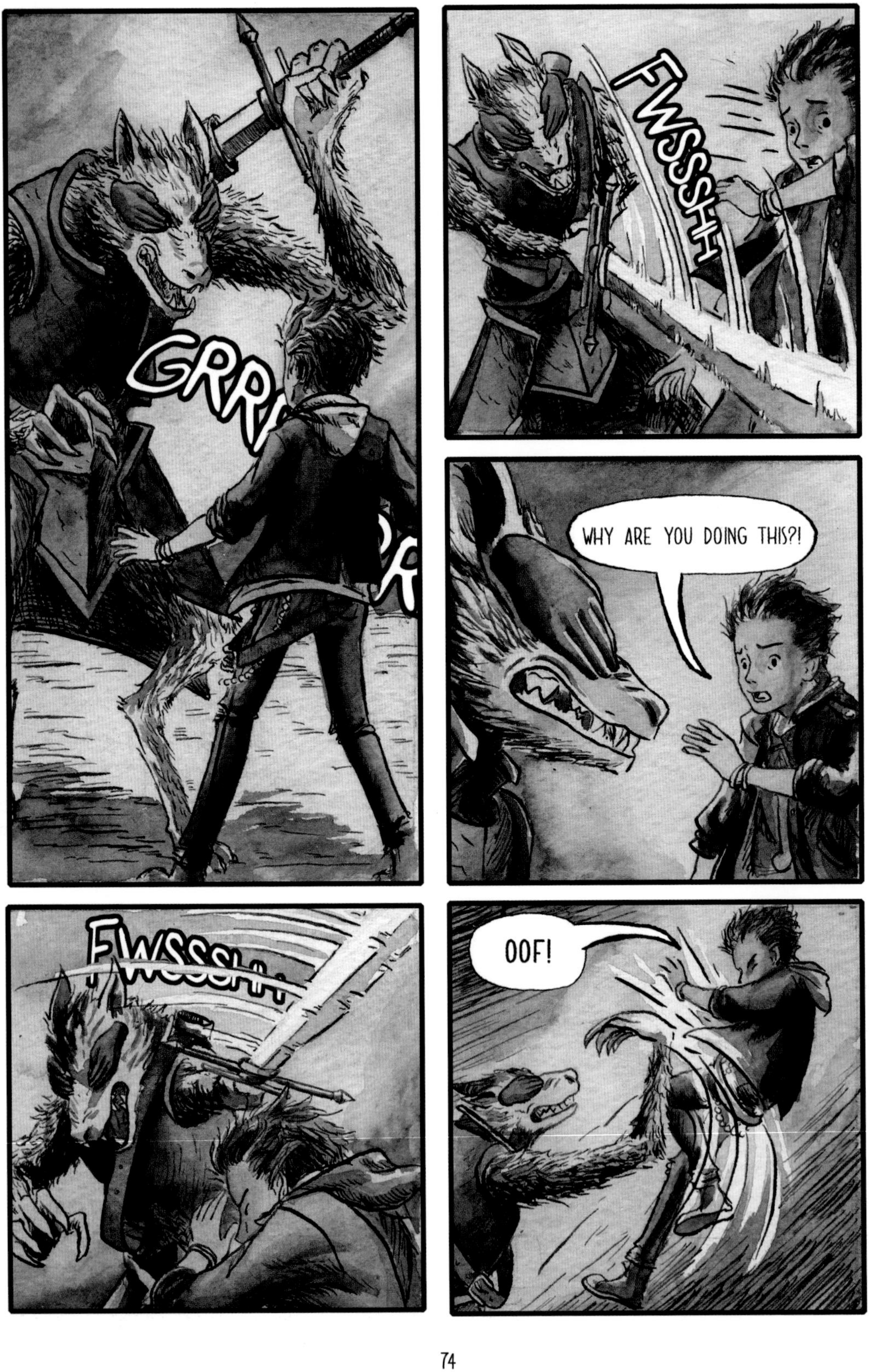
GRR
FWSSSH
WHY ARE YOU DOING THIS?!
OOF!

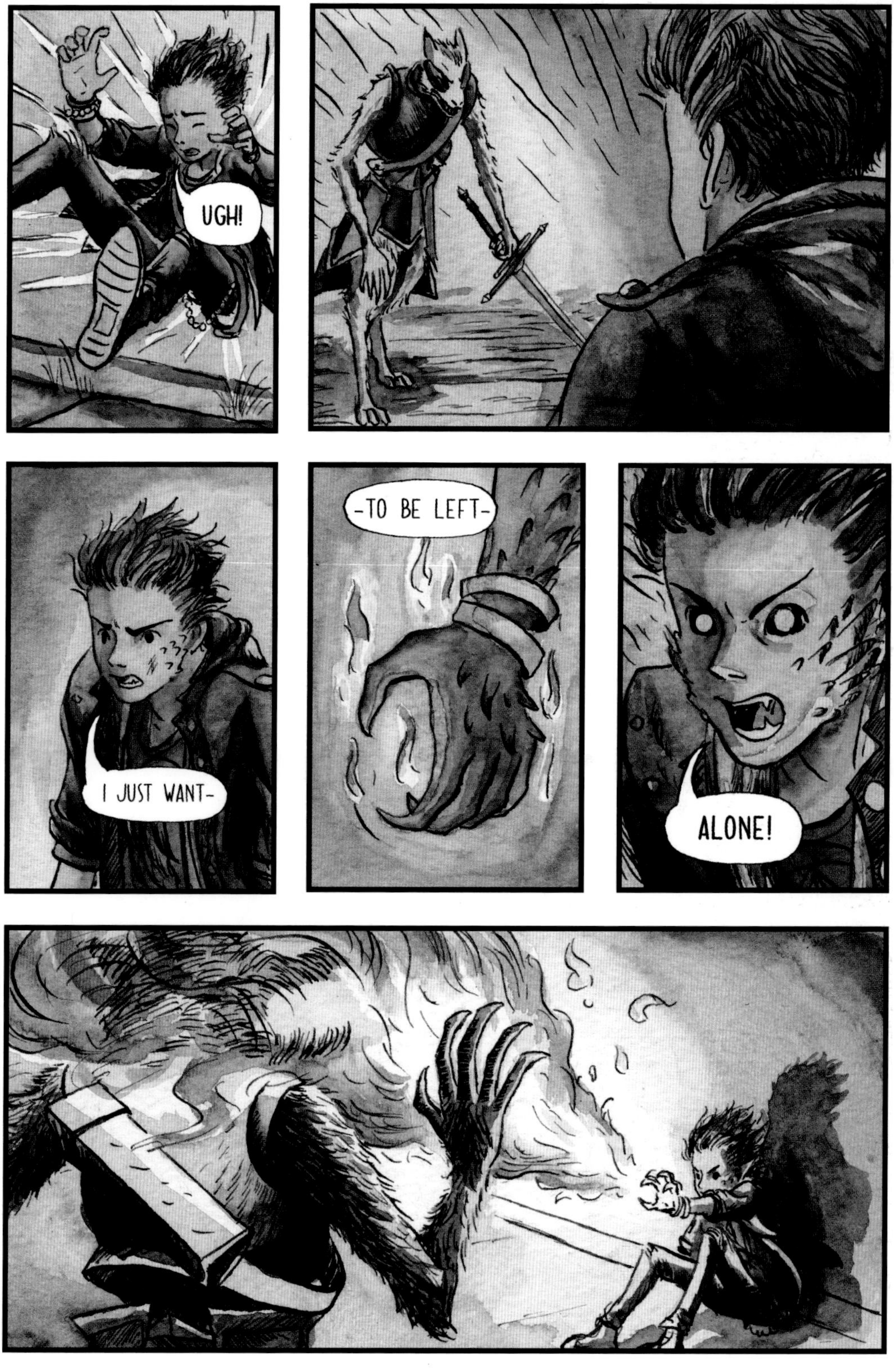
UGH!
I JUST WANT-
-TO BE LEFT-
ALONE!

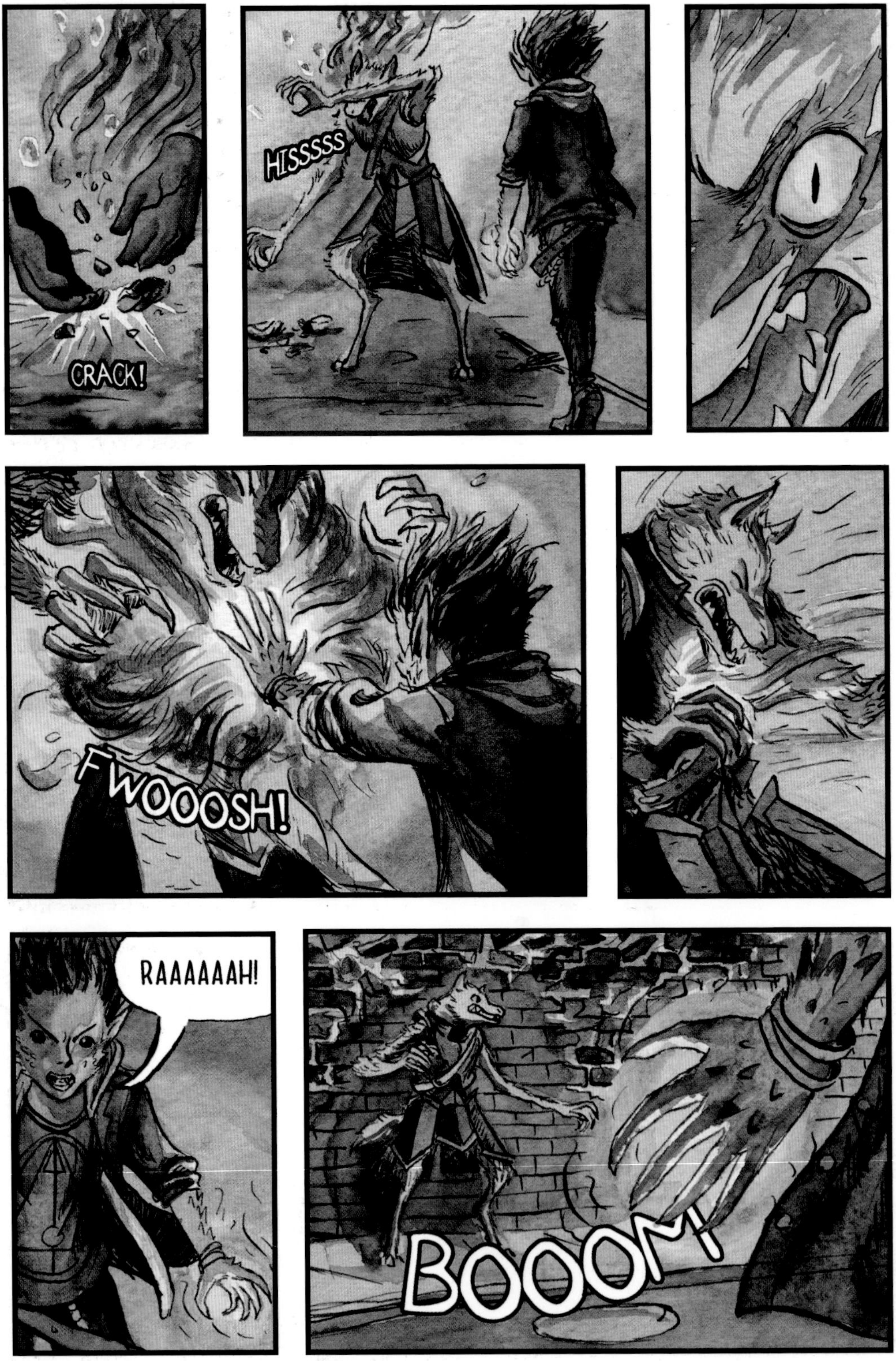
CRACK!
HISSSSS
FWOOOSH!
RAAAAAAH!
BOOOM!

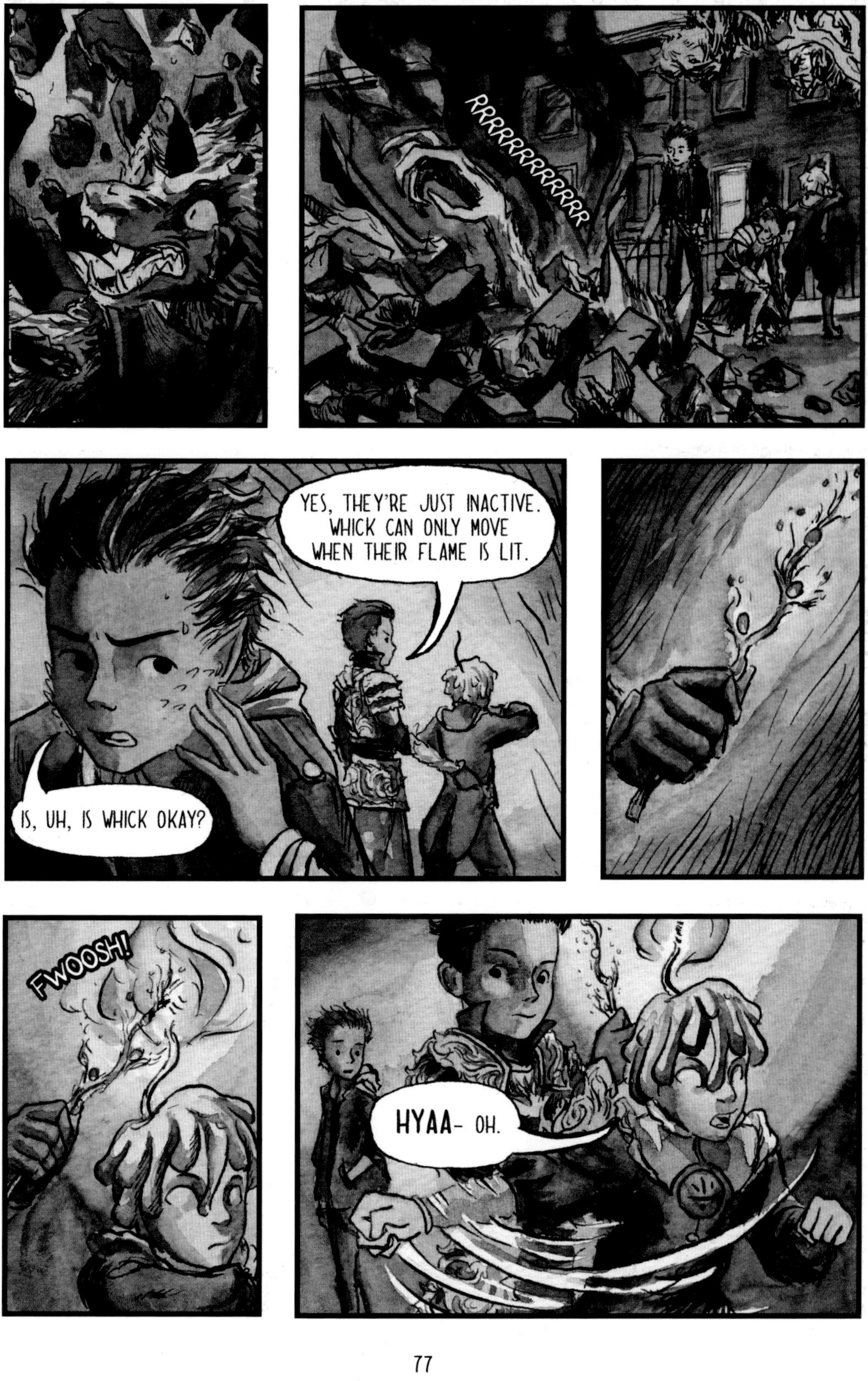
RRRRRRRRRRRR
YES, THEY'RE JUST INACTIVE. WHICK CAN ONLY MOVE WHEN THEIR FLAME IS LIT.
IS, UH, IS WHICK OKAY?
FWOOSH!
HYAA- OH.

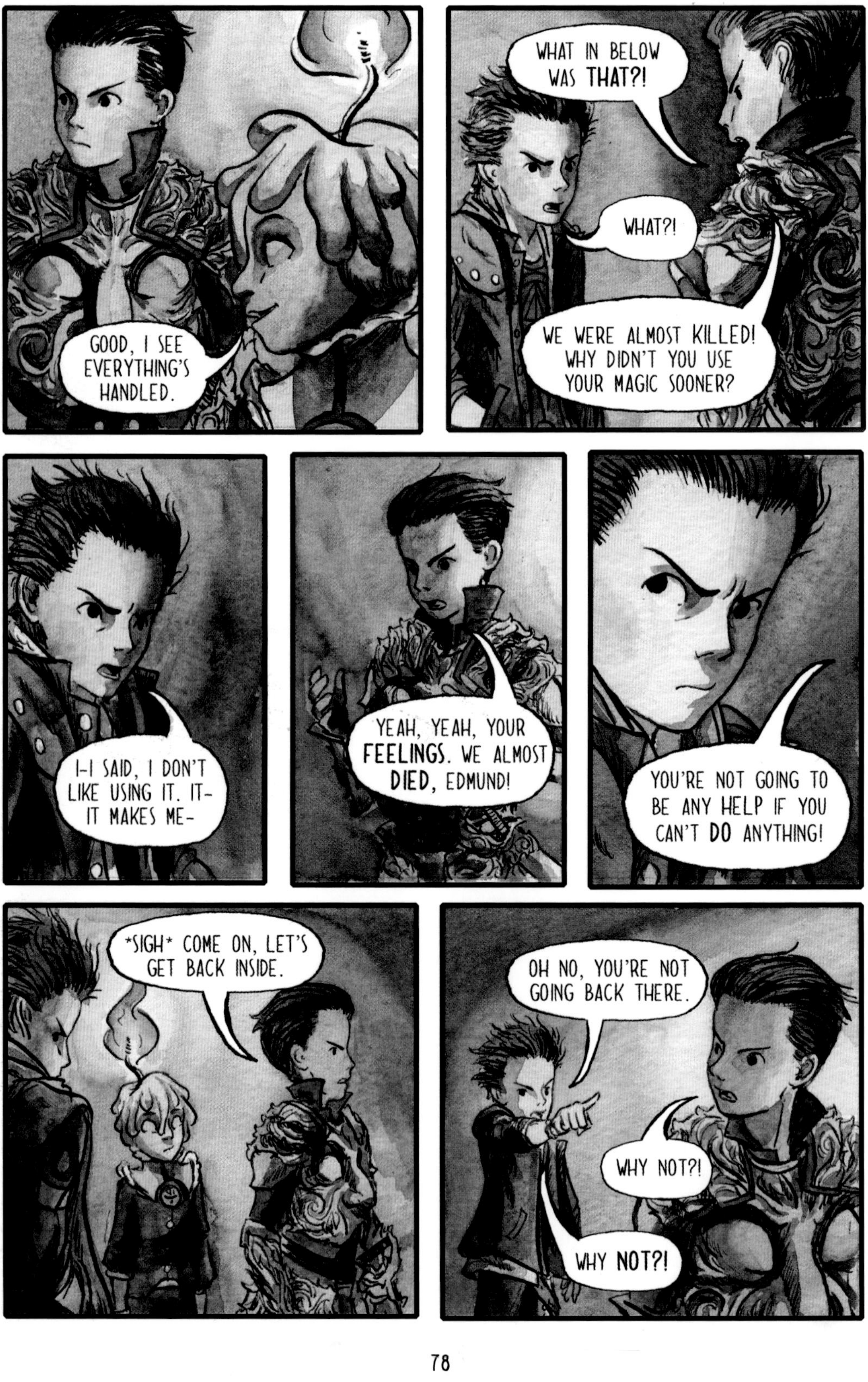
GOOD, I SEE EVERYTHING'S HANDLED.
WHAT IN BELOW WAS THAT?!
WHAT?!
WE WERE ALMOST KILLED! WHY DIDN'T YOU USE YOUR MAGIC SOONER?
I-I SAID, I DON'T LIKE USING IT. IT- IT MAKES ME-
YEAH, YEAH, YOUR FEELINGS. WE ALMOST DIED, EDMUND!
YOU'RE NOT GOING TO BE ANY HELP IF YOU CAN'T DO ANYTHING!
SIGH COME ON, LET'S GET BACK INSIDE.
OH NO, YOU'RE NOT GOING BACK THERE.
WHY NOT?!
WHY NOT?!

Chapter Six

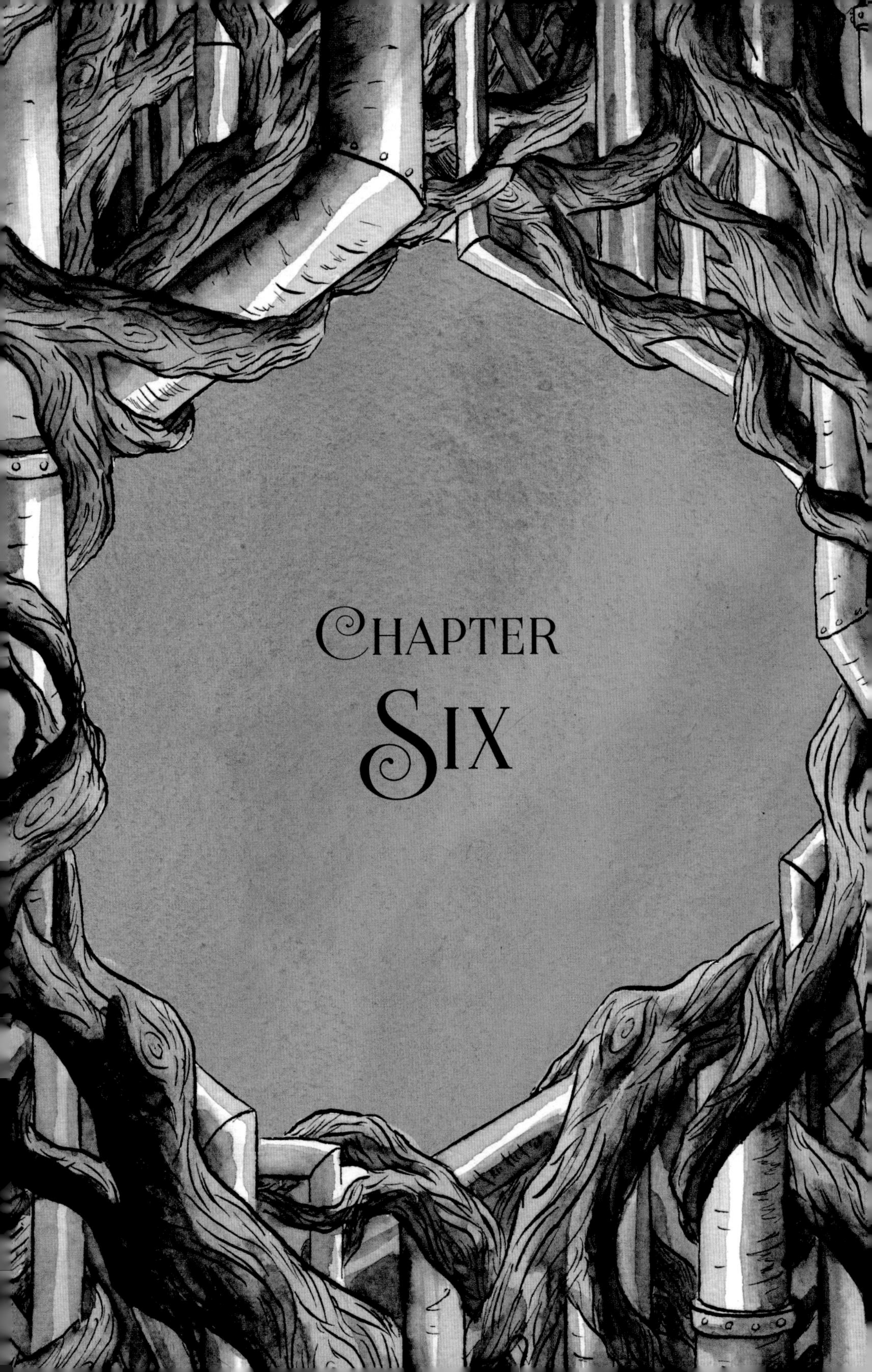

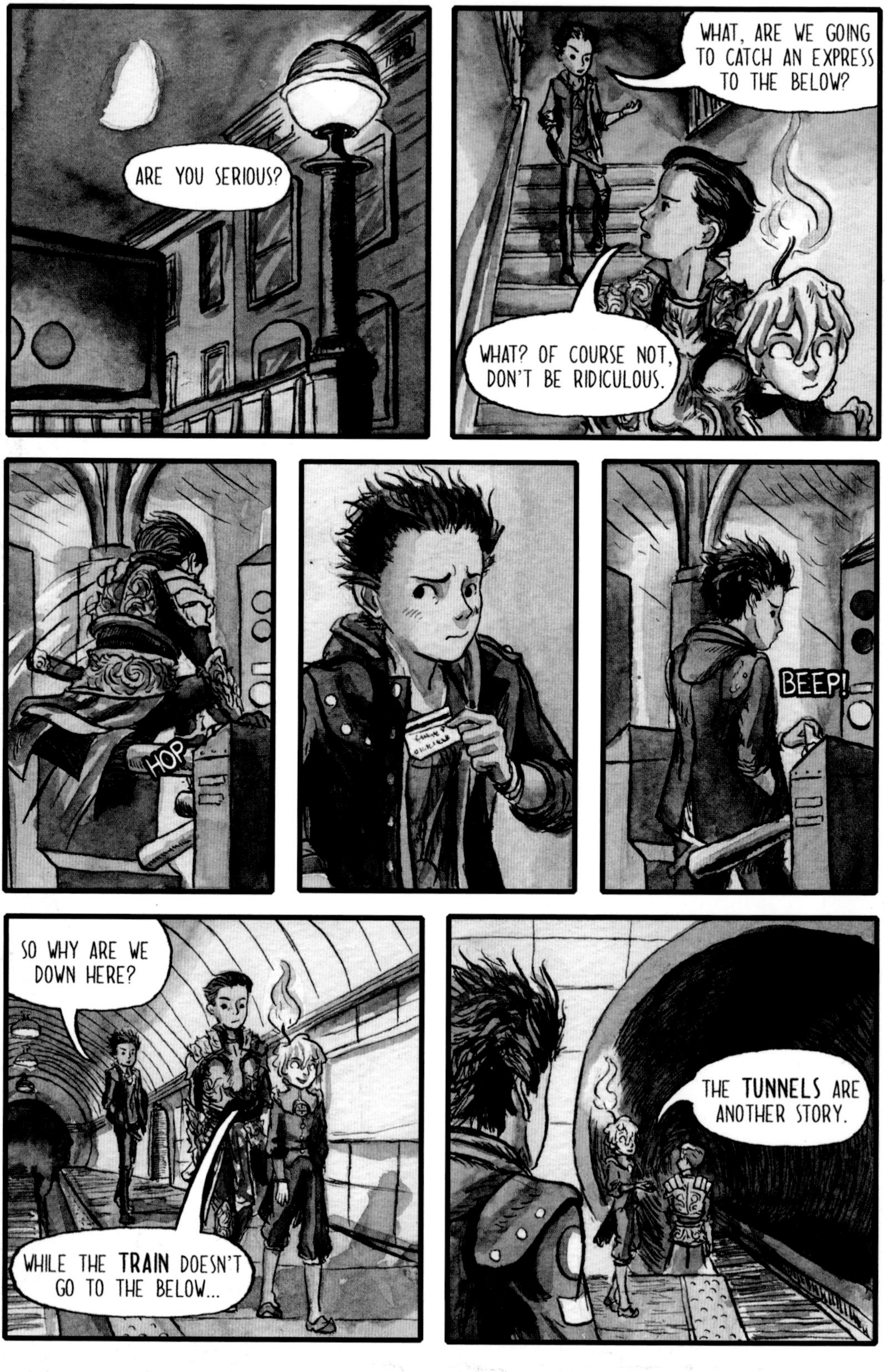
ARE YOU SERIOUS?
WHAT, ARE WE GOING TO CATCH AN EXPRESS TO THE BELOW?
WHAT? OF COURSE NOT, DON'T BE RIDICULOUS.
HOP
BEEP!
SO WHY ARE WE DOWN HERE?
WHILE THE **TRAIN** DOESN'T GO TO THE BELOW...
THE **TUNNELS** ARE ANOTHER STORY.

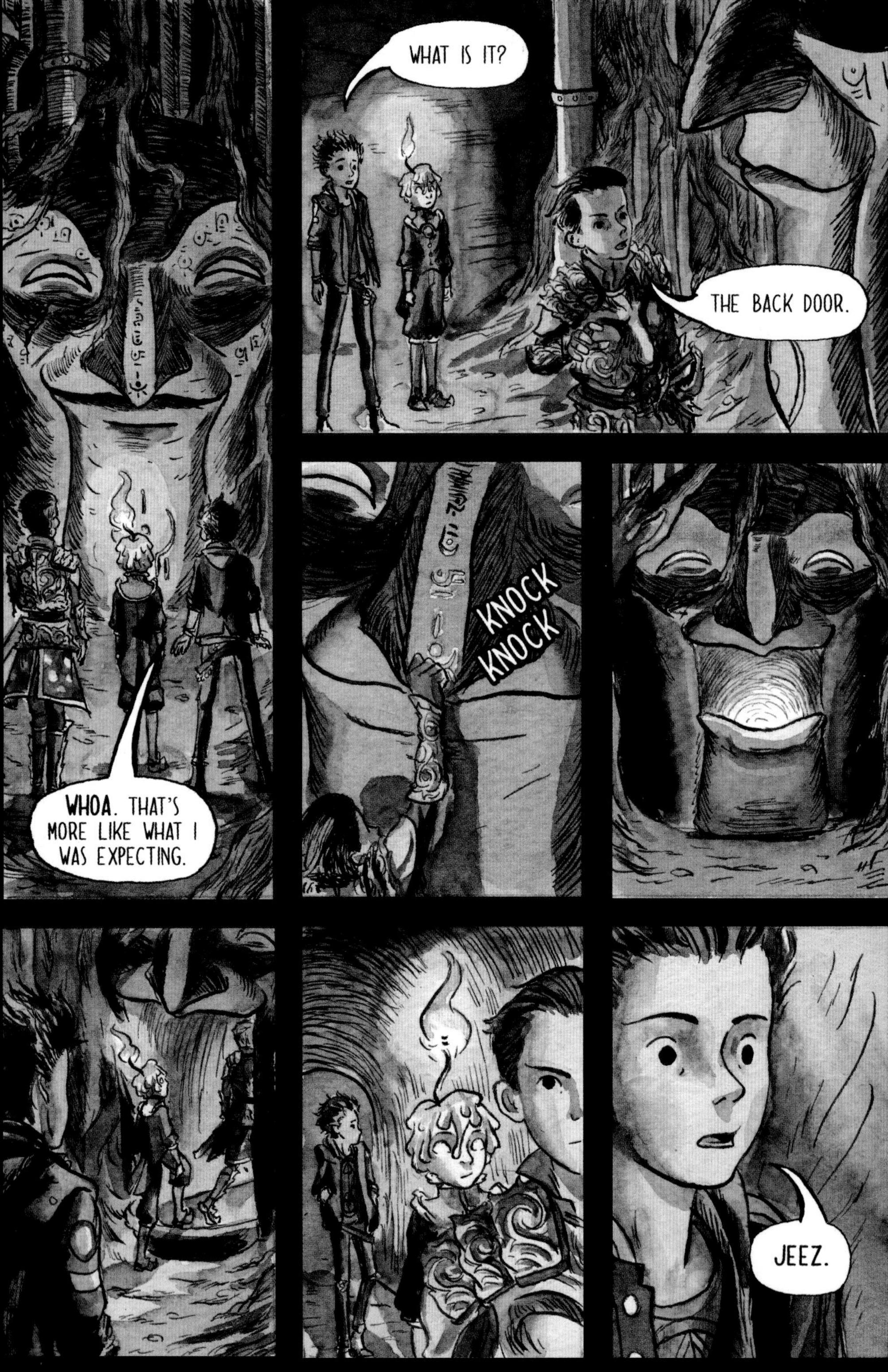
WHOA. THAT'S MORE LIKE WHAT I WAS EXPECTING.
WHAT IS IT?
THE BACK DOOR.
KNOCK KNOCK
JEEZ.

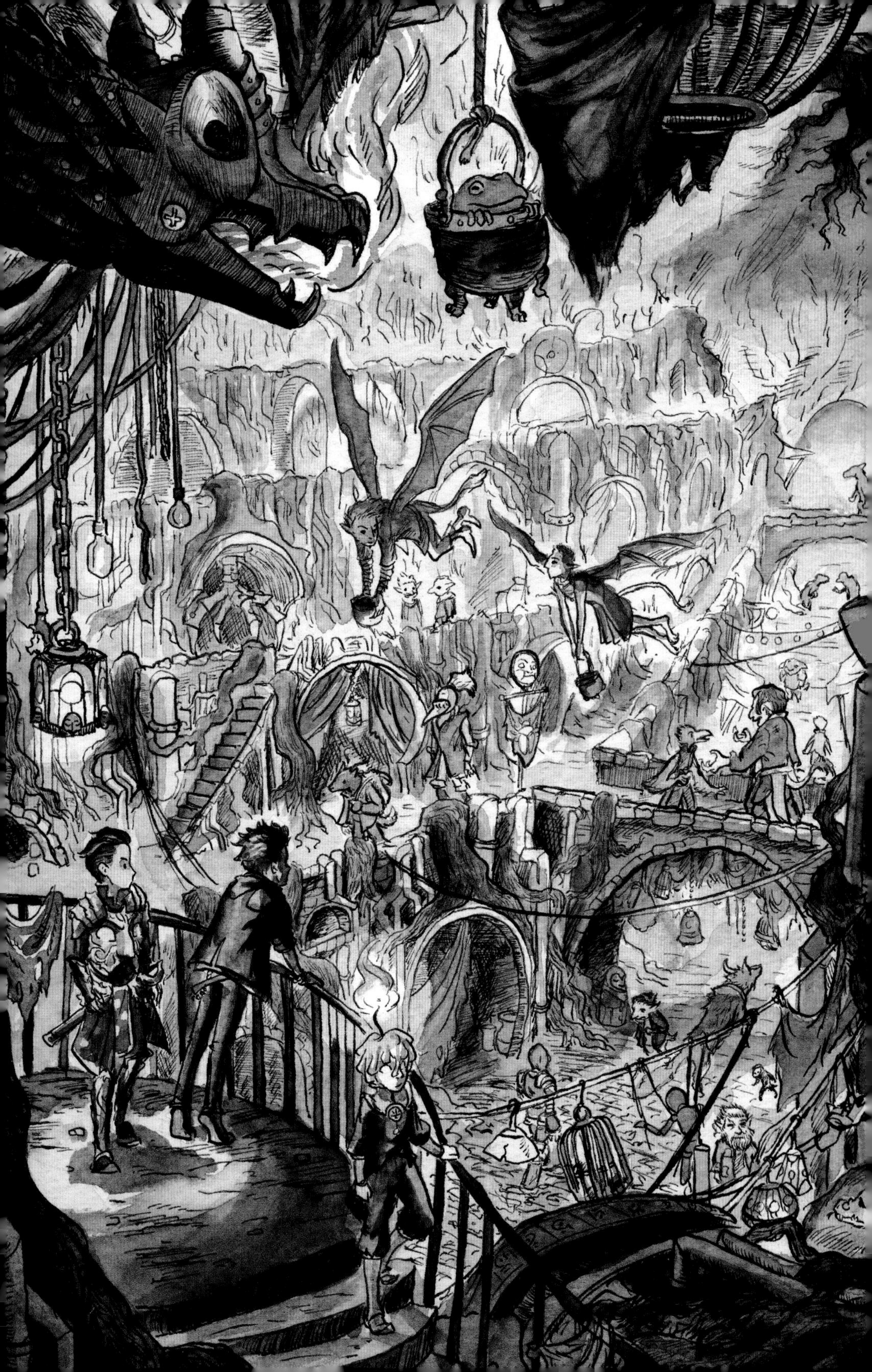

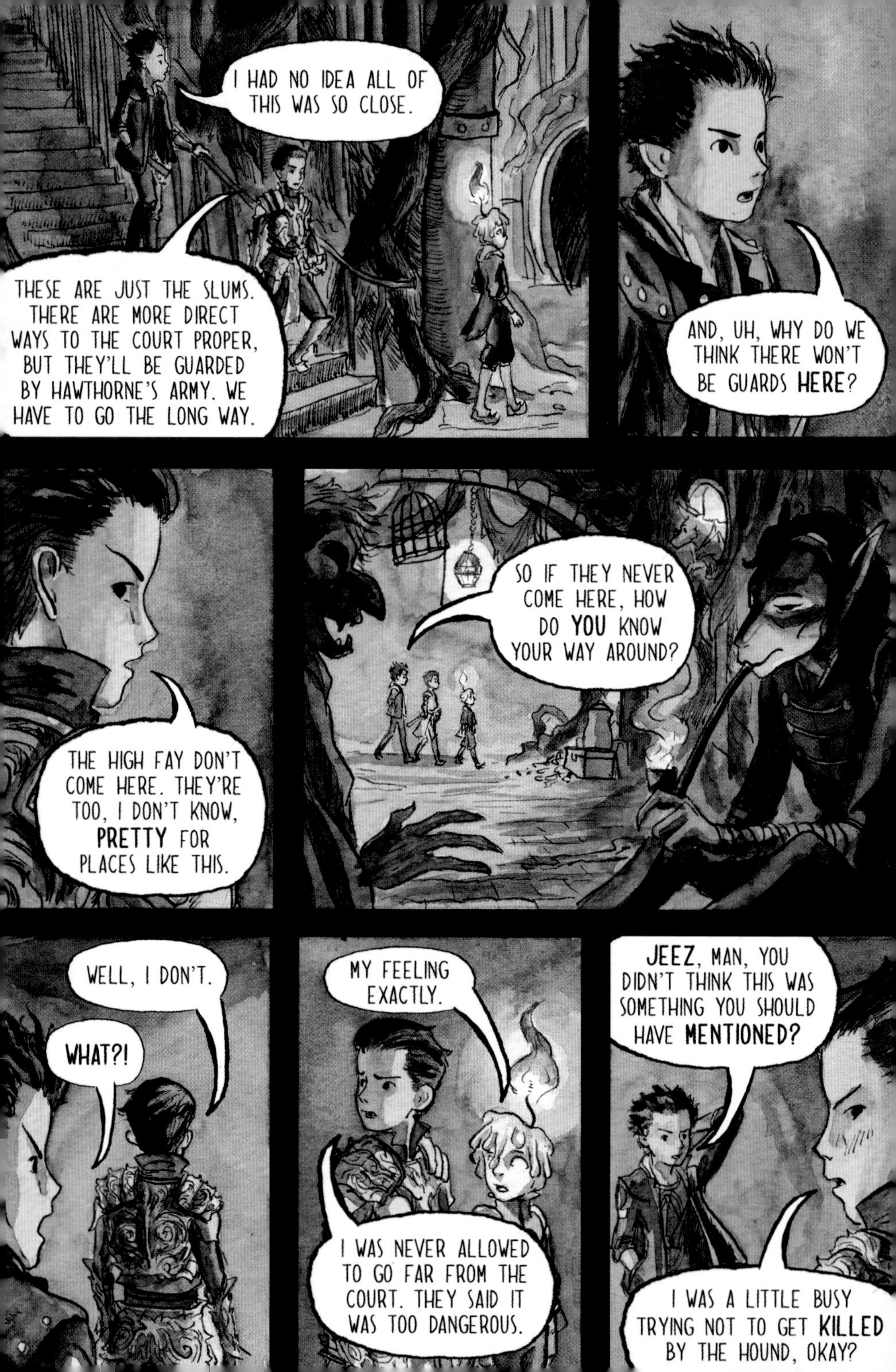
I HAD NO IDEA ALL OF THIS WAS SO CLOSE.
THESE ARE JUST THE SLUMS. THERE ARE MORE DIRECT WAYS TO THE COURT PROPER, BUT THEY'LL BE GUARDED BY HAWTHORNE'S ARMY. WE HAVE TO GO THE LONG WAY.
AND, UH, WHY DO WE THINK THERE WON'T BE GUARDS **HERE**?
THE HIGH FAY DON'T COME HERE. THEY'RE TOO, I DON'T KNOW, **PRETTY** FOR PLACES LIKE THIS.
SO IF THEY NEVER COME HERE, HOW DO **YOU** KNOW YOUR WAY AROUND?
WELL, I DON'T.
WHAT?!
MY FEELING EXACTLY.
I WAS NEVER ALLOWED TO GO FAR FROM THE COURT. THEY SAID IT WAS TOO DANGEROUS.
JEEZ, MAN, YOU DIDN'T THINK THIS WAS SOMETHING YOU SHOULD HAVE **MENTIONED?**
I WAS A LITTLE BUSY TRYING NOT TO GET **KILLED** BY THE HOUND, OKAY?

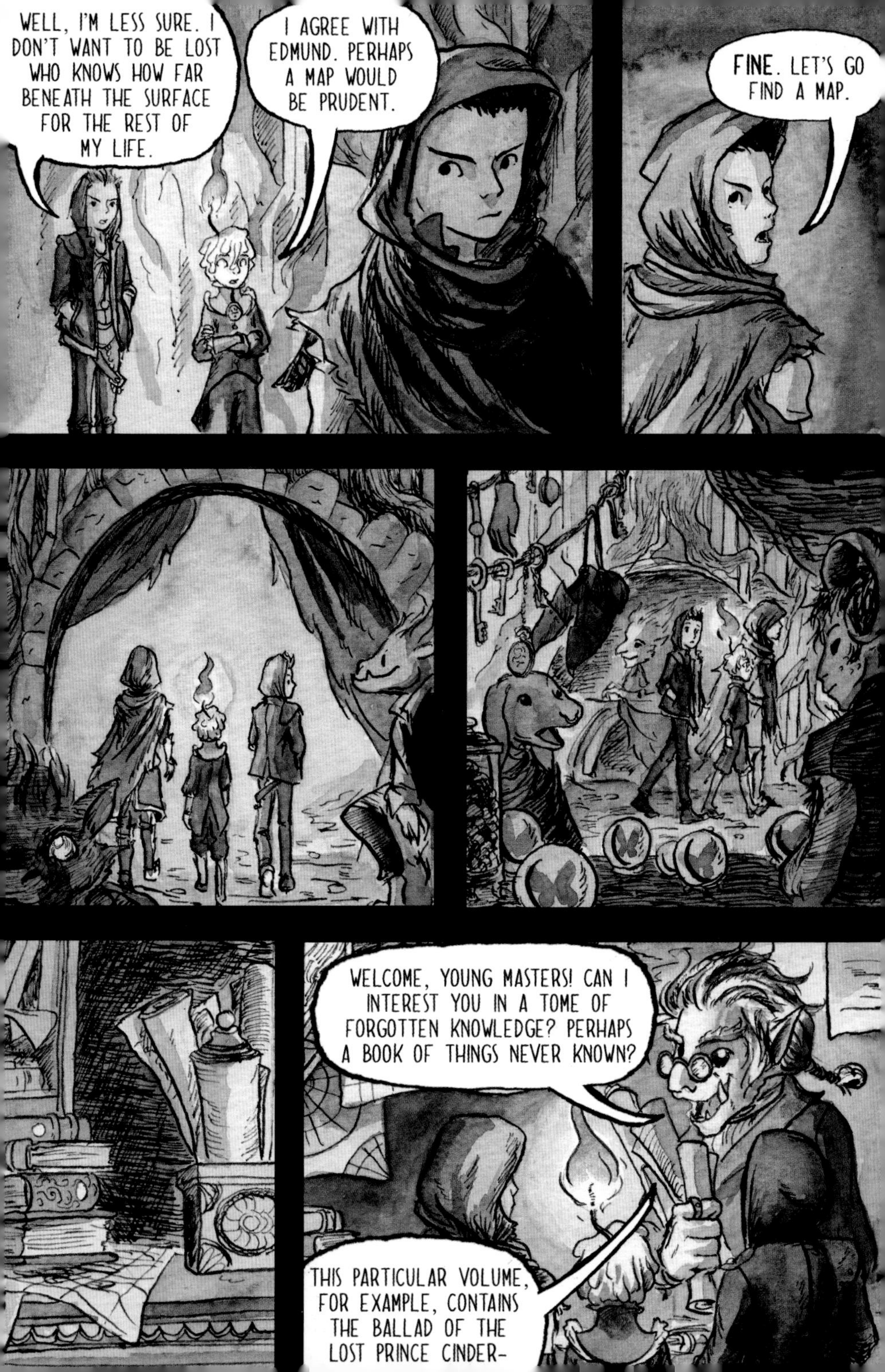

WELL, I'M LESS SURE. I DON'T WANT TO BE LOST WHO KNOWS HOW FAR BENEATH THE SURFACE FOR THE REST OF MY LIFE.
I AGREE WITH EDMUND. PERHAPS A MAP WOULD BE PRUDENT.
FINE. LET'S GO FIND A MAP.
WELCOME, YOUNG MASTERS! CAN I INTEREST YOU IN A TOME OF FORGOTTEN KNOWLEDGE? PERHAPS A BOOK OF THINGS NEVER KNOWN?
THIS PARTICULAR VOLUME, FOR EXAMPLE, CONTAINS THE BALLAD OF THE LOST PRINCE CINDER-

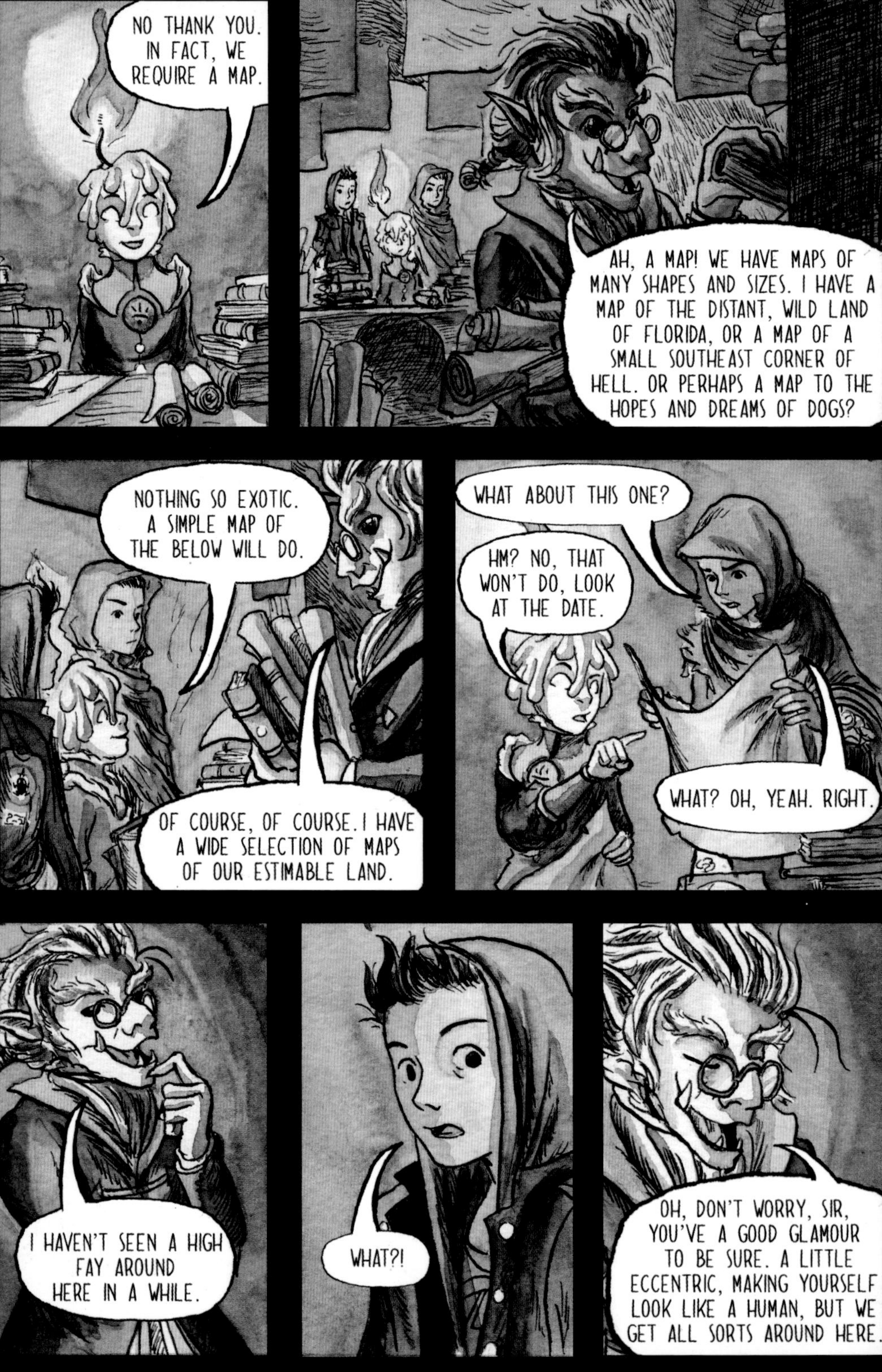
NO THANK YOU. IN FACT, WE REQUIRE A MAP.
AH, A MAP! WE HAVE MAPS OF MANY SHAPES AND SIZES. I HAVE A MAP OF THE DISTANT, WILD LAND OF FLORIDA, OR A MAP OF A SMALL SOUTHEAST CORNER OF HELL. OR PERHAPS A MAP TO THE HOPES AND DREAMS OF DOGS?
NOTHING SO EXOTIC. A SIMPLE MAP OF THE BELOW WILL DO.
OF COURSE, OF COURSE. I HAVE A WIDE SELECTION OF MAPS OF OUR ESTIMABLE LAND.
WHAT ABOUT THIS ONE?
HM? NO, THAT WON'T DO, LOOK AT THE DATE.
WHAT? OH, YEAH. RIGHT.
I HAVEN'T SEEN A HIGH FAY AROUND HERE IN A WHILE.
WHAT?!
OH, DON'T WORRY, SIR, YOU'VE A GOOD GLAMOUR TO BE SURE. A LITTLE ECCENTRIC, MAKING YOURSELF LOOK LIKE A HUMAN, BUT WE GET ALL SORTS AROUND HERE.

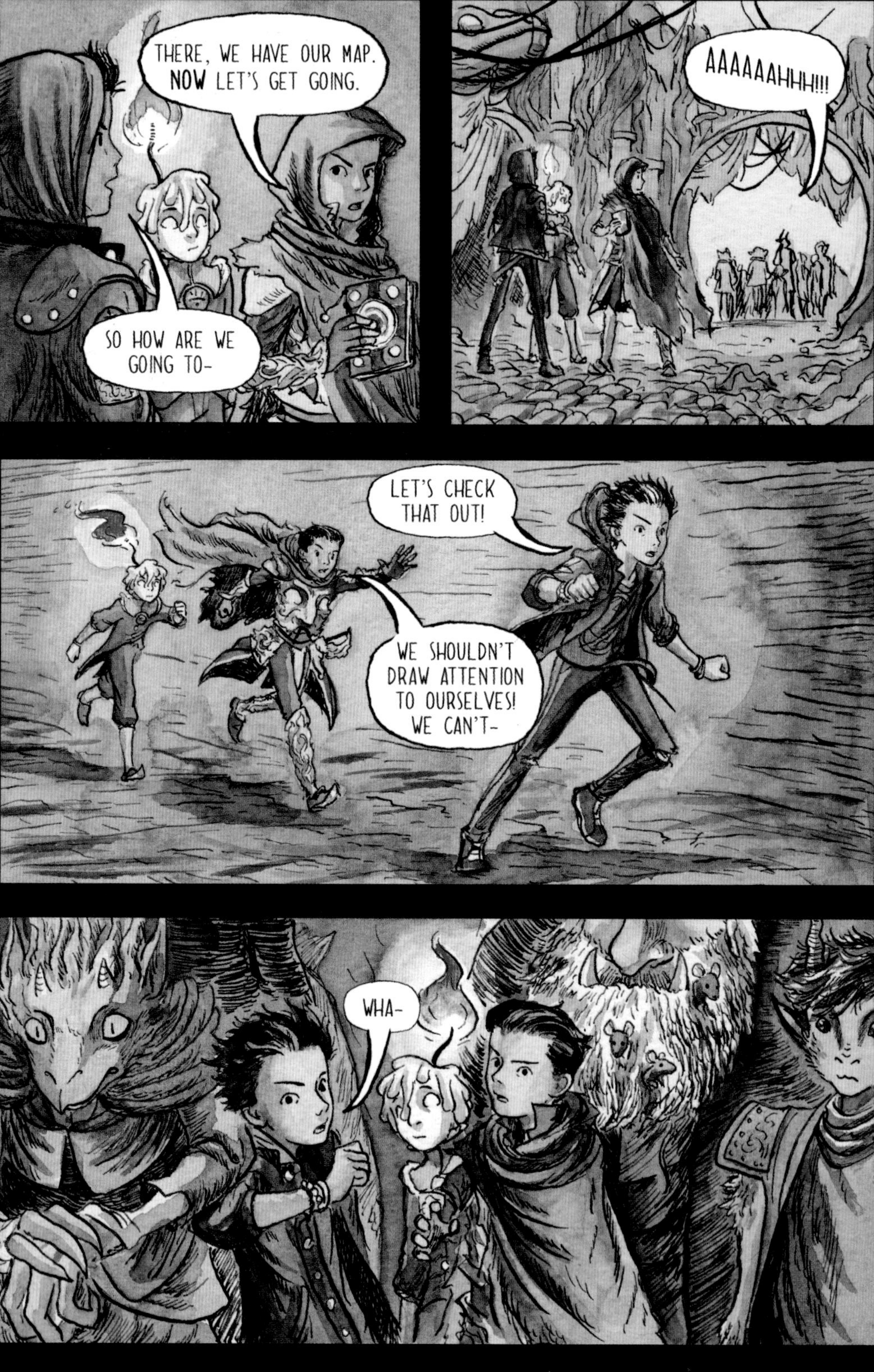

THERE, WE HAVE OUR MAP. NOW LET'S GET GOING.
SO HOW ARE WE GOING TO-
AAAAAAHHH!!!
LET'S CHECK THAT OUT!
WE SHOULDN'T DRAW ATTENTION TO OURSELVES! WE CAN'T-
WHA-

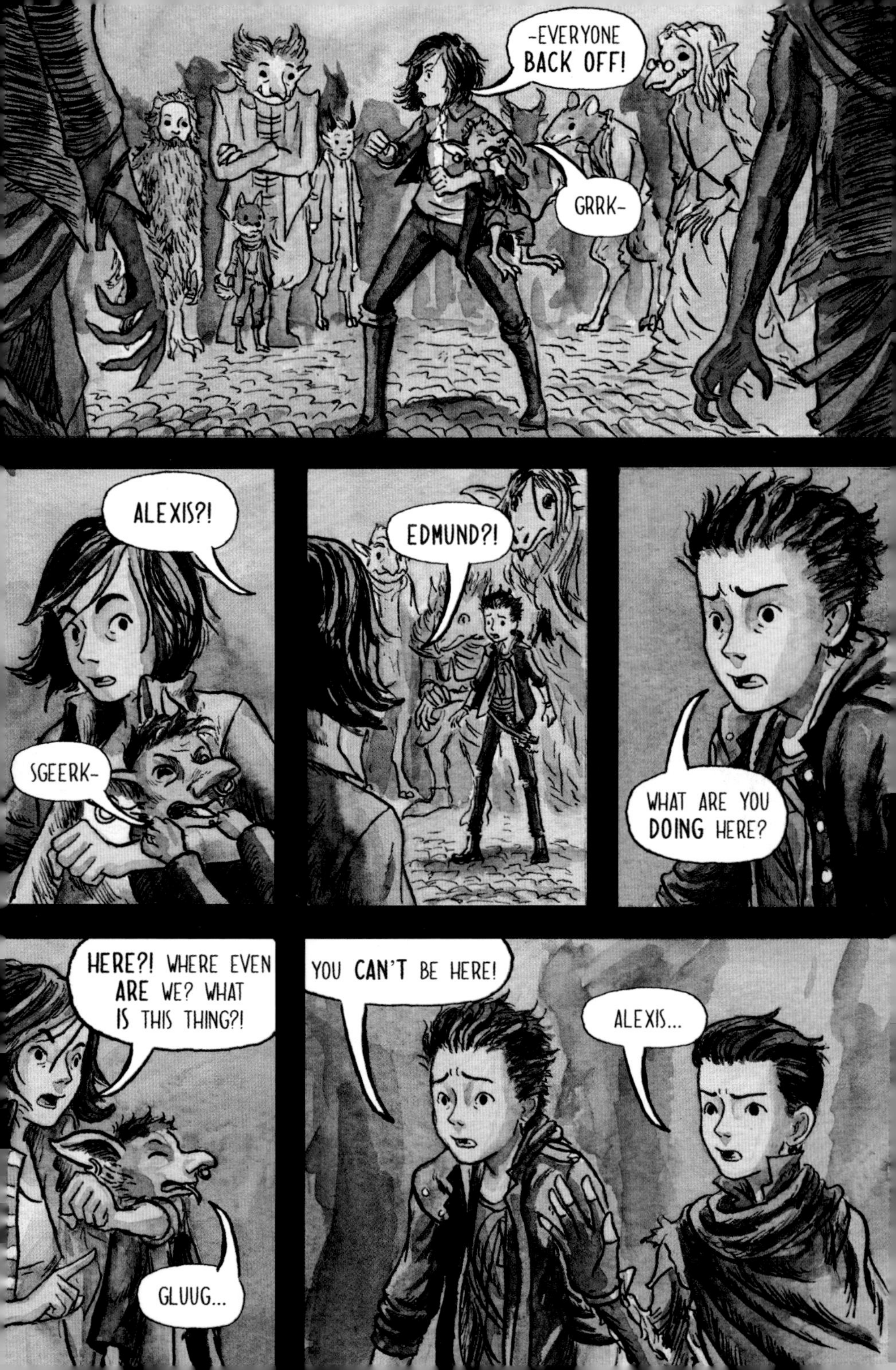
-EVERYONE BACK OFF!
GRRK-
ALEXIS?!
SGEERK-
EDMUND?!
WHAT ARE YOU DOING HERE?
HERE?! WHERE EVEN ARE WE? WHAT IS THIS THING?!
GLUUG...
YOU CAN'T BE HERE!
ALEXIS...

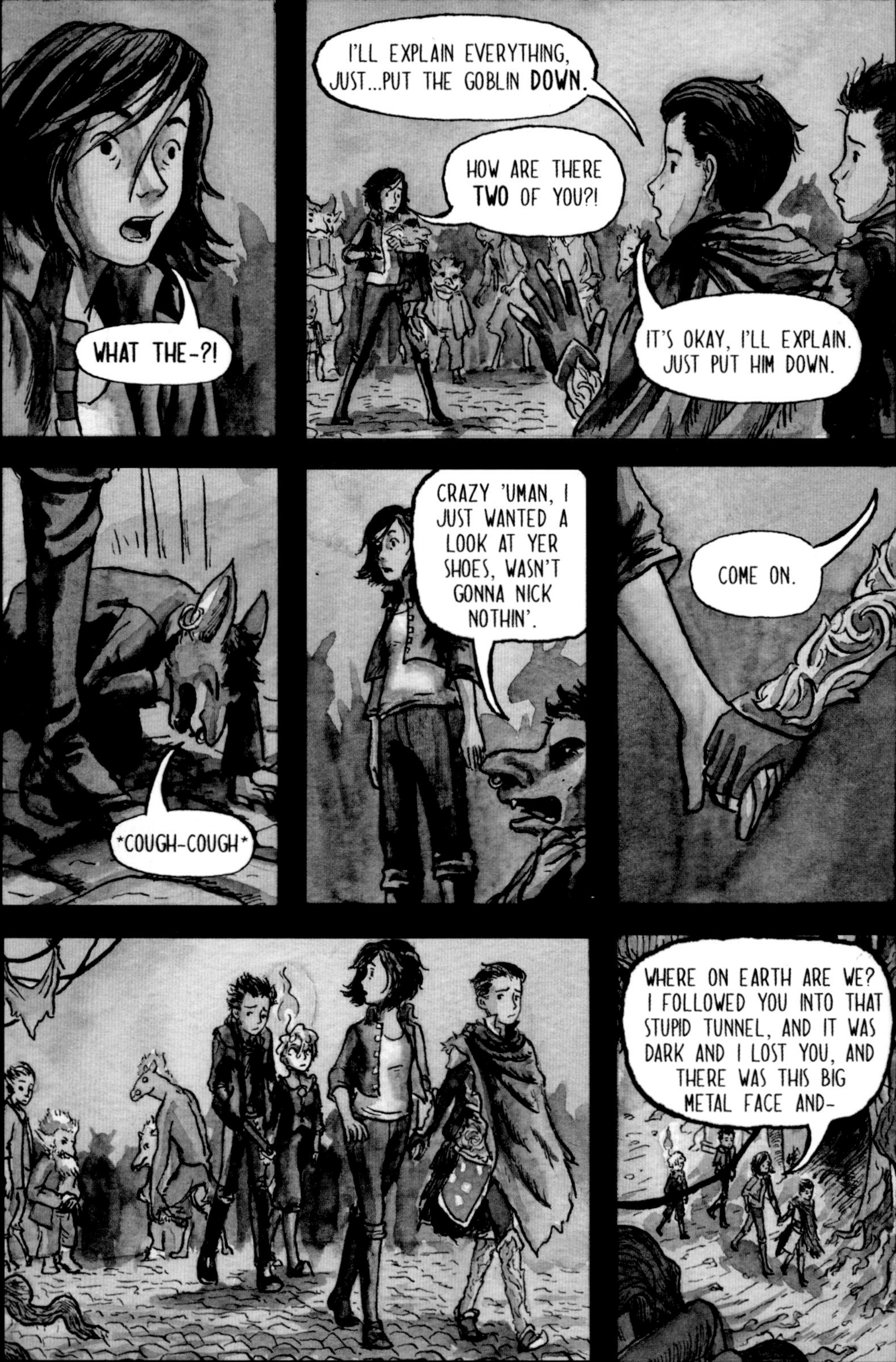
WHAT THE-?!
I'LL EXPLAIN EVERYTHING, JUST...PUT THE GOBLIN **DOWN**.
HOW ARE THERE **TWO** OF YOU?!
IT'S OKAY, I'LL EXPLAIN. JUST PUT HIM DOWN.
COUGH-COUGH
CRAZY 'UMAN, I JUST WANTED A LOOK AT YER SHOES, WASN'T GONNA NICK NOTHIN'.
COME ON.
WHERE ON EARTH ARE WE? I FOLLOWED YOU INTO THAT STUPID TUNNEL, AND IT WAS DARK AND I LOST YOU, AND THERE WAS THIS BIG METAL FACE AND-

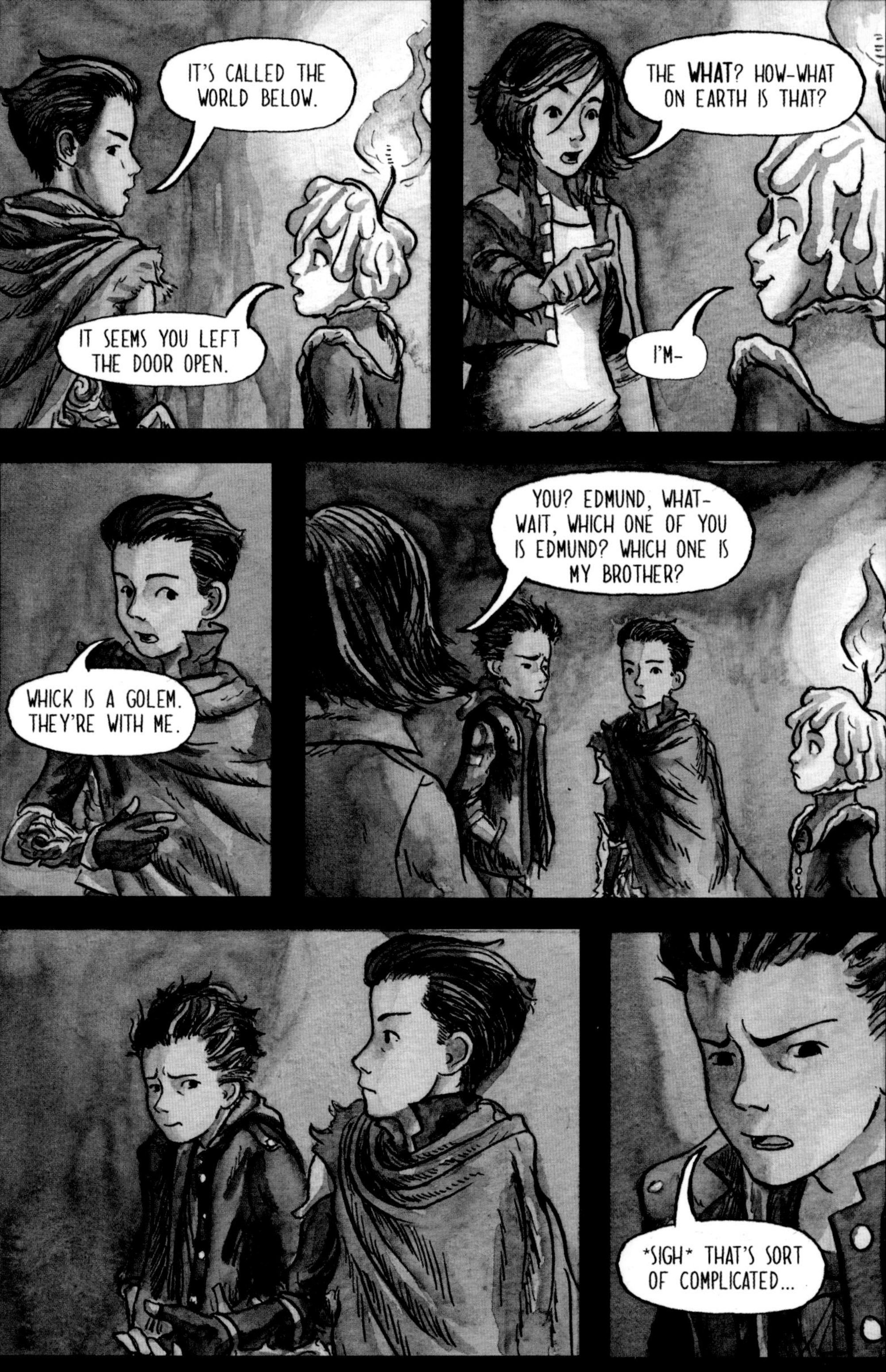
IT'S CALLED THE WORLD BELOW.
IT SEEMS YOU LEFT THE DOOR OPEN.
THE **WHAT**? HOW-WHAT ON EARTH IS THAT?
I'M-
WHICK IS A GOLEM. THEY'RE WITH ME.
YOU? EDMUND, WHAT- WAIT, WHICH ONE OF YOU IS EDMUND? WHICH ONE IS MY BROTHER?
SIGH THAT'S SORT OF COMPLICATED...

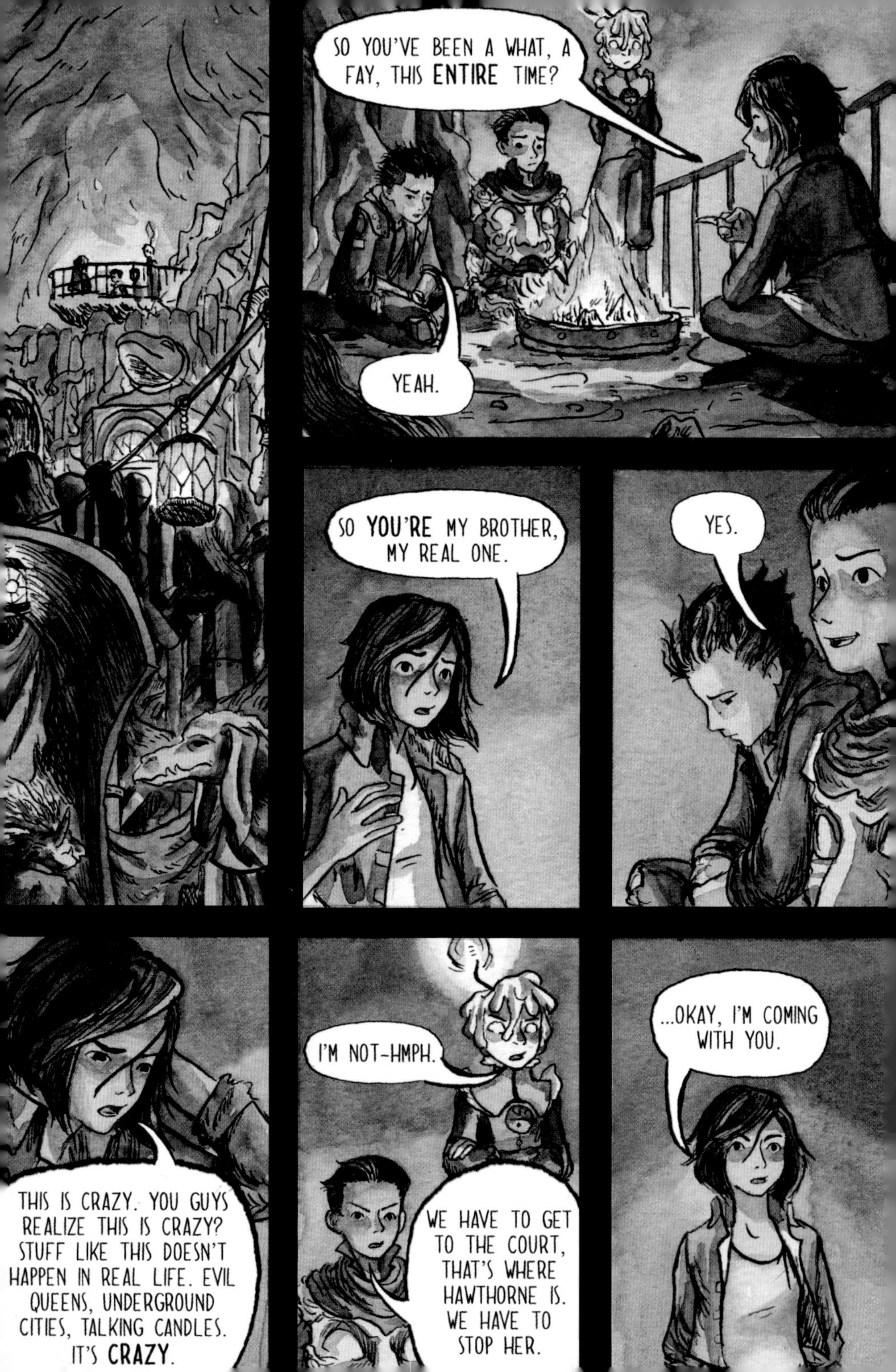
SO YOU'VE BEEN A WHAT, A FAY, THIS **ENTIRE** TIME?
YEAH.
SO **YOU'RE** MY BROTHER, MY REAL ONE.
YES.
THIS IS CRAZY. YOU GUYS REALIZE THIS IS CRAZY? STUFF LIKE THIS DOESN'T HAPPEN IN REAL LIFE. EVIL QUEENS, UNDERGROUND CITIES, TALKING CANDLES. IT'S **CRAZY**.
I'M NOT—HMPH.
WE HAVE TO GET TO THE COURT, THAT'S WHERE HAWTHORNE IS. WE HAVE TO STOP HER.
...OKAY, I'M COMING WITH YOU.

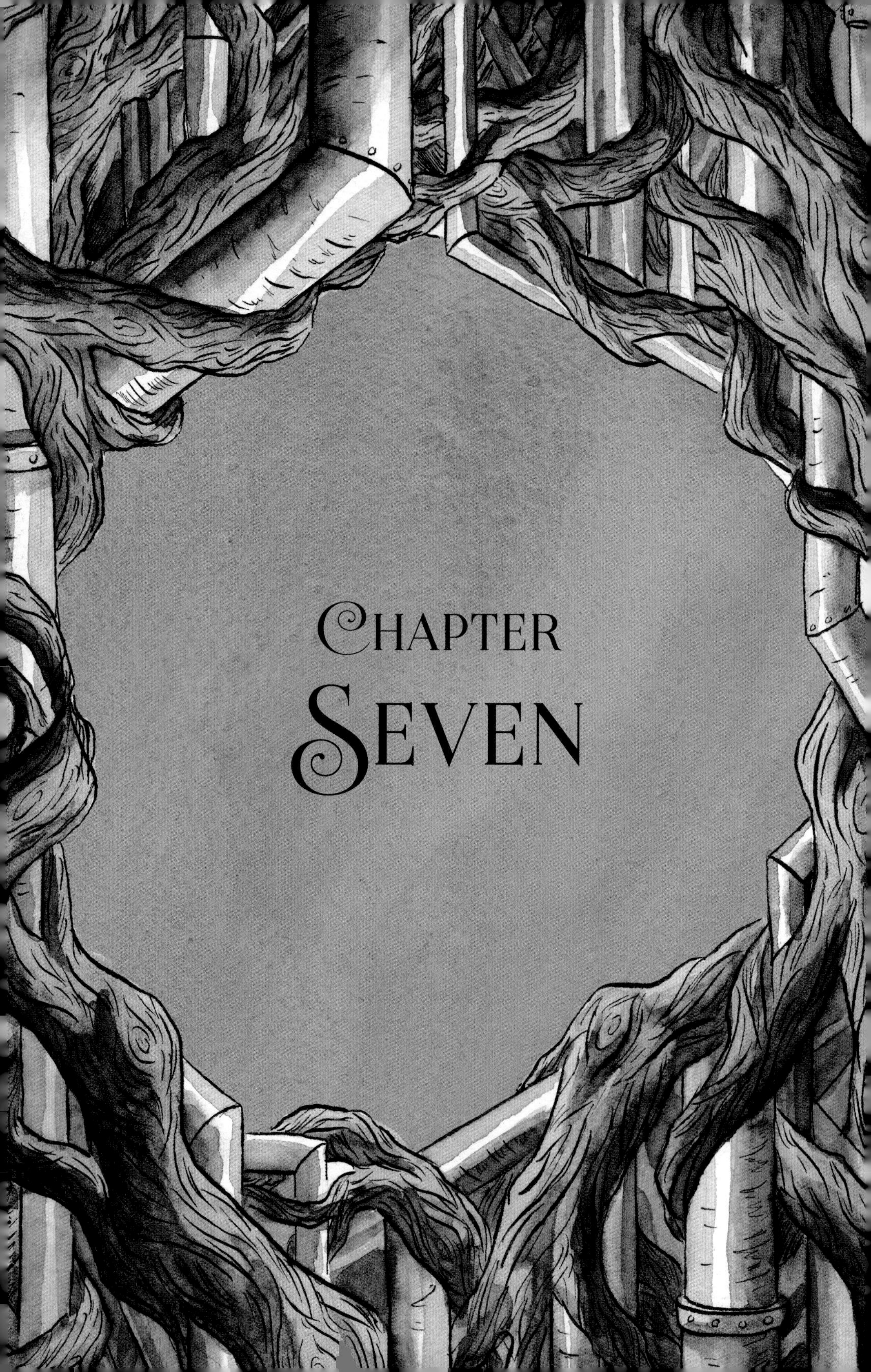

Chapter Seven

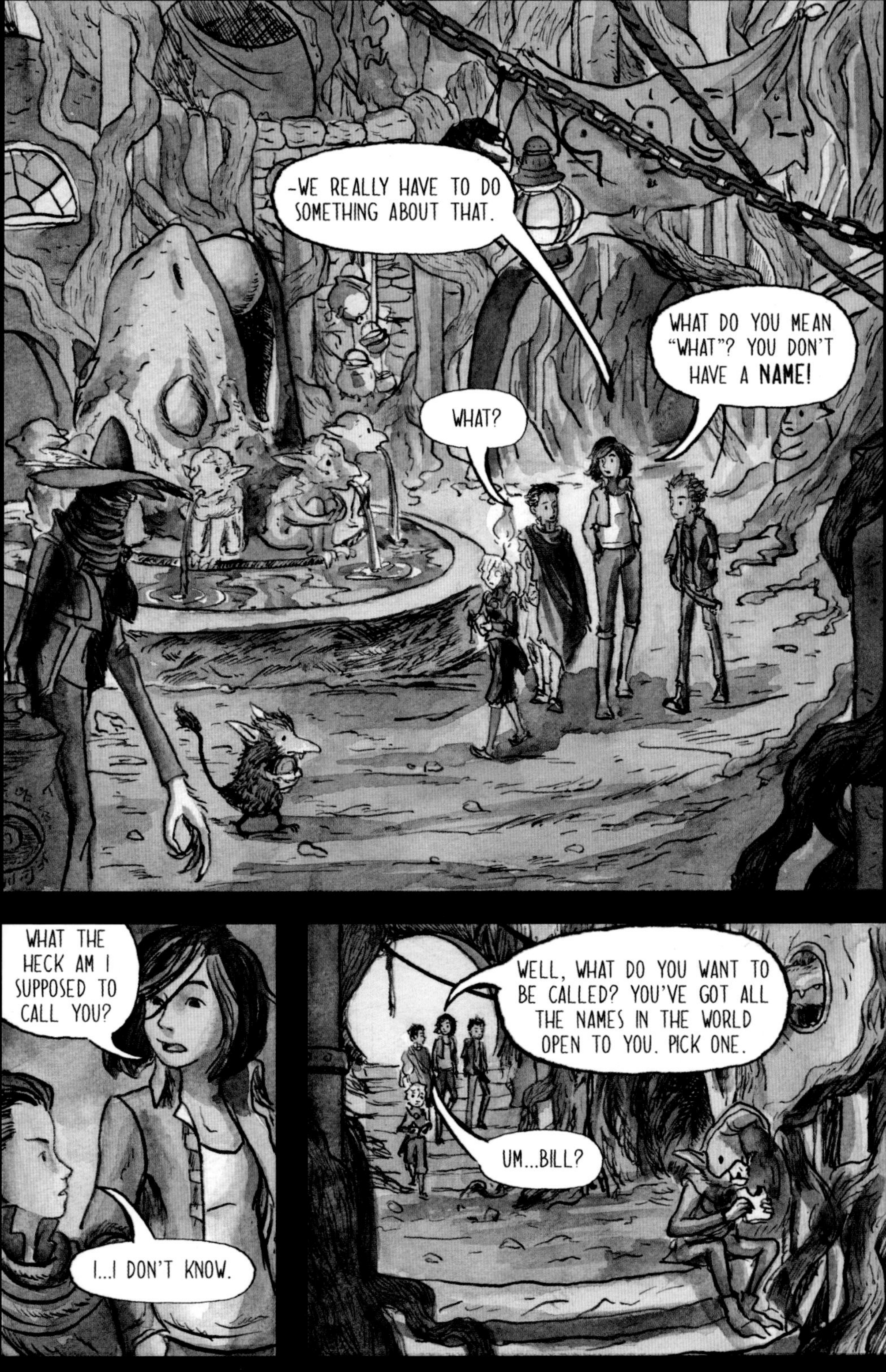
-WE REALLY HAVE TO DO SOMETHING ABOUT THAT.
WHAT?
WHAT DO YOU MEAN "WHAT"? YOU DON'T HAVE A **NAME!**
WHAT THE HECK AM I SUPPOSED TO CALL YOU?
I...I DON'T KNOW.
WELL, WHAT DO YOU WANT TO BE CALLED? YOU'VE GOT ALL THE NAMES IN THE WORLD OPEN TO YOU. PICK ONE.
UM...BILL?

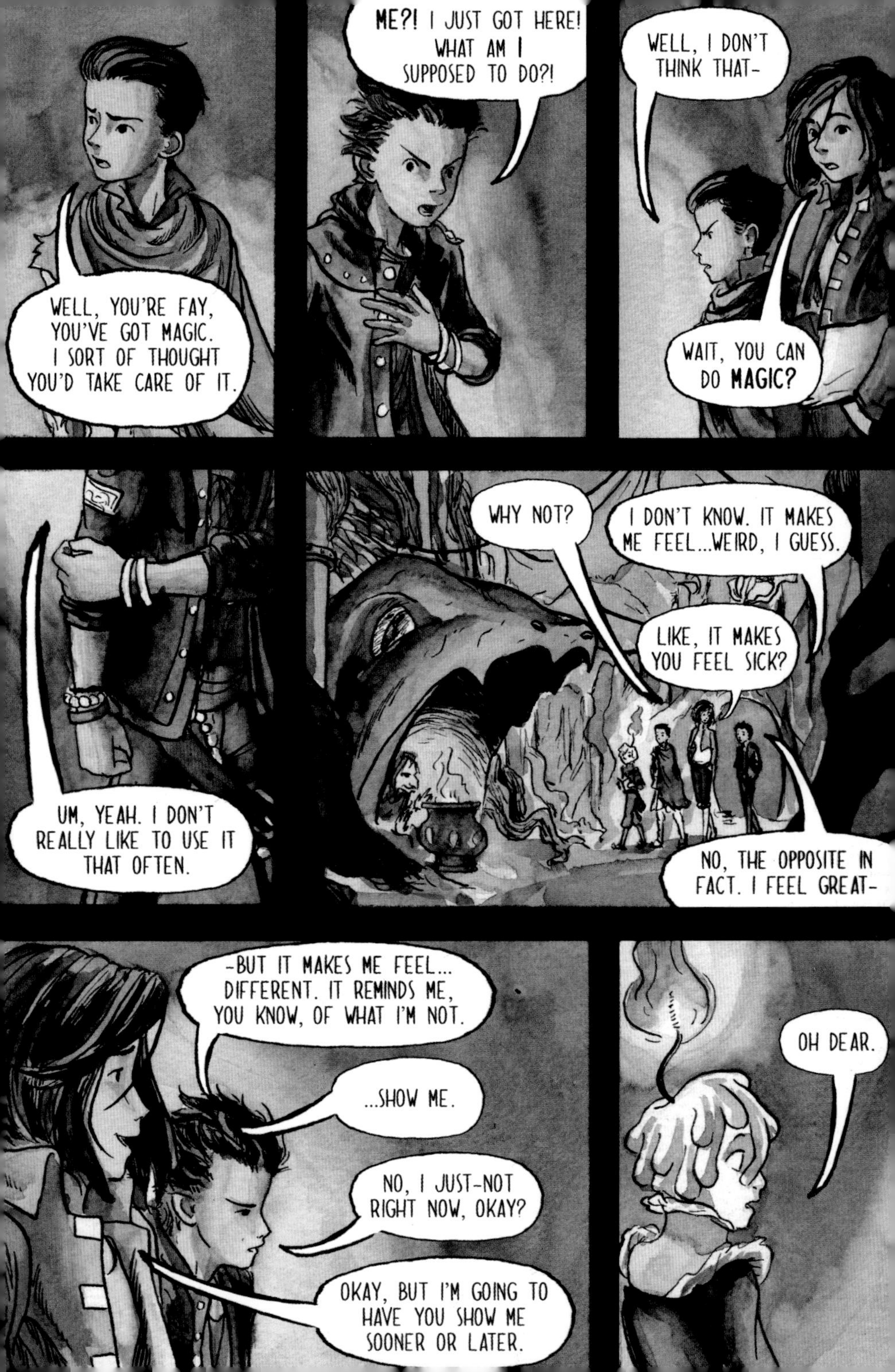
WELL, YOU'RE FAY, YOU'VE GOT MAGIC. I SORT OF THOUGHT YOU'D TAKE CARE OF IT.
ME?! I JUST GOT HERE! WHAT AM I SUPPOSED TO DO?!
WELL, I DON'T THINK THAT-
WAIT, YOU CAN DO MAGIC?
UM, YEAH. I DON'T REALLY LIKE TO USE IT THAT OFTEN.
WHY NOT?
I DON'T KNOW. IT MAKES ME FEEL...WEIRD, I GUESS.
LIKE, IT MAKES YOU FEEL SICK?
NO, THE OPPOSITE IN FACT. I FEEL GREAT-
-BUT IT MAKES ME FEEL... DIFFERENT. IT REMINDS ME, YOU KNOW, OF WHAT I'M NOT.
...SHOW ME.
NO, I JUST-NOT RIGHT NOW, OKAY?
OKAY, BUT I'M GOING TO HAVE YOU SHOW ME SOONER OR LATER.
OH DEAR.

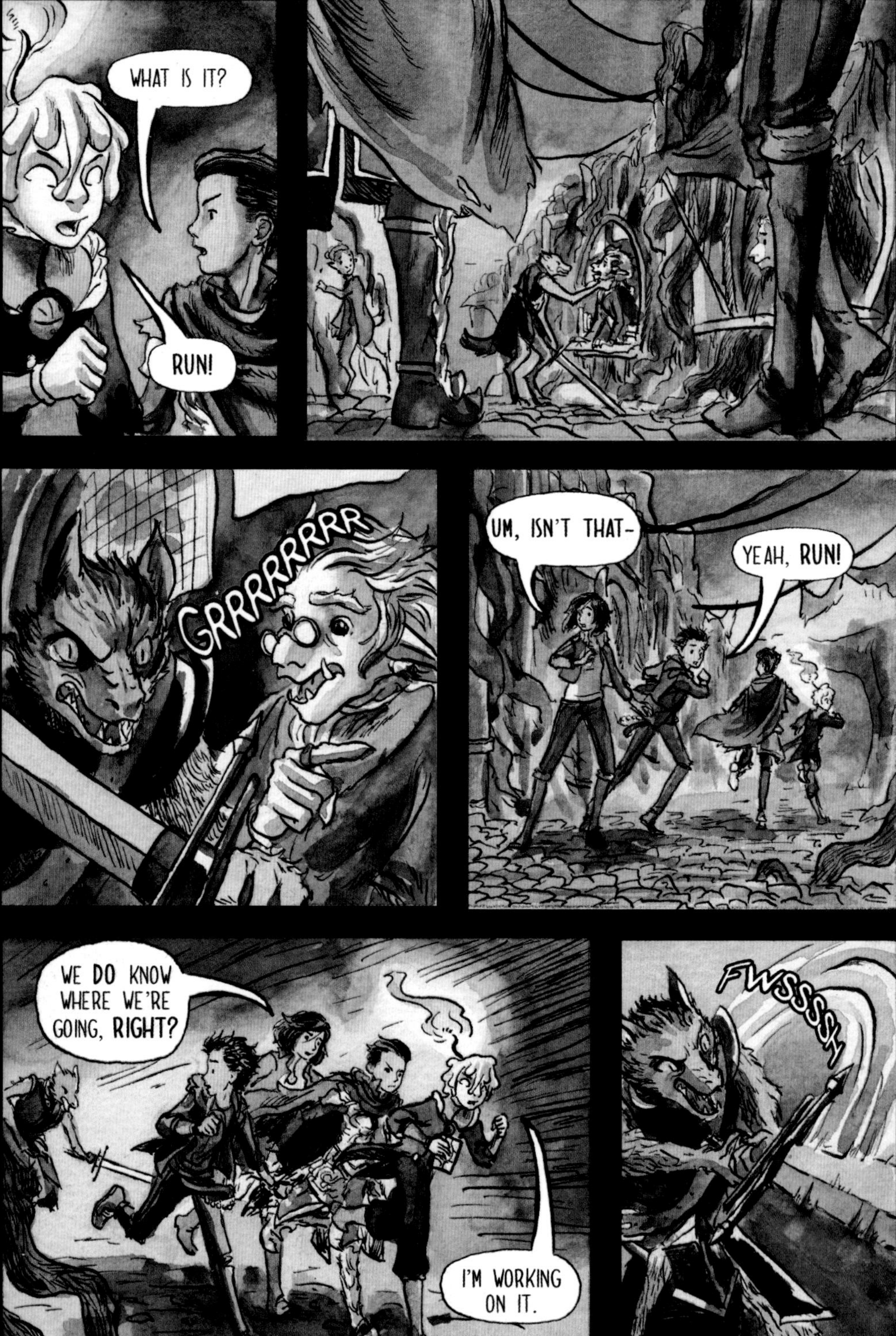
WHAT IS IT?
RUN!
GRRRRRRRR
UM, ISN'T THAT-
YEAH, RUN!
WE DO KNOW WHERE WE'RE GOING, RIGHT?
I'M WORKING ON IT.
FWSSSSH

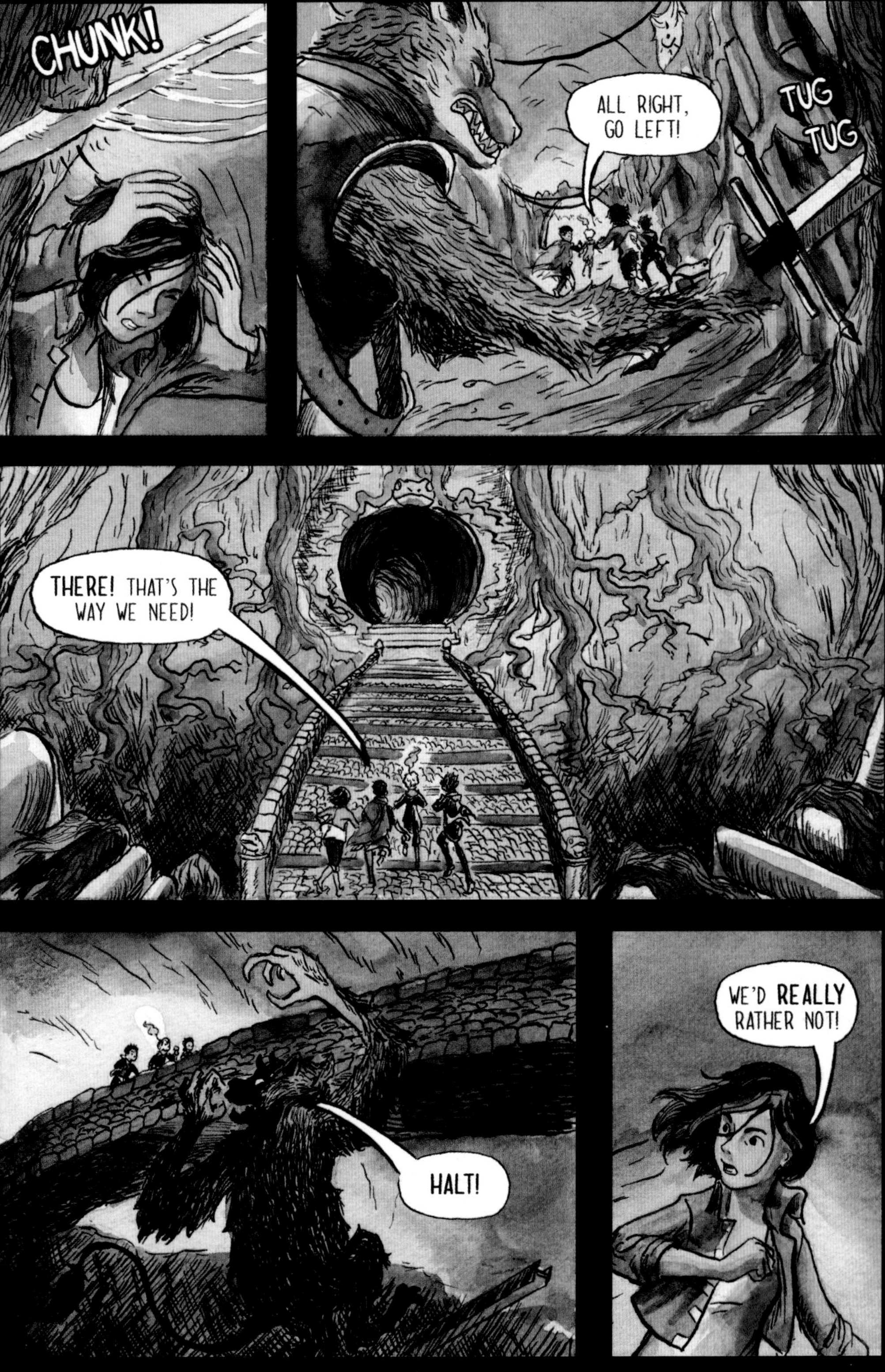
CHUNK!
ALL RIGHT, GO LEFT!
TUG
TUG
THERE! THAT'S THE WAY WE NEED!
HALT!
WE'D REALLY RATHER NOT!

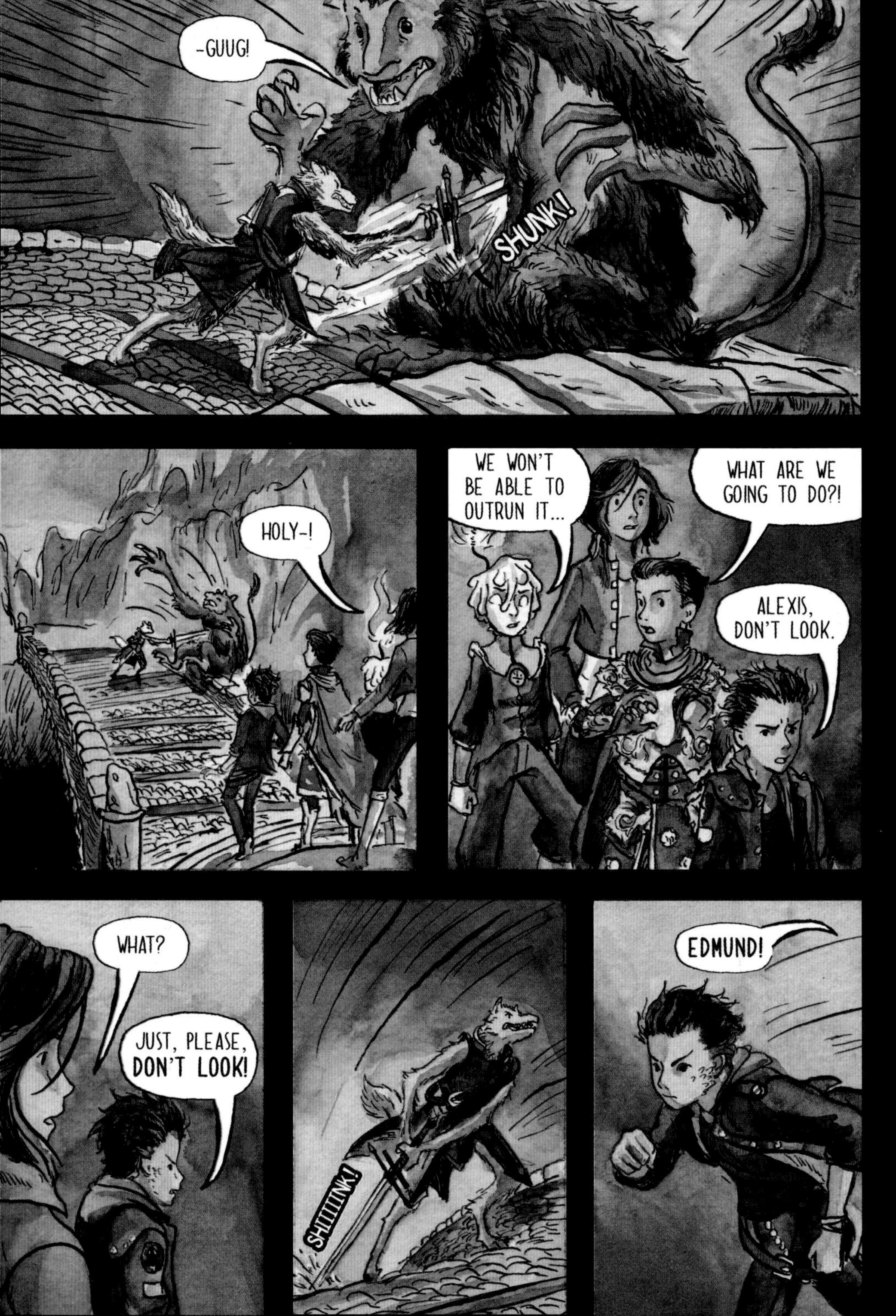

-GUUG!
SHUNK!
HOLY-!
WE WON'T BE ABLE TO OUTRUN IT...
WHAT ARE WE GOING TO DO?!
ALEXIS, DON'T LOOK.
WHAT?
JUST, PLEASE, DON'T LOOK!
SHIIIIINK!
EDMUND!

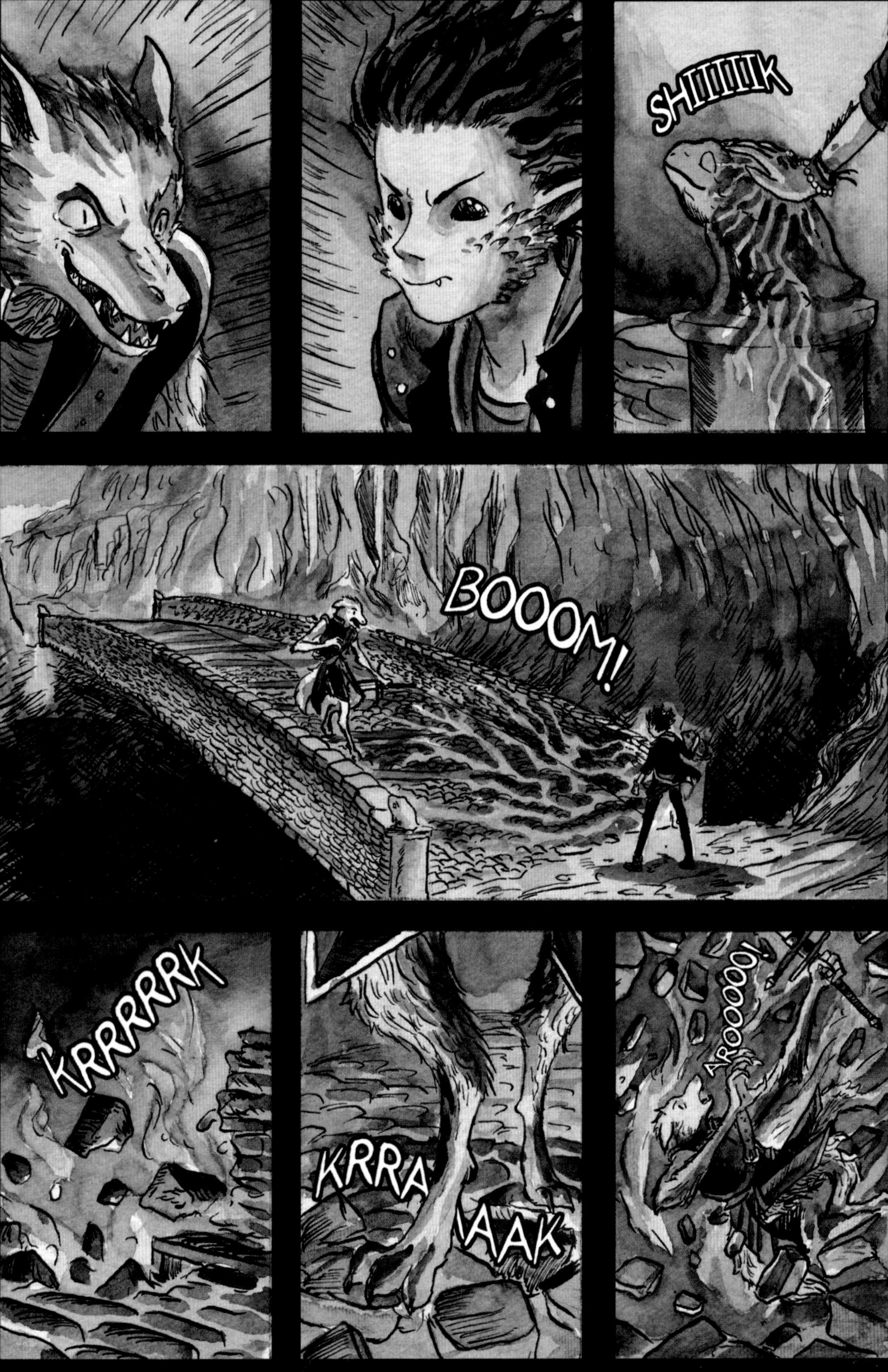
SHIIIIIK
BOOOM!
KRRRRRK
KRRA
AAK
AROOOOO!

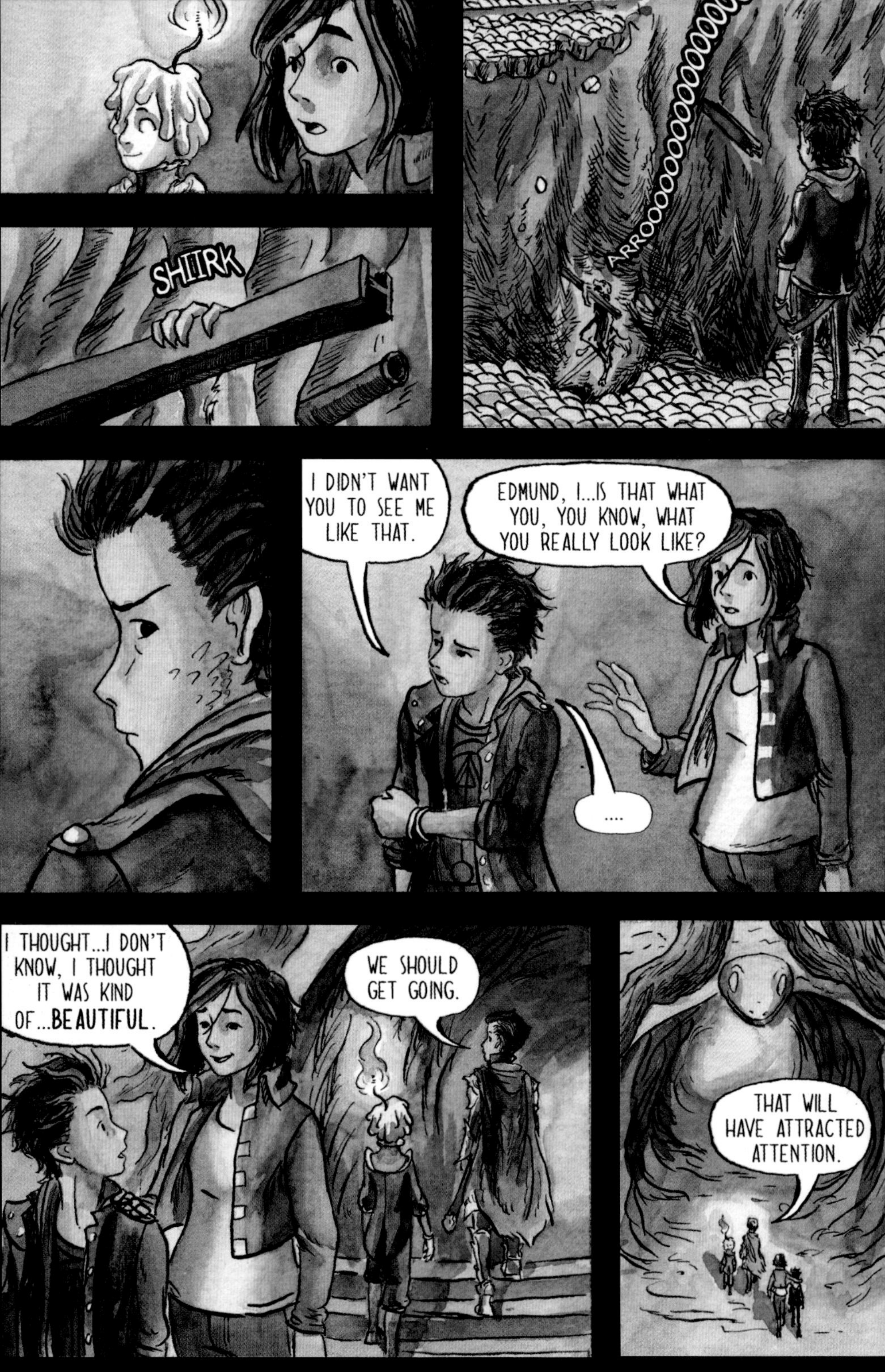
SHIIRK
ARROOOOOOOOOOOOOO
I DIDN'T WANT YOU TO SEE ME LIKE THAT.
EDMUND, I...IS THAT WHAT YOU, YOU KNOW, WHAT YOU REALLY LOOK LIKE?
....
I THOUGHT...I DON'T KNOW, I THOUGHT IT WAS KIND OF...**BEAUTIFUL**.
WE SHOULD GET GOING.
THAT WILL HAVE ATTRACTED ATTENTION.

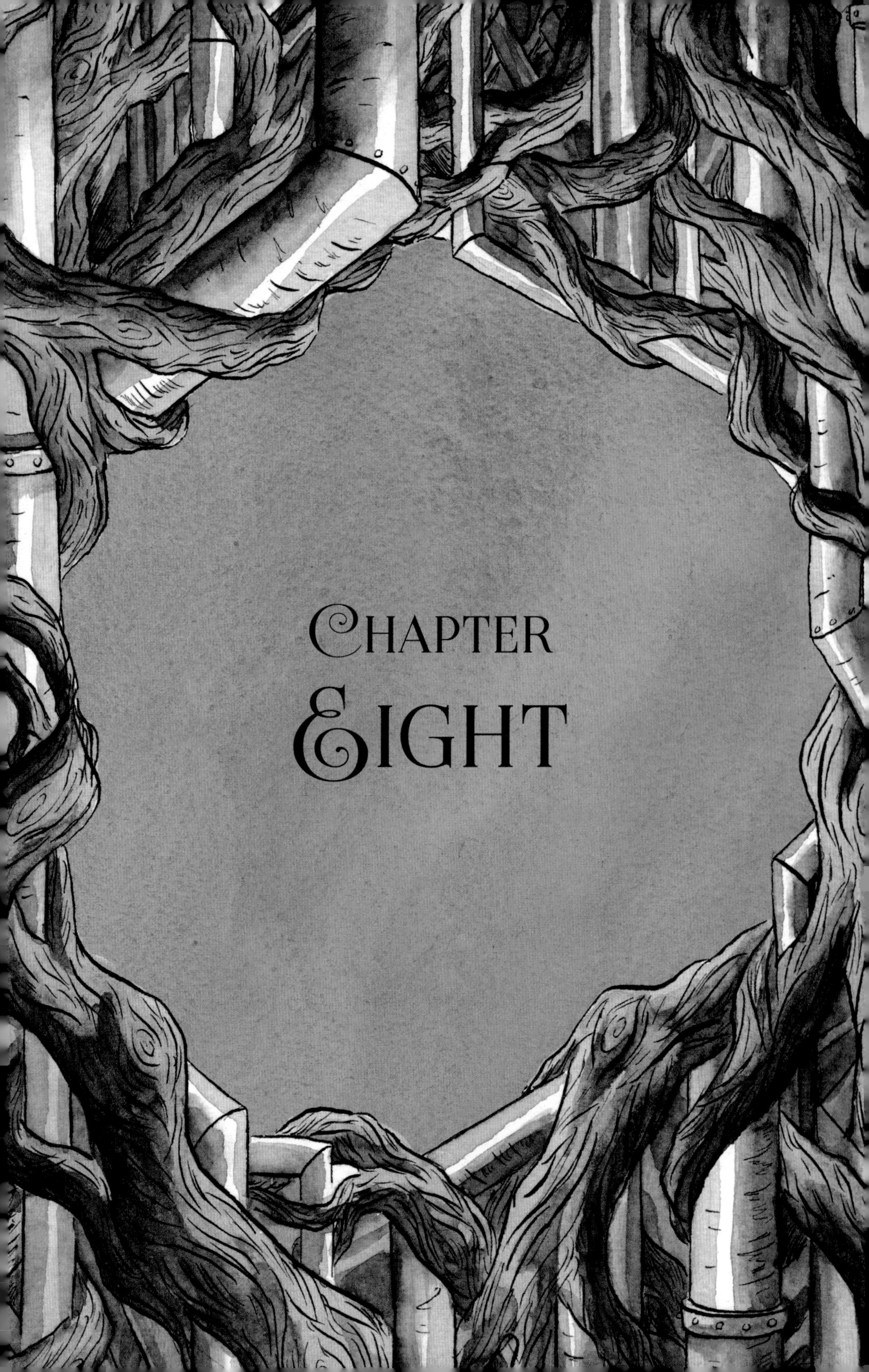

Chapter Eight

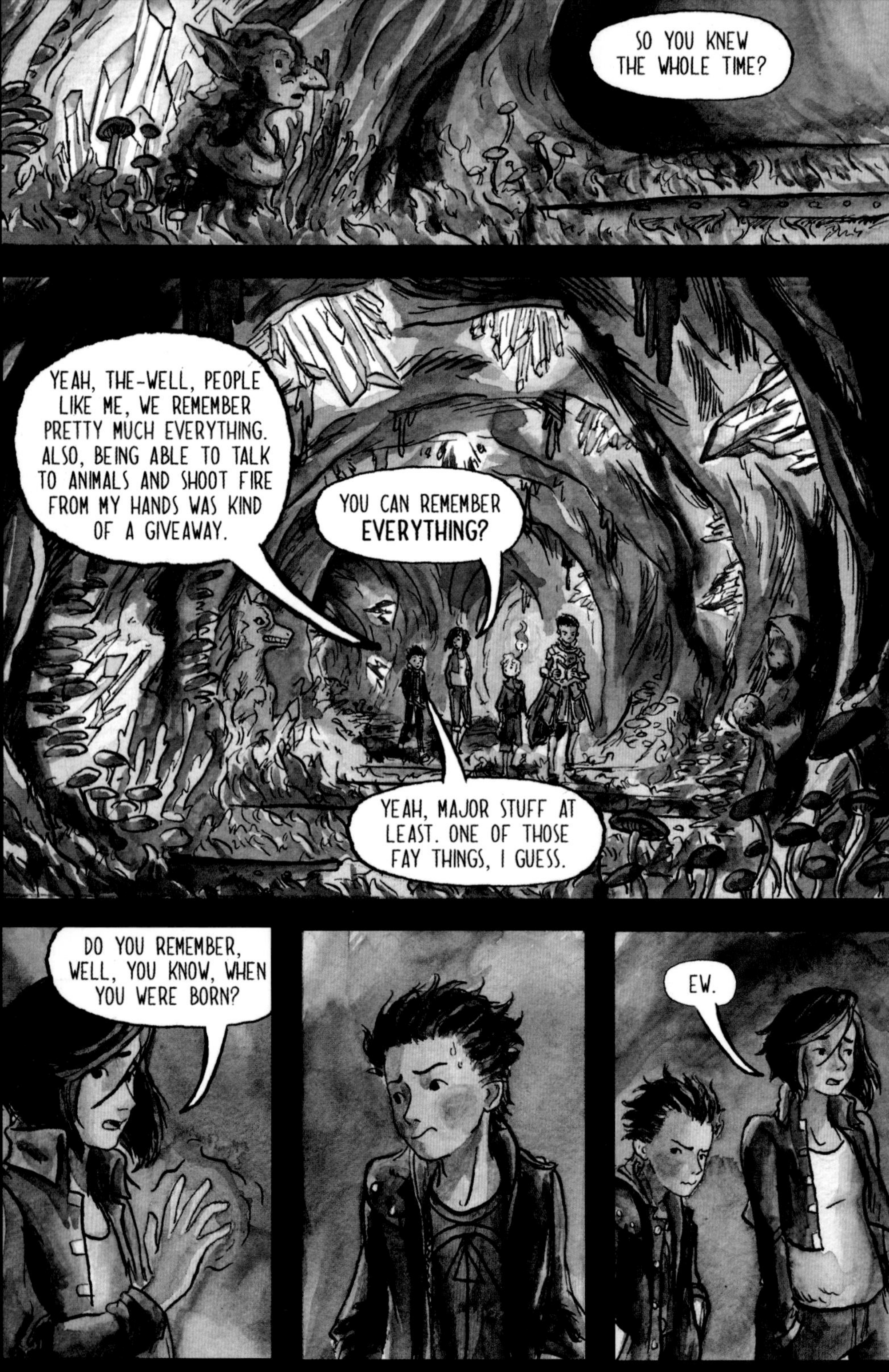
SO YOU KNEW THE WHOLE TIME?
YEAH, THE-WELL, PEOPLE LIKE ME, WE REMEMBER PRETTY MUCH EVERYTHING. ALSO, BEING ABLE TO TALK TO ANIMALS AND SHOOT FIRE FROM MY HANDS WAS KIND OF A GIVEAWAY.
YOU CAN REMEMBER **EVERYTHING?**
YEAH, MAJOR STUFF AT LEAST. ONE OF THOSE FAY THINGS, I GUESS.
DO YOU REMEMBER, WELL, YOU KNOW, WHEN YOU WERE BORN?
EW.

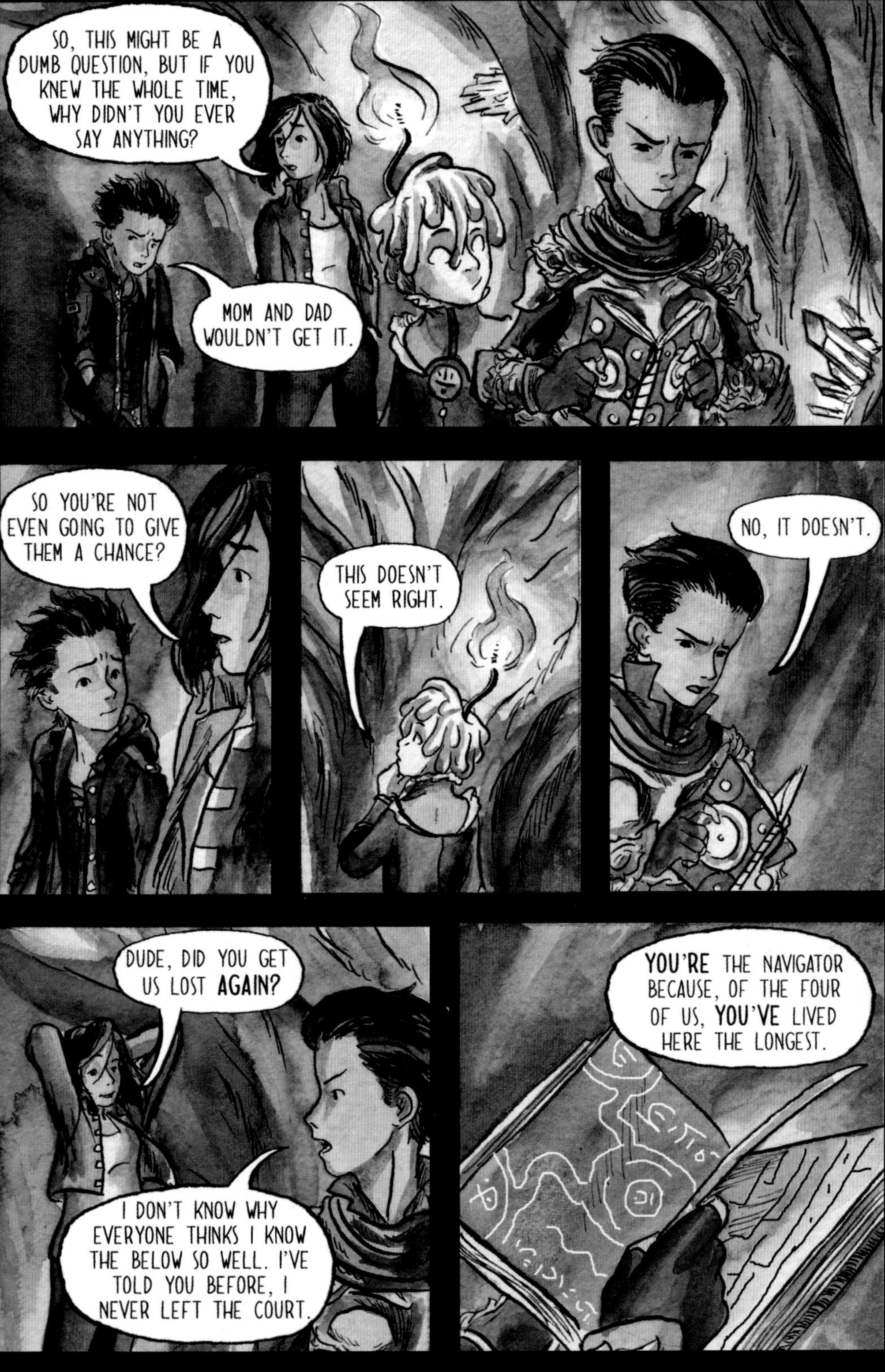
SO, THIS MIGHT BE A DUMB QUESTION, BUT IF YOU KNEW THE WHOLE TIME, WHY DIDN'T YOU EVER SAY ANYTHING?
MOM AND DAD WOULDN'T GET IT.
SO YOU'RE NOT EVEN GOING TO GIVE THEM A CHANCE?
THIS DOESN'T SEEM RIGHT.
NO, IT DOESN'T.
DUDE, DID YOU GET US LOST **AGAIN?**
I DON'T KNOW WHY EVERYONE THINKS I KNOW THE BELOW SO WELL. I'VE TOLD YOU BEFORE, I NEVER LEFT THE COURT.
YOU'RE THE NAVIGATOR BECAUSE, OF THE FOUR OF US, **YOU'VE** LIVED HERE THE LONGEST.

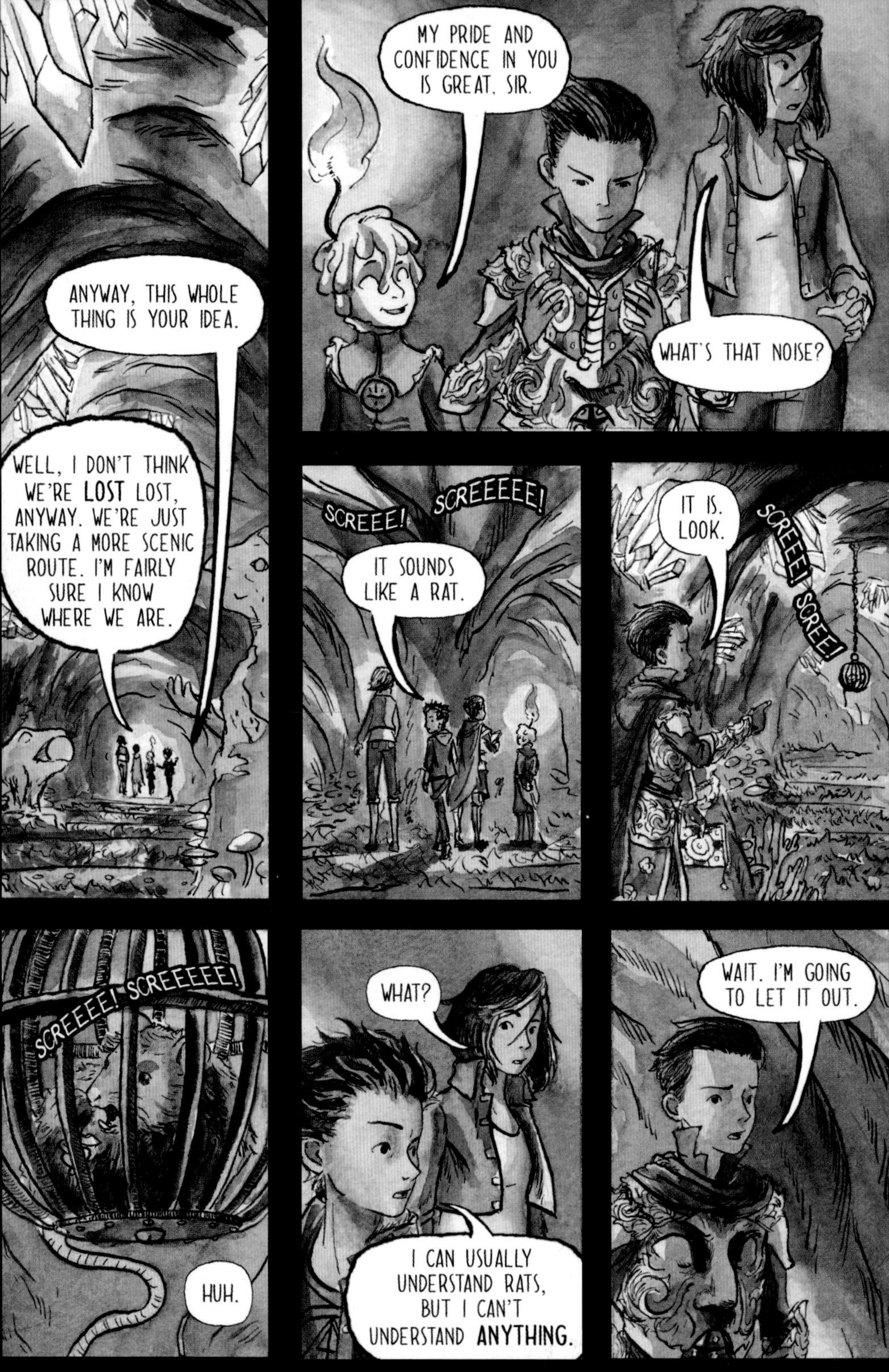

ANYWAY, THIS WHOLE THING IS YOUR IDEA.
WELL, I DON'T THINK WE'RE **LOST** LOST, ANYWAY. WE'RE JUST TAKING A MORE SCENIC ROUTE. I'M FAIRLY SURE I KNOW WHERE WE ARE.
MY PRIDE AND CONFIDENCE IN YOU IS GREAT, SIR.
WHAT'S THAT NOISE?
SCREEE!
SCREEEEEE!
IT SOUNDS LIKE A RAT.
IT IS. LOOK.
SCREEEE!
SCREE!
SCREEEE! SCREEEEEE!
HUH.
WHAT?
I CAN USUALLY UNDERSTAND RATS, BUT I CAN'T UNDERSTAND **ANYTHING**.
WAIT. I'M GOING TO LET IT OUT.

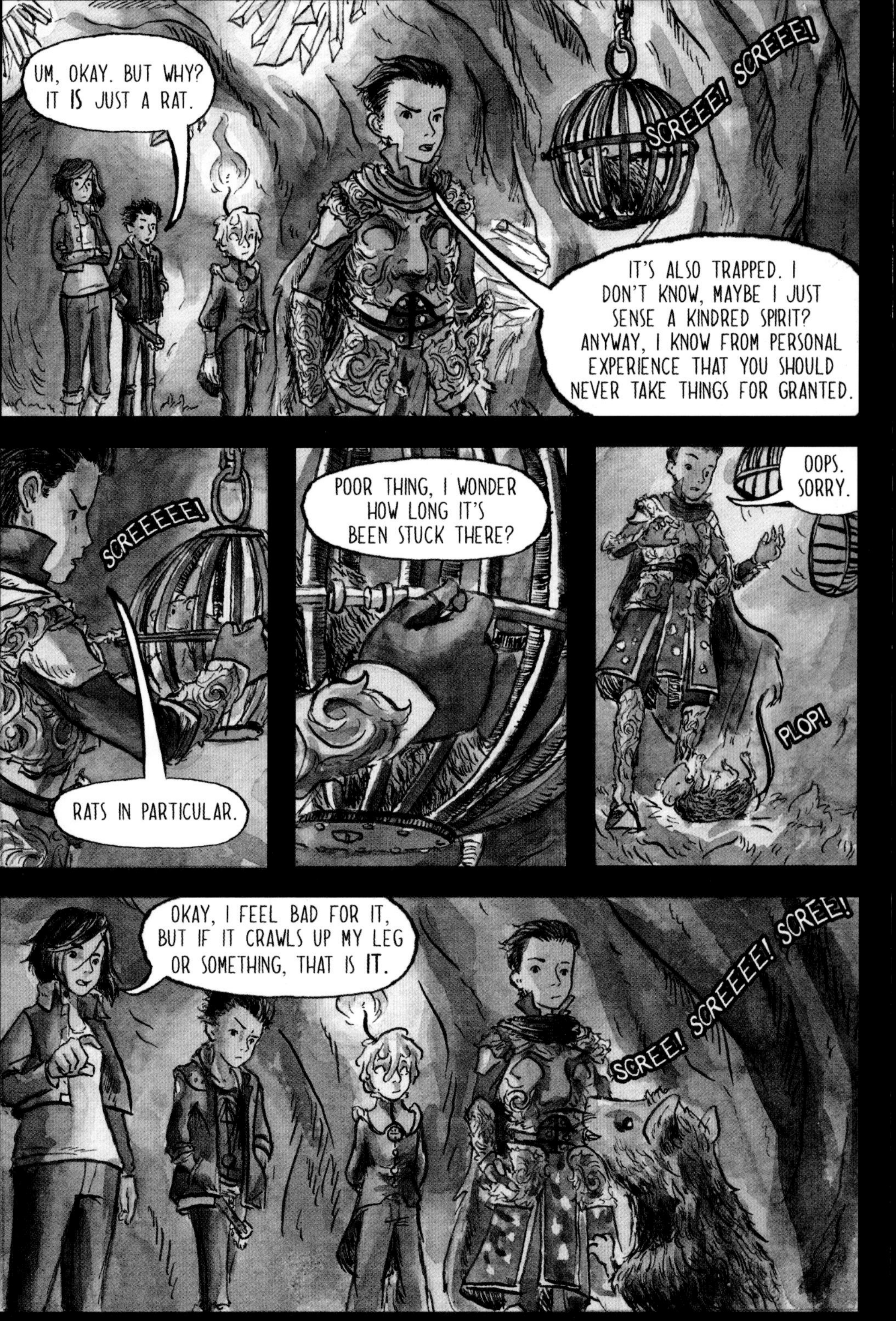
UM, OKAY. BUT WHY? IT IS JUST A RAT.
SCREEE! SCREEE! SCREEE!
IT'S ALSO TRAPPED. I DON'T KNOW, MAYBE I JUST SENSE A KINDRED SPIRIT? ANYWAY, I KNOW FROM PERSONAL EXPERIENCE THAT YOU SHOULD NEVER TAKE THINGS FOR GRANTED.
SCREEEEEE!
RATS IN PARTICULAR.
POOR THING, I WONDER HOW LONG IT'S BEEN STUCK THERE?
OOPS. SORRY.
PLOP!
OKAY, I FEEL BAD FOR IT, BUT IF IT CRAWLS UP MY LEG OR SOMETHING, THAT IS IT.
SCREE! SCREEEE! SCREE!

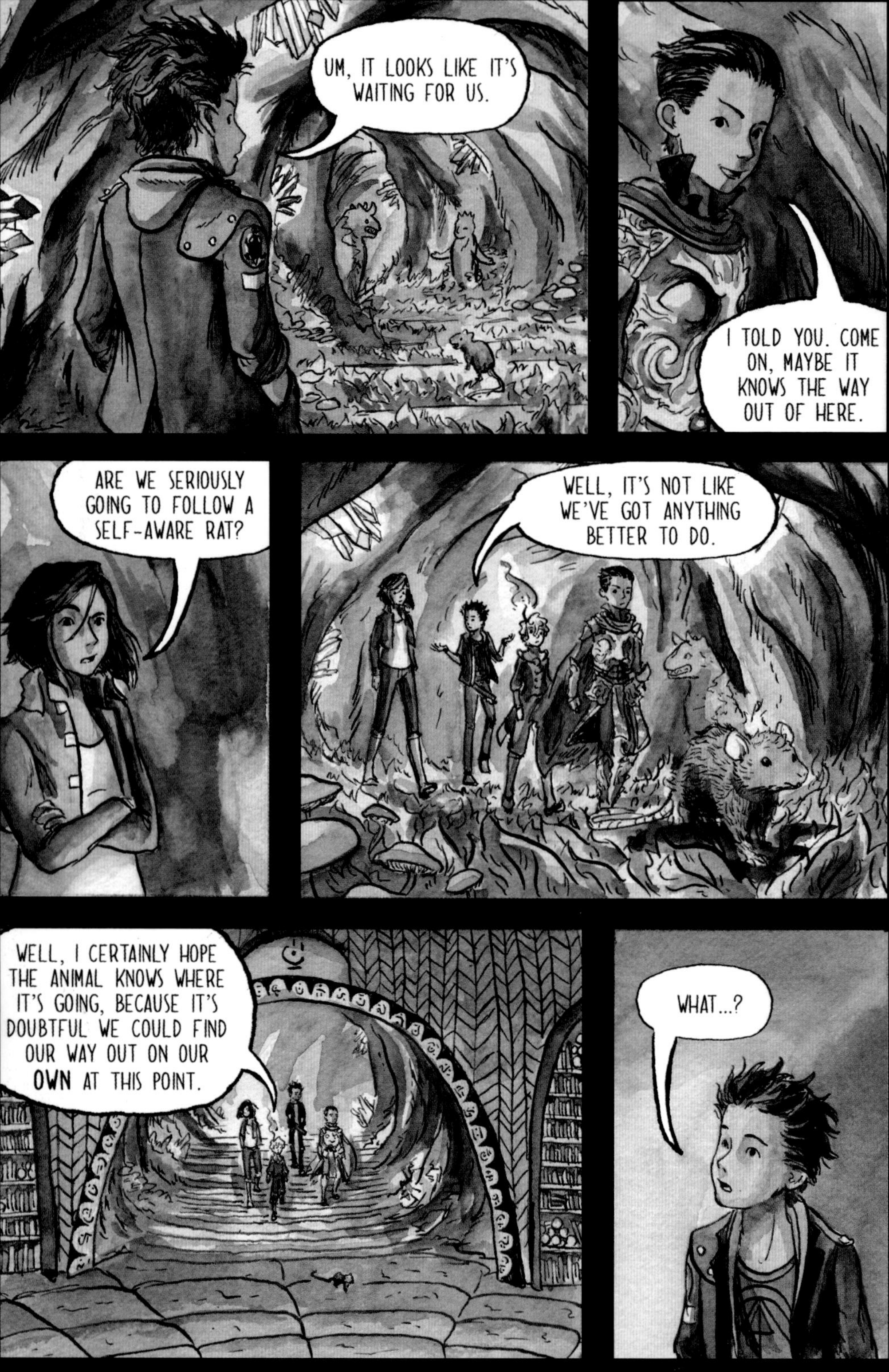
UM, IT LOOKS LIKE IT'S WAITING FOR US.
I TOLD YOU. COME ON, MAYBE IT KNOWS THE WAY OUT OF HERE.
ARE WE SERIOUSLY GOING TO FOLLOW A SELF-AWARE RAT?
WELL, IT'S NOT LIKE WE'VE GOT ANYTHING BETTER TO DO.
WELL, I CERTAINLY HOPE THE ANIMAL KNOWS WHERE IT'S GOING, BECAUSE IT'S DOUBTFUL WE COULD FIND OUR WAY OUT ON OUR **OWN** AT THIS POINT.
WHAT...?

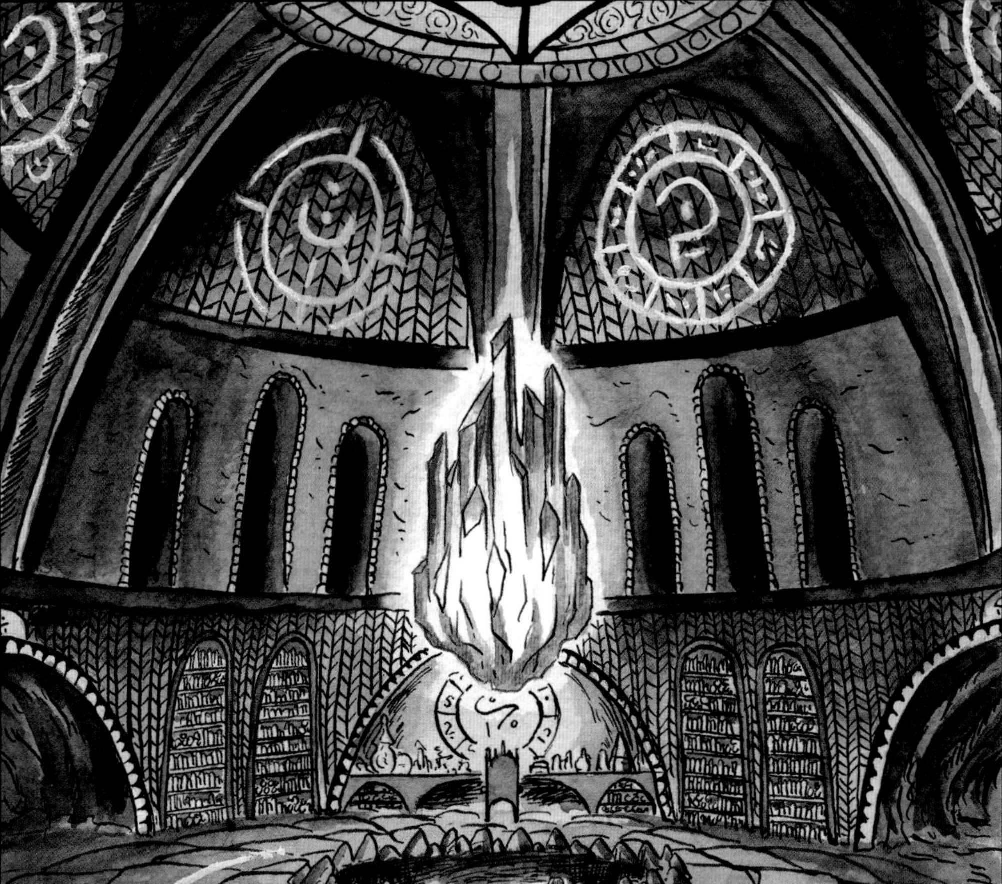

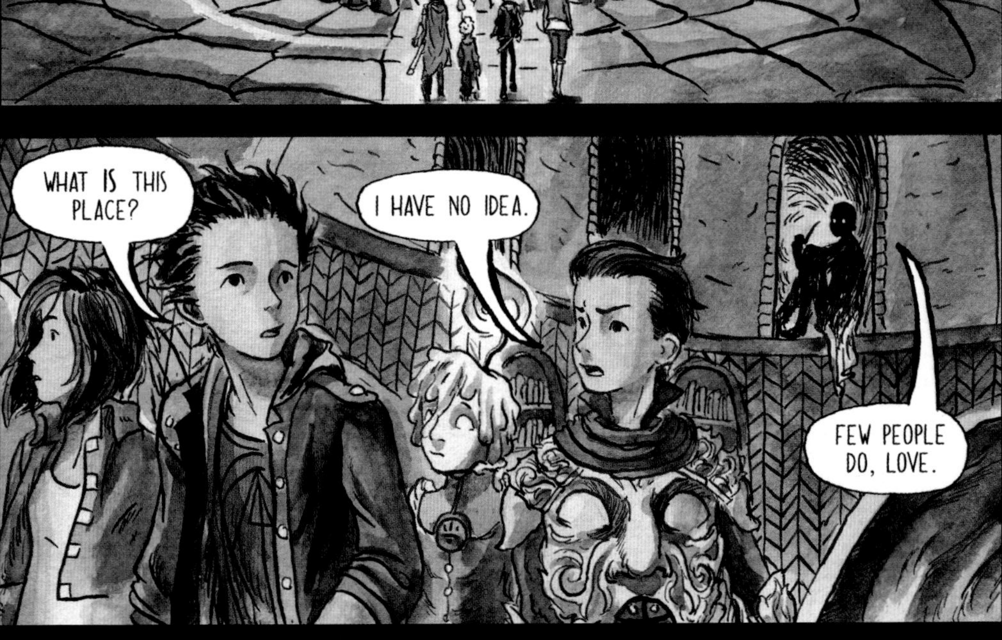
WHAT IS THIS PLACE?
I HAVE NO IDEA.
FEW PEOPLE DO, LOVE.

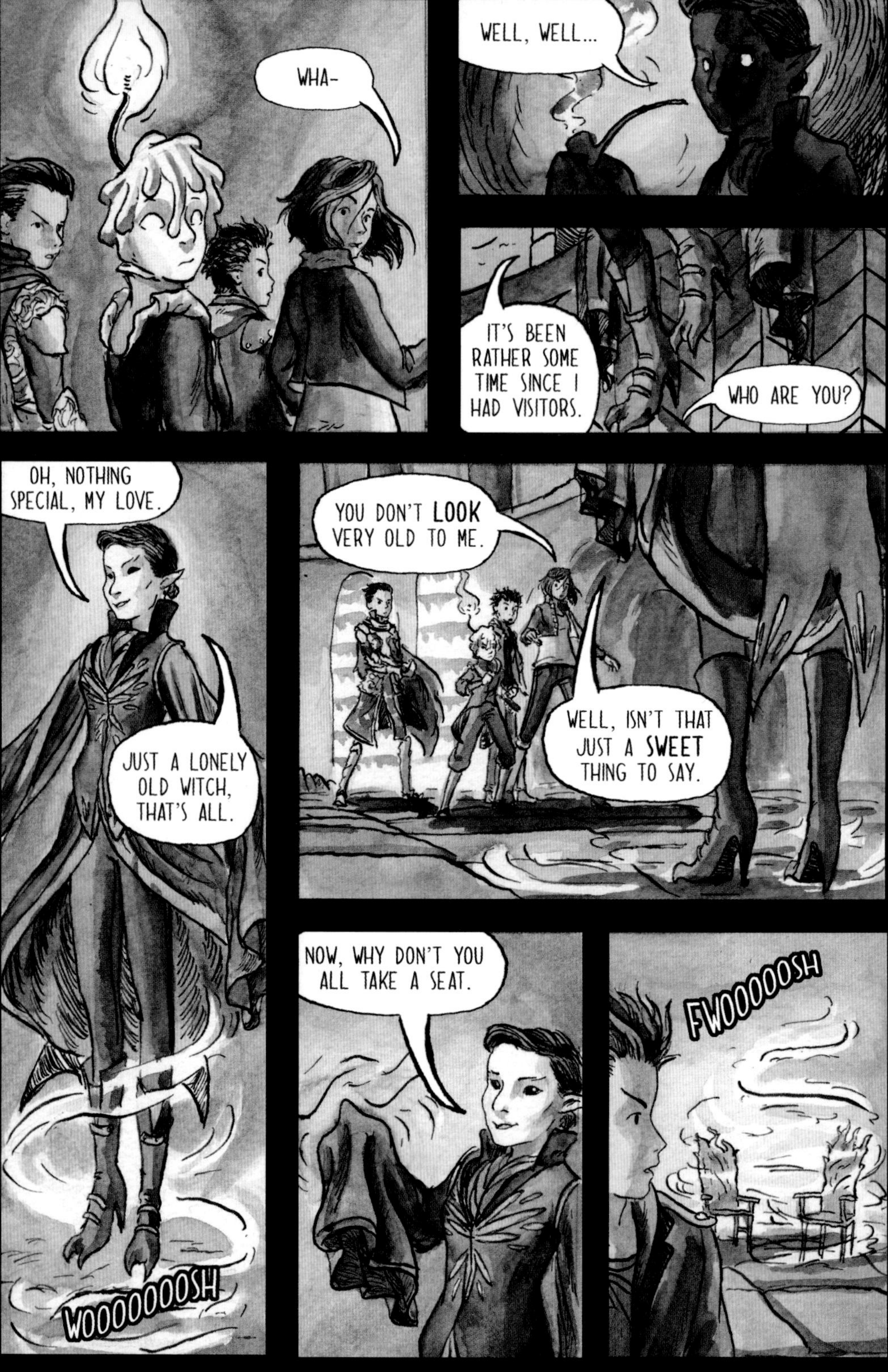
WHA-
WELL, WELL...
IT'S BEEN RATHER SOME TIME SINCE I HAD VISITORS.
WHO ARE YOU?
OH, NOTHING SPECIAL, MY LOVE.
JUST A LONELY OLD WITCH, THAT'S ALL.
WOOOOOOOSH
YOU DON'T **LOOK** VERY OLD TO ME.
WELL, ISN'T THAT JUST A **SWEET** THING TO SAY.
NOW, WHY DON'T YOU ALL TAKE A SEAT.
FWOOOOOSH

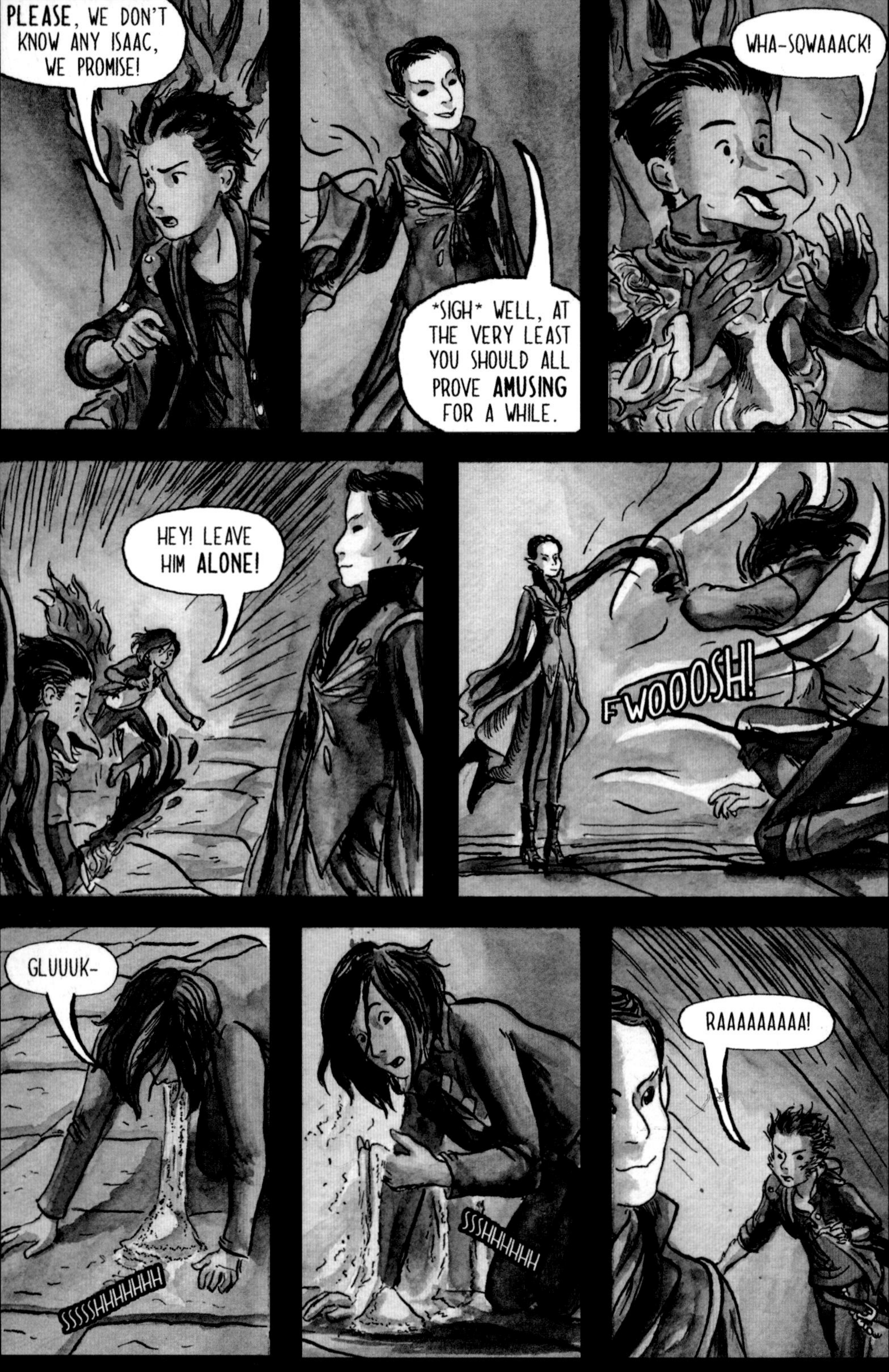
PLEASE, WE DON'T KNOW ANY ISAAC, WE PROMISE!
SIGH WELL, AT THE VERY LEAST YOU SHOULD ALL PROVE AMUSING FOR A WHILE.
WHA-SQWAAACK!
HEY! LEAVE HIM ALONE!
FWOOOSH!
GLUUUK-
SSSSSHHHHHHH
SSSHHHHHH
RAAAAAAAAA!

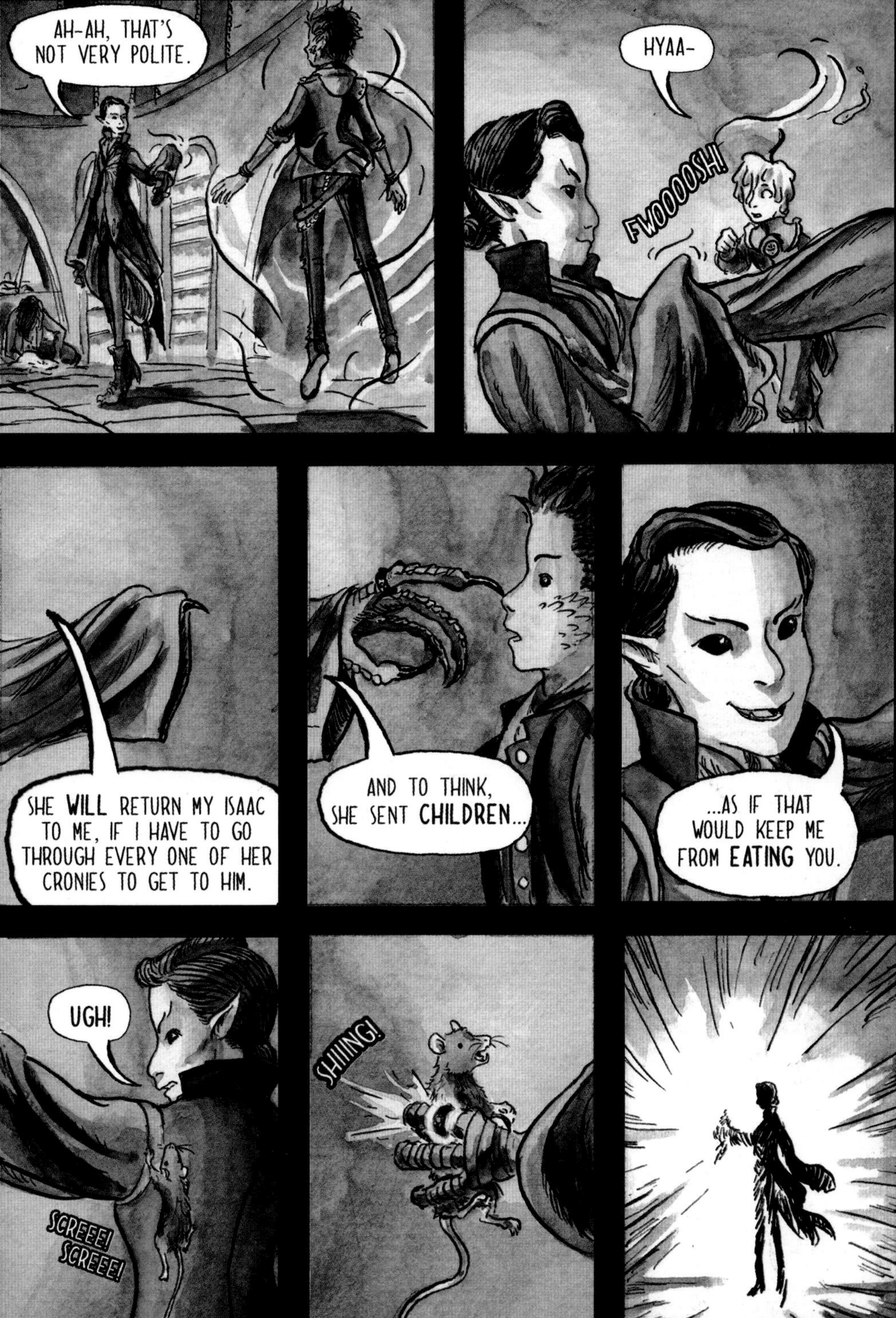
AH-AH, THAT'S NOT VERY POLITE.
HYAA-
FWOOOOSH!
SHE WILL RETURN MY ISAAC TO ME, IF I HAVE TO GO THROUGH EVERY ONE OF HER CRONIES TO GET TO HIM.
AND TO THINK, SHE SENT CHILDREN...
...AS IF THAT WOULD KEEP ME FROM EATING YOU.
UGH!
SCREEE! SCREEE!
SHIING!

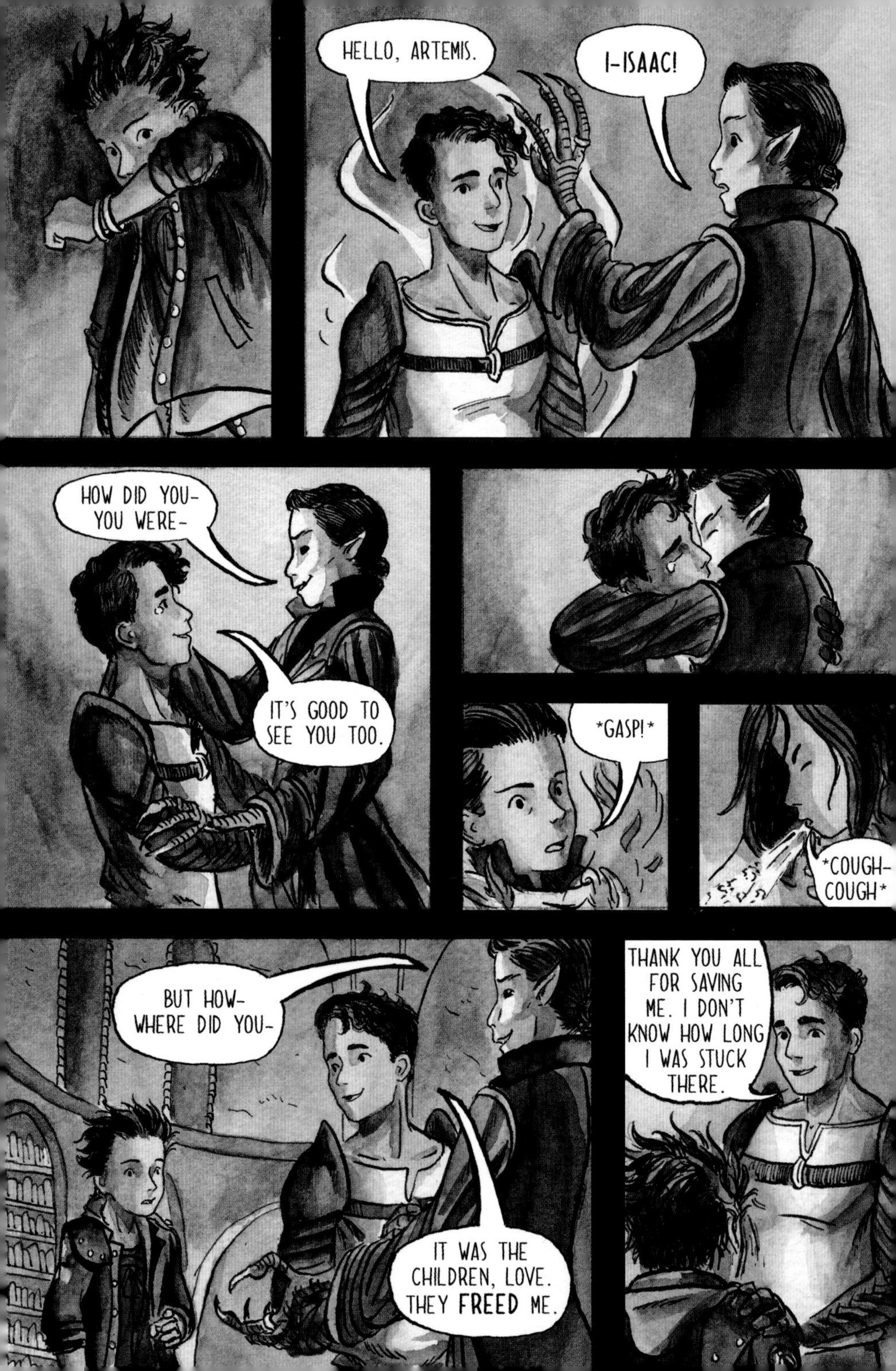
HELLO, ARTEMIS.
I-ISAAC!
HOW DID YOU- YOU WERE-
IT'S GOOD TO SEE YOU TOO.
GASP!
COUGH- COUGH
BUT HOW- WHERE DID YOU-
IT WAS THE CHILDREN, LOVE. THEY **FREED** ME.
THANK YOU ALL FOR SAVING ME. I DON'T KNOW HOW LONG I WAS STUCK THERE.

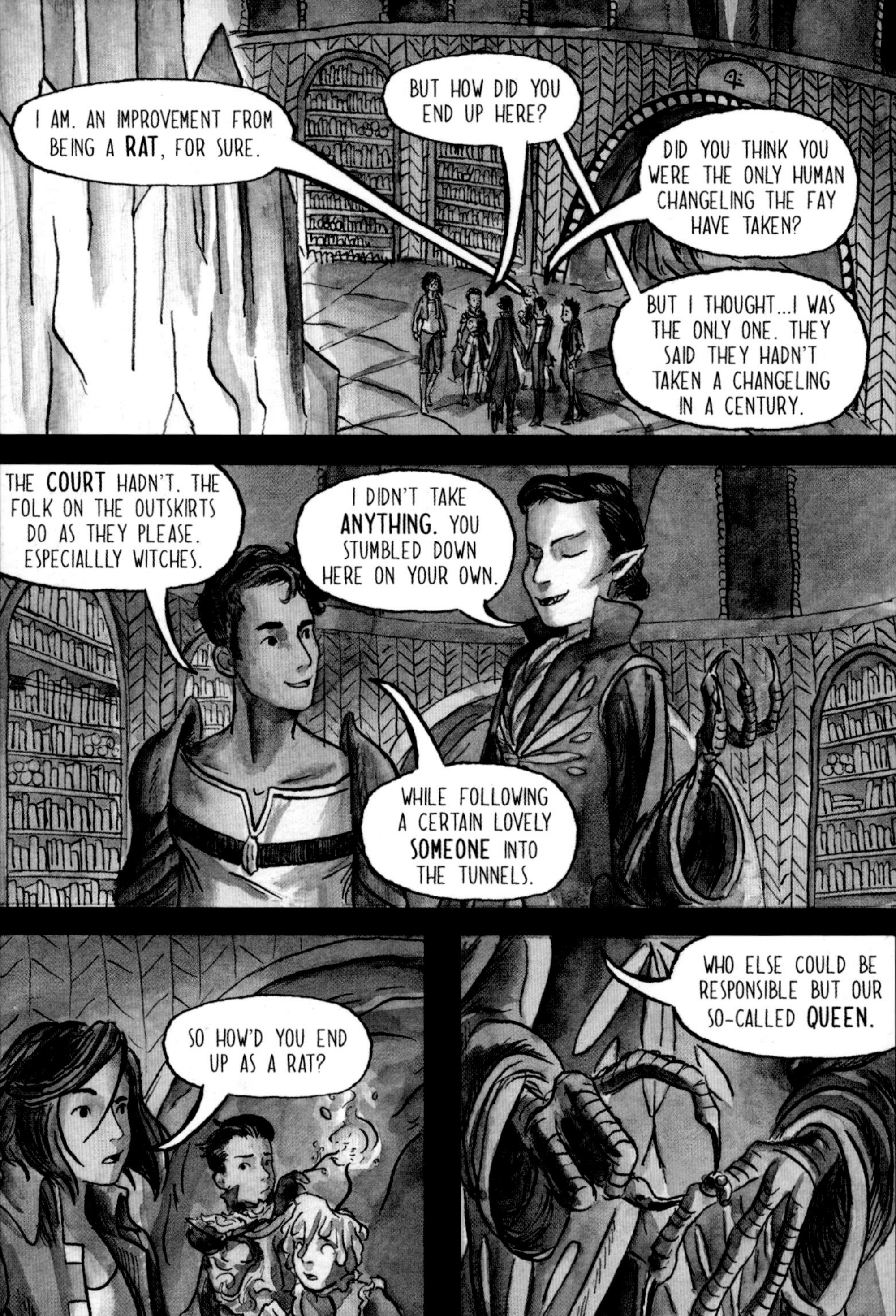
I AM. AN IMPROVEMENT FROM BEING A RAT, FOR SURE.
BUT HOW DID YOU END UP HERE?
DID YOU THINK YOU WERE THE ONLY HUMAN CHANGELING THE FAY HAVE TAKEN?
BUT I THOUGHT...I WAS THE ONLY ONE. THEY SAID THEY HADN'T TAKEN A CHANGELING IN A CENTURY.
THE COURT HADN'T. THE FOLK ON THE OUTSKIRTS DO AS THEY PLEASE. ESPECIALLLY WITCHES.
I DIDN'T TAKE ANYTHING. YOU STUMBLED DOWN HERE ON YOUR OWN.
WHILE FOLLOWING A CERTAIN LOVELY SOMEONE INTO THE TUNNELS.
SO HOW'D YOU END UP AS A RAT?
WHO ELSE COULD BE RESPONSIBLE BUT OUR SO-CALLED QUEEN.

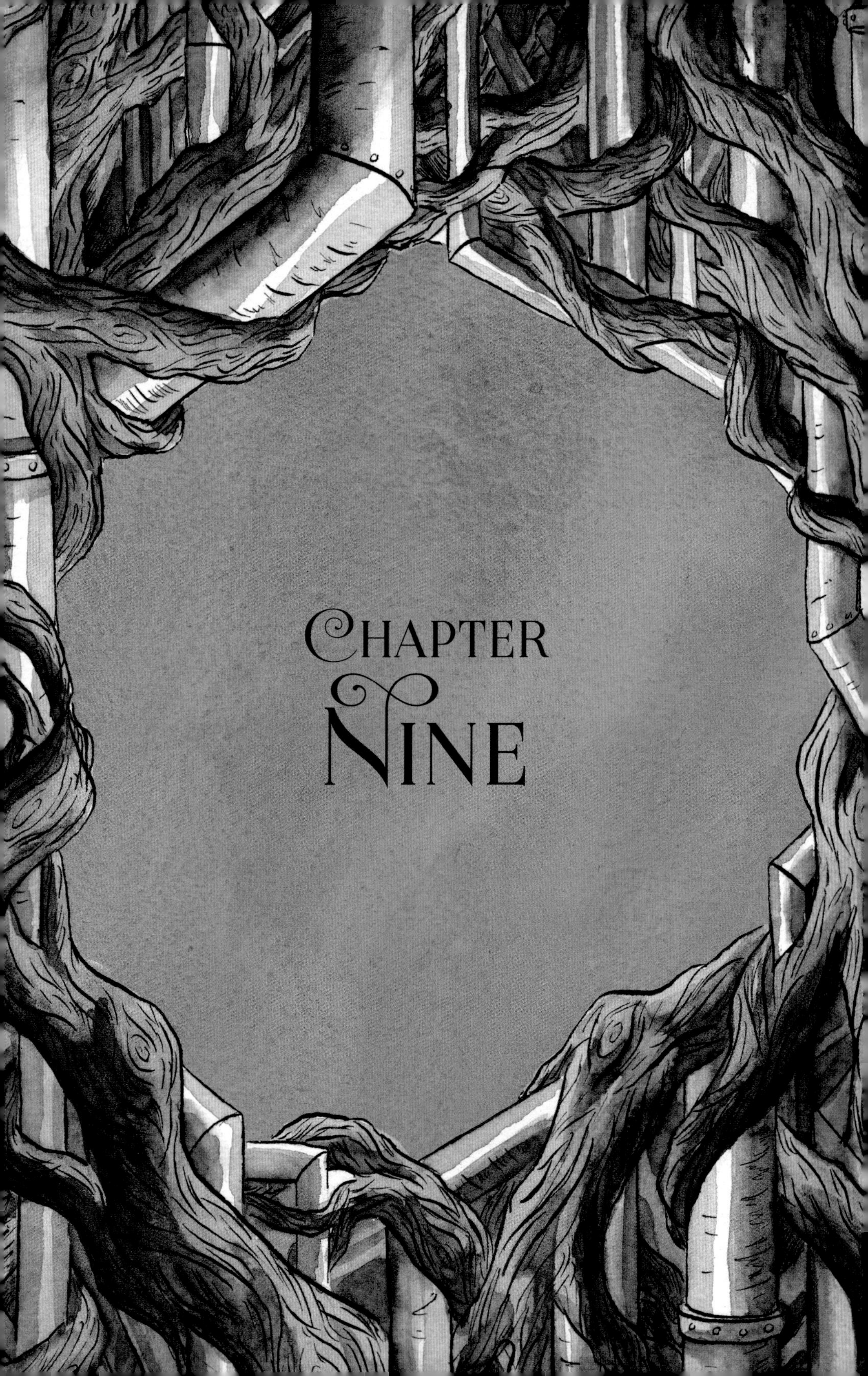

Chapter Nine

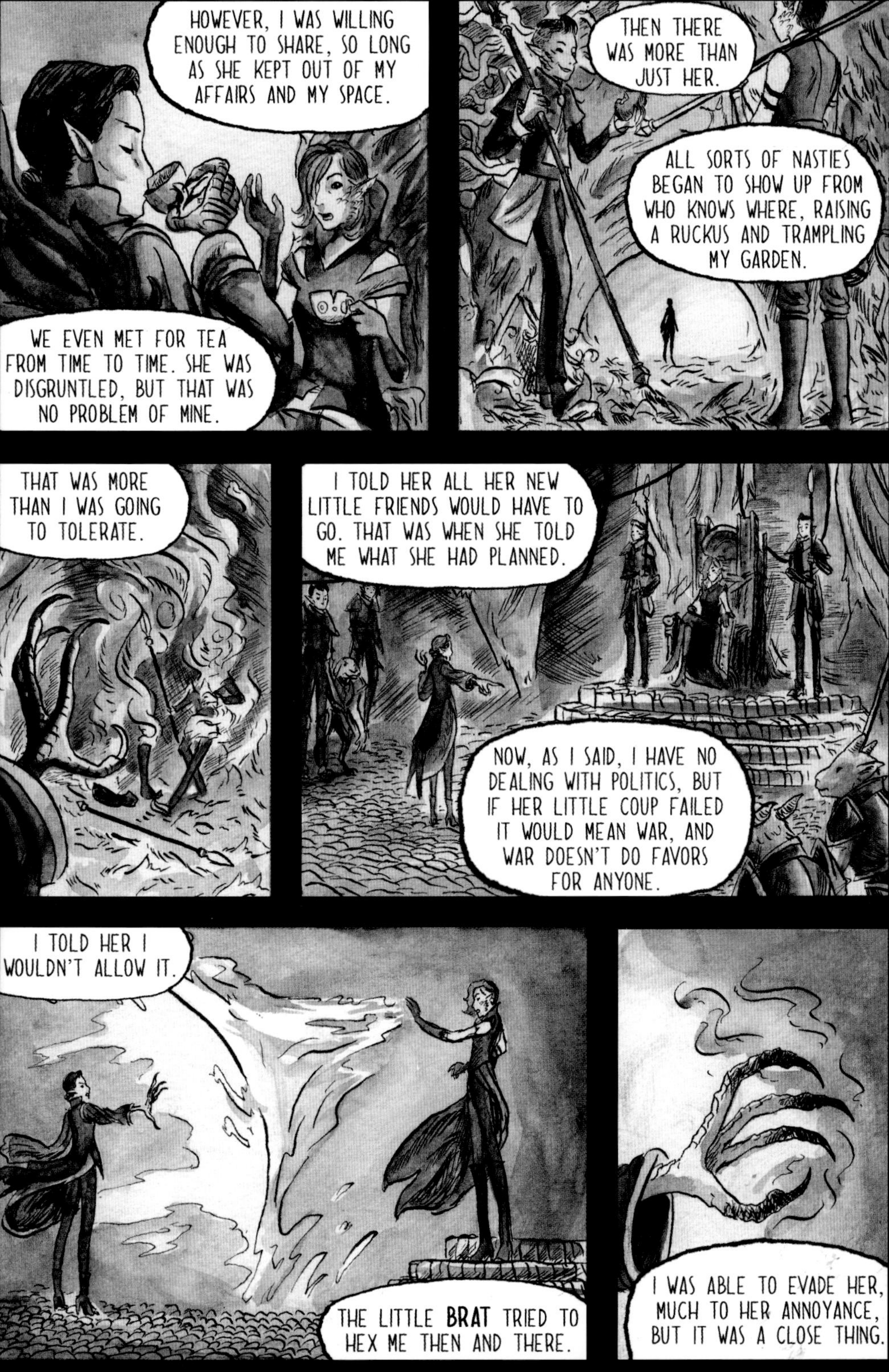
HOWEVER, I WAS WILLING ENOUGH TO SHARE, SO LONG AS SHE KEPT OUT OF MY AFFAIRS AND MY SPACE.
WE EVEN MET FOR TEA FROM TIME TO TIME. SHE WAS DISGRUNTLED, BUT THAT WAS NO PROBLEM OF MINE.
THEN THERE WAS MORE THAN JUST HER.
ALL SORTS OF NASTIES BEGAN TO SHOW UP FROM WHO KNOWS WHERE, RAISING A RUCKUS AND TRAMPLING MY GARDEN.
THAT WAS MORE THAN I WAS GOING TO TOLERATE.
I TOLD HER ALL HER NEW LITTLE FRIENDS WOULD HAVE TO GO. THAT WAS WHEN SHE TOLD ME WHAT SHE HAD PLANNED.
NOW, AS I SAID, I HAVE NO DEALING WITH POLITICS, BUT IF HER LITTLE COUP FAILED IT WOULD MEAN WAR, AND WAR DOESN'T DO FAVORS FOR ANYONE.
I TOLD HER I WOULDN'T ALLOW IT.
THE LITTLE **BRAT** TRIED TO HEX ME THEN AND THERE.
I WAS ABLE TO EVADE HER, MUCH TO HER ANNOYANCE, BUT IT WAS A CLOSE THING.

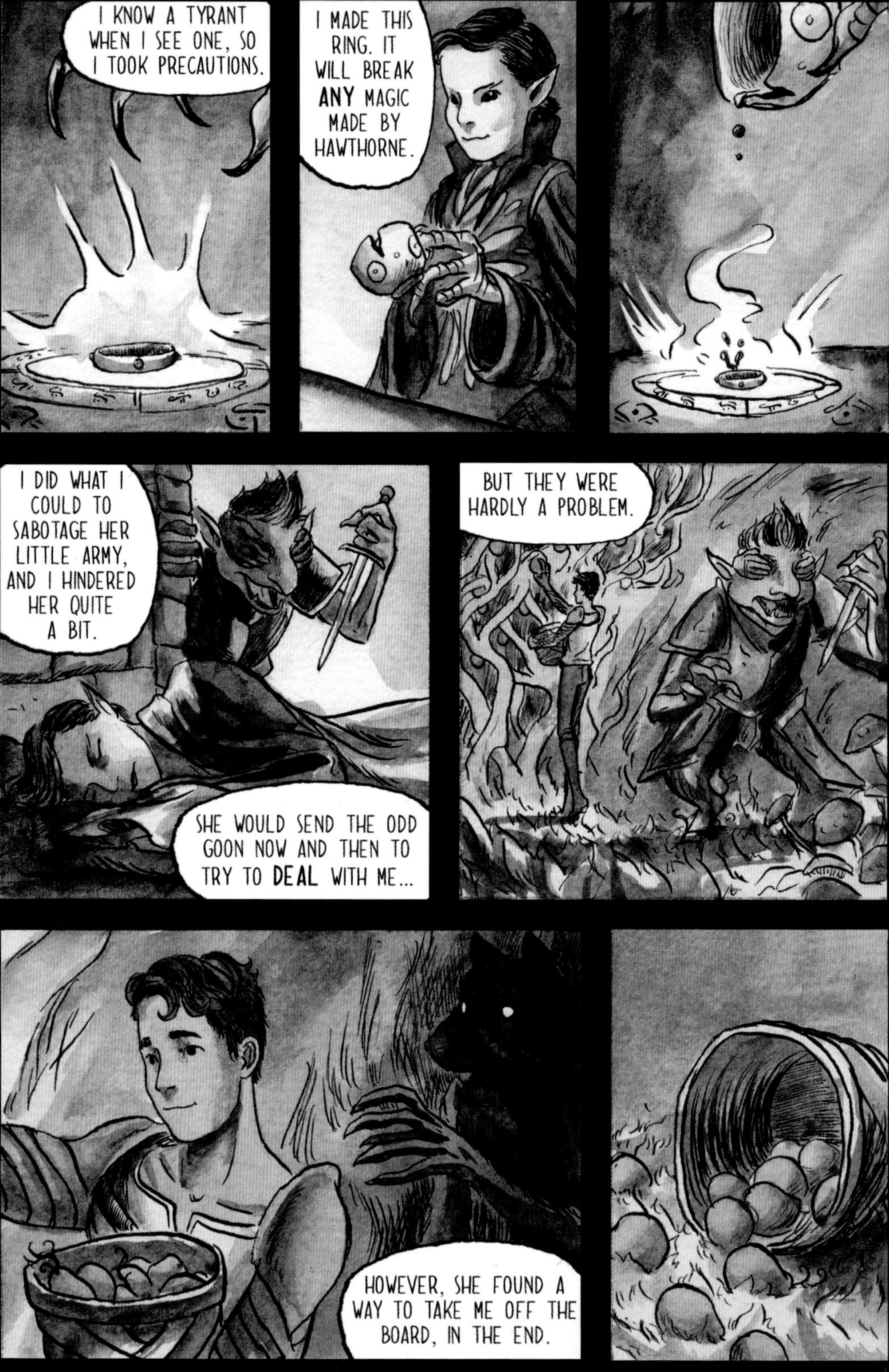
I KNOW A TYRANT WHEN I SEE ONE, SO I TOOK PRECAUTIONS.
I MADE THIS RING. IT WILL BREAK **ANY** MAGIC MADE BY HAWTHORNE.
I DID WHAT I COULD TO SABOTAGE HER LITTLE ARMY, AND I HINDERED HER QUITE A BIT.
SHE WOULD SEND THE ODD GOON NOW AND THEN TO TRY TO **DEAL** WITH ME...
BUT THEY WERE HARDLY A PROBLEM.
HOWEVER, SHE FOUND A WAY TO TAKE ME OFF THE BOARD, IN THE END.

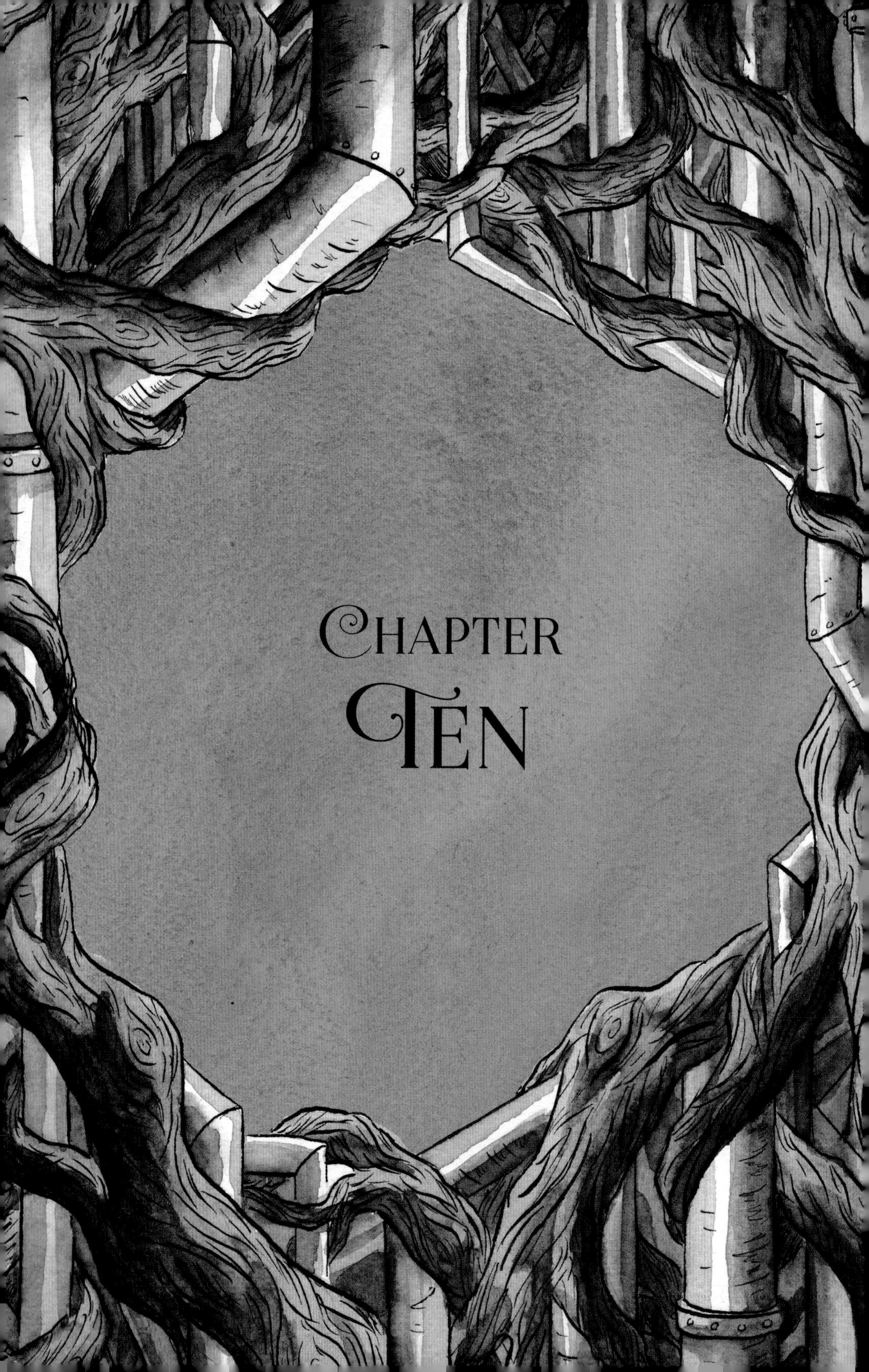

Chapter Ten

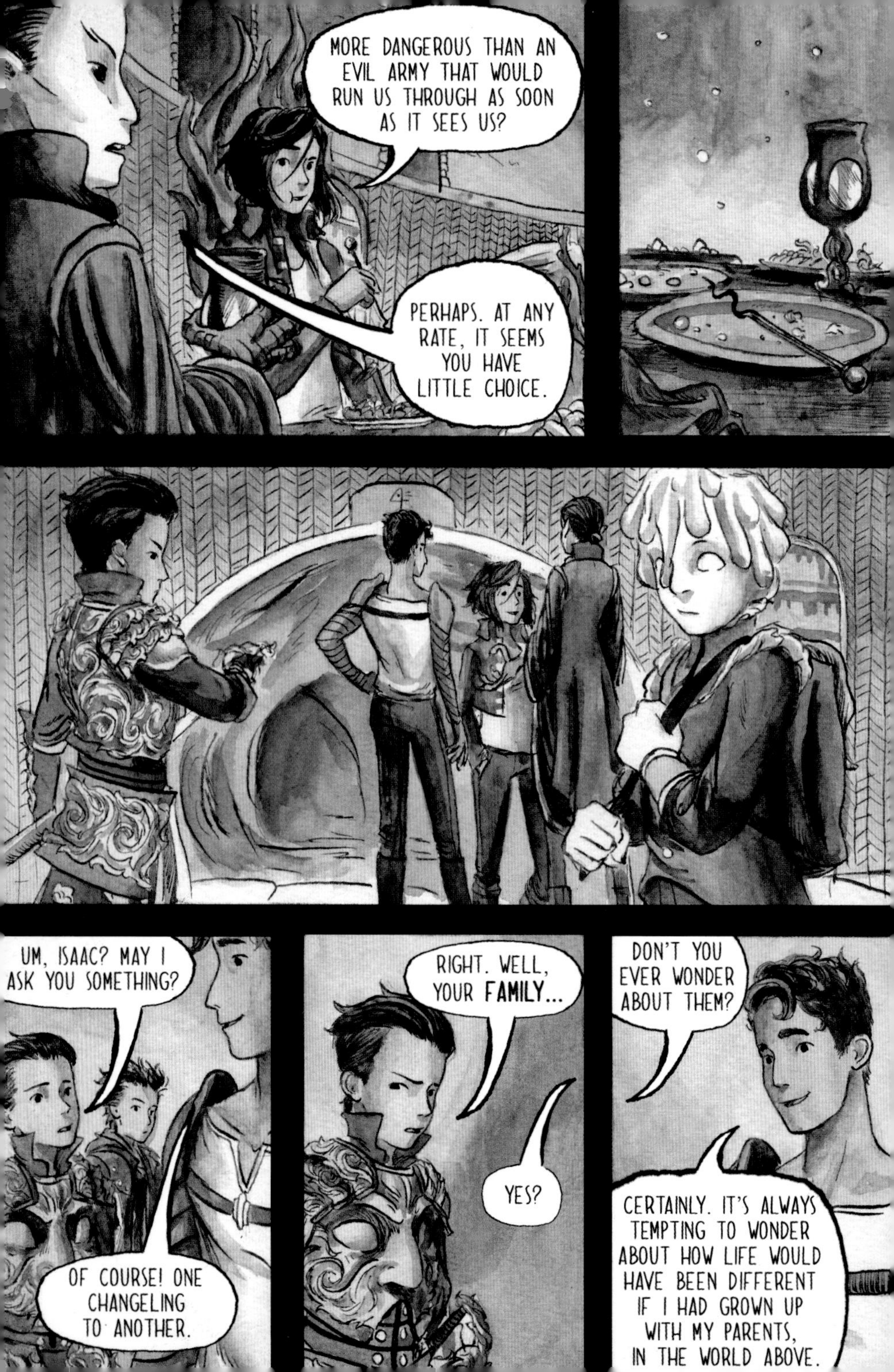
MORE DANGEROUS THAN AN EVIL ARMY THAT WOULD RUN US THROUGH AS SOON AS IT SEES US?
PERHAPS. AT ANY RATE, IT SEEMS YOU HAVE LITTLE CHOICE.
UM, ISAAC? MAY I ASK YOU SOMETHING?
OF COURSE! ONE CHANGELING TO ANOTHER.
RIGHT. WELL, YOUR **FAMILY**...
YES?
DON'T YOU EVER WONDER ABOUT THEM?
CERTAINLY. IT'S ALWAYS TEMPTING TO WONDER ABOUT HOW LIFE WOULD HAVE BEEN DIFFERENT IF I HAD GROWN UP WITH MY PARENTS, IN THE WORLD ABOVE.

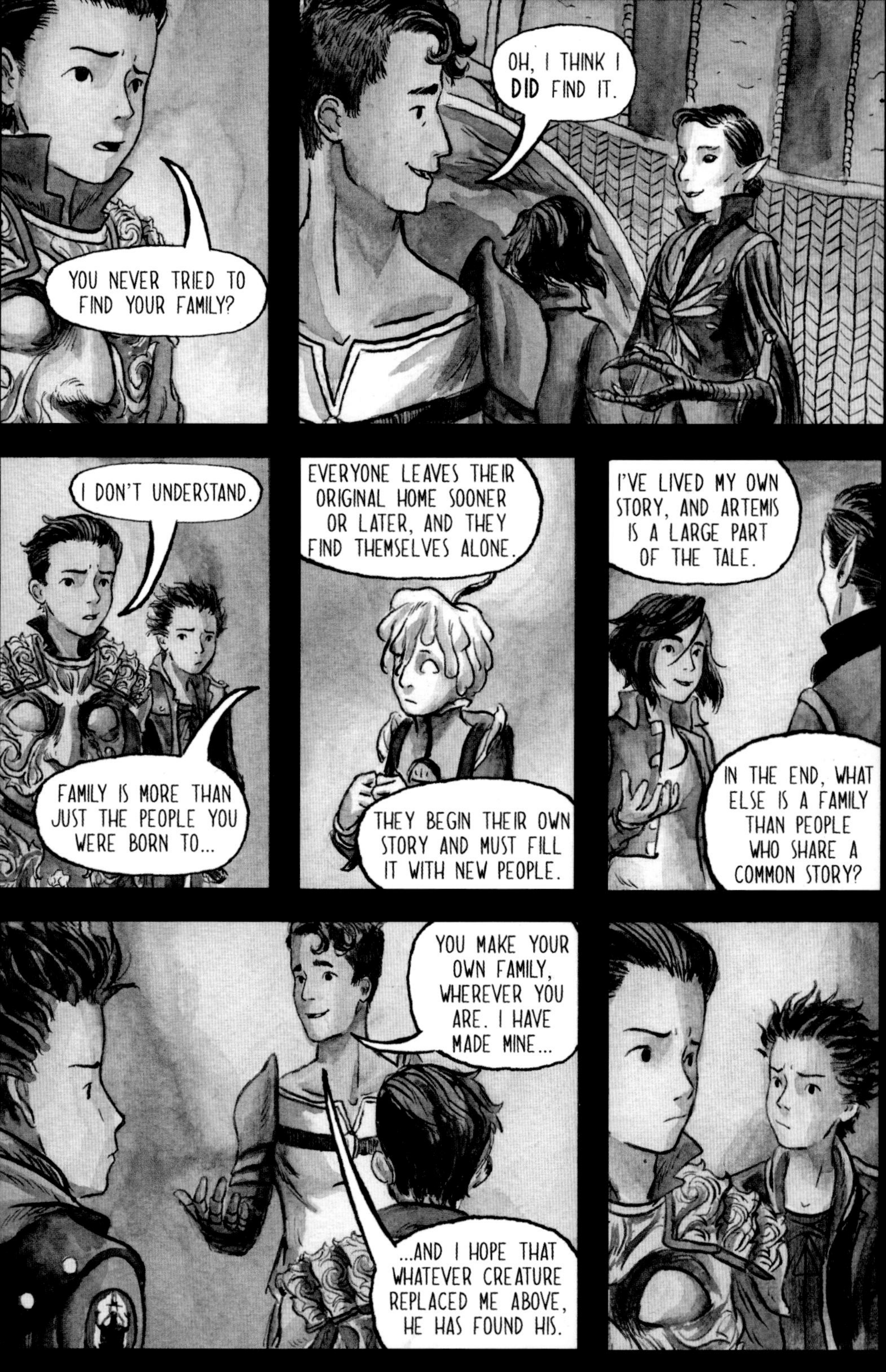
YOU NEVER TRIED TO FIND YOUR FAMILY?
OH, I THINK I **DID** FIND IT.
I DON'T UNDERSTAND.
FAMILY IS MORE THAN JUST THE PEOPLE YOU WERE BORN TO...
EVERYONE LEAVES THEIR ORIGINAL HOME SOONER OR LATER, AND THEY FIND THEMSELVES ALONE.
THEY BEGIN THEIR OWN STORY AND MUST FILL IT WITH NEW PEOPLE.
I'VE LIVED MY OWN STORY, AND ARTEMIS IS A LARGE PART OF THE TALE.
IN THE END, WHAT ELSE IS A FAMILY THAN PEOPLE WHO SHARE A COMMON STORY?
YOU MAKE YOUR OWN FAMILY, WHEREVER YOU ARE. I HAVE MADE MINE...
...AND I HOPE THAT WHATEVER CREATURE REPLACED ME ABOVE, HE HAS FOUND HIS.

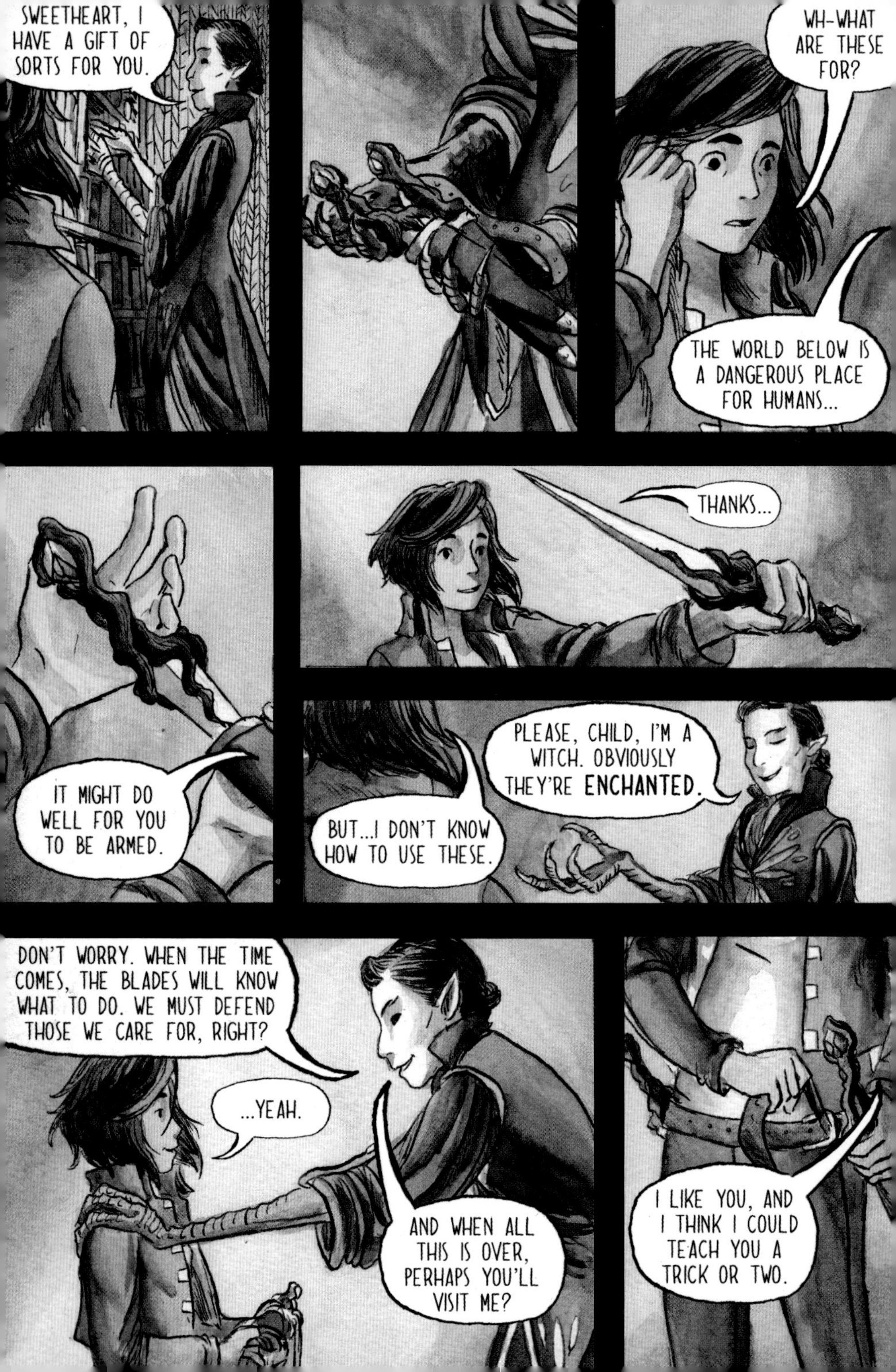
SWEETHEART, I HAVE A GIFT OF SORTS FOR YOU.
WH-WHAT ARE THESE FOR?
THE WORLD BELOW IS A DANGEROUS PLACE FOR HUMANS...
IT MIGHT DO WELL FOR YOU TO BE ARMED.
THANKS...
BUT...I DON'T KNOW HOW TO USE THESE.
PLEASE, CHILD, I'M A WITCH. OBVIOUSLY THEY'RE **ENCHANTED**.
DON'T WORRY. WHEN THE TIME COMES, THE BLADES WILL KNOW WHAT TO DO. WE MUST DEFEND THOSE WE CARE FOR, RIGHT?
...YEAH.
AND WHEN ALL THIS IS OVER, PERHAPS YOU'LL VISIT ME?
I LIKE YOU, AND I THINK I COULD TEACH YOU A TRICK OR TWO.

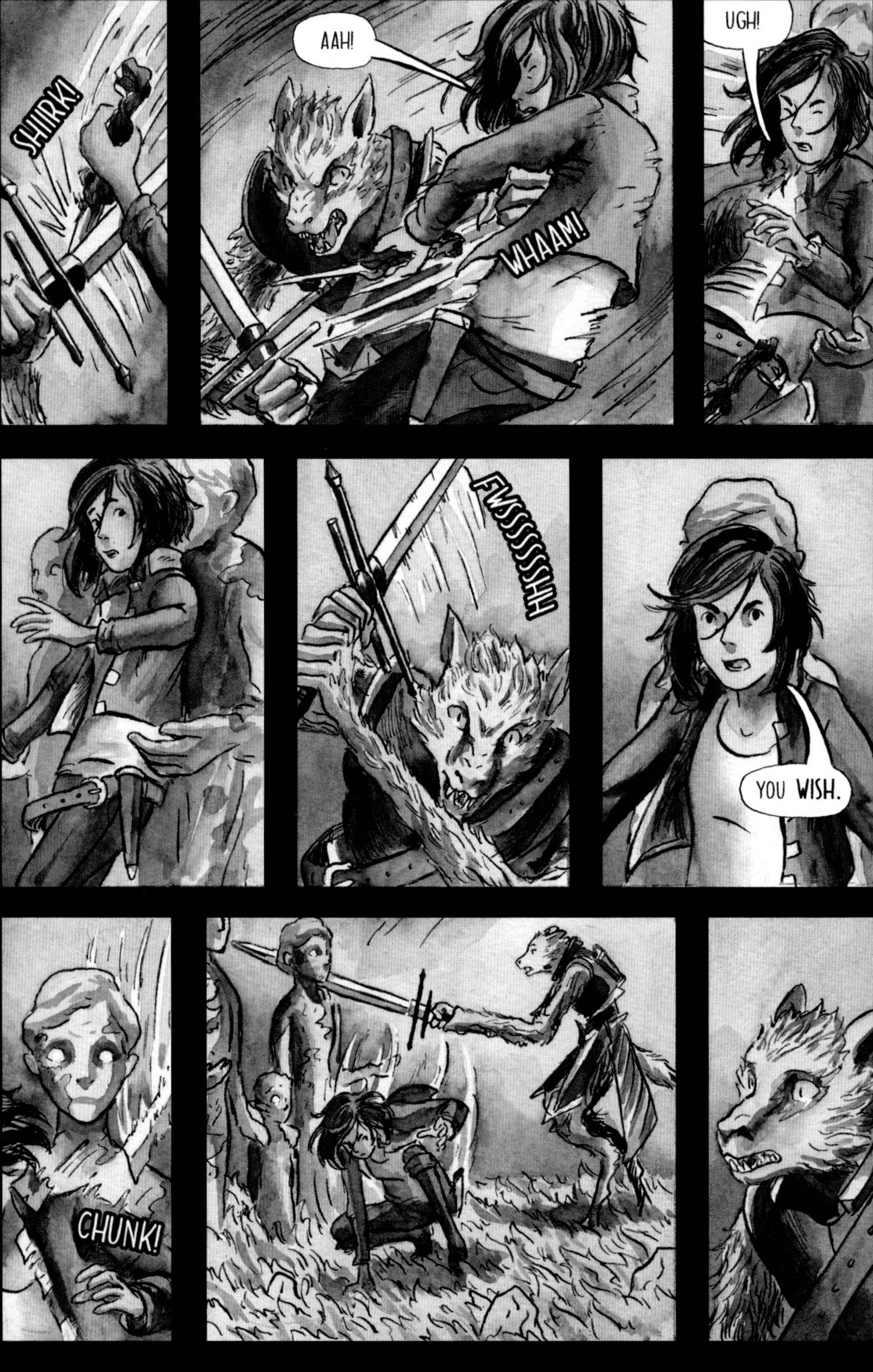
SHIRK!
AAH!
WHAAM!
UGH!
FWSSSSSSHH
YOU WISH.
CHUNK!

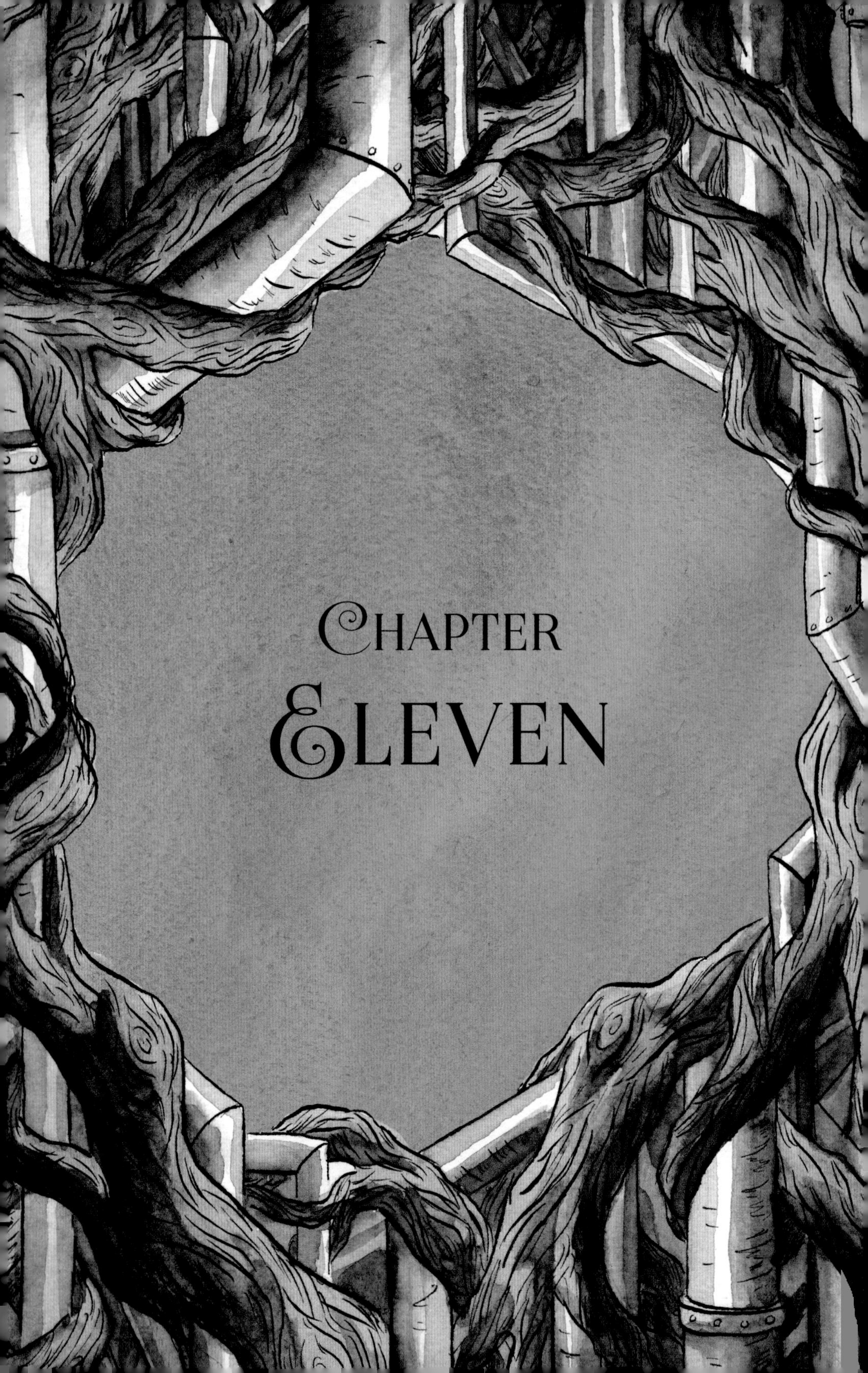

Chapter Eleven

WE'RE VERY CLOSE TO THE SERVANTS' ENTRANCE. ONCE INSIDE, WE'LL HAVE TO BE **VERY** QUIET...

WE STAND A CHANCE IF IT'S JUST US AND HAWTHORNE, BUT IF HER CRONIES SHOW UP, WE'RE DONE FOR.

RIGHT. SO, AFTER WE— WHAT'S THAT SOUND?

HMM, IT **SOUNDS** LIKE—

RRRRRRR-RRRRRRR-RRRRRRR-RRRRRRR

DON'T SAY BREATHING.

O...KAY.

RRRRRRR-RRRRRRR-

...IT'S BREATHING, ISN'T IT? IT'S SOMETHING **HUGE** BREATHING.

LET'S SEE.

RRRRR-R'

OH **NO**...

RRRRR-RRRRRRR-RRRR

NO, NO, NO, NO.

RRRRRR-RRRRRRR-RRRRRRR-RRRRRRR-RRRRRR

RRRRRR-RRRRRRR-RRRRRRR

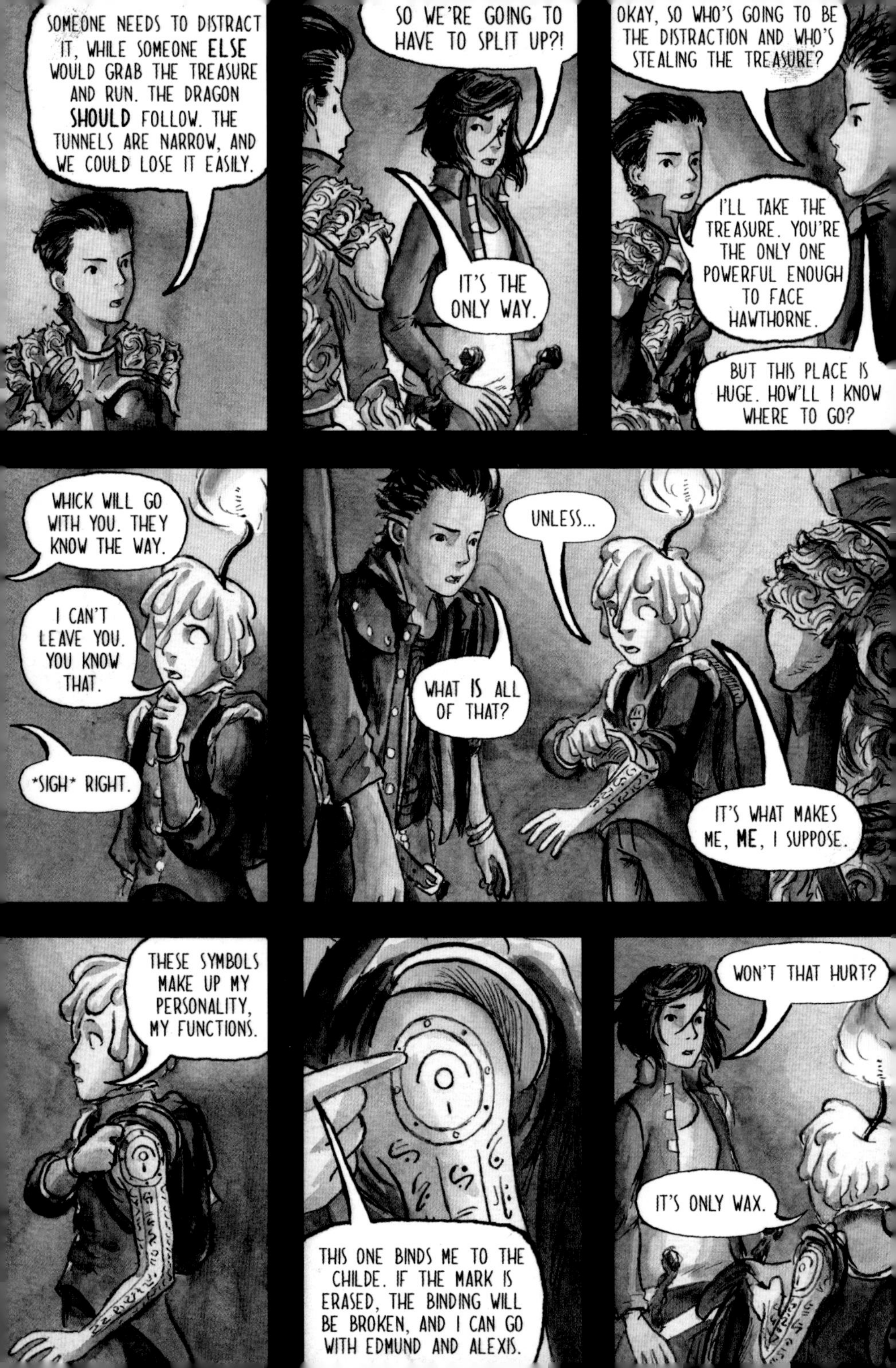
SOMEONE NEEDS TO DISTRACT IT, WHILE SOMEONE ELSE WOULD GRAB THE TREASURE AND RUN. THE DRAGON SHOULD FOLLOW. THE TUNNELS ARE NARROW, AND WE COULD LOSE IT EASILY.
SO WE'RE GOING TO HAVE TO SPLIT UP?!
IT'S THE ONLY WAY.
OKAY, SO WHO'S GOING TO BE THE DISTRACTION AND WHO'S STEALING THE TREASURE?
I'LL TAKE THE TREASURE. YOU'RE THE ONLY ONE POWERFUL ENOUGH TO FACE HAWTHORNE.
BUT THIS PLACE IS HUGE. HOW'LL I KNOW WHERE TO GO?
WHICK WILL GO WITH YOU. THEY KNOW THE WAY.
I CAN'T LEAVE YOU. YOU KNOW THAT.
SIGH RIGHT.
UNLESS...
WHAT IS ALL OF THAT?
IT'S WHAT MAKES ME, ME, I SUPPOSE.
THESE SYMBOLS MAKE UP MY PERSONALITY, MY FUNCTIONS.
THIS ONE BINDS ME TO THE CHILDE. IF THE MARK IS ERASED, THE BINDING WILL BE BROKEN, AND I CAN GO WITH EDMUND AND ALEXIS.
WON'T THAT HURT?
IT'S ONLY WAX.

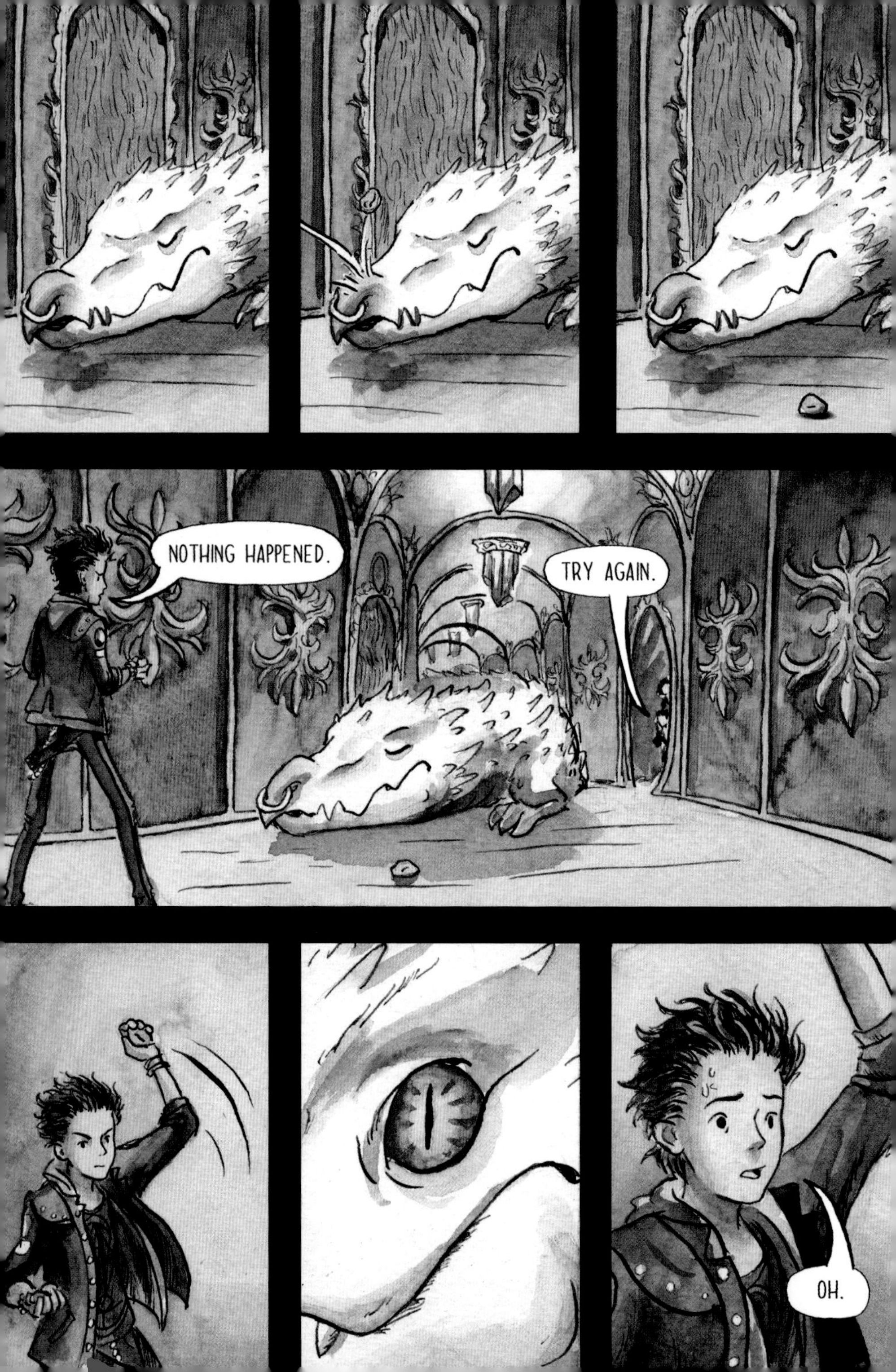
NOTHING HAPPENED.
TRY AGAIN.
OH.

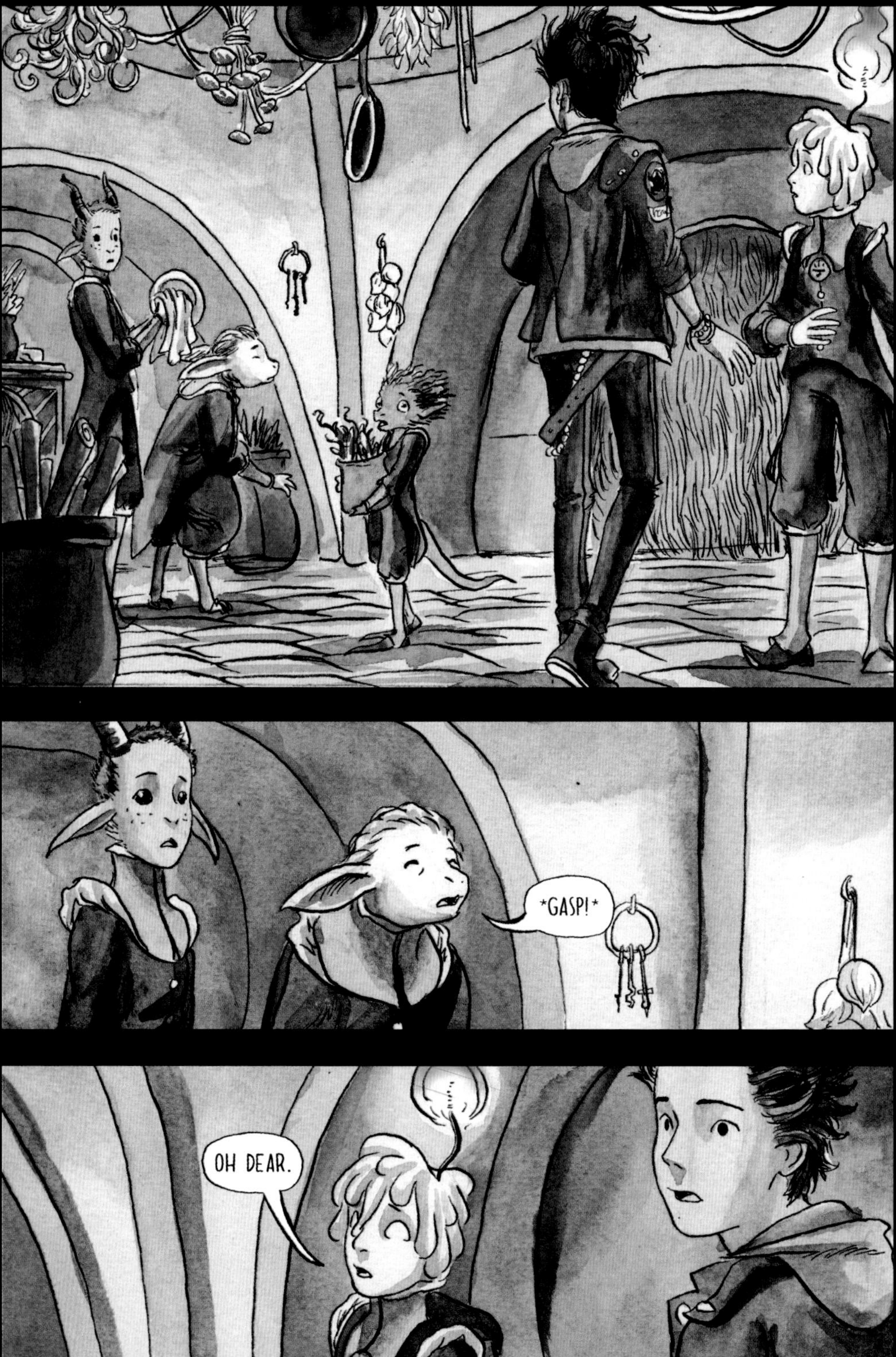
GASP!
OH DEAR.

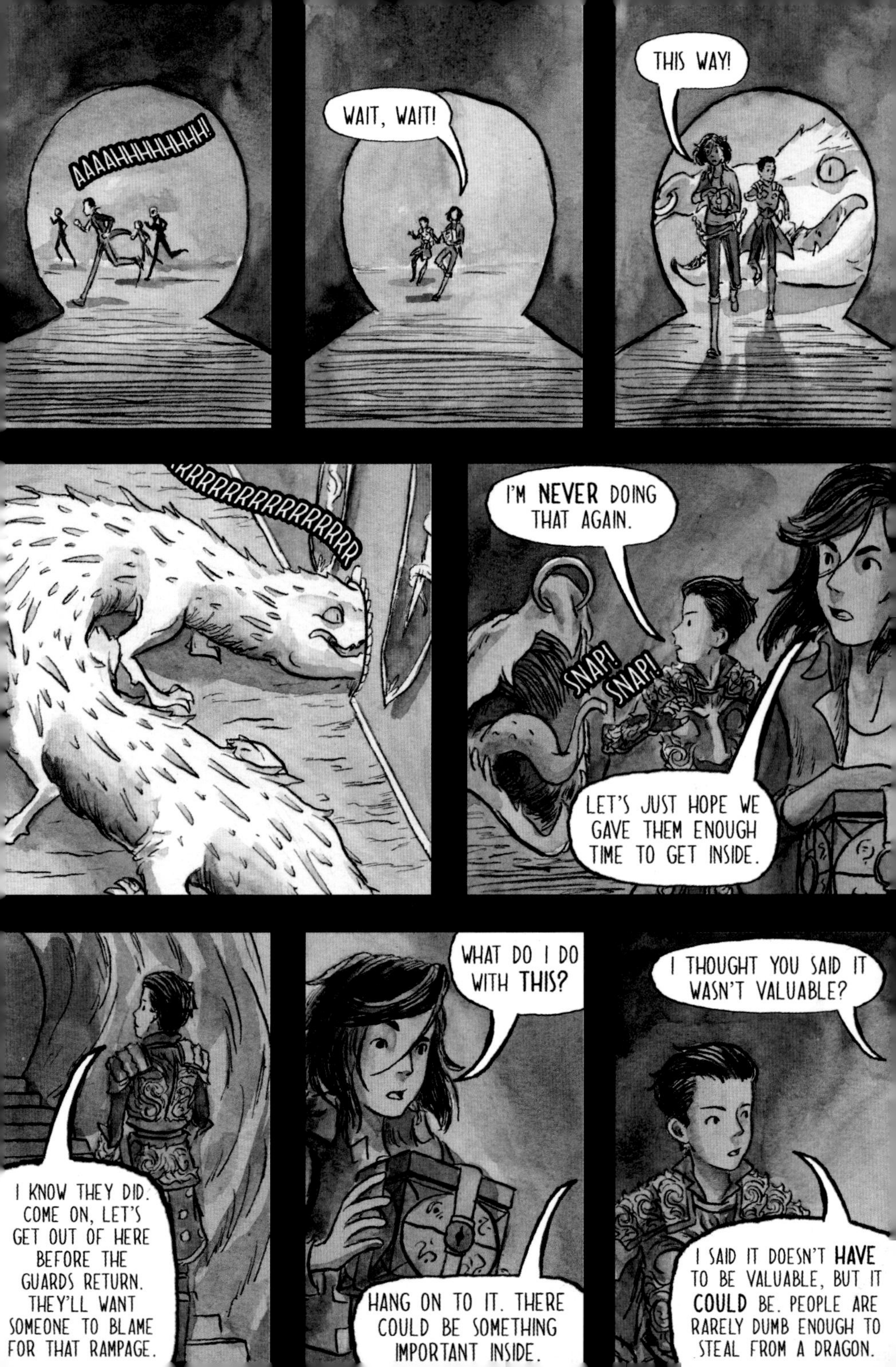
AAAAHHHHHHHH!
WAIT, WAIT!
THIS WAY!
RRRRRRRRRRRRRRRRR
I'M **NEVER** DOING THAT AGAIN.
SNAP!
SNAP!
LET'S JUST HOPE WE GAVE THEM ENOUGH TIME TO GET INSIDE.
I KNOW THEY DID. COME ON, LET'S GET OUT OF HERE BEFORE THE GUARDS RETURN. THEY'LL WANT SOMEONE TO BLAME FOR THAT RAMPAGE.
WHAT DO I DO WITH **THIS**?
HANG ON TO IT. THERE COULD BE SOMETHING IMPORTANT INSIDE.
I THOUGHT YOU SAID IT WASN'T VALUABLE?
I SAID IT DOESN'T **HAVE** TO BE VALUABLE, BUT IT **COULD** BE. PEOPLE ARE RARELY DUMB ENOUGH TO STEAL FROM A DRAGON.

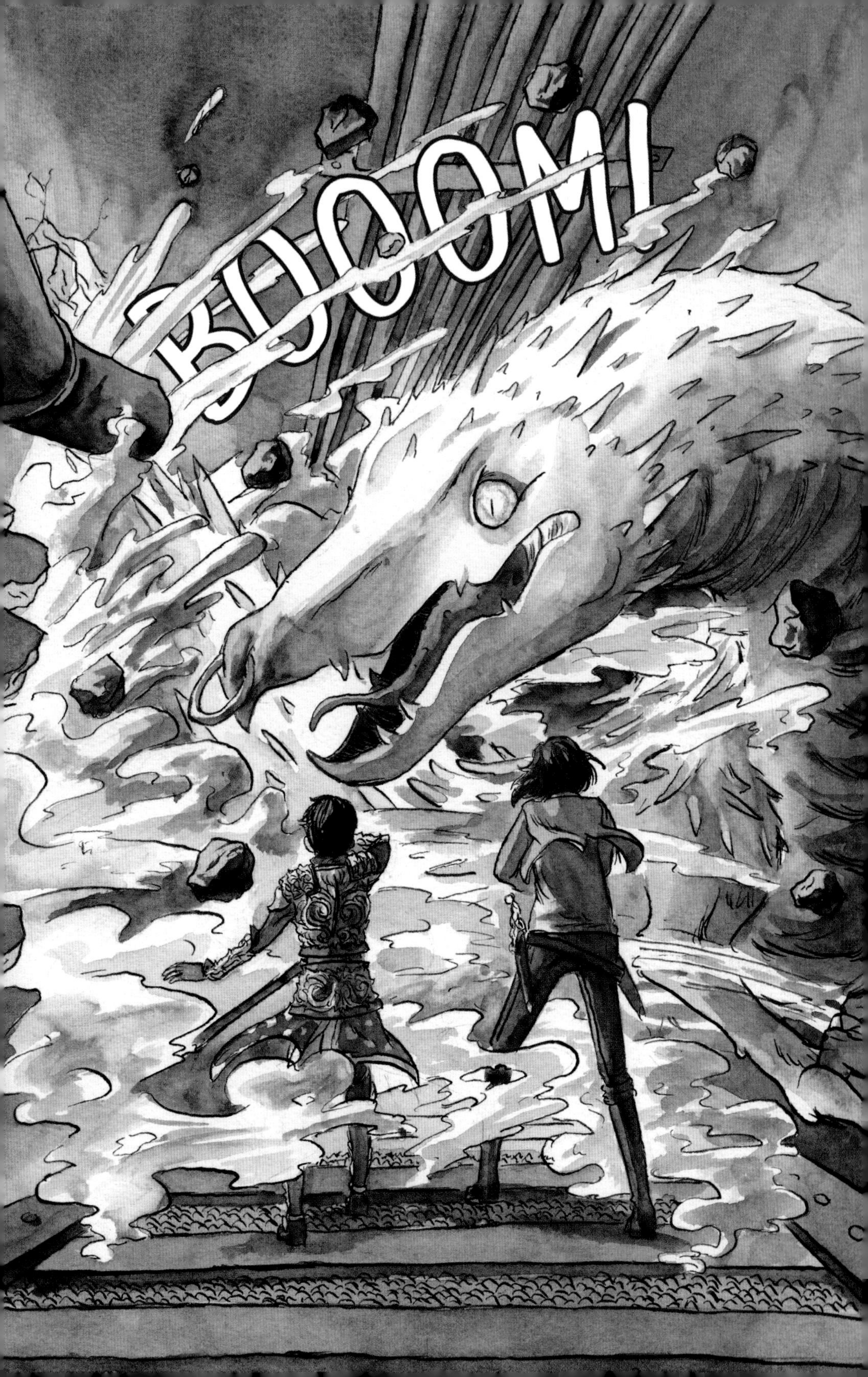
BOOOOM!

Chapter Twelve

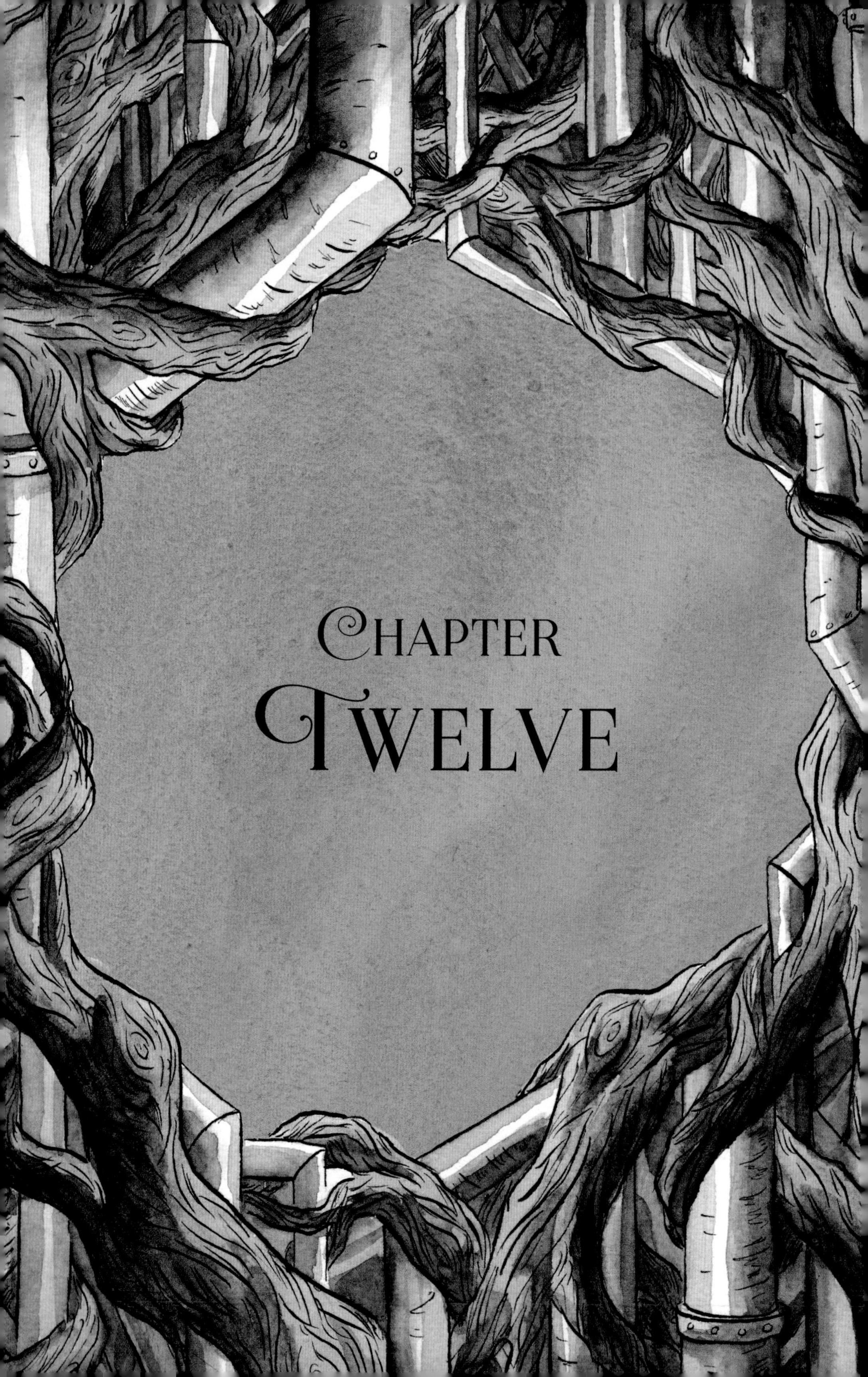

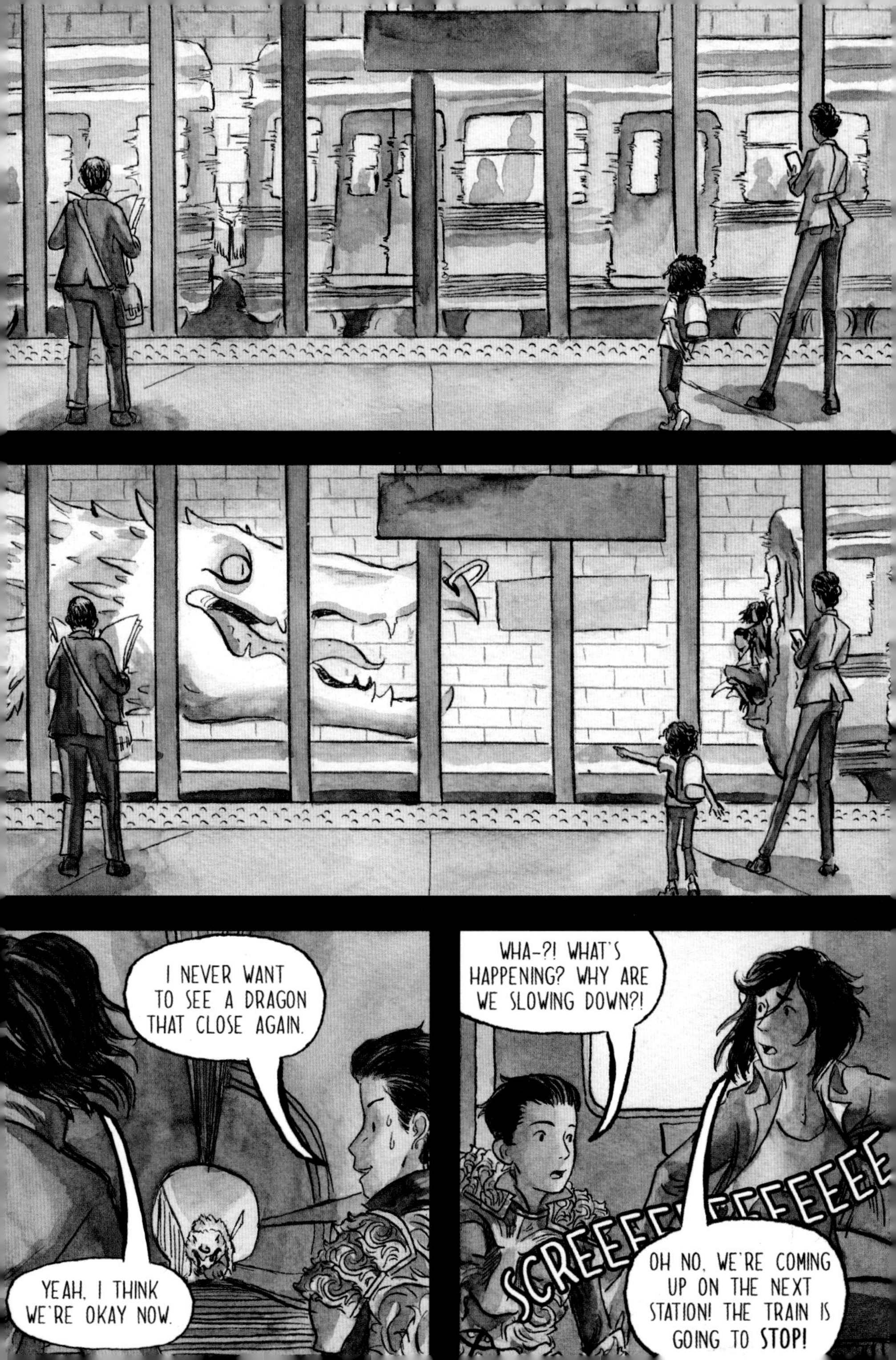

I NEVER WANT TO SEE A DRAGON THAT CLOSE AGAIN.
YEAH, I THINK WE'RE OKAY NOW.
WHA-?! WHAT'S HAPPENING? WHY ARE WE SLOWING DOWN?!
SCREEEEEEEEEEEEE
OH NO, WE'RE COMING UP ON THE NEXT STATION! THE TRAIN IS GOING TO STOP!

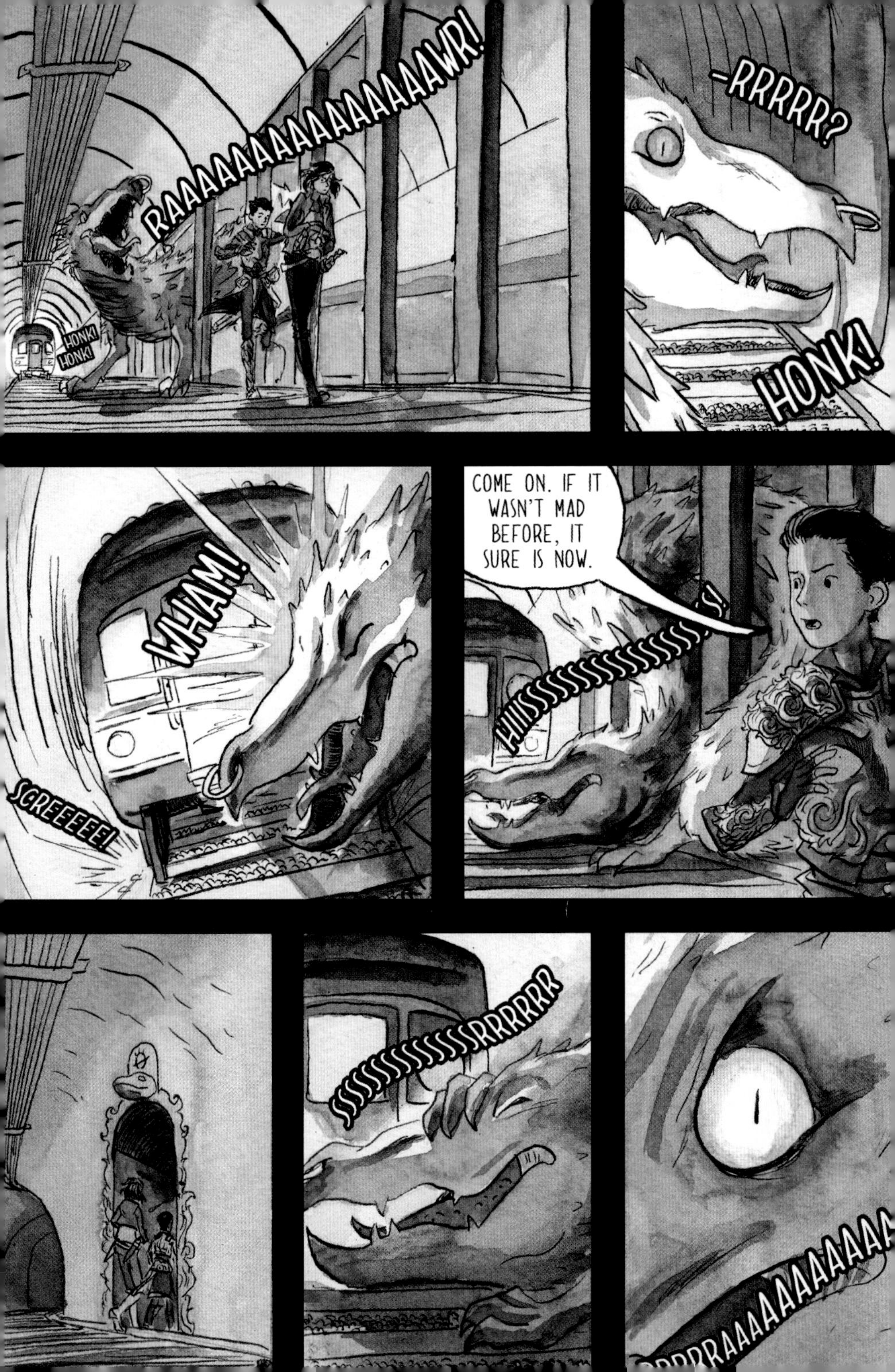
RAAAAAAAAAAAAAAAAAWR!
HONK! HONK!
-RRRRRR?
HONK!
WHAM!
SCREEEEEE!
COME ON. IF IT WASN'T MAD BEFORE, IT SURE IS NOW.
HIISSSSSSSSSSSSSSSSSS!
SSSSSSSSSSSSRRRRRR
RRRRRAAAAAAAAAAAA

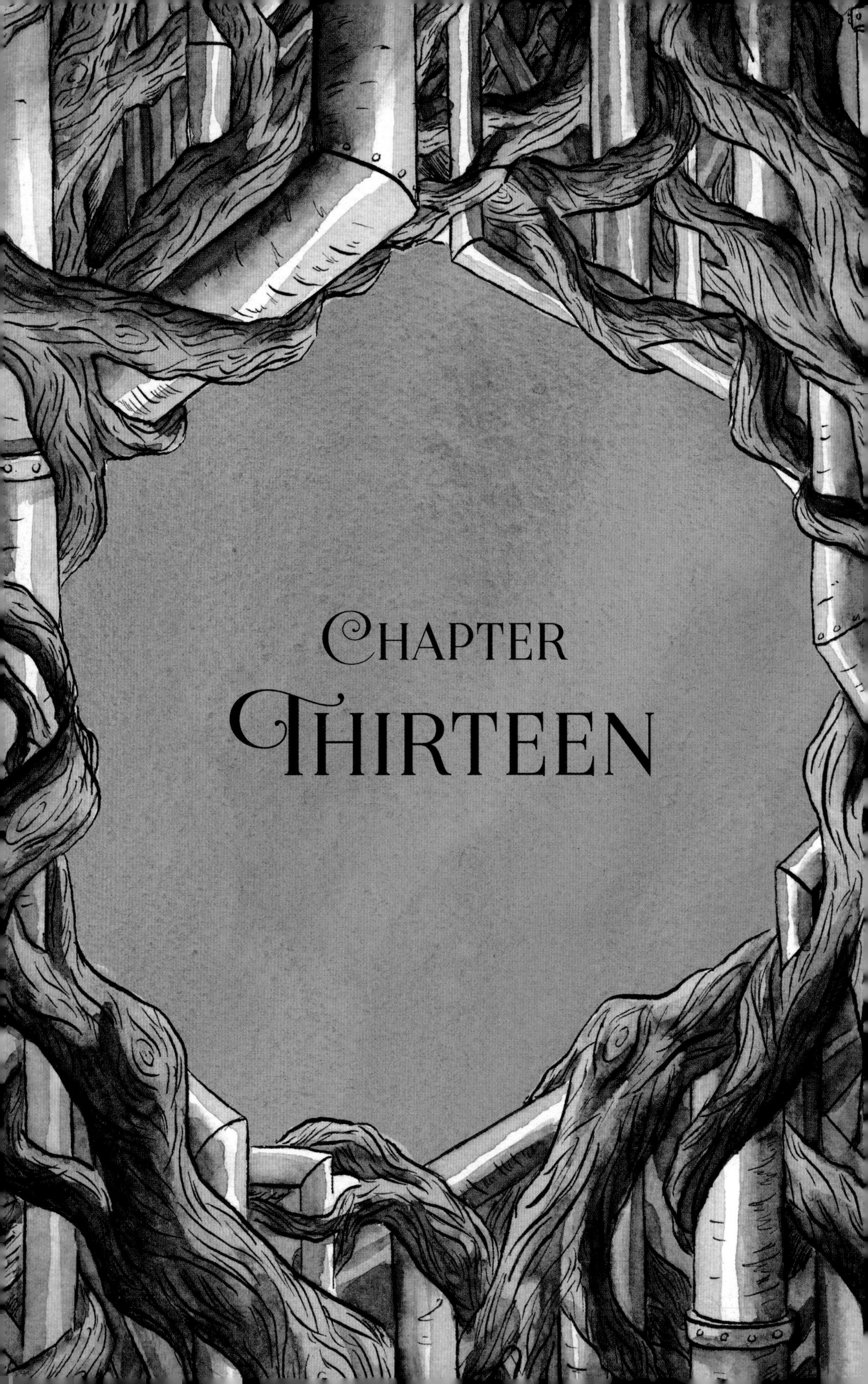

Chapter Thirteen

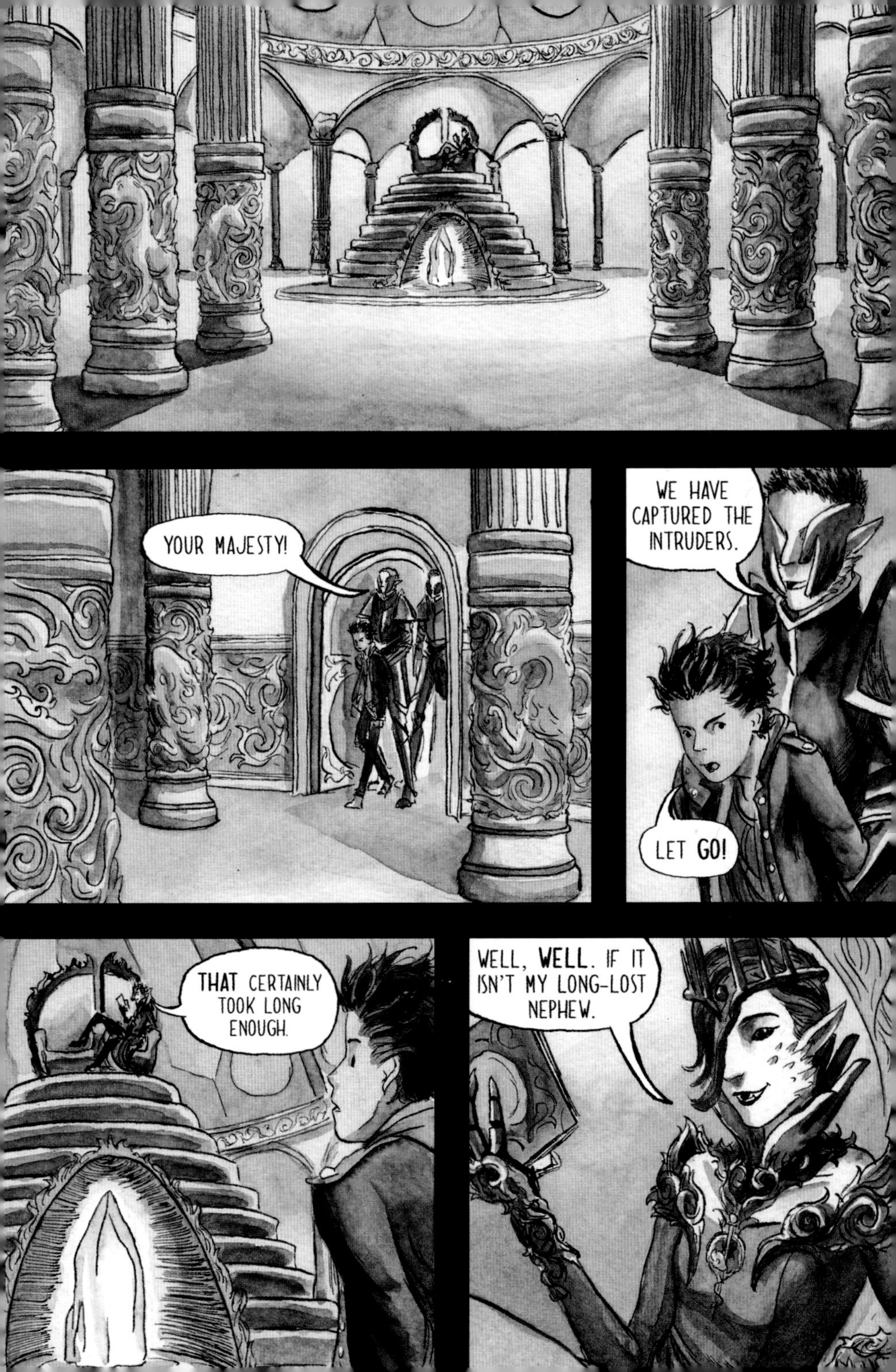

YOUR MAJESTY!
WE HAVE CAPTURED THE INTRUDERS.
LET **GO**!
THAT CERTAINLY TOOK LONG ENOUGH.
WELL, **WELL**. IF IT ISN'T MY LONG-LOST NEPHEW.

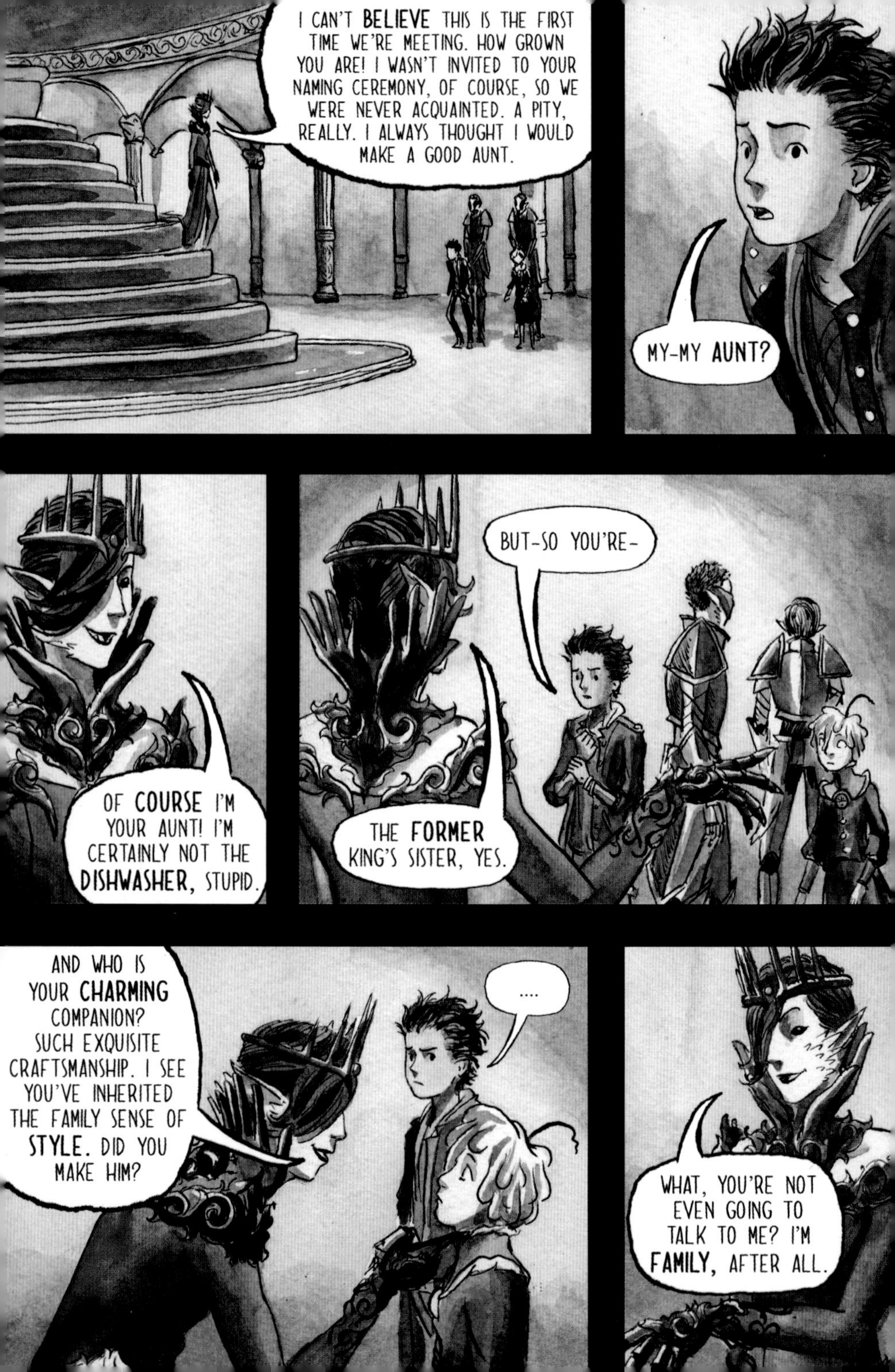
I CAN'T **BELIEVE** THIS IS THE FIRST TIME WE'RE MEETING. HOW GROWN YOU ARE! I WASN'T INVITED TO YOUR NAMING CEREMONY, OF COURSE, SO WE WERE NEVER ACQUAINTED. A PITY, REALLY. I ALWAYS THOUGHT I WOULD MAKE A GOOD AUNT.
MY-MY **AUNT**?
OF **COURSE** I'M YOUR AUNT! I'M CERTAINLY NOT THE **DISHWASHER**, STUPID.
BUT-SO YOU'RE-
THE **FORMER** KING'S SISTER, YES.
AND WHO IS YOUR **CHARMING** COMPANION? SUCH EXQUISITE CRAFTSMANSHIP. I SEE YOU'VE INHERITED THE FAMILY SENSE OF **STYLE.** DID YOU MAKE HIM?
....
WHAT, YOU'RE NOT EVEN GOING TO TALK TO ME? I'M **FAMILY,** AFTER ALL.

WHAT?

THEY DIDN'T WANT YOU, BUT **I** DO. I PUNISHED THEM, FOR **BOTH** OF US, AND NOW WE CAN HAVE OUR FAMILY, OUR **HOME**. ISN'T THAT WHAT YOU WANT?

YES, BUT...BUT-

BUT **WHAT**? NO ONE IS GOING TO GIVE US A PLACE IN THIS WORLD. WE HAVE TO **TAKE** IT.

COME ON, LET'S BE THE FAMILY WE NEVER HAD, THE ONE WE **DESERVE**.

NO.

PARDON?

AND YOU'RE RIGHT, I WANT THAT TOO. BUT NOT LIKE THIS.

AND I **WON'T** LET YOU TAKE MY HOME FROM ME.

NO. I'M SORRY. I KNOW YOU WANT A HOME...

I...I SEE. IT BREAKS MY HEART TO HEAR YOU SAY THAT, IT REALLY DOES. I GUESS YOU'RE JUST LIKE THE REST OF THEM AFTER ALL.

MY WORD, HUMANS! LIVING, BREATHING, BLEEDING HUMANS! I HAVEN'T SEEN ONE OF YOU SINCE THE CHI–

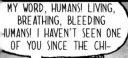

WELL, BLAST ME DOWN, IT'S **YOU**!

MY MY, THE QUEEN **WILL** BE INTERESTED–

–UGH!

I DON'T **THINK** SO, YOU–

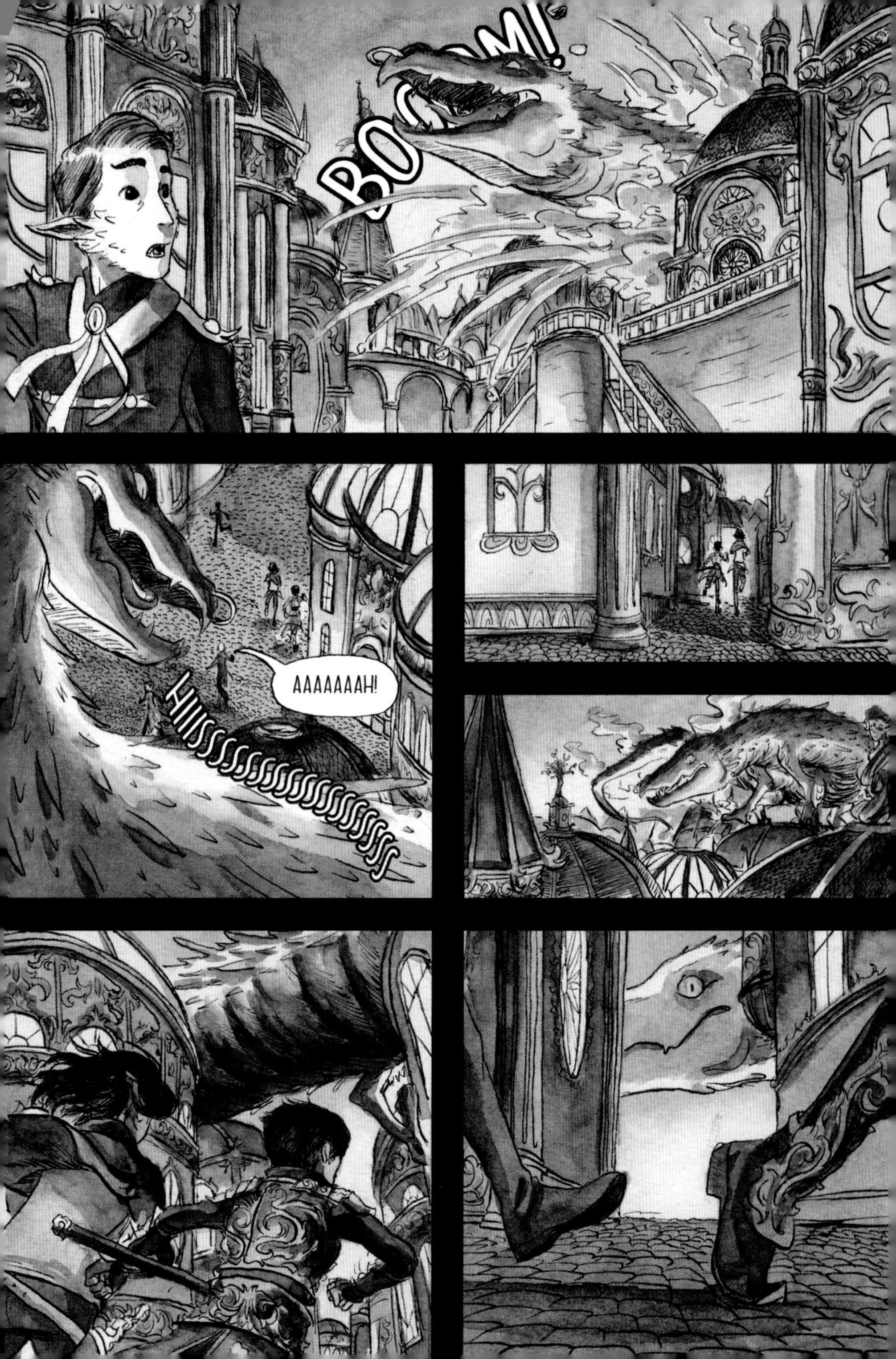
BO M!
HIISSSSSSSSSSSSSSSSS
AAAAAAAH!

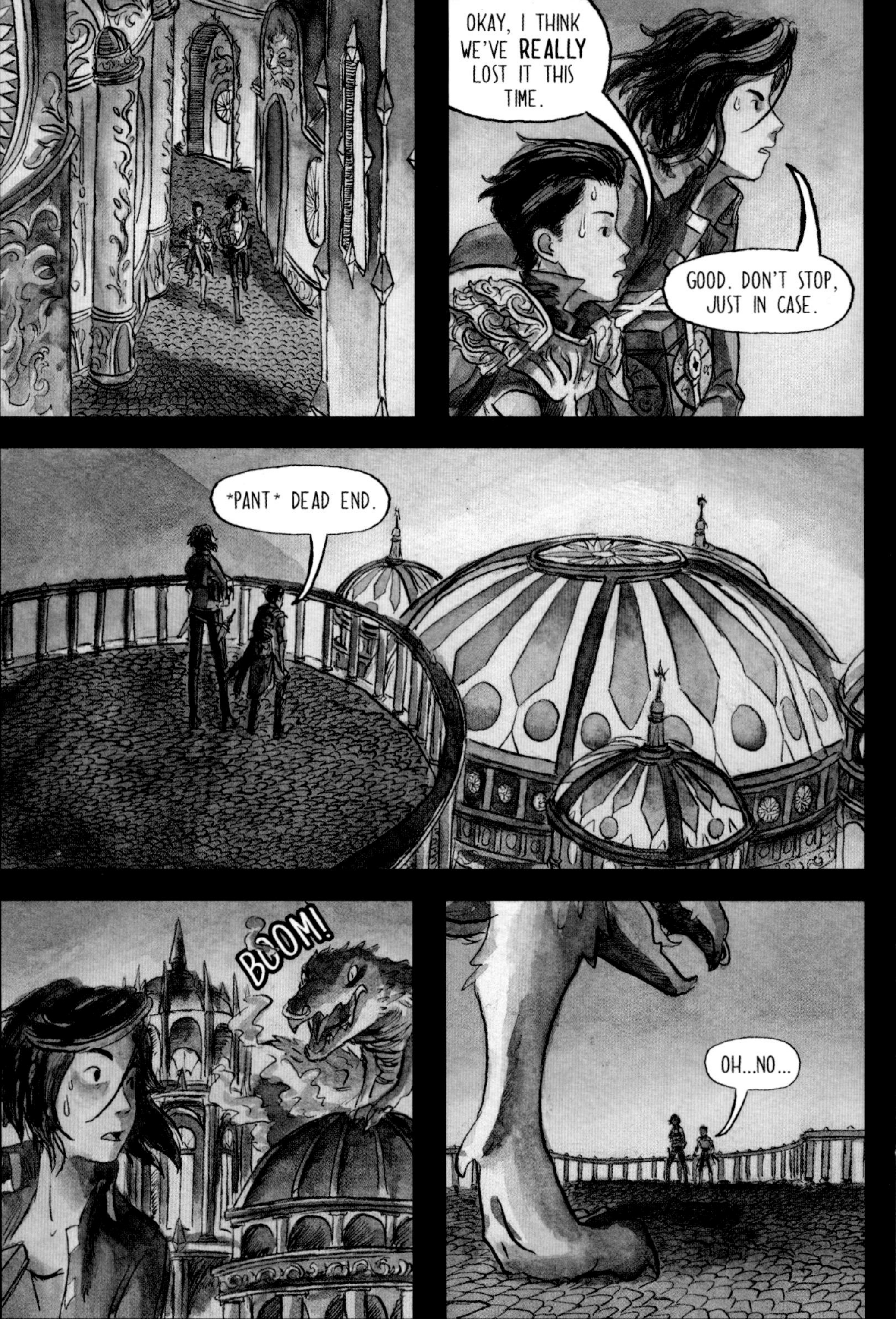
OKAY, I THINK WE'VE **REALLY** LOST IT THIS TIME.
GOOD. DON'T STOP, JUST IN CASE.
PANT DEAD END.
BOOM!
OH...NO...

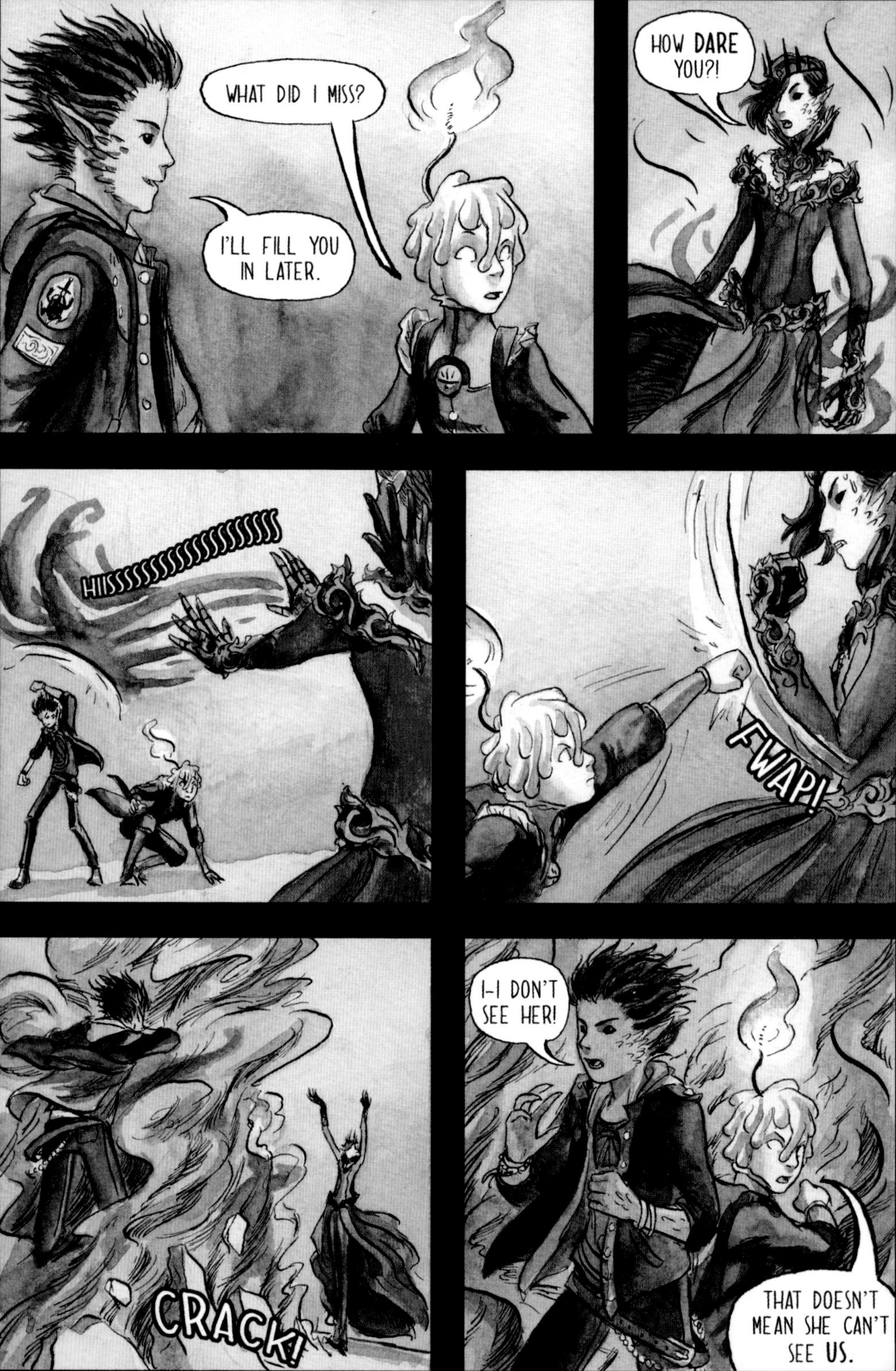

WHAT DID I MISS?
I'LL FILL YOU IN LATER.
HOW DARE YOU?!
HIISSSSSSSSSSSSSSSSSSS
FWAP!
CRACK!
I-I DON'T SEE HER!
THAT DOESN'T MEAN SHE CAN'T SEE US.

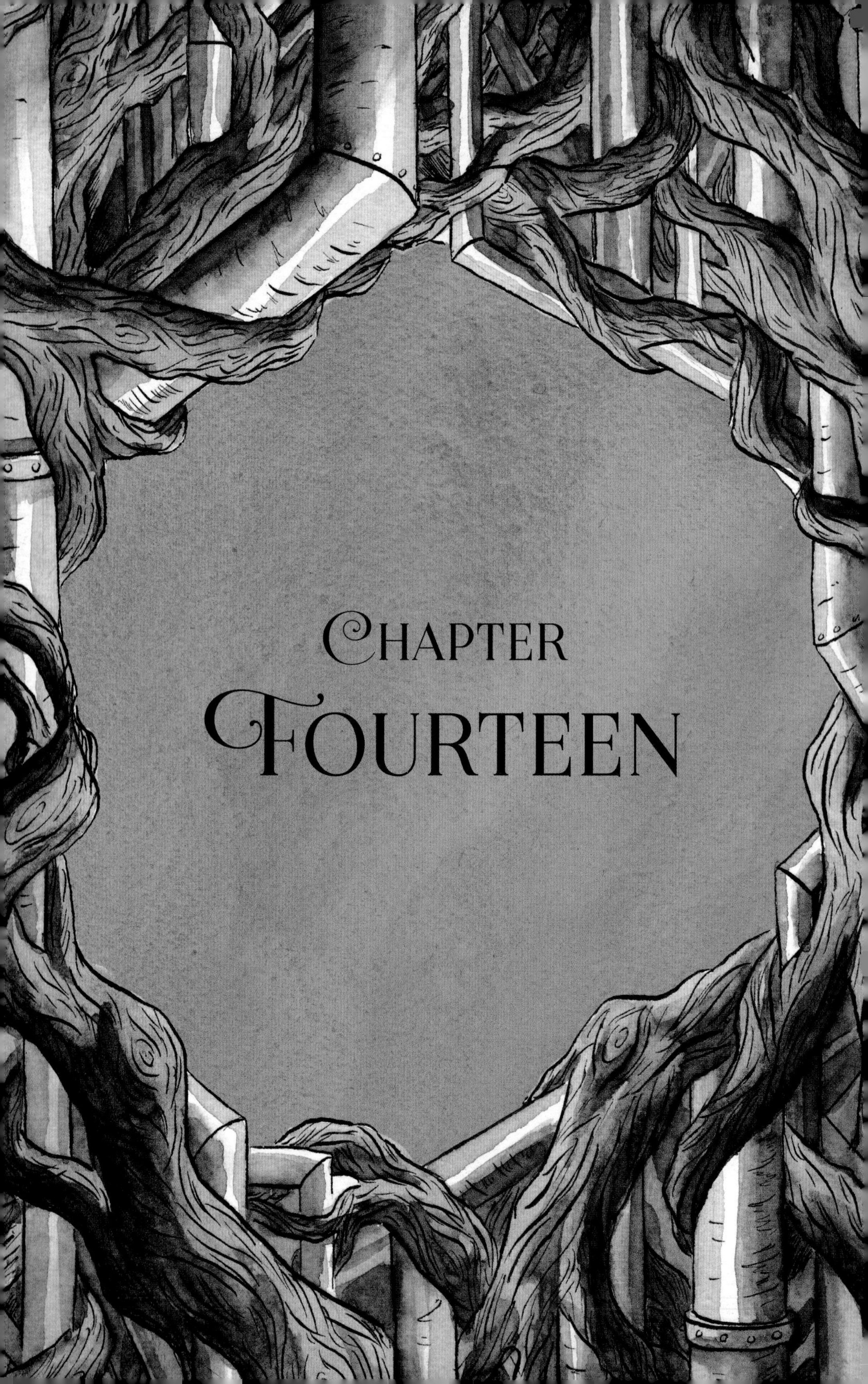

Chapter Fourteen

WE'RE TRAPPED!

YEAH, LOOKS THAT WAY!

WHAT ARE WE GOING TO DO?!

IT...IT DOESN'T WANT US. IT WANTS ITS TREASURE.

RRRRRRRRRRR

I DON'T THINK IT WOULD MIND GETTING US TOO!

RRAAAAA

WH-WHAT ARE YOU DOING?!

GAMBLING.

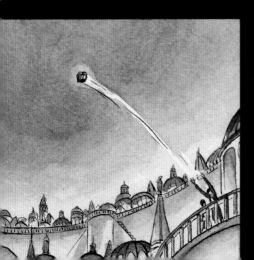

SCREEEEEE!

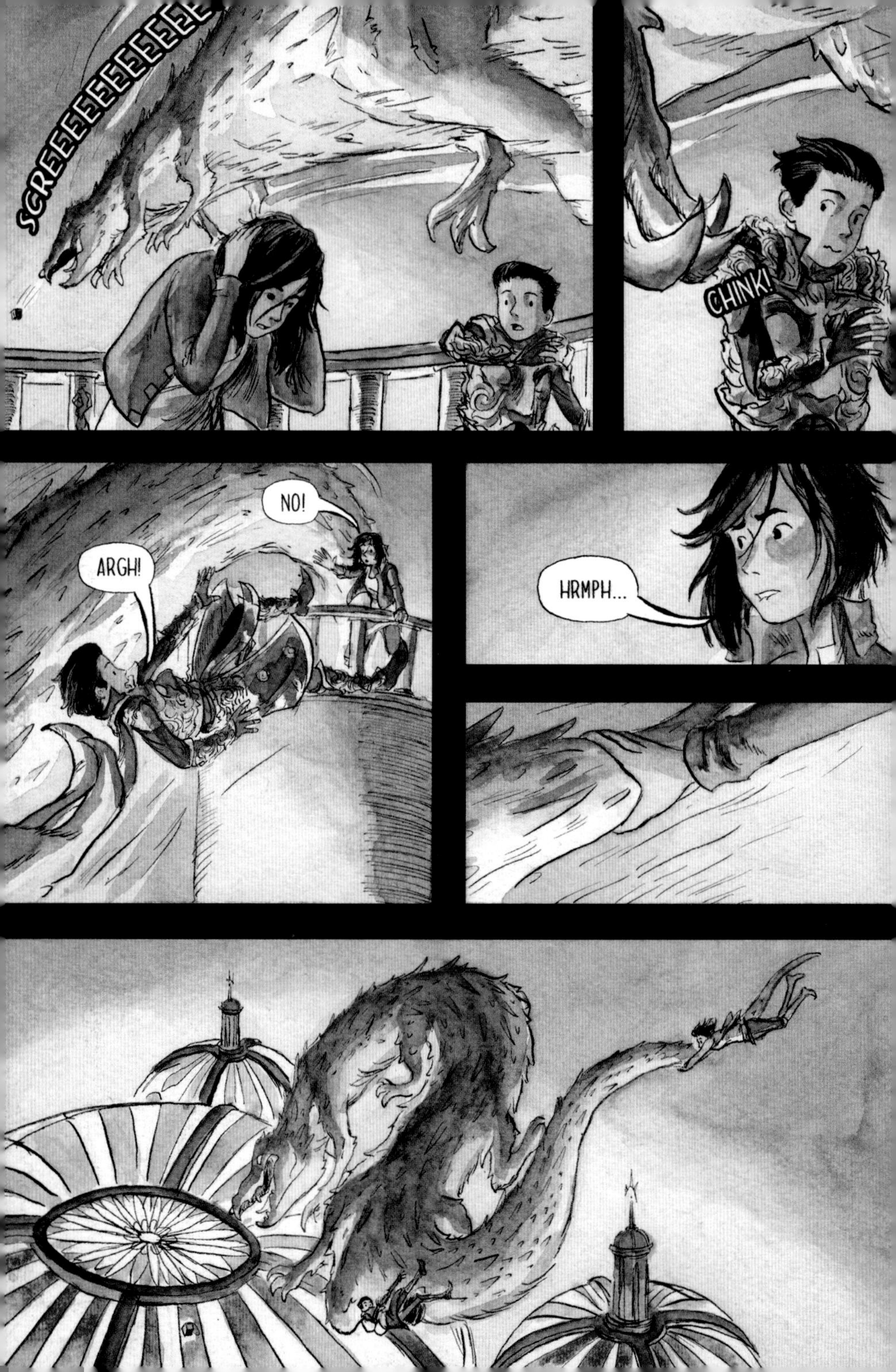
SCREEEEEEEEEEE
CHINK!
NO!
ARGH!
HRMPH...

SHINK!

HUMANS! HOW DELIGHTFUL!

HIIIIISSSSSSSSSSSSSSSSSSS

AND **YOU!** OH, I'VE HEARD **SO MUCH** ABOUT YOU. AREN'T YOU CLEVER. I WAS **SURE** YOU'D DIED IN THE TUNNELS.

WELL, WE'LL HAVE TO RECTIFY **THAT**, WON'T WE?

STOP!

OKAY, YOU **WIN.** DON'T HURT HIM. I'LL JOIN YOU, I'LL BE YOUR **FAMILY.**

IT'S A BIT LATE FOR **THAT.**

THEN I'LL BE YOUR **SERVANT!**

I'LL BE YOUR SERVANT. I'LL DO **WHATEVER** YOU WANT. JUST DON'T HURT THEM.

WHAT?

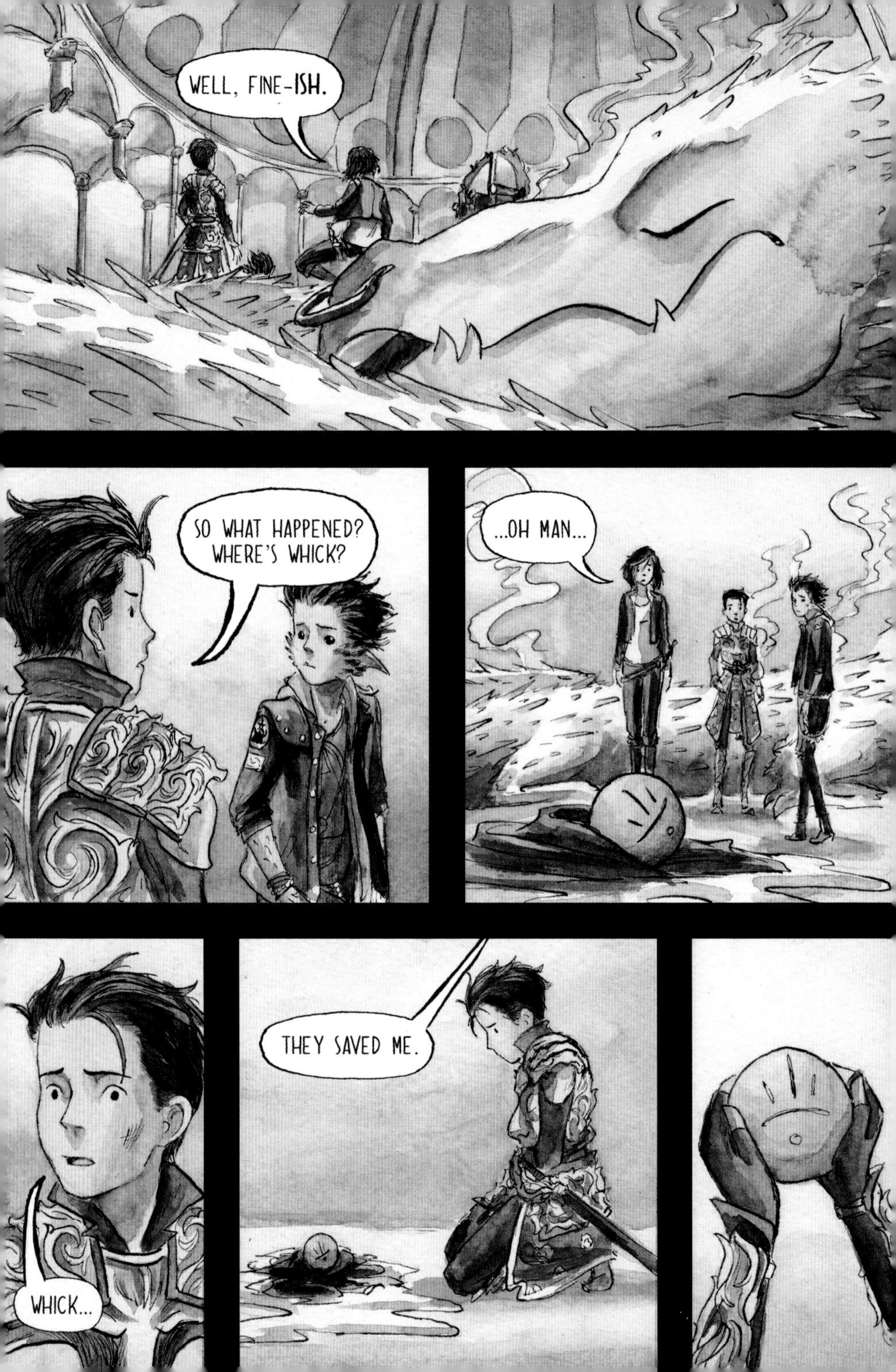
WELL, FINE-ISH.
SO WHAT HAPPENED? WHERE'S WHICK?
...OH MAN...
WHICK...
THEY SAVED ME.

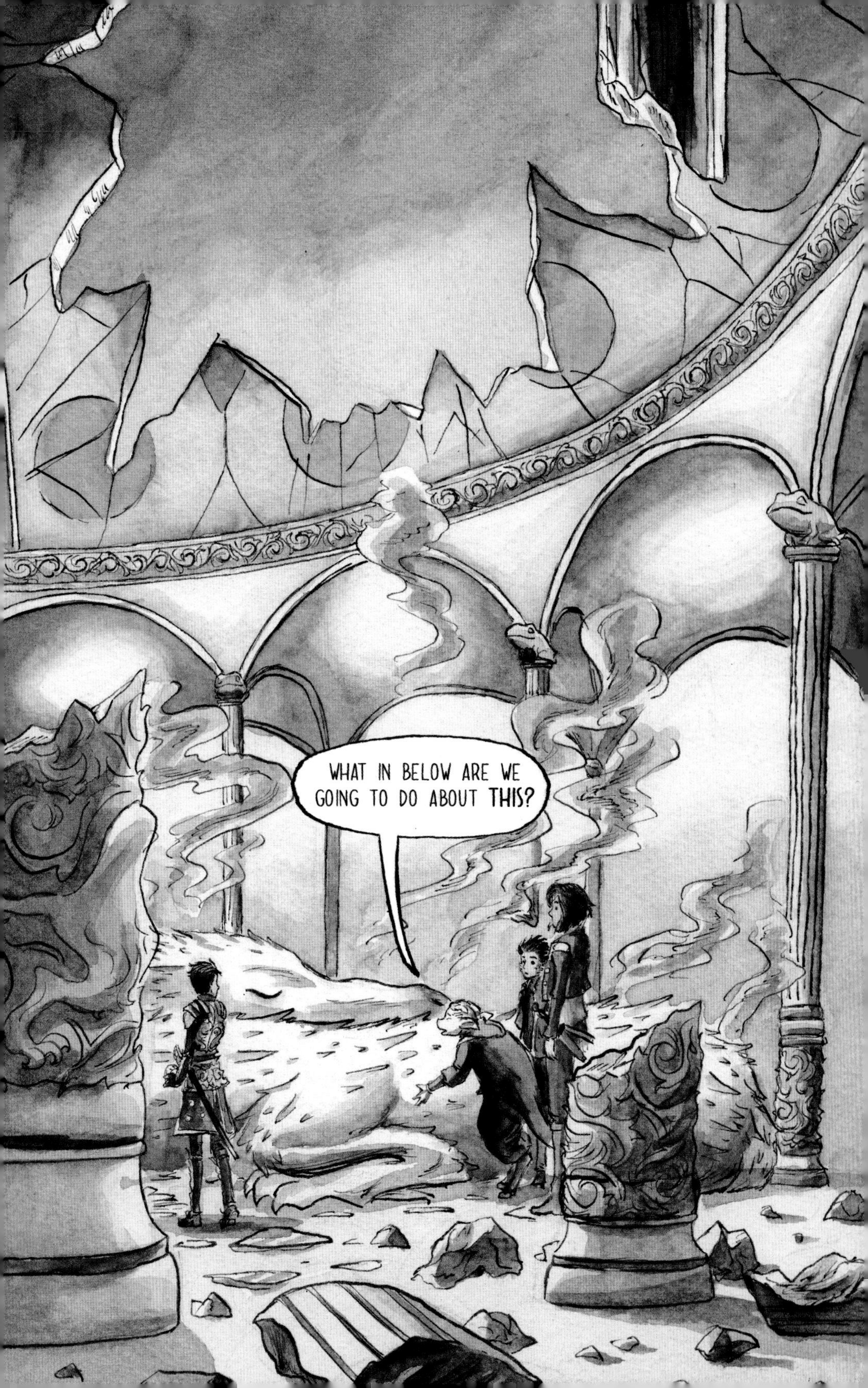
WHAT IN BELOW ARE WE GOING TO DO ABOUT THIS?

Chapter Fifteen

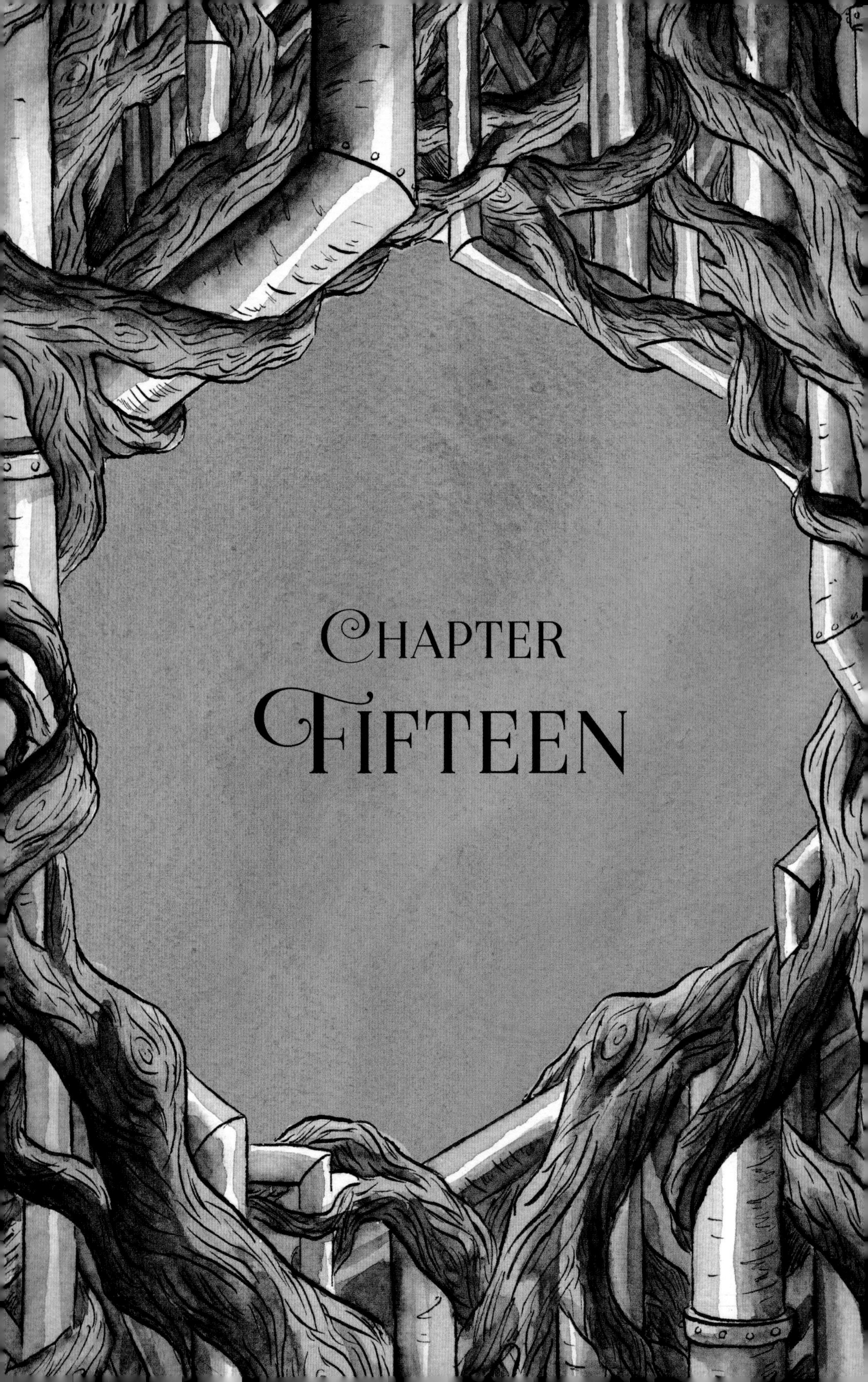

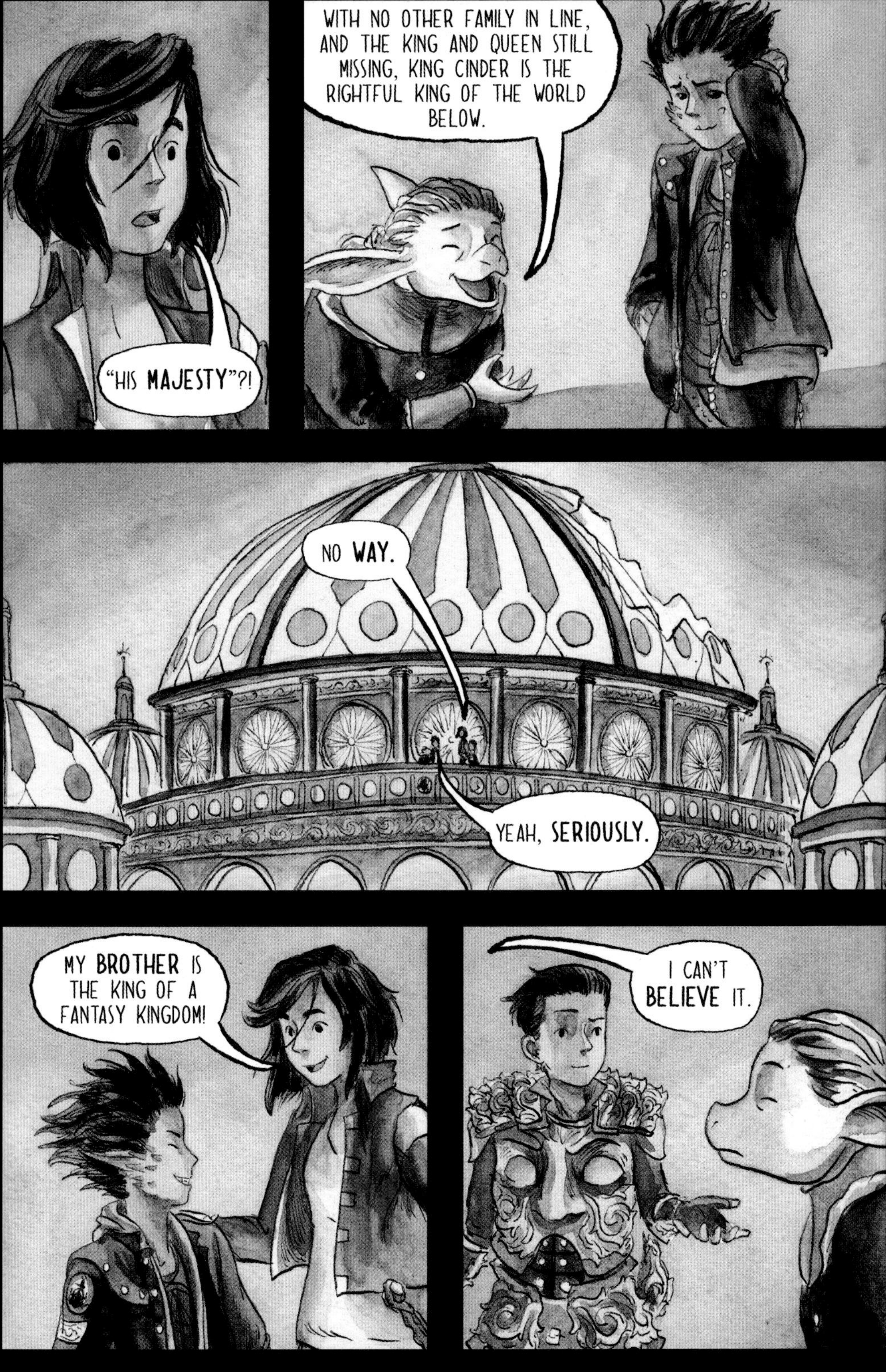
"HIS **MAJESTY**"?!
WITH NO OTHER FAMILY IN LINE, AND THE KING AND QUEEN STILL MISSING, KING CINDER IS THE RIGHTFUL KING OF THE WORLD BELOW.
NO **WAY**.
YEAH, **SERIOUSLY**.
MY **BROTHER** IS THE KING OF A FANTASY KINGDOM!
I CAN'T **BELIEVE** IT.

EPILOGUE

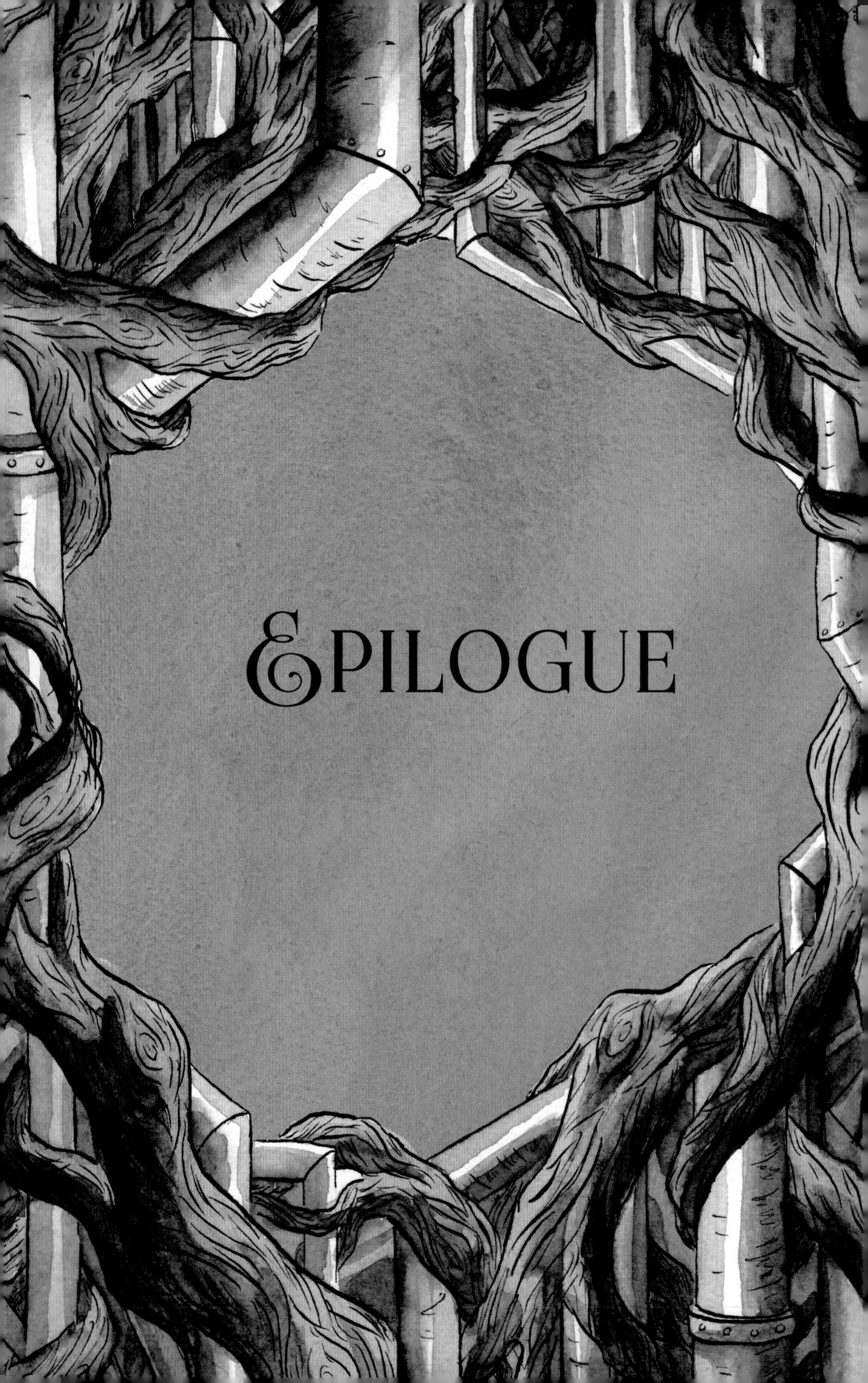

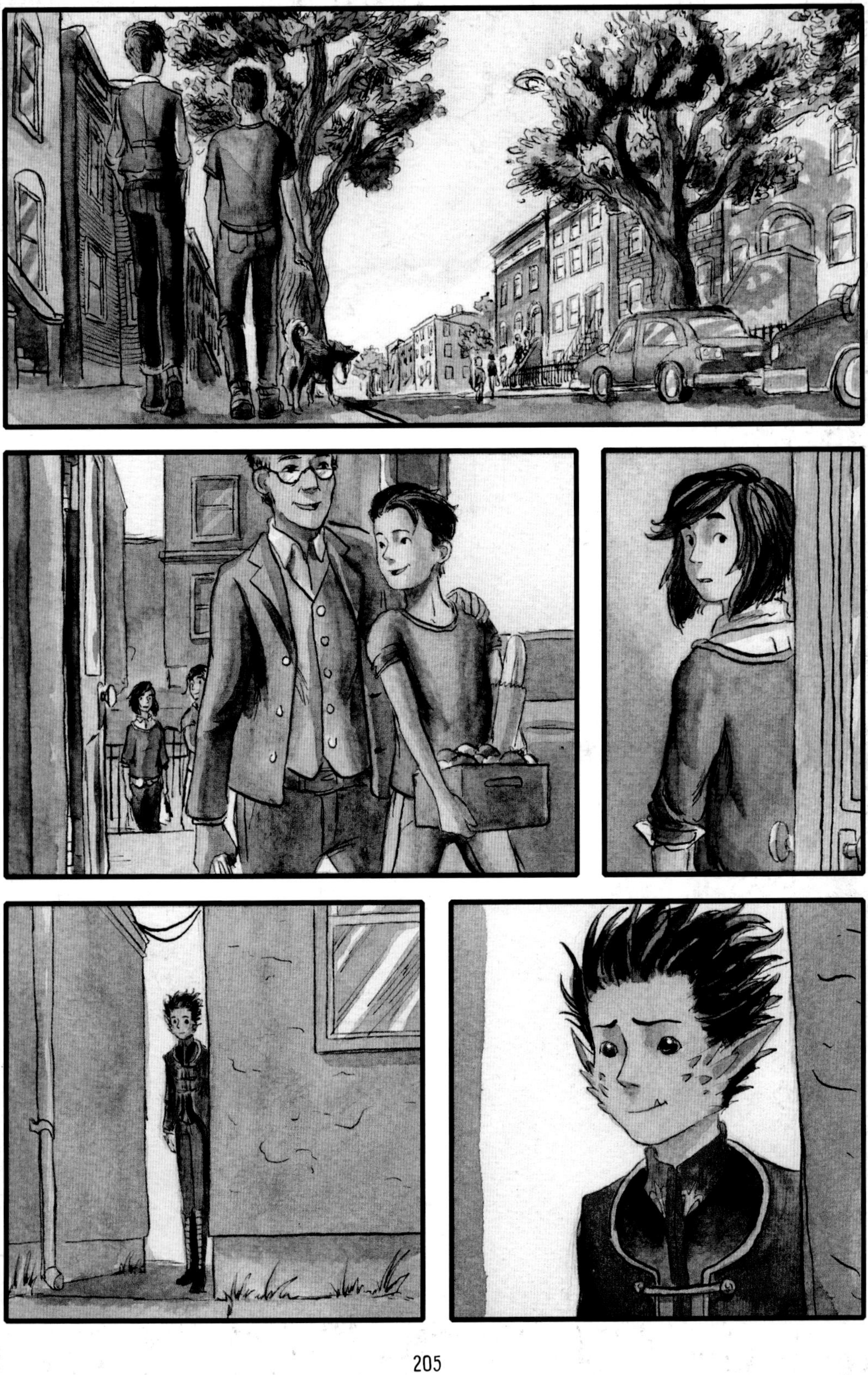

208

THE END

ACKNOWLEDGMENTS

First, to my parents, **BRAD** and **JULIA**, who went out of their way to make sure our home was always filled with good stories and that there was always plenty of blank paper and usable pencils lying about, in case any child should have the impulse to doodle.

To those who encouraged my ideas (no matter how strange) and helped me to make them better, including **PAUL ALLRED, SCOTT ALLRED, ADAM LARSEN, DUSTIN HANSEN, BRAD TAGGART**, and **CHARLIE OLSEN**.

To **JULIE DANIELSON**, who liked my work and introduced me to the wider publishing world at a time when no one else knew who I was.

To my wonderful agent, **STEPHEN BARBARA**, who remains my constant guide through the often confusing labyrinth of publishing.

To **BRITTANY RAGLIN**, who patiently listened to long rambling explanations of the early development of this story, and responded with insight, cleverness, and wit.

To **ANDREW ELIOPULOS, ERIN FITZSIMMONS**, and the entire team at Harper, for their wisdom, expertise, and unfailing dedication to making good books.

And finally to my incredible husband, **MATTHEW**, for his unwavering support, brilliant understanding of narrative, and for bringing me food when I forgot to eat, deep in what he lovingly calls my "cave-goblin" mode. This book literally could not have been made without him.

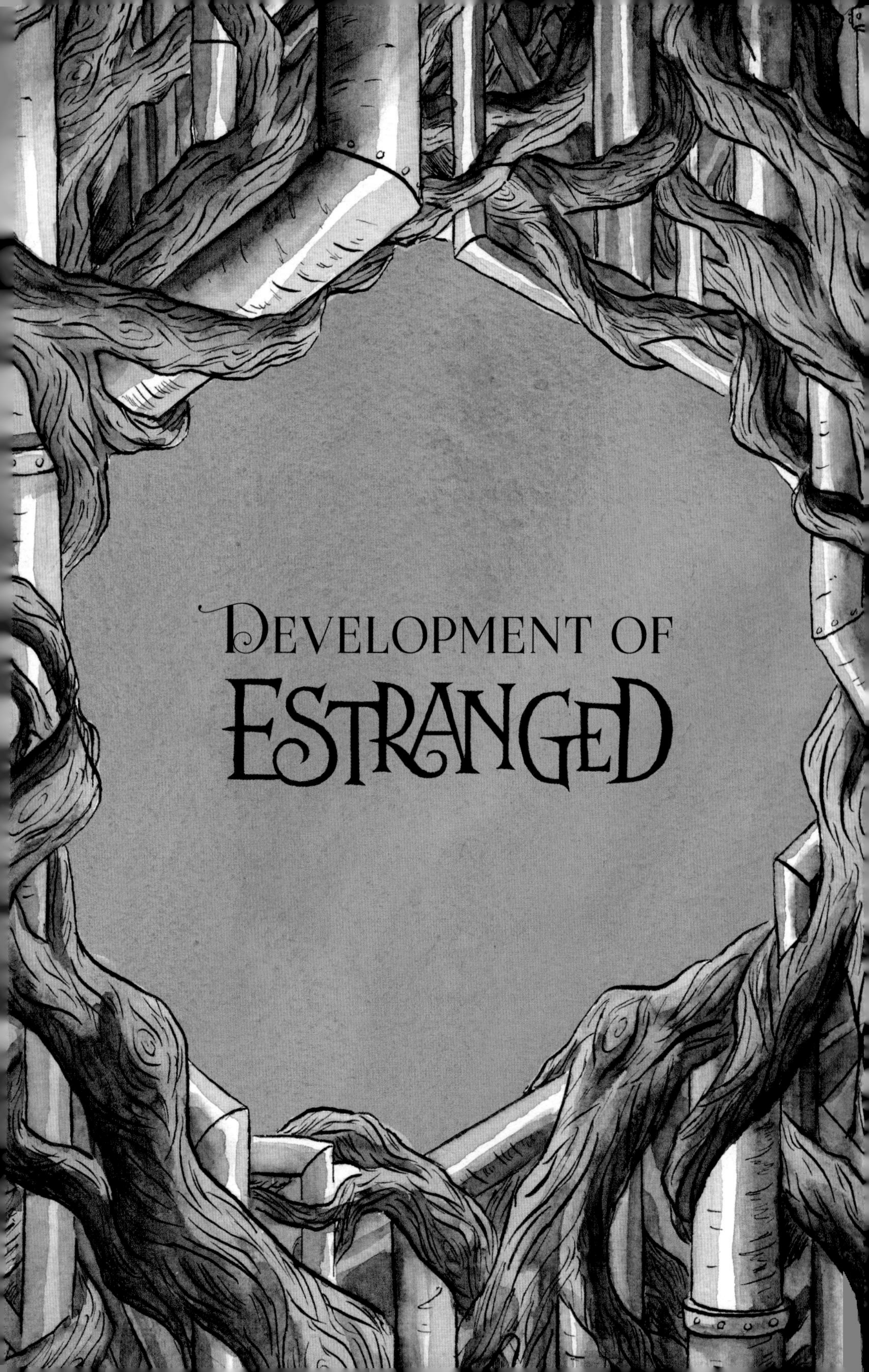

Development of Estranged

THE CHILDE

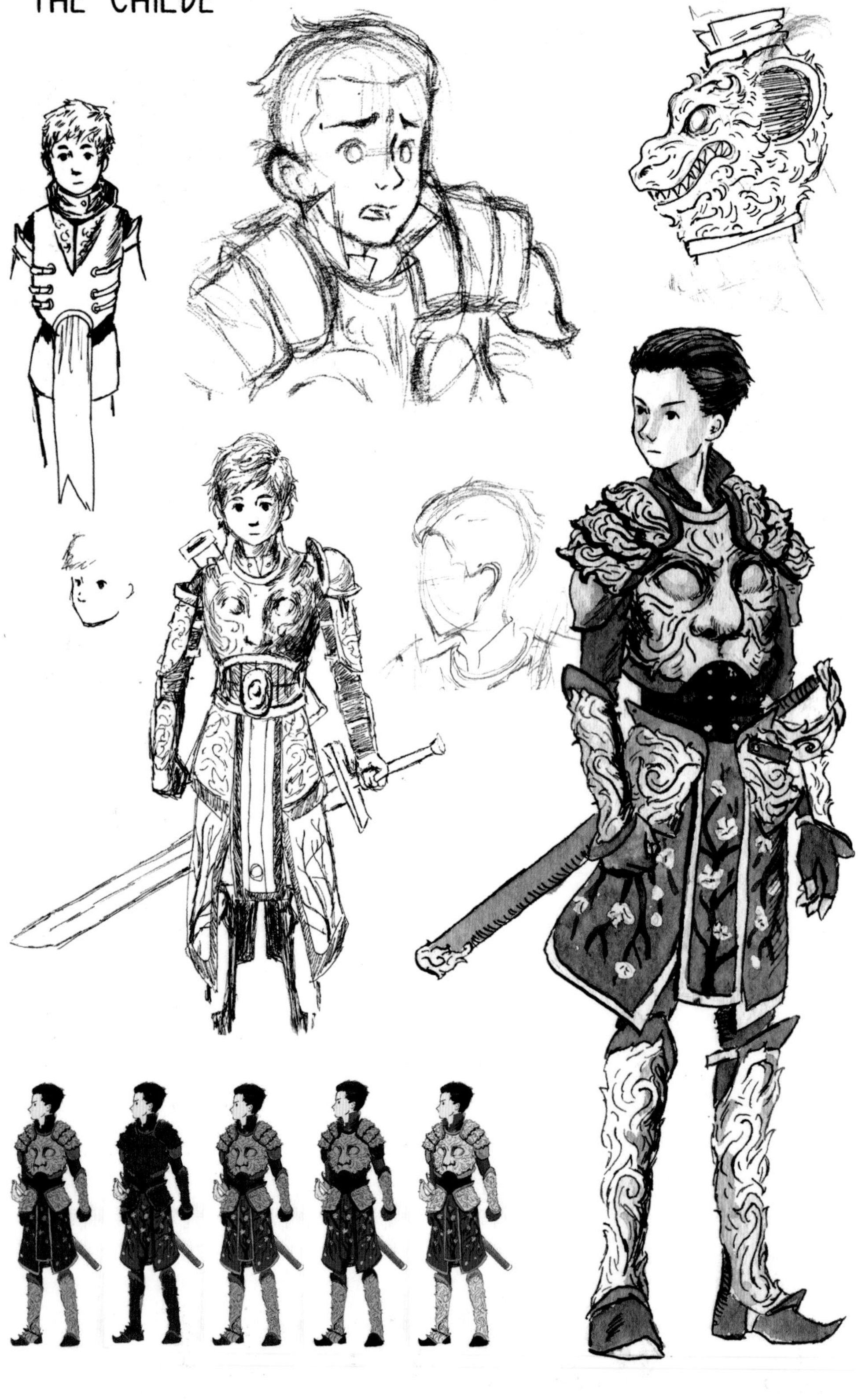

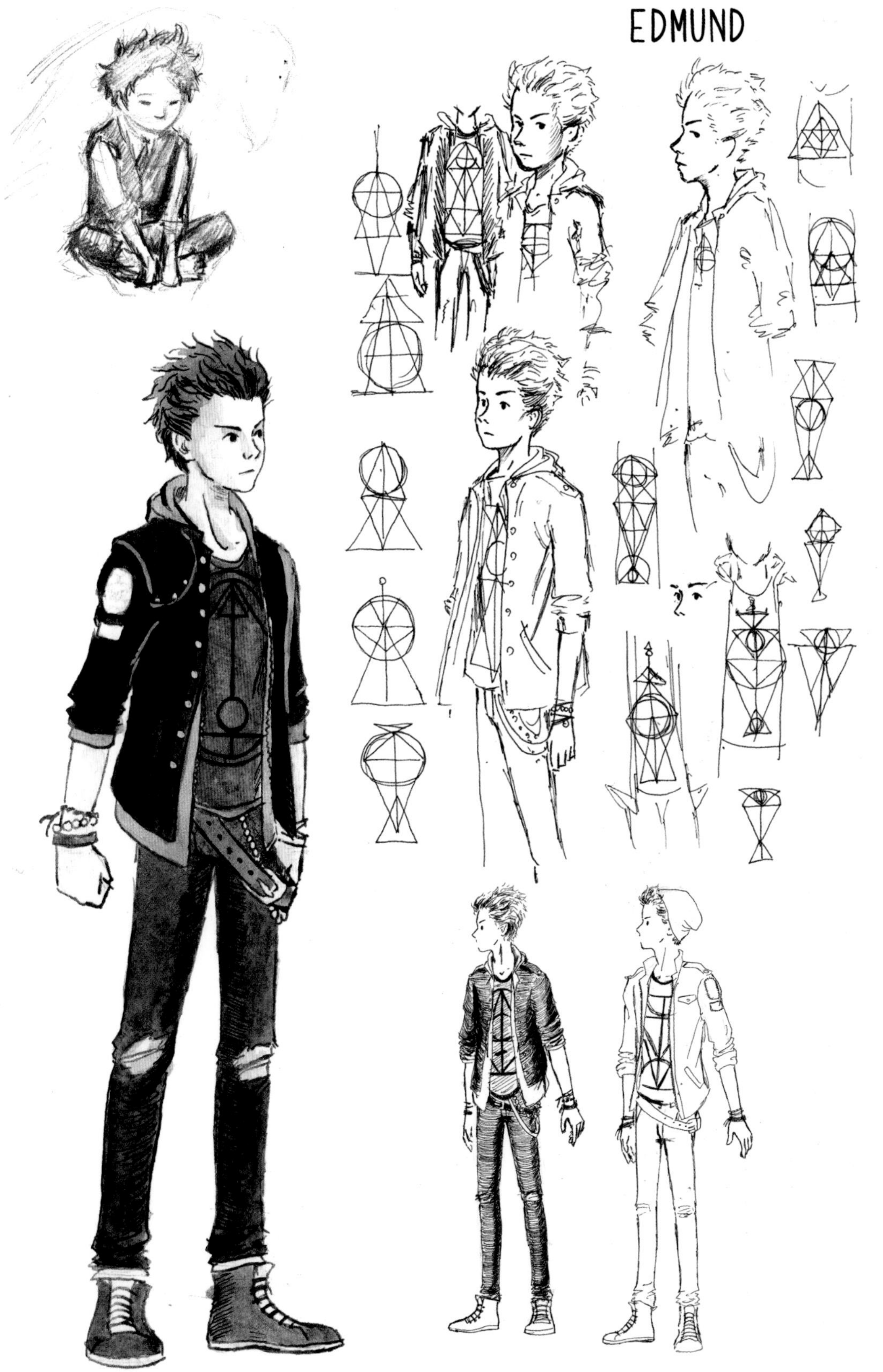
EDMUND

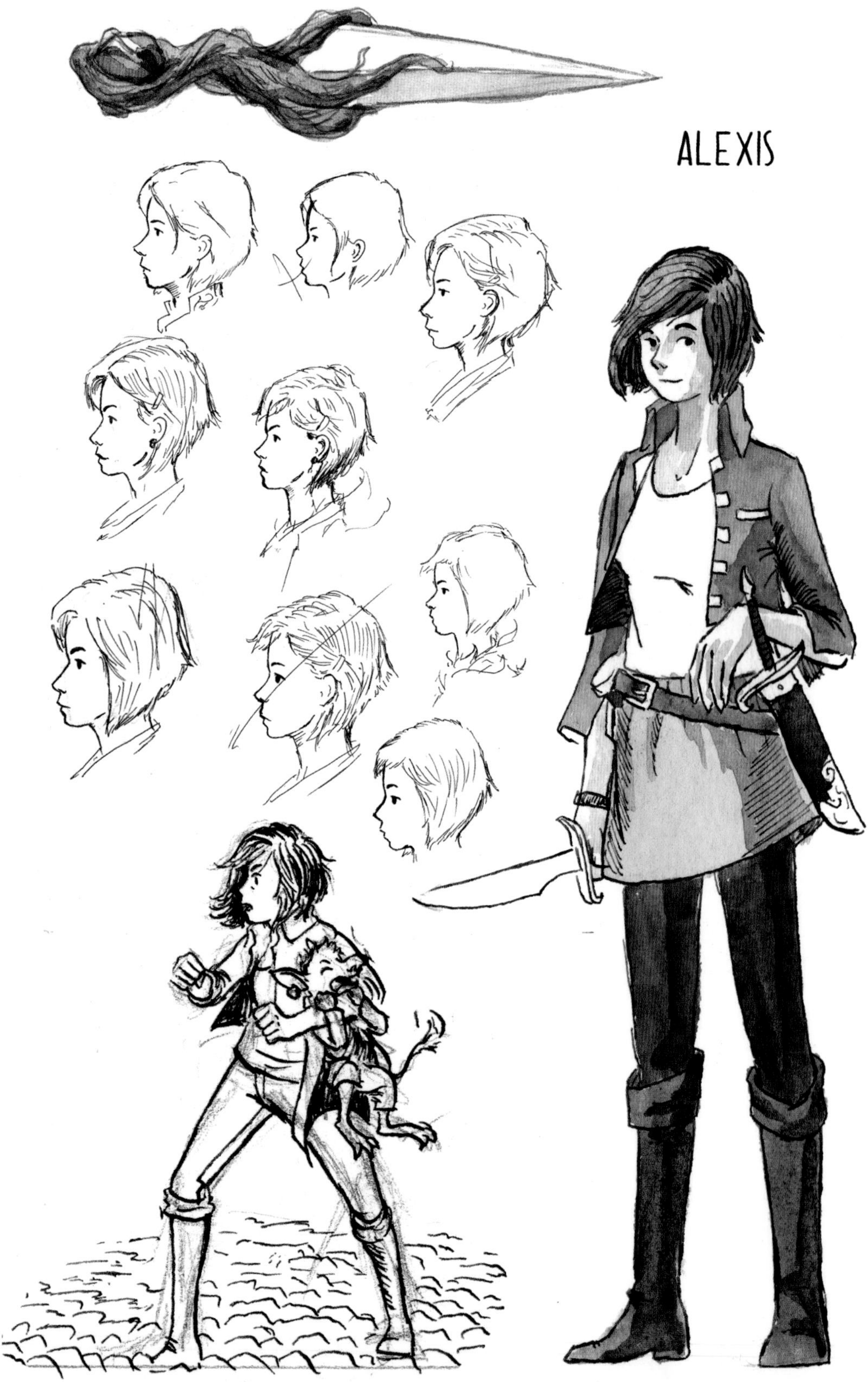
ALEXIS

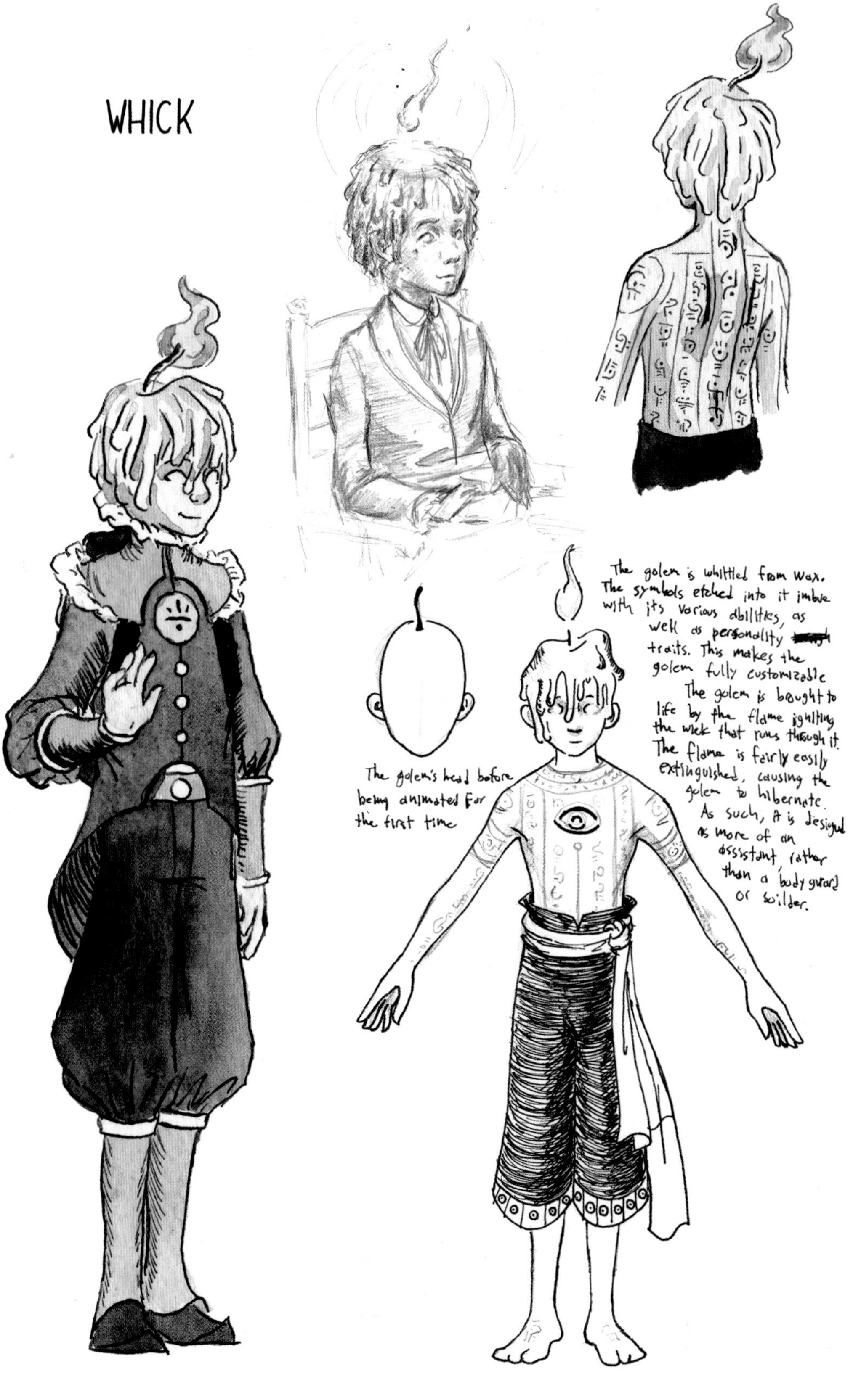
WHICK
The golem's head before being animated for the first time
The golem is whittled from wax. The symbols etched into it imbue with its various abilities, as well as personality [redacted] traits. This makes the golem fully customizable
The golem is brought to life by the flame igniting the wick that runs through it. The flame is fairly easily extinguished, causing the golem to hibernate. As such, it is designed as more of an assistant, rather than a bodyguard or soilder.

THE WORLD BELOW

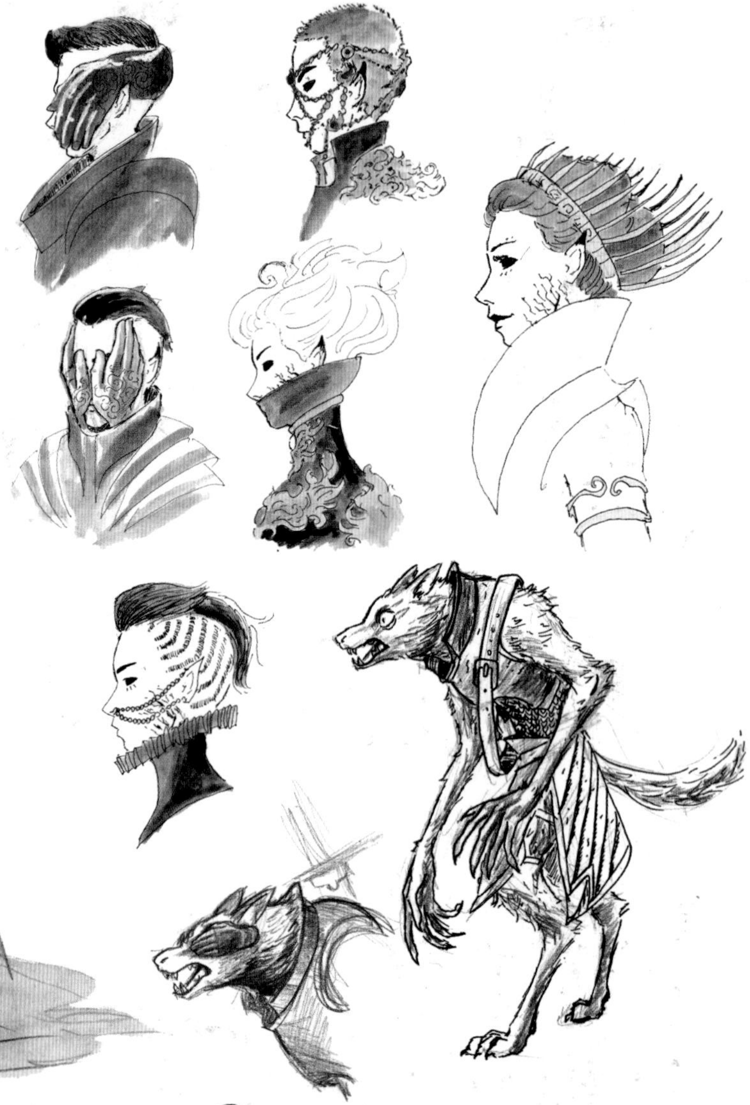

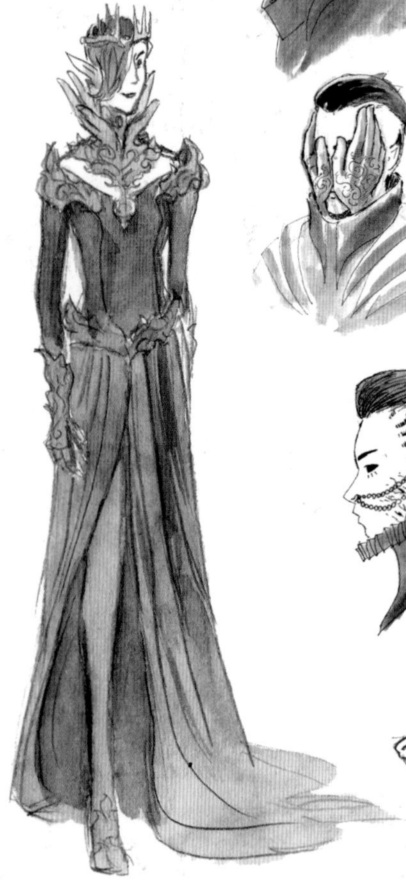

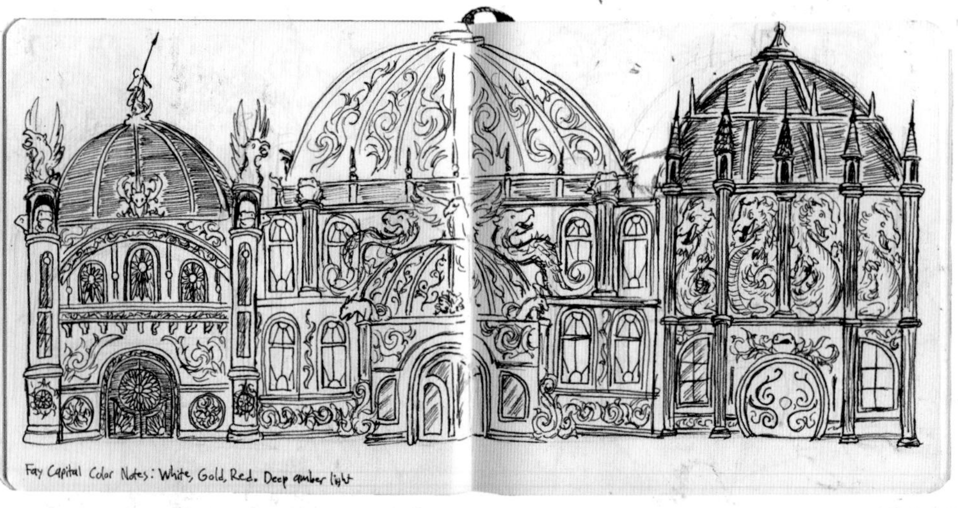
Fay Capital Color Notes: White, Gold, Red. Deep amber light

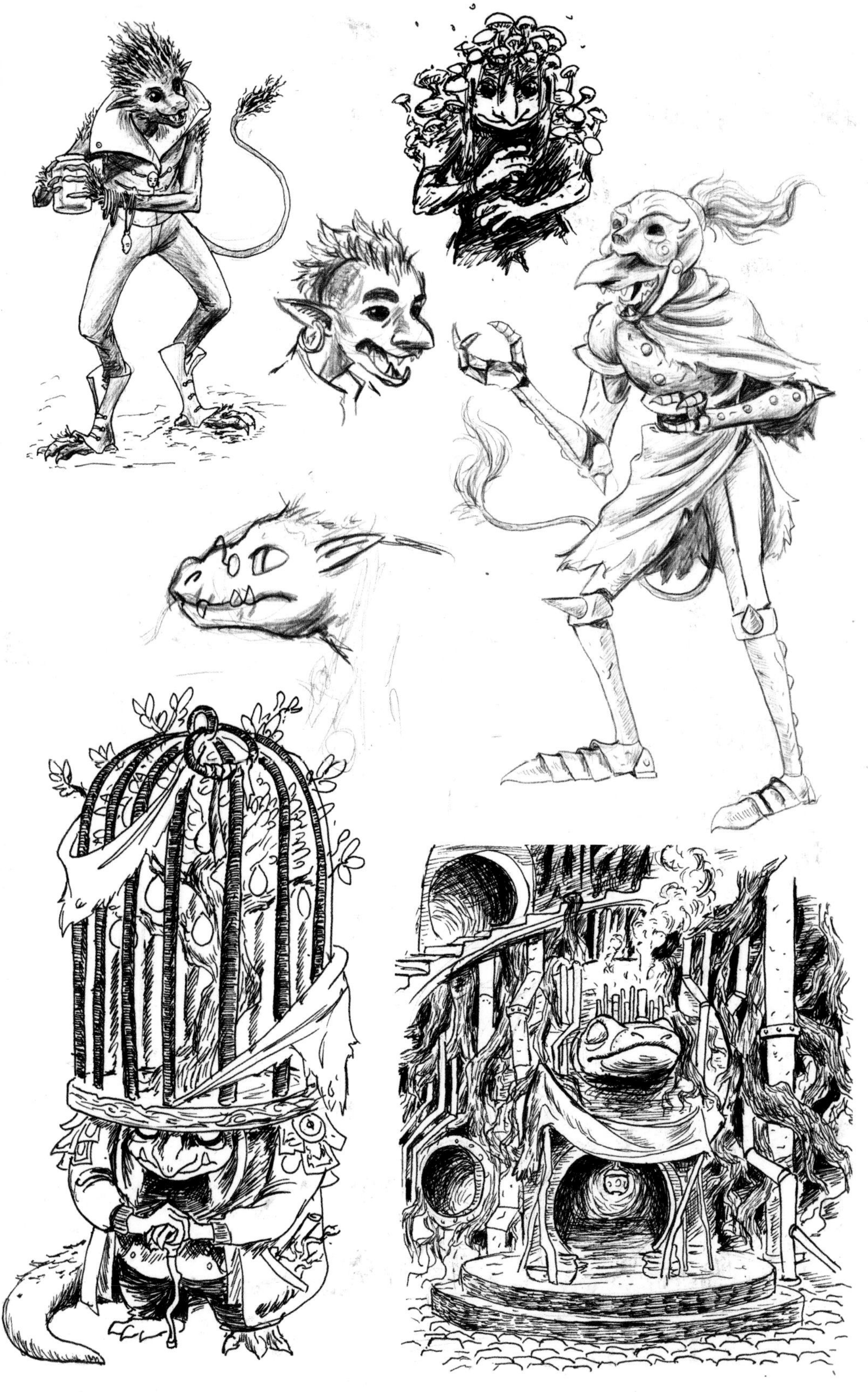

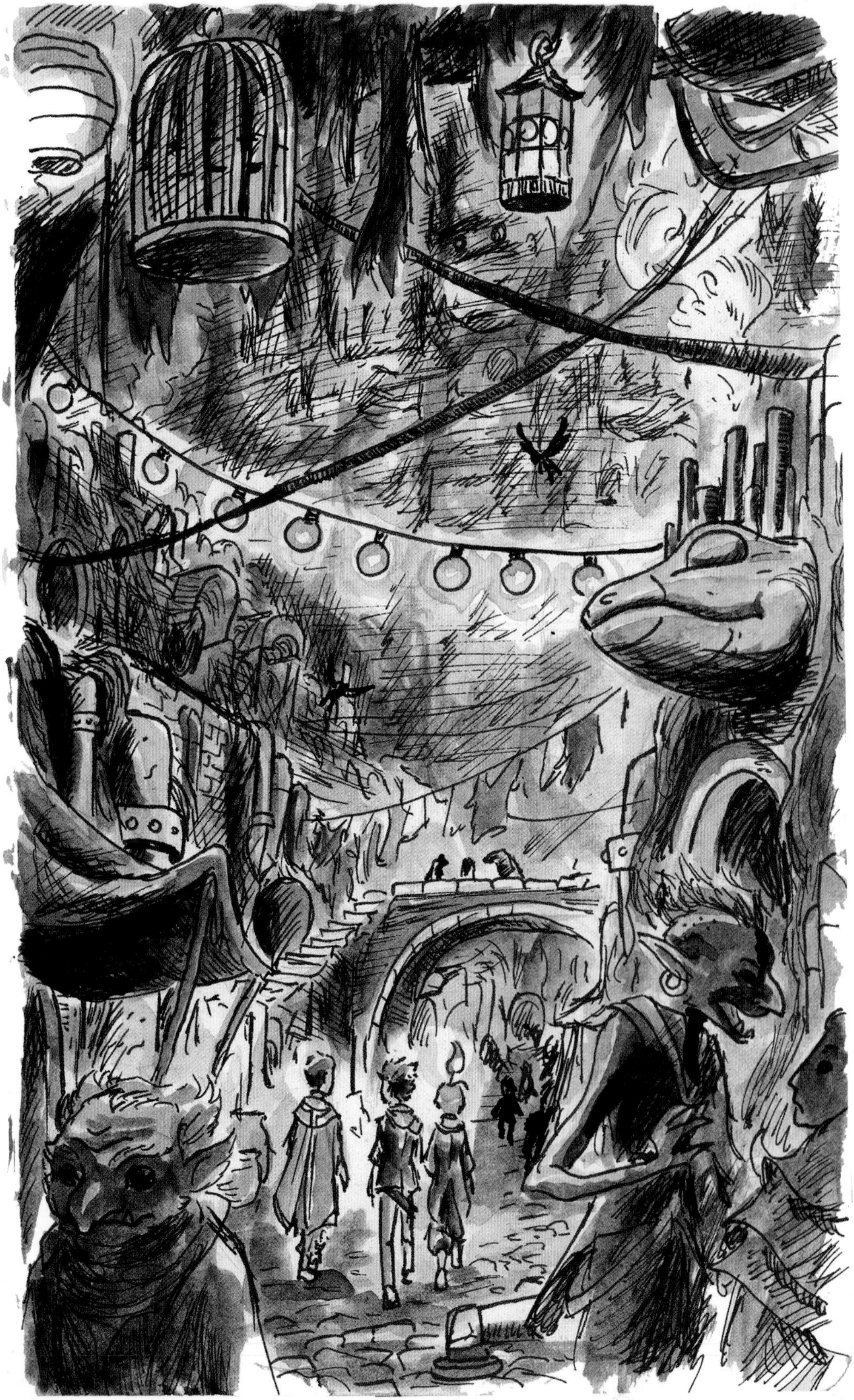